And so

A distant bark echoed through the P̶̶̶̶̶̶ ̶̶̶̶̶ later, a not so small puppy rushed down the hallway, three servants in pursuit.

Gerald knelt, letting the creature rush into his arms. "Have you decided on a name?"

"Not yet. I'm afraid I'm at a loss when it comes to names."

"You named your son."

"Yes, but even that took weeks."

"He's only a pup," said Gerald. "He doesn't care what you call him."

"I know, but a name defines a person, or in this case, a dog, and I want to get it right." She looked at him and smiled. "I'm open to suggestions?"

"Oh, no you don't. You're not foisting this off on me. He's your dog. You name him."

"But he likes you so much!"

"Well, let's see now. Do you remember how Tempus got his name?"

"Of course," said Anna. "Albreda told us he was named Tempest, but his first owner couldn't pronounce it. Why, what are you thinking?"

He smiled. "How about Storm?"

"I like that, and it suits him, as he's forever storming around the Palace. Very well. Storm it is."

The arrival of a guard interrupted their conversation.

"Your Majesty," the fellow said, bowing deeply. "Albreda has just arrived."

"By way of magic?"

"Yes, Majesty. She instructed me to inform you she bears important news."

"Very well, tell her to meet us in my study." She turned to Gerald. "Where's Beverly?"

"She and Aldwin are up in Hawksburg, visiting Aubrey. Why? Do you think you'll need her? I can send Revi to fetch her if you wish."

"Not just yet. Let's find out what news Albreda brings before we jump to any conclusions. In the meantime, I'd like you with me for this meeting."

"And Alric?"

"He's still in Weldwyn and not expected to return until this evening." She set off for her study at a fast pace, Gerald hurrying after her, the pup cradled in his arms.

Also by Paul J Bennett

GUARDIAN OF THE CROWN

Heir to the Crown: Book Eleven

PAUL J BENNETT

Dedication

To my wife, Carol.

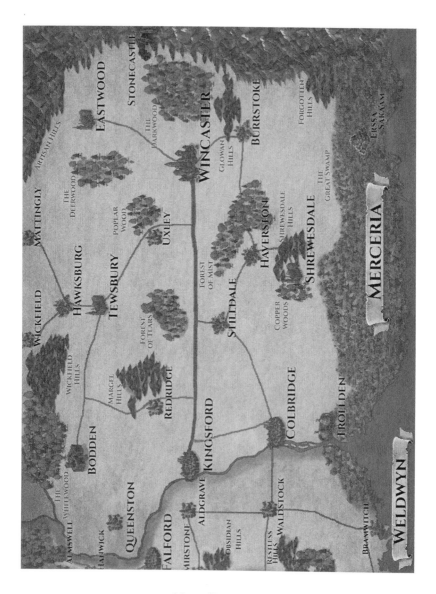

Map of Merceria

Map of Norland

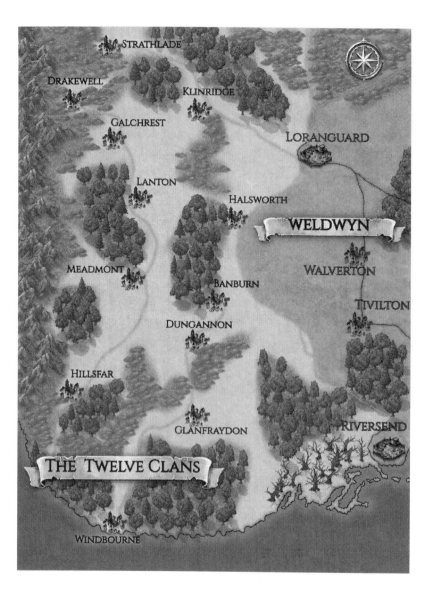

Map of The Twelve Clans

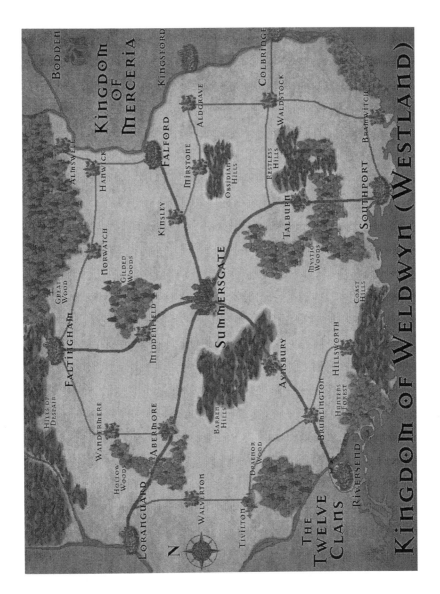

Map of Weldwyn

ONE

Wincaster

AUTUMN 966 MC* (*MERCERIAN CALENDAR)

G erald Matheson, Marshal of Merceria, yawned. The realm was theoretically at peace with Kythelia's defeat and the Twelve Clans' capitulation. Yet, you would've never known it from how the members of the Nobles Council argued over every detail.

Queen Anna glanced his way, noting his tiredness. "Perhaps a break will serve us well," she said. "We shall reconvene tomorrow." With that, she rose, the signal the discussion was over.

Everyone stood as she walked from the room, but as she neared the door, she slowed, turning back and looking at her advisors. "Lord Gerald, I wonder if I might have a word?"

"Of course, Majesty," he replied. He soon joined her, happy to be free of the cloying atmosphere.

"You looked like you needed rescuing," she said as they wandered down the hall.

"You must admit, it's not the most exciting place to be."

"True, but it can't be helped. The war put many issues aside, things we must now deal with."

"You're the queen. Couldn't you just delegate and disappear?"

She chuckled. "You and I both know I would never do that. The people deserve a chance to be heard."

"And by people, you mean nobles."

"I might remind you they're not all nobles."

"You make a good point, Anna, but sometimes it just feels like the same old problems. Every time the nobles get together, all they want to do is push their own agendas."

"I suppose that's Human nature. They say power corrupts, and the nobles of Merceria wield a great deal of that. My job, as queen, is to ensure they don't get carried away."

"Easier said than done."

"I'm surprised you're not more involved. After all, you are the Duke of Wincaster, and you have the queen's ear. I think that would add a lot of weight to your words."

"I'm not one to throw around my weight, as you well know."

She smiled. "And for that, I am truly thankful. Now, tell me, how was Braedon last night? I hope he didn't give you and Lady Jane any difficulty?"

"Not at all. Truth is, he slept most of the night. How was the play?"

"Quite entertaining. I never thought someone could take one of Califax's comedies and translate it to the present day, but it worked nicely. Not bad for a story written over three hundred years ago."

"I hear the Grand is reviving *The King's Mistress*. I hope you're not considering shutting it down like King Andred did?"

She chuckled. "No, though perhaps you and I should go and see it. We never did find out how it ended. Do you think Lady Jane would enjoy it?"

"I think so. Underneath that formal exterior is a heart full of passion." His went red in the face as he realized what he'd revealed.

"Good. Then I'll bring Alric, and we can watch from the best seat in the house."

"What about Braedon?"

"He's much too young for a play like that. Don't worry. There are plenty of people around here to look after him for an afternoon."

A distant bark echoed through the Palace, and then, moments later, a not so small puppy rushed down the hallway, three servants in pursuit.

Gerald knelt, letting the creature rush into his arms. "Have you decided on a name?"

"Not yet. I'm afraid I'm at a loss when it comes to names."

"You named your son."

"Yes, but even that took weeks."

"He's only a pup," said Gerald. "He doesn't care what you call him."

"I know, but a name defines a person, or in this case, a dog, and I want to get it right." She looked at him and smiled. "I'm open to suggestions?"

"Oh, no you don't. You're not foisting this off on me. He's your dog. You name him."

"But he likes you so much!"

"Well, let's see now. Do you remember how Tempus got his name?"

"Of course," said Anna. "Albreda told us he was named Tempest, but his first owner couldn't pronounce it. Why, what are you thinking?"

He smiled. "How about Storm?"

"I like that, and it suits him, as he's forever storming around the Palace. Very well. Storm it is."

The arrival of a guard interrupted their conversation.

"Your Majesty," the fellow said, bowing deeply. "Albreda has just arrived."

"By way of magic?"

"Yes, Majesty. She instructed me to inform you she bears important news."

"Very well, tell her to meet us in my study." She turned to Gerald. "Where's Beverly?"

"She and Aldwin are up in Hawksburg, visiting Aubrey. Why? Do you think you'll need her? I can send Revi to fetch her if you wish."

"Not just yet. Let's find out what news Albreda brings before we jump to any conclusions. In the meantime, I'd like you with me for this meeting."

"And Alric?"

"He's still in Weldwyn and not expected to return until this evening." She set off for her study at a fast pace, Gerald hurrying after her, the pup cradled in his arms.

They'd just sat down when Albreda entered. Gerald, noticing how haggard she appeared, was immediately concerned.

"Your Majesty," Albreda began, her voice breaking ever so slightly. "I regret to inform you Lord Richard Fitzwilliam, Baron of Bodden, is dead. He passed away peacefully in his sleep sometime last night."

Gerald gasped. "Fitz? Dead? How? He was healthy as an ox!" A great sadness rose within him, his voice choking as he tried to continue. "He… was only a few years older than me."

"Even an ox has a natural life-span, and magic must inevitably bow to the ravages of time."

Anna reached out, placing her hand on Gerald's. "He was a great man," she said, "and your mentor. Perhaps it might be best to take a few days to mourn your loss?"

"I don't understand," he persisted. "Was he ill?"

"Not as far as I'm aware," replied the Druid. "We dined last evening, and he was in fine spirits."

"I'm sorry for your loss, Albreda," said Anna. "I know you and he were very close. It must've been devastating to find he'd passed."

"It was," said Albreda, her calm breaking for a moment as a tear ran down her cheek. "I've lost loved ones before, but this time it's different. We

were, as you say, very close, and the thought of living without him feels...
empty."

Gerald nodded. "I know exactly how you feel. I, too, have lost loved
ones, and it never leaves you."

"Yet," said Anna, "Fitz would be the first to tell you both that life must go
on." She squeezed his hand.

"Yes, of course, although I can't help but hope I'll see him again one day
in the Afterlife."

"Have you told Beverly?"

"Not yet," replied Albreda. "I only just returned from Bodden. Is she here
in the capital?"

"I'm afraid she's in Hawksburg," said the queen. "Shall I send for her?"

"No. I'll go there myself. Such news is best delivered in the presence of
friends, and Aubrey, being her cousin, must be told as well."

"Please convey our deepest condolences on the loss of her father."

"I will."

"Are you sure you're up to it?" said Gerald. "You look... tired."

"Sad tidings are not a cause for celebration!" she snapped back. "How
would you expect me to look? Exuberant?" Albreda took a deep breath.
"Sorry, Gerald. That was uncalled for, but it's been a difficult morning. Fear
not. I shall recover. With your permission, Majesty, I'll recall to Hawksburg
immediately."

"Of course," said Anna. "I'll send word you'll be using the magic circle."

"Thank you." The Druid turned, leaving the room with no further
discussion.

"She's hurting," said Gerald. "She and Fitz were together for quite a
while. I can well imagine the loss she's feeling right now."

"We must keep an eye on her," said Anna. "Such a loss can drive a person
to despair."

"Surely you're not suggesting anything bad?"

"Only that I fear loneliness will see her once again withdraw into the
Whitewood and a life of solitude. If you recall, that was her life before she
met Lord Richard. We must be sure she doesn't slip back into old habits."

Aubrey reached across the table, spearing a choice cut of beef. "And what's
happening in Summersgate of late? I would've gone there myself if I hadn't
been busy preparing the Conservatory of Magic."

"Not much," replied Beverly. "Prince Alric went there to see about
sorting out the Twelve Clans, but we've no word on his progress of late."

"Speaking of the conservatory," said Aldwin, "how is that going?"

"Well," said Aubrey, "we're not ready to begin classes yet, but the old Royal Estate will suit us well once we've finished cleaning things up a bit."

"Meaning?"

"We're stripping out some rooms to use as classrooms. We also thought we'd knock down a few walls and make bigger rooms for sleeping, something like those barracks of yours in Wincaster, Beverly."

"They're not my barracks, but I understand what you mean. And on the topic of students, you were trying to detect magical ability using a spell. Did you get that working?"

"I did, though it's a little more difficult than I anticipated."

"Oh? In what way?"

"The concept is simple," explained Aubrey. "I use a variation on the spell that lets me enter the spirit realm. Only this one allows me to remain in the material world and merely peek into it."

"I'm not sure I understand," said Aldwin. "Are you suggesting it lets you see spirits without entering their world?"

"That is precisely the case. My theory is that anyone capable of using magic has a distinctly coloured aura."

"So, what's the problem?"

"A fully trained mage has a bright aura, the colour of which reveals their magical power. It appears, however, the untrained possess auras much paler, so pale it's tough to identify."

"And what does this mean for the future of your conservatory?"

"I don't know yet. I identified five people I believe are potential mages, two of them Orcs, but only time will tell if I'm correct."

"That's still better than how the Weldwyn mages do it," said Beverly. "Might I ask what type of mages you identified?"

"Two earth, one fire, one life, and of course, Princess Edwina, who has the potential to use Air Magic."

"I'd heard of Edwina's discovery, but fire? That's the last type I would've expected. There's no history of Fire Mages in Merceria, is there?"

"No," replied Aubrey, "but it's not unknown amongst the Orcs, just not in recent memory."

"And will you teach them the magical alphabet first, or use the Orcs' methods?"

"A little of both. There are many what we call universal spells, those which any type of mage can use. I thought we'd start with the orb of light. At least that way, they'll have a light source for further study."

They heard a familiar voice in the hallway: "I hope I'm not interrupting?"

"Albreda," said Aubrey. "Come in and join us. We were just chatting about—" The sight of the pale, unsteady Druid took her by surprise.

"I'm afraid I am the bearer of sad tidings," said Albreda.

Beverly drew a sharp breath, holding tight to her fear. "It's Father, isn't it? What's happened?"

"I'm afraid he's taken the final trip to the Afterlife. He passed peacefully in his sleep last night."

Aubrey reached out, touching her cousin's arm. "Beverly, I'm so sorry."

"I should've been there," said Beverly, a sob escaping her lips.

"There's nothing you could've done," said Albreda. "The Afterlife waits for no one."

Beverly stood, crossing the room to embrace the Druid. She wanted to say more but couldn't find the words. Instead, she held the woman tightly, her tears flowing freely.

Albreda squeezed her back. It was a strange sensation for the Mistress of the Whitewood, for she'd lost her own family when she was but a young girl.

"I'm here for you," she said finally. "And know that the Whitewood will always welcome you."

Beverly released her and wiped her tears. "Thank you. That means a lot to me. I know you and Father never married, but I've always considered you family. I hope my father's passing won't change that?"

The old woman straightened her back, but her eyes held little of their usual fire, a stark change from her typical appearance. "Family? Yes. I'd like that very much."

"Come, sit," said Aubrey, her voice barely above a whisper. "You must be devastated."

Albreda joined them at the table, looking small as if she were somehow diminished, despite being the most powerful mage in the kingdom.

"I think I'd convinced myself he'd live forever," said Beverly, "but I should've known better."

"I'll miss him too," said Aubrey. "He was the last family I had left."

"Not quite. I'm still here, but my father's left some formidable boots to fill."

"You are so much like him," said Albreda. "You have his heart and the same dedication to duty."

Beverly chuckled, releasing some of the tension. "Yes, but apparently not his appetite for cheese."

"You'll get over his death, as we all must, but his spirit lives on inside you. As for me, I shall return to the Whitewood for a time to grieve in solitude. You?"

"There were no secrets between my father and me, no words left unspoken. I shall miss him dearly, but I'm happy he was in good company when the end came. It's what he would've wanted."

"Well said," added the Druid.

"Come," said Aubrey. "Let us sit awhile and reminisce about Uncle Richard. I'm sure there must be plenty of tales between us?"

The hour grew late, and Albreda departed before the moon reached its height, leaving the other three to talk into the wee hours of the morning.

"I suppose that makes you baroness now," said Aubrey.

"Not quite," said Beverly. "I'm not officially baroness until after my investiture, and the date for that will be in the queen's hands. Until then, I shall only be the acting baroness."

"You've looked into it?"

"When Aldwin and I married, Father took great pains to ensure I understood what would happen in the event of his death. He also left instructions for his interment."

"Was he ill?"

"No, only thorough."

"He was always like that," added Aldwin. "Planning for everything."

"And if I might ask," said Aubrey, "what exactly were his plans?"

"To be interred beneath Bodden, in the family crypt. He'd picked a space beside my mother."

"I wish I'd been able to bury my own family, but by the time we retook Hawksburg, they were gone."

"Gone?" said Aldwin.

"Valmar built a large fire and burned all the bodies."

"I'm so sorry."

Aubrey forced a smile. "There was nothing you could've done about it. Will there be a ceremony for your father, Beverly?"

"Naturally. In fact, I may need your help creating a list of whom to invite. Let's not make it too long, though. My father would hate the idea of a great spectacle."

"So, no parade through Wincaster?"

Beverly laughed. "That would've driven him to distraction."

"We should get to Bodden soon," said Aubrey. "I can use a preserve spell to keep the body intact until we arrange everything. In the meantime, I'll see about enlisting a few mages to organize transportation for all the guests."

"But there's no circle in Bodden," said Aldwin.

"True, but the one in the Whitewood is close enough. I'm sure Albreda won't mind us using it."

"What can I do to help?"

"Keep me company," replied Beverly. "The next few days are bound to be filled with all manner of tasks."

The days soon became a week, and Beverly began to wonder if there was any end to it. Invitations needed to be sent out, people to be collected, and a barony didn't run itself. She'd always looked up to her father but never realized the depth of commitment it took to manage a place like Bodden.

Since the civil war and the founding of Queenston, traffic to the barony had increased substantially, growing it beyond its modest walls. For the first time, she realized it was no longer a small frontier village but a growing town bustling with newcomers. The influx brought in plenty of coins, filling the coffers, yet there were endless requests for audiences from those seeking reassurance that nothing would change once she became baroness.

The people she'd grown up with respected her father, loved him even, but those new to Bodden held no such loyalties. Beverly struggled to come to grips with it all, doing her best to reassure them, but they were worried about their futures.

Finally, on the day set aside to honour her father, the guests crowded into the great hall in Bodden Keep. They'd entombed Fitz days earlier with only a few close friends in attendance, but this larger assembly gathered to celebrate his life rather than mourn it.

Beverly looked in the mirror, straightening her dress.

"I like the sword," said Aldwin. "It's a nice touch."

"You should—you made it."

"Still, it's a fitting tribute to your father, wouldn't you say? After all, he encouraged you to become a knight."

"There's a lot to be thankful for when it comes to my father, including that he brought you to Bodden." She moved closer, embracing him.

"You've faced terror on the battlefield, fought countless times. Why so nervous now?"

"I've a lot to live up to. My father was well-respected, even by his enemies."

"The same can be said of you. And I shouldn't need to remind you—I'm here to help."

"I know you are, and I'm truly thankful for that, but it all feels so different without him."

"Bodden was part of him, and to an extent, he shall always be part of Bodden, especially this keep."

"So why am I so nervous?"

"You spent your childhood here but most of your adult life elsewhere. It's only natural you feel out of place. Now, come. Aubrey is waiting to escort us down to the great hall." He took her hand, guiding her into the hallway, where her cousin stood.

"All set?" asked the mage.

Beverly turned, looking back at her room. "I suppose I'll be expected to move into the master bedroom once I'm the baroness."

"Nonsense," said Aldwin. "The choice of rooms is completely up to you. If you don't want to move, then don't."

"But it barely fits the two of us."

"I might remind you I spent most of my life sleeping on the smithy floor. Besides, it's not the size of the room that matters so much as who you share it with."

Beverly smiled. "You're right, of course." She straightened her back, then waited as her husband tucked away a strand of red hair that had worked its way loose from her braid.

They descended the steps, Aubrey leading as they entered the great hall. People had travelled from all over the kingdom to pay their respects, including Elves, Dwarves, and even Orcs. Added to that were many of the nobles of Merceria and the queen herself.

They made their way to the head table, and all assembled stood, save for Her Majesty. Beverly sat, Aldwin to her right and Aubrey to her left. The guests followed suit, their attention all on Beverly.

"We are here today," she began, "to remember my father, Lord Richard Fitzwilliam, Baron of Bodden."

A cheer went up, and the soldiers amongst the audience raised their cups in salute. Beverly smiled, for her father had always been popular with his warriors, particularly the Bodden horse. She raised her own cup on high, then waited as others rushed to do likewise. "To my father," she said, then tipped the tankard back, pouring the ale down her throat.

Everyone mimicked her actions, and then they slammed their mugs down on the table and cheered. People began talking amongst themselves, sharing fond stories of her father.

She turned to Aubrey, only to notice her staring off at the great doors leading outside. Beverly followed her cousin's gaze to where someone had slipped into the room and now advanced towards the head table. His clothing marked him as a man of means, and though she was sure they'd never met, there was something familiar about him.

All in the room fell silent as he halted before the head table. He scanned the great hall but ignored Beverly, focusing instead on the queen.

"My name is Sir Randolf Blackburn," he announced, his voice loud and clear, "and I come here today to claim my birthright: the Barony of Bodden!"

TWO

Weldwyn

AUTUMN 966 MC

Alric, Prince of Weldwyn, shifted in his seat. As the only surviving son of King Leofric, he was attending the meeting of the Earls Council, but only as an observer. The earls' duty as the guardians of the kingdom was to select their next ruler. Although normally a quick and easy decision, things were proceeding much slower today.

The council usually consisted of five members, but the recent invasion had reduced that number to three. According to ancient tradition, they only needed three votes to proclaim a king, yet Lord Elgin Warford, the Earl of Riversend, could not make up his mind.

"But His Highness has proven his leadership prowess in countless battles," said Lord Julian, the youngest son of the previous Earl of Falford and the only surviving family member.

"I recognize his military accomplishments," said Lord Elgin, "but we're talking of leading the kingdom, not an army. There's a vast difference between fighting battles and navigating the pitfalls of politics here in the capital. And what of his loyalty?"

"Come now," soothed Lord Oliver. "How can you even call that into question?"

"It's quite simple. He's wed to Queen Anna of Merceria. How do we know his loyalty to her won't precede the needs of Weldwyn?"

"I'm sorry you feel that way. This means we are at an impasse." Oliver turned to the scribe taking notes. "Have we any word on Canning or Mainbridge?"

"No, my lord. Both heirs are still unaccounted for."

"Then I suppose we must await their presence."

"There's too much at stake," said Lord Julian. "We can't just let the kingdom fall to pieces."

"I might remind you," said Lord Elgin, "that we, as the council, are more than capable of ruling without a king. It wouldn't be the first time, nor, I think, will it be the last. With all due apologies to His Highness, it's our responsibility to select the ruler who best represents the interests of this realm."

"And, just out of curiosity, who do you propose? Yourself?"

"No, of course not. All I'm saying is we must consider other potential candidates. Perhaps a distant cousin of the king?"

"Don't be ridiculous," said Oliver. "You know full well Brida went to great lengths to kill off as many as possible. The only heir left is Alric."

"And his two sisters," added Lord Julian. "Let's not forget them."

"A woman can never rule Weldwyn," countered Lord Elgin. "You know the law as well as I do."

"Were my father here, I'm sure he'd be able to settle our differences."

"Well, he's not, nor is mine, nor Oliver's. None of us possess much experience as earls, which is why we must choose someone with the knowledge to rule Weldwyn."

They all nodded in agreement, the first sign they shared a common belief. As they sat in silence, each contemplated the table. Alric wanted to get out of his seat and give them a good shake but knew that would only make matters worse. Instead, he straightened in his seat, drawing their attention.

"It appears, my noble lords, that you are at an impasse. Might I suggest you postpone the matter of succession until you locate the missing members of this esteemed council?"

"An excellent idea, Your Highness," said Lord Elgin, "and one that allows us to move on to another matter that has come to our attention."

"Which is?"

"The acts of treachery committed by Lord James Goodwin and his associates."

"And what is the precise nature of this treachery?" asked Lord Julian.

"Treason," said Lord Elgin. "He's been accused of conspiring with the enemy to allow the invaders entry into Summersgate without opposition."

"A most serious charge. Have we proof?"

"That is for the courts to decide."

"Then why bring it to us?" asked Lord Oliver.

"As a noble, only his peers can judge him. It thus falls to us to name three barons or viscounts to oversee the trial. It will, in turn, be up to them to appoint investigators to gather the facts."

"Then whom do we choose?"

"Good question," said Lord Julian, "although a better question might be who's left to pick from?"

"What about Lady Lindsey Martindale?" suggested Lord Elgin. "She survived, didn't she?"

"I believe so, but that still leaves us two short."

"Lord Tulfar is still with us," noted Lord Oliver, "although he is a Dwarf. I'm not sure he'd be my first choice."

"Wait a moment," said Lord Elgin, his gaze flicking to Prince Alric. "We forgot about Jack Marlowe."

"That would be Lord Jack, now that his father is dead, but yes, that's an excellent choice."

"That settles it, then. The three of them will form the court."

Lord Oliver pursed his lips. "I thought we agreed not to use Lord Tulfar?"

"No. You're the one who suggested we might not want him. Personally, I'm fine with him."

"I second that motion," added Lord Julian.

Lord Oliver sighed. "Very well. It appears we have our selection. I only hope you two know what you're doing."

"Meaning?"

Lord Oliver lowered his voice. "Lord Tulfar has been trying to throw his weight around."

"In what way?"

"He wants a seat on the council, says he has Princess Althea's backing."

At that revelation, Alric suddenly took more interest in the proceedings.

"He can say what he wants," said Lord Elgin. "It doesn't make it true. Besides, Althea doesn't rule in Weldwyn, nor will she ever, unless we change the laws, and I don't see that happening any time soon."

They all nodded in agreement.

Alric, despite his interest in the coming trial, found his thoughts drifting elsewhere. "You must excuse me, noble lords," he said, "for there are other things I must attend to."

They all stood as he left the room.

Jack waited in the hallway. "Ah, there you are," said the cavalier. "I thought I'd lost you. Managed to stay awake, did you?"

Alric chuckled. "Not so much, but I overheard a tidbit or two."

The cavalier rubbed his hands together. "Ah, there's nothing quite like a nice bit of gossip. What is it? Someone found a new mistress or something?"

"No, not that."

"Then what?"

"It appears my sister may have made some promises."

"What kind of promises?"

"Let's go find out, shall we, while you still have time."

"What do you mean by that?"

Alric smiled. "Let's just say you may soon find yourself very busy."

The Grand Edifice of the Arcane Wizards Council, better known as 'the Dome', had seen better days. During the occupation, Kythelia sought to gain the knowledge stored therein, but Tyrell Caracticus, the chief administrator, took steps to deny her of her prize, losing his life in the process. Most of the shelves now sat empty, the rooms still littered with bloodstains and broken furniture.

Princess Althea had spent the last three months cleaning up pockets of Clan resistance in the south, but with that campaign now over, she'd taken up temporary residence in the Dome. Alric respected her decision, but the sight of Dwarven warriors in front of the place upon his arrival surprised him.

The guards stepped aside, allowing Jack and him entrance without a challenge. It was heartbreaking to see the damage wrought by Kythelia's warriors. The fighting had been brutal during the last stages of the assault, but even worse was the discovery of the torture that preceded it. Of all the mages and apprentices from the Dome, only those who fled to Merceria still lived. The loss to the kingdom was profound, and Alric wondered if Weldwyn would ever see their like again.

"We're here," said Jack.

The pair of Dwarves guarding the door eyed them suspiciously. Alric moved to open it, but the two guards stepped closer together, crossing their axes to block his advance.

"And who might you be?" asked the taller of the two.

"Althea's brother, Prince Alric."

"How do I know you're telling the truth?"

The prince stared back, unsure how to react.

"He bears a resemblance to her," noted the shorter guard.

His companion shrugged. "What do I know? Humans all look alike to me." They stood aside, allowing the visitors entry.

Alric opened the door, revealing a modest apartment, with Althea sitting at a table, examining some papers. She waved her hand in irritation but didn't deign to look up. "Not now. I'm busy."

"Is that how you treat your only remaining brother?"

She looked up in surprise. "Alric! What are you doing in Summersgate?"

"Meeting with the Earls Council. You?"

"A great number of things. It appears the kingdom has almost come to a complete standstill in our absence."

"I can well believe that," he replied. "They killed all the earls, not to mention half the barons. The council is now comprised of little more than boys."

"Hardly," said Althea. "I might remind you they're close to you in age."

"Yes. You're right. I suppose I just feel older."

"It's all the campaigning you've been doing."

He moved closer, gazing down at the notes scattered around her table. "What's all this?"

"Pleas for help, for the most part. The entire population is struggling, those in the capital even more so. The invaders destroyed everything they couldn't steal and killed all who resisted."

"It will be a lot of work to restore the kingdom," he agreed, "but that's not why I'm here."

"Then speak plainly, dear brother. Let there be no secrets between us."

"I'm curious about your relationship with Lord Tulfar."

"He's a good friend and a stalwart ally. Malin knows we had few of them during the war. Why? What are you getting at?"

"It's been implied you made certain promises to him concerning the Dwarves."

"What promises?"

"Representation on the Earls Council, for one." Alric chuckled.

"You find that amusing?"

"Only in that the very same idea occurred to me. I even talked it over with Anna."

"And what conclusion did you come to?"

"That our kingdom needs to be more inclusive. The Dwarves of Mirstone carried out an active campaign against our enemies under your direction. We must reward that."

"Yet…"

"What makes you think there's a yet?"

"I recognize that look," said Althea. "You are my brother after all."

"I agree with the idea, but I can do nothing about it until the Earls Council is properly reconstituted."

"Weldwyn only has five earldoms. What gives these five individuals the right to decide on the next king? That's what this is about, isn't it?"

He grinned. "Well, I can hardly make changes if I'm not king."

"I think you underestimate your influence. You are the last heir to the Throne of Weldwyn. Who else could the council choose?"

"You'd be surprised what an ambitious noble can come up with. In any case, there's little I can do to change their opinions."

"Isn't there?"

"What are you suggesting?"

"The Mercerians carry a lot of influence in Weldwyn, especially their marshal. Everyone knows his leadership enabled our liberation, and that's not even including his part in defeating the previous invasion."

"So, you suggest I use Gerald to influence the earls?"

"That's what I would do, were I you."

"Since when did you become so clever?"

"I've had a lot of time to think of late."

"Tell me more."

"The very concept of the Earls Council is outdated. It should be redesigned. You're familiar with the Nobles Council of Merceria; how does that work?"

"It has more voices," said Alric, "and that often leads to more arguments."

"But is it effective?"

"Yes, though I believe that has more to do with Anna's allies on the council. She's experienced her fair share of discontent since her coronation, but she's kept them in line so far."

"Do you believe something like that would work in Weldwyn?"

"We'd have difficulty convincing the earls to give up any of their power. We also have more barons than the Mercerians, which would make for crowded council chambers."

"There are Dwarves on their council, aren't there?"

"Yes," said Alric. "That would be Herdwin, but he represents the opinion of a foreign ruler, the King of Stonecastle. He's not a baron."

"He gets a vote, though, doesn't he?"

"Yes."

"Then it amounts to the same thing. The truth is, it's not about the earls but representation. Between them, the earls control the five largest cities in Weldwyn, but there's more to this kingdom than those. Why should they get to dictate what the rest of the realm does?"

She paused a moment, giving him time to mull things over, but continued before he could say anything. "You realize all of this is just postponing the inevitable."

"I'm not sure I understand what you're suggesting?"

"You and Anna have a son. One day, he'll inherit the Thrones of both Weldwyn and Merceria. That means we'll eventually be a single, united kingdom."

He smiled. "Of course it does. The Earls Council must learn to adapt, or it will eventually be swept away when the two kingdoms merge."

"Providing the current council chooses you to rule, and therein lies the problem. They may see that inevitability as an affront to their power and influence. Perhaps that's why they won't give you the Crown?"

"And you believe I can convince them otherwise?"

"You'd know better than I," said Althea. "I never took much of an interest in our politics."

Alric laughed. "How things have changed. It used to be, you wanted to be a warrior princess, even more so once you met Anna."

"Well, you must admit, she sets a fine example. The question now is how you proceed from this point forward?"

"Thank you," said Alric. "You've helped me clear my mind. I may not be the king at the moment, but being prince still gives me quite a few powers. I shall use those to do what I can to ease the suffering of our people."

"And when you become king, Brother, what will you do with me?"

"I don't have the faintest idea, but I'm guessing you might have some thoughts on the subject?"

"I do, though I'm loathe to speak of them until I do a bit more work."

"Work? You sound like a merchant."

"Then call it research, if you like. One thing I've learned from the Dwarves is to be prepared."

"For what? The war is over."

"The war may be over, but there are plenty of battles ahead."

The words stuck with Alric as he returned to his lodgings, Jack still by his side. With the Palace destroyed, they'd taken up residence at the Drake, a luxurious place that, before the war, catered to an exclusive clientele—the nobles of Weldwyn.

Jack went in first, and Alric paused as he entered, suddenly realizing he'd neglected his duty as a friend.

"I'm sorry, Jack," he said at last. "With all that's been going on of late, I haven't offered my condolences on your father's loss."

"Quite all right, Highness. After all, he and I seldom got along. I loathed the man, if truth be told, but now that he's gone, I feel a strange sense of... emptiness. Still, I suppose that makes me the Viscount Aynsbury, or at least it will once I'm confirmed. How does that work, by the way?"

"I'm surprised you don't already know."

"I never paid much attention to my father's lessons. I preferred to spend my time out riding, which led to no end of arguments, but what else could I do? The man was an ogre."

"Was he always like that?" asked Alric.

"I seem to recall him more kind-hearted when I was a young lad, but I fear my mother's death put an end to such things."

"As to your assumption of title, you may begin using it at your earliest convenience."

Jack straightened. "I daresay that ought to impress the ladies."

"Are you suggesting you couldn't impress them without it?"

"No, of course not, but it puts another arrow in my quiver, if you get my meaning."

"Yes, well, don't let it go to your head."

"I suppose I should visit Aynsbury and see to the estate."

"Have you any family left?"

"A few distant cousins, provided they still live, but I honestly don't remember their names. They'll undoubtedly crawl out of the woodwork now that I've inherited my father's estate." He paused a moment. "Say, why don't you come with me? We can make an adventure of it."

"I'd love to, Jack, but I'm afraid I have duties here, not to mention back in Wincaster. Perhaps another time?"

"Of course, Highness."

"I should give you fair warning, Jack. The Twelve Clans ravaged the countryside. There's a distinct possibility you might not find things as you last saw them."

"Meaning?"

"Your father was renowned for his horses. I doubt the invaders left such a prize unattended."

The cavalier scowled. "Yes. I suppose you're right. I hadn't considered such an eventuality. Ah well, if they're gone, they're gone."

"You can always get more. You might even breed Mercerian Chargers. Malin knows we need more of them."

"That's an excellent idea, but we'll have to change their name. What do you think about calling them Jack's Chargers? Or perhaps Marlowe's Mighty Mounts? That has a certain ring to it."

Alric laughed. "I'll leave that entirely in your charge, my lord."

THREE

Lochlan

AUTUMN 966 MC

Lochlan, now chieftain of Clan Dungannon, looked out over the encampment. His fellow Clansmen wandered around aimlessly, living a miserable existence under the watchful eye of Weldwyn warriors. He'd promised a truce when the war ended, that his men would march back to their homes, but that agreement required the King of Weldwyn's approval, and to date, no one had been named. As a result, the Clansmen now lived in a makeshift village of tents five miles north of Summersgate. Though it was only supposed to be a temporary measure, they'd remained in this stinking hole for almost three months.

He spotted Ellis, the Weldwyn captain, walking through the camp with guards following in his wake.

"Captain," Lochlan called out. "I wonder if I might have a word?"

Upon hearing his request, Ellis turned, heading directly for the Clansman, his heavy steps indicating he was in his usual foul mood.

"Well?" the fellow snapped. "What is it this time?"

"I need to talk to your superior. It's a matter of great importance."

"You'll speak to me, or you'll speak to no one," the captain snarled. "Now, what is it?"

"The Clan folk need to return home. Winter is fast approaching, and these tents will do little to keep us warm."

"Perhaps you should've thought of that before you invaded our land?"

"I am Lochlan, Chief of Clan Dungannon," Lochlan said, straightening his back. "I demand to speak to your superior."

"You're no one here. Why, if it were within my power, I'd string up the lot of you filthy—"

A distant horn blast interrupted his words.

"What's this, now?" The captain whirled around, his discussion forgotten. "Come," he said to his entourage of guards. "We must see who's deigned to visit this stinking pit of filth."

He strode off, his men following. Lochlan understood the captain intended the order for his guards but chose to play ignorant, following in their wake, eager for the opportunity to make contact with an outsider—any outsider.

A hastily constructed wooden fence demarked the camp's outer perimeter, and a man could easily climb over such an obstacle were it not for the archers who stood watch fifty paces farther out. In the early days of their internment, several Clansmen had tried to escape, but only one survived. Thanks to the arrow to his leg, he was forever crippled.

The captain suddenly picked up his pace, and Lochlan wondered who commanded such attention. Other Clansmen, eager to discover what the Clan Chief was up to, followed, creating a sea of people who would, no doubt, raise Captain Ellis' ire.

As the entrance to the camp came into view, an unexpected sight greeted Lochlan—that of a young woman around his own age astride a horse. That, by itself, was strange enough way out here, but adding to the mystery was the group of short, mail-clad warriors surrounding her. As he drew closer, he realized they had to be mountain folk, although he'd never met one in person.

Captain Ellis bowed deeply. "Greetings."

"Who commands here?" the mysterious woman replied.

"I do. Captain Ellis, at your service, my lady."

"That's Your Highness," barked out the rough voice of a Dwarf. "Mind your manners, Human."

The captain stiffened but held his tongue.

"I come seeking someone who speaks for the Twelve Clans. I believe it's a man going by the name of Lochlan."

"That's me," the Clan Chief called out, pushing his way forward.

The woman dismounted and came to stand before him, looking him up and down. "You're younger than I expected."

"I've lived eighteen summers, and we have that in common by the look of it."

"I'll have you know I'm twenty."

"And someone who lives in splendour. Who are you that comes to this place in the company of the mountain folk?"

A wry smile escaped her lips. "I am Althea, Warrior Princess of Weldwyn and Dwarf friend."

He bowed. "Pleased to meet you, Highness. Might I ask why you came all this way? You could've easily summoned me to your Palace."

"Palace? There is no Palace. Your dragon saw to that."

"A dragon your own people destroyed. I shall not apologize for the sins of my sister. She did what she believed right for her people."

"They are your people now," said Althea. "How they live, going forward, is for you to decide."

"I cannot decide anything as a prisoner."

"Walk with me," she said, then turned, making her way out of the encampment.

Lochlan looked at his jailer, but the captain merely nodded.

"What is it you want?" he said, rushing to catch up.

"Peace."

"Then it appears we have something else in common."

"Why did your people invade Weldwyn?" asked the princess.

"An Elf led us astray. You must understand that my father, King Dathen, was imprisoned in Summersgate."

"Only after he invaded us back in sixty-one. Are you suggesting the Elves had something to do with that as well?"

"I wouldn't know. The king did not take me into his confidence."

"It seems to me, there's always been conflict between our respective people. It's about time we got to the bottom of it, don't you think?"

Lochlan shrugged. "It's no secret. We live in a harsh land, scrabbling to survive, while your kingdom has lush fields and plentiful crops."

"You could've offered something in trade for food. Instead, you rode across the river and raided. Why?"

"It's our way. If we're not fighting you, we're fighting amongst ourselves. The truth is, Weldwyn is a common enemy, something to bring our people together."

"And what if there was a better way?" asked Althea.

"I'm listening."

"I propose a new era in relations between the Clanholdings and Weld-wyn, one of peace and co-operation."

"I see much to recommend this plan of yours," said Lochlan, "but we've been enemies for generations. It would be difficult to convince my countrymen."

"Would you be willing to try?"

He stopped walking and looked back at the camp. Everyone within sight watched them, no doubt wondering what they were discussing.

"Well?" she pressed.

Lochlan returned his gaze to the princess but perceived no signs of deceit. "I am a scholar at heart and not used to the ways of court."

"Then I appeal to your intellect. What do you think of this idea?"

"It would be easier if there was a show of good faith."

"Such as?"

"Well, for one, you could replace Captain Ellis with someone a little more sympathetic to our plight."

"Your plight?"

"Yes. We live in tents, and the winter winds will soon blow down from the north. We shall likely perish beneath winter's grip if nothing is done."

"I will inform my brother of what I discovered here today. It's safe to say the captain will find his tenure cut short in the next day or two."

"And the tents?"

"I think it's high time we sent your people home, don't you?"

"Will your brother agree to that?"

"I'm hopeful. Make no mistake, it will be a difficult task and require an army to escort them, but I believe it's a far better solution in the long run. In the meantime, I suggest you stop trying to antagonize the captain."

"I shall do what I can."

"That's encouraging. I'll send for you in a day or two to discuss the matter further."

"I look forward to it, Highness."

She turned to her escort. "Brogar. Would you come here a moment?"

A Dwarf stepped forward, bowing deeply.

"This is Brogar Hammerhand, one of my most trusted warriors. I will send him to escort you to Summersgate when the time comes."

"Why are you telling me this?" asked Lochlan.

"I've recently learned the politics of Weldwyn can often be deceitful. No doubt, some might attempt to take advantage of your presence."

"Are you suggesting someone might attempt to kill me?"

"Kill, no, but were they to discover my plan, they'd oppose the idea of sending you home. I wouldn't put it past them to create an incident that incited some sort of violence so that there's a reason to keep you here. I shall talk to Captain Ellis, ensuring your safety while in his care, and inform him that only Brogar is authorized to remove you from this camp."

"Thank you, Highness," said Lochlan, bowing deeply.

She gently touched his shoulder. "I would have you stand, Lochlan. If there is to be peace between our lands, then we must be seen as equals, else all this will be for naught."

"I understand, but first, you need to know that, while I am Chief of Dungannon, I am not the High King. That title died with my sister."

"And how is a High King chosen?"

"By a gathering of the Clans, which has only happened a few times in our long history."

"Then we'll start with Dungannon. Tell me, do they accept you as their chief?"

"They do, although they're not all happy about it."

"Why is that?" she asked.

"I am no warrior."

"And they see no honour in a scholar?"

"That's the gist of it, yes."

She stared at him, deep in thought. "They will see you differently once you secure their release."

"Once I secure their release? I've done nothing."

Althea glanced at the distant crowd. "They don't need to know that."

Alric looked up as Althea entered his room. "Trouble?" he asked.

"Can't a sister simply drop by to visit?"

He set down his correspondence. "We both know that's out of character for you. There's obviously something troubling you; let me ease you of that burden."

"It's the Twelve Clans."

"What about the Clans?"

"We can't just sit back and watch them all die off as winter settles in."

"There are some who might argue otherwise."

"Can you honestly tell me you're happy with that?"

"No," said Alric. "Of course not."

"I think it's time we send them home."

"As do I, but how do we ensure they don't simply rebuild and try again?"

"We help them."

"And how do we do that?"

"They live in a harsh landscape; we could trade them food."

"And what would we get in return?"

"Who knows? They must possess something of worth."

"You, dear sister, have uncovered the uncomfortable truth about our relations with the Twelve Clans."

"Which is?"

"That we know next to nothing about them."

"Then we must change that."

"We've tried in the past, and all our envoys were either driven out or murdered."

"Lochlan wouldn't do that."

"Oh? On a first-name basis with the Clan Chief, are we now?"

"For Malin's sake, what else would I call him?"

"How about, Chieftain? That is his title, or is it Clan leader? I've never been entirely sure what their customs are in that regard."

"This is not a laughing matter."

Alric sobered. "No, you're right, it's not. Please excuse my behaviour."

"How would Father have handled this?"

"Probably at the end of a sword, but I am not him. Once king, I must somehow peacefully coexist with these people. I would prefer to do so without the necessity of maintaining a large army on their border."

"I still believe an envoy is a better solution than constant war."

"And I agree, but the risk to whoever goes there is enormous." He sat for a moment, mulling things over. "What about a marriage?"

"A marriage?"

"Yes. We could marry this Lochlan fellow into one of the noble families of Weldwyn. There must be a surviving daughter around somewhere who's the right age."

"No, it has to be someone of Royal Blood. It's the only thing that would demonstrate our commitment to peace."

"Surely you're not suggesting yourself?"

"Why not? Am I not a Royal Princess?"

"But you'd be putting yourself in danger!"

"I shall take some bodyguards to keep me safe."

Alric shook his head. "I never expected you, of all people, to throw away your life in so callous a manner."

She moved closer, holding his hands in hers. "You will have the Crown," she said, "but even if they deny you, you still have Anna and a place in Wincaster. Deep down, I've always known that, as a princess, I was destined to be married—if not to a noble of Weldwyn, then to some foreign lord. This way, I'm at least taking charge of my destiny."

"But you'd be marrying a Clansman!"

"Not so long ago, even the mention of Merceria filled us with disgust, and now, here you are, married to their queen."

He chuckled. "Yes. I suppose that's true, and Malin knows you've proven your worth over the last few months. I will consider your request, but I have a few caveats of my own."

"Such as?"

"I'll send riders with you to carry dispatches, and I expect you to report regularly on your efforts to bring about peaceful relations."

"I can live with that, but don't we need to gain approval from the Earls Council?"

"Not at all. As the senior male of our family, it's entirely within my purview as to whom you marry. I would insist, however, that Lochlan agrees to this. I'm not about to force him into anything distasteful."

"You think me distasteful?"

"That's not what I meant. I merely wished to imply his heart must be in it, or it will be bound to fail. I met him during the war, although I spent little time in his company. I suppose if we are to propose a marriage between the two of you, we should rectify that?"

"We could arrange a meeting here, in Summersgate," offered Althea. "Do you think Anna would come?"

"I'm returning to Wincaster this evening. I'll ask her myself."

"You're coming back, I hope?"

"Naturally. There's too much to do here in Summersgate. Not that it's a big imposition when there are mages to transport me back and forth in the blink of an eye. I tell you what. You pick a date, and I'll work around it."

"Shall we say two days hence?"

"Two days, then, and let's make it dinner, shall we? Much easier to free up time in the evening. I'll leave it to you to arrange it."

"Thank you, Alric."

"Don't mention it. Oh, I just had a thought. Should I bring Edwina?"

"If you can, although by now, she's probably deep in her studies."

"I'm sure they can spare her for an evening." He paused a moment. "Something wrong?"

"It just occurred to me this will be the first time the three of us have been together for… well, let's say it's been quite some time. I would suggest we make it more of a regular occurrence now that the war's over, but with you traipsing off to the Clan holdings, I suppose we must postpone any family gatherings for the time being."

"I'm hardly traipsing," said Althea. "And who knows, someday I might convince them to build a magic circle in Dungannon, and then a visit will be a simple matter of finding an available mage."

"Perhaps, but from my understanding, creating such a thing carries an enormous expense."

"Why is that?"

"I'm told gold is required to hold the magic—the more powerful the circle, the greater the expense. There's also the problem of having available mages. I'm afraid Kythelia killed off most of the Dome's residents."

"Yes, but the Mercerians have them in abundance, don't they?"

"They have some, but hardly what I'd call an abundance. Lady Aubrey's starting her Conservatory of Magic soon, but from what I understand, it takes years to train a mage."

"And has she any students?"

"I assume she does, though it hasn't exactly been the object of my attention of late. Events here in Summersgate saw to that."

"But you've kept in touch with Edwina, surely?"

"I have, indeed. That's how I know they've been working on readying the conservatory. She's been helping Lady Aubrey with things. She's also learning Orcish."

"The language of the Orcs? Why in Malin's name would she need that?"

"The Army of Merceria uses it for all of its written correspondence, making it much harder for intercepted messages to reveal important information."

"I suppose that makes sense. I myself have been learning the basics of the Dwarven tongue, but I must admit, it's challenging."

"Why's that?"

"It's an ancient language bearing little resemblance to our own."

"You could say the same of the Orcs," said Alric. "Anna tells me their language is descended from the ancients, as is that of the Dwarves and Elves."

"I find that difficult to believe," said Althea.

"No, it's true. I've become fluent in Orcish, and it's made learning Elvish so much easier."

"And have you tackled the language of Dwarves yet?"

"No, but that matters little. The Dwarves in service to Merceria all speak our language, and they generally speak it when outside their own realms."

"Yes, and inside as well. Lord Tulfar says they primarily use Dwarvish only for ceremonial occasions."

"Then why learn it?"

"They've made me their protector," she replied, "and I take that obligation seriously. They also possess a fascinating culture."

"Yet you'd prefer to travel into Clan territory instead of returning to Mirstone?"

"I have a lifetime to learn more about the Dwarves. The Clan holdings need my help now if we are to end this constant strife that has set our two kingdoms at each other's throats."

"Well, I look forward to seeing what Lord Lochlan thinks of all this. Or would that be His Highness? Do we even know the correct form of address for a Clan Chief?"

"Come to think of it, no, we don't."

FOUR

Claimant

B everly entered the map room where the Queen of Merceria sat at the table, along with Gerald and Aubrey. The only other occupant, Sir Randolf Blackburn, stood off to one side. The solemn mood of those in the room surprised the knight as she settled in beside her cousin.

"Now," said the queen. "Let's get to the bottom of this, shall we? Sir Randolf, you claim Bodden is your birthright but have so far produced nothing to prove your claim."

"Yes," added Gerald, "and how is it that a Blackburn should claim a title that's been in the Fitzwilliam family for generations?"

"My father was Lord Edward Fitzwilliam, Baron of Bodden. He named me after one of his closest friends, Sir Randolf of Burrstoke."

"But Lord Edward died in thirty-three during the siege."

"Then where is his body?" replied Sir Randolf.

"He was blown to bits igniting the combustibles that destroyed the wall."

"No, he wasn't. They bore him away on a makeshift stretcher and took him prisoner."

"Are you suggesting he somehow survived?"

"Am I not living proof?"

"He lies!" said Beverly. "It's taken me a moment to place the name, but this man is the brother of Celia Blackburn, the traitor who died in Norwatch."

"Brother?" said Anna. "What have you to say for yourself, Sir Randolf?"

"I do not defend my sister's actions. She was always headstrong and rash, and there was no excuse for her behaviour."

"Yet you now claim Bodden as your own?"

"She did, too," added Beverly. "Before she died, she said Bodden was promised to her."

"By whom?" asked Gerald.

"She didn't say."

"I can answer that," said Sir Randolf. "My father wished that she inherit the title."

"Why not you? After all, the old laws of succession would have been in place. You, as his son, would be the logical pick."

"I didn't want it."

"Yet you try to claim it now," said Beverly.

"I was content to live out my life in Norland until recent events made it clear the influence of Merceria is spreading throughout the region. There is no longer a king in Norland, only a queen who has no interest in bestowing titles or rewards upon her people. Merceria, on the other hand, is a kingdom of laws, is it not?"

"It is," said Anna.

"Then I only ask a fair chance to prove my claim."

"Lady Beverly has served this Crown for a long time."

"I will not speak ill of Dame Beverly, for everyone knows she's been a faithful servant to Your Majesty. However, that doesn't mean I'll give up my legal claim to Bodden."

"You can't be taking this seriously?" said Aubrey. "Lord Richard was the Baron of Bodden, Beverly, his only child. Surely his recognition as baron supersedes this man's claim to the title?"

"Would you now throw away the very laws that define your reign?" asked Sir Randolf. "I readily admit my claim is not convenient or particularly timely, but from all accounts, you wish Merceria to be a land ruled by law. Would you put that aside simply for the sake of friendship? What kind of example would that set?"

"You still haven't fully explained your presence," said Gerald. "You claim Lord Edward was your father, yet you bear the name Blackburn."

"My apologies, but the name Fitzwilliam was loathed in Norland for many years. After Lord Hollis took him in and had him nursed back to health, my father married the lord's cousin."

"And you were born shortly afterwards—is that what you're trying to tell us?"

"Celia came first. I followed two years later."

"And where is your father now?"

"Dead, I'm afraid. He was never in good health after the severe burns he suffered at Bodden. In the end, a cold snap proved too much for him. I remember it well, although I was only seven at the time."

"And his body?"

"Interred in a crypt in Beaconsgate."

"What of your mother?" asked the queen.

"She, too, eventually passed, succumbing to a fever two years ago."

The silence in the room was deafening. Anna had much to consider, and no one wanted to interrupt her thoughts. Beverly stared daggers at Sir Randolf, but something in his manner stilled them. Was he telling the truth? Could he have a lawful claim against Bodden? Part of her raged at the unfairness of it all, yet she had to admit the story seemed plausible.

She knew little of her uncle's life and even less about his death. Her father always spoke fondly of his elder brother, lamenting that there was no body to place in the family crypt.

She looked at Gerald, but he appeared uncomfortable, shuffling his feet, and avoiding eye contact. Did he know something? He'd been there at the siege when Lord Edward died. What was he hiding?

"I must give this matter a great deal of thought," Anna finally said. "In the meantime, Dame Beverly will continue overseeing things as the Lady of Bodden." Her gaze swept the room. "You three may leave us now so that Gerald and I can discuss the matter privately."

Gerald watched them depart, with some trepidation. He knew what was coming, and part of him loathed the very idea of dragging up such old memories.

"Well?" said Anna. "What do you think?"

"You should ignore the man and give Bodden to Beverly. She's certainly earned it."

"But..." added the queen.

"What makes you believe there's a but?"

"Your manner, for one. Gerald, I've known you since I was a little girl. You're Braedon's grandfather, for Saxnor's sake. You don't think I can tell when you're holding something back?"

He took a deep breath and let it out slowly, trying to fight down the rising panic. "There may be some truth to Sir Randolf's claims. There. I've said it."

"Care to explain?"

"I've told you before about that night."

"Refresh my memory."

"You don't forget anything," said Gerald. "You're cursed with a perfect memory."

"I am, but I haven't all the details of the night in question. Perhaps, in the retelling, it will help you remember everything that transpired. Lord Edward told you and Fitz not to enter the enemy encampment, didn't he?"

"That's true. Fitz planned on going in alone, but a small group of us insisted on accompanying him. You must realize the keep was doomed. Lord Edward was considering surrendering Bodden. Fitz knew if we destroyed the enemy's catapults, it would buy us time."

He closed his eyes and took another deep breath, reliving the moment. "I can still see their faces. Fletcher, whose wife had been injured by a horse. Blackwood, of course, along with Cooper and Graves, both of whom died that night. We climbed down the south wall, the better to avoid Lord Edward's gaze, and then crept along in the dark until we found the catapults. We intended to set fire to them, but to do that, we had to take out the sentries first."

His hands began to shake.

She moved closer, taking his arm and guiding him to a chair. "Was it bad?"

"I've killed many men in my time, Anna, but that night will forever haunt me. I saw the look in Cooper's eyes as an arrow took his life. It's one thing to lose a comrade in battle, quite another when they're a lifelong friend."

"You destroyed the catapults, didn't you?"

"We did, then we were moving off into the darkness to escape a counterattack when we saw a brilliant flash as fire lit up the wall. Lord Edward had ordered anything that could burn to be placed in readiness for the expected assault. The plan was always to light it at the last possible moment to destroy the attack. We learned later that Lord Edward lit the fuse, only to be blown up in the process."

"Who reported that?"

"Sir James, if I recall correctly. Why?"

"The court will need to determine if the baron was indeed killed. They never found a body, remember?"

"No one could've survived that explosion."

"You might be surprised by what people survive should the circumstances be favourable. Now tell me, did you see anyone carried from the field?"

"I... I think perhaps I did right after the explosion. I seem to recall someone borne away on a stretcher, but we assumed it was one of the Norlanders."

"That makes perfect sense," said Anna. "You had no reason to suspect Lord Edward incapacitated instead of killed."

"For Saxnor's sake, was he truly in the Norlanders' hands all those years?"

"I cannot deny the possibility, but it will take more than mere speculation to determine the truth."

"So you mean to investigate?"

"I shall send word to Hayley. In her capacity as High Ranger, it will be her responsibility to delve into this mystery."

"Beverly won't like this."

"Nor do I, but if this kingdom is to prosper after my death, I must put aside my personal feelings on the matter in the interest of fairness."

"And if his claim is recognized, what happens to Beverly?"

"Beverly will be ennobled eventually, even if I must create a new barony for just that purpose."

"Let's hope it doesn't come to that."

"There is something else to consider," said Anna.

"Which is?"

"How is it Sir Randolf arrived in Bodden just in time to announce his claim? All the other guests were brought here by magic."

"Could it be a coincidence?"

"The war's been over for months. Why press his claim now rather than when Lord Richard still lived?"

"I can't answer that," said Gerald, "but I sense you have a theory."

"I do. There are very few people alive today who knew Lord Edward well. In fact, Fitz himself may have been the last person who could refute Sir Randolf's story."

"But he didn't know about the man's existence."

"True," said Anna, "but he could've dispelled such tales by asking about his brother, things we would expect a son to know, don't you see?"

"I suppose, but it's too late now. I suggest you pass your theories on to Hayley, but ultimately, it'll be her task to determine the truth, not ours."

Lady Hayley Chambers, Baroness of Queenston and High Ranger, drew back the arrow, took careful aim, then let loose. It sailed through the air, striking the centre of the target.

"Very good," said Gorath. "That new bow suits you well."

"I should hope so. It cost a lot more than I expected."

"Come now. You are the High Ranger. What else have you to spend your coins on?"

"Believe it or not, I still have to survive. That means I have to eat, not to mention sleep somewhere. Houses don't grow on trees, you know."

He stared at her before breaking into a smile. "You are hoping to win the archery contest next week."

"There's a contest next week?"

"You know full well there is. You yourself sanctioned it in the queen's name."

"Oh, that contest. Well, it is the responsibility of rangers to keep up with their skills. I assume you'll be competing?"

"I had not planned on it."

Hayley spotted Bertram Ayles coming towards them with a note in hand. He'd taken a crossbow bolt to the chest at the attack on Ravensguard and had been shy of bows ever since. She lowered her own bow as he approached. "Is that for me?"

"It is," the fellow replied, handing it over. "Just came in."

She looked at the seal. "It seems the queen has some pressing need, else she would've waited until the next meeting of the Nobles Council."

She broke the seal, carefully unfolded it, and scanned its contents.

"Trouble?" asked Gorath.

She read it a second time, ensuring she'd not misinterpreted anything. "Someone has come forward to claim the Barony of Bodden."

"But that's Dame Beverly's," said Ayles. "Who would do such a thing?"

"According to this, a man named Sir Randolf Blackburn."

"Blackburn?"

"Yes, brother to Celia Blackburn. Do you know the name?"

"Who doesn't?" said Ayles. "It's not every day a Knight of the Hound betrays the Crown."

"He claims to be the son of Lord Edward Fitzwilliam, Beverly's uncle."

"But he died in a siege, didn't he?"

"That's what we were all led to believe."

"So, what is it the queen expects us to do?"

"Investigate," said Hayley. "More specifically, test the validity of his claims."

"And how do we go about doing that?"

"Well, we can begin by locating Sir James."

"Who is?" asked Bertram.

"An older knight who served in Bodden at the time of Lord Edward's purported death. There is reason to believe he may have witnessed the baron's demise first-hand. If that's true, we can easily put this entire matter to rest."

"And if not?"

"Then we must travel to Norland."

"Whatever for?"

"To corroborate Sir Randolf's story," replied Hayley. "Go and find me Sam, would you? I'd like her to lend a hand in this."

"Why?"

"Because she served in Bodden during the civil war when Sir James and his companions showed up to help Lord Richard."

"How does that help us?"

"Well," said Hayley, "for one thing, she knows what the fellow looks like, and it wouldn't hurt to have a friendly face when we finally track him down."

"I'll get right on it," replied Ayles. He turned, running back towards the building.

"He wants to know everything," said Gorath.

"That's precisely why I want him helping us with this. Don't get me wrong, all our rangers are good at keeping the roads safe, but this task may require a little more depth."

"Where would you like me to start?"

Hayley handed over the letter. "We need to create a list of anybody who served at Bodden back in thirty-three. I suggest you start with the Palace archives."

"That will list everyone?"

"No, only those the king sent. I know Lord Richard kept precise records, but I'm unaware how good his brother was at recording things of that nature."

"That was over thirty years ago. Will anyone still be alive?"

"I know that's old for an Orc, but Humans often live longer. The marshal was at Bodden then, and he still lives. Let's hope others do as well."

"Do you think we will need help from Lord Arnim and Lady Nicole?"

"Not at the moment, but if we run into trouble in Norland, we may have no other choice."

"Then I shall let them know we might require their services in the future."

"That's a reasonable precaution," said Hayley. She looked at the archery target. "I suppose this means my practice is over." She headed off to retrieve her arrows, calling for Gryph. The wolf, lounging in the sun, lifted its head before jumping up and running across the field towards her.

"Well," she said. "It's about time you woke up."

She pulled out her arrows, examining each for damage. "You know, I should teach you to retrieve these. It would make my life so much easier."

Gryph sat on his haunches, looking at her and licking his chops.

"I suppose it's well past that time, isn't it? Come on, then. Let's fetch my horse, and then we'll do a little hunting. There's nothing quite like fresh meat."

The wolf bounded off towards the stables.

"He understands you," said Gorath.

"You have wolves in your villages," said Hayley. "How does Gryph compare to them?"

"The master of wolves cares for them in our tribe. They are kept separate from the rest of the tribe, though that is not the case when Zhura is present. She claims they calm the spirits."

"You don't believe her?"

"It is not my place to speak ill of a ghostwalker," said Gorath, "but it has always been this way to hone their hunting instincts."

"An interesting theory, but Gryph's hunting instincts seem intact, even though he wasn't raised in a pack."

"Ah, but he was."

"No, he wasn't. Norland raiders killed his pack."

"Yes, but the rangers have become his pack."

"I suppose I hadn't thought of things that way. It also helps that Albreda talks to him on occasion."

"Now, that," said the Orc, "is a frightening thought."

"You don't like the idea that she can talk with wolves?"

"It is not wolves so much as other animals. We Orcs like to hunt, but it is unsettling to think a Druid can talk to animals."

"Why is that?"

"Do you really want to know what your dinner is thinking before you cook it?"

"Now that you mention it, I suppose not."

"Then you understand my revulsion."

"Just because she can doesn't mean she will."

"Also true, yet the very fact it is even possible suggests a certain intelligence on the part of a deer, not to mention other animals we consume. That makes me wonder if they think as we do. Do they love their families? Have friends? Do they gather round with other members of their herd and tell stories of times long past?"

"You've given this entire concept far too much consideration," said Hayley. "I'm surprised you haven't stopped eating meat entirely."

Gorath frowned. "Why would I do that?"

"You were just wondering about their lives. I only assumed you felt some guilt."

He laughed. "Wonderment, yes, but guilt? Not at all. I like the taste of venison too much!"

FIVE

A Country in Ruins

AUTUMN 966 MC

"May I say," said Lord Elgin, "it's a pleasure to welcome you to this council."

"I wish I could say the same," replied Beric Canning as he took a seat. "I was fifth in line to the Earldom of Southport. I should never have inherited."

"We are all in a similar situation, Lord Beric. Yours is not the only family to suffer."

"My apologies. I meant no offence."

"Tell me," said Lord Oliver, "has anyone heard of what's happening with the Earldom of Loranguard?"

"Lord Garret had a nephew. I believe he was visiting Aynsbury."

"That bodes ill," said Lord Julian. "The Clans occupied it."

"True, but he was alive and well, last I heard."

"What was his name again?"

"Dryden, Dryden Wentworth."

"Not a Mainbridge, then?" said Julian.

"No. He inherits the title through the earl's sister."

"What in the name of the Gods was he doing down in Aynsbury?"

"Trying to buy some horses, or so I'm led to believe."

"For Malin's sake," said Elgin. "Does the man not realize the Clans took anything of value?"

"I suppose not. In any case, word's been sent. By now, he should be on his way back to Summersgate."

"Should we wait for him?"

"No," said Lord Beric. "The country is a mess. The sooner we sort things out, the better. What's first on the agenda for today?"

Lord Elgin looked down at his list. "There are several items requiring our attention, but might we address the matter of the Throne first?"

"Again?" said Julian. "We've already discussed it in some detail."

"Yes, but Lord Beric was not yet amongst us. Perhaps you might summarize for his sake?"

Lord Julian shifted his seat to face their newest member. "As you know, one of the most important roles of the Earls Council is to select the next king. Ordinarily, this is not a difficult task, as the presumptive heir is prepared to take on the role."

"I sense a but," said Beric.

"Lord Elgin doesn't believe Prince Alric is a good choice."

"Why ever not?"

"He's spent considerable time in Merceria, even commanding a portion of their army."

"I imagine that would be desirable. It means he has battle experience."

"He does," said Elgin. "And if we were looking for someone to lead the army, he's the best choice. The problem, you see, is we don't need a general; we need a diplomat who can navigate the complexities of court. His Highness, as Leofric's third son, was never properly prepared to take on this responsibility."

"Your concerns are duly noted," said Beric.

"There's more."

"Go on."

"As the Queen of Merceria's husband, what guarantee do we have that he'd put the needs of his own people above those of our new ally?"

"Who else is there to choose from?"

"That," said Elgin, "is an interesting matter. I propose we find a suitable candidate and marry him to Princess Althea."

"And by suitable candidate, you mean yourself?"

"If such was in the kingdom's best interests, then certainly. Why not?"

"This is ridiculous," said Julian. "Alric is the rightful heir. I propose we select him immediately. Let's have a show of hands, shall we? All those in favour?" He raised his hand.

Lord Oliver followed his example, but Beric and Elgin did not.

"It appears," said Lord Elgin, "that we are at an impasse."

"Not necessarily," replied Julian. "Once Lord Dryden shows up, he'll carry the deciding vote. Who knows? With a little persuasion, we might even be able to convince Beric here to change his mind."

"I stand by my opposition," said Beric. "Alric's lack of courtly experience is a considerable detriment, as is his reliance on the Queen of Merceria."

"And who would you suggest in his place?"

"On that, I am undecided. We are dealing with the future of Weldwyn, gentlemen, which is not a burden I take lightly. Have we any information on the king's extended family? Cousins and whatnot?"

"The Palace archives contained most of that. Unfortunately, they're buried beneath rubble."

"Then I suggest we start by making a list of all surviving nobles and go from there."

"Already done," said Elgin. "The list, that is, but we're still waiting for word on a few. Brida was very thorough in her scouring of the nobility."

"How did Brida even know who was who? It's not as if she spent much time in Weldwyn."

"I believe that was because of the efforts of Lord James Goodwin."

"That," said Oliver, "is for the tribunal to decide. Your statement is nothing more than conjecture."

"Tribunal?" asked Beric.

"Yes. We intend to convene a trio of nobles to determine the truth of these accusations."

"Which nobles?"

"Jack Marlowe is the best choice to lead them."

"The cavalier?"

"Yes," said Oliver, "though I suppose we should call him Lord Jack now that he's inherited his father's title."

"And the others?"

"Lord Tulfar and Lady Lindsey Martindale."

"Lady Lindsey? Surely not?"

"Why?" said Lord Oliver. "Do you have an objection?"

"She's a woman!"

"And Tulfar a Dwarf. Look, I know it's not the ideal tribunal, but it's the best we could do under the circumstances."

"No other barons were available?" replied Beric.

"I'm afraid we're still trying to determine who lives. It didn't help that the Clans burned their records before surrendering—not that they kept many to begin with."

"So, a cavalier, a Dwarf, and an old woman will determine Lord James' guilt? I wouldn't want to be in his shoes."

"Nor I," said Lord Oliver.

"Have the members of the tribunal been informed of your decision?"

"Letters were sent out this very morning."

"And when is it to convene?" asked Beric.

"That largely depends on how soon its members can return to Summersgate. I believe Lord Jack recently travelled to Aynsbury to oversee his new estates."

"And Lord Tulfar?"

"He's in Mirstone. It will likely be more than a week before he arrives. As to Lady Lindsey, she is already here in the capital. I spoke with her this morning."

"You've been busy," said Lord Julian.

"As was stated earlier," replied Oliver, "there is much to do. On that note, we'd best move on to the next topic."

"Which is?"

"Restoring the Royal Army."

Jack Marlowe stared at the ruins of the stables. After taking all the horses, the invaders had reduced it to little more than ash and burned timbers. The house, at least, had more or less survived, though they'd thoroughly plundered it.

The town of Aynsbury fared a little better than the Viscount's estate. When word came of the Twelve Clans's surrender, those occupying the town fled, carting off anything of value they could get their hands on. They later abandoned much of it in their rush to return home, leaving most of the town's wealth scattered across miles of wilderness.

A few of the more adventurous townsfolk ventured west in search of the expected riches, but they'd located nothing of value so far. Dead horses and wrecked carriages were mixed in with piles of burned furniture and linen.

Thankfully, the staff at the Aynsbury Estate survived by hiding out in the Barren Hills, using the extensive cave systems there to keep them safe from the marauders. They returned when the flag of Weldwyn flew once more from the rooftops, but there was little they could do to restore the house to its former glory.

Jack had seen the face of war, but this was something else. A sense of emptiness overwhelmed him as if a great storm had just swept away his childhood.

"My lord?"

The words made him jump. "Murton," said Jack. "I didn't see you there."

"Cook wondered if you might like dinner served, my lord."

"Dinner? The house lies there ransacked, and all you can think about is food?"

"I realize this is a lot to take in, Lord, but even in the face of adversity, we still need to eat."

"You have a point," said Jack. "Very well, I shall come in for a meal." He walked towards the estate, then slowed, causing his servant to do likewise. "Tell me, Murton, where am I to eat? They destroyed the dining hall and broke all the chairs to feed fires."

"Fear not, my lord, we've made do."

"With what?"

"We found an old crate in the cellars that will suffice for a table and a small chest on which you can sit. Think of it not as an inconvenience so much as an adventure. I have no doubt the child in you will be excited by our efforts."

"Yes, I suppose he would. Very well, lead on."

The Clansmen had stripped the room of all save the makeshift table and chair, yet somehow, Cook prepared him a feast. It must have used up half the remaining food stocks, but Jack wasn't about to complain. He ate sparingly, knowing full well the servants would partake of the leftovers. With his last mouthful, he looked up to see Murton hovering over him, ready to whisk away the plates.

"Tell me," said Jack. "Was there any area of the house they didn't plunder?"

"Oh yes, my lord. They failed to gain entry to your father's private study."

"But he never locked it."

"True," said Murton, "but that's not the room of which I speak. Your father maintained another, hidden from view."

"Why?"

"He was distrustful of others, particularly family members."

"Others? There were no others." Jack paused a moment as the truth settled. "You mean me?"

"I'm afraid so, my lord."

"Well, if I am to be the new Viscount Aynsbury, you best show me where it is."

"Of course. If you'll follow me, I'll take you there." Murton took a moment to pick up a candlestick before heading upstairs, using his other hand to shield the tiny flame.

Jack had spent most of his younger years in Aynsbury, the estate's halls so familiar to him he could've navigated them in the dark.

Murton led him to his father's regular study, wherein the servant moved to the fireplace and reached under the mantle. Part of it came loose, acting as a lever. "This opens the wall, my lord." He pulled back on it, producing a loud click, and then a section of the panelling moved slightly. Upon releasing the lever, Murton grasped the edge of the panel and pulled it open.

Jack moved closer, peering within. It was odd to see such a well-furnished room after the desolation in the rest of the house, and for a moment, he wondered if he might be imagining things.

A large portrait of his mother hung on the wall, her eyes following his every move. Jack couldn't imagine how they got the ornate desk into the room, for it was far wider than the entrance. Before it, sat a pair of cushioned chairs, with a small table beside them bearing a lamp. Murton moved in, using his candle to light the lamp, illuminating all within the room.

"This is remarkable," said Jack. "I had no idea this was here."

"Nor did the Clansmen, Lord, and we staff went out of our way to keep it so."

"What's in this desk?"

"I believe you'll find papers of a personal nature, though I can't say for sure."

"Have we a key?"

"Alas, no. Your father insisted on carrying that on him at all times, and as far as I know, there were no others. I'm afraid if you want to find out what's in that desk, you'll need someone to pry open the drawers."

"Or pick the lock," replied Jack. "Unfortunately, the only people I know who can do that are back in Merceria."

A collection of shelves filled with books lined one wall, and as Jack moved closer to take a look, Murton brought the lantern.

"I never knew my father was such a prolific reader."

"He was not, my lord."

"These books say otherwise."

"He inherited those from your grandfather."

Jack pulled forth a book and skimmed its contents. "This appears to be written in another language, although I have no idea which one."

"This is your study now, my lord. What do you want done with it?"

"Well, for a start, let's get somebody up here to pry open that desk and see what's inside."

"And the books?"

"They should be shared with someone who will appreciate them."

"I'm not sure I follow, Lord?"

"I'll give them to Lady Aubrey Brandon."

"Who?"

"The Baroness of Hawksburg, back in Merceria. She's a powerful Life Mage."

"And you believe these books might be of some use to her?"

"Maybe. I know she's getting ready to train some new mages, so they'll need to learn how to read. At least this way, they'll have something to pick from."

"I shall make arrangements for them to be delivered, Lord."

Lord Tulfar sat in a dark room, lit by a single candle, within a warehouse located in one of the seedier districts of Summersgate. He'd chosen this meeting place for its privacy. Two knocks followed by a pause, then a third let him know his guest had arrived.

The Dwarf stood and moved to the doorway, throwing back the latch to peer outside into the darkness. A dark green cloak covered most of Lord Parvan Luminor, Baron of Tivilton, but there was no mistaking his face.

"Come in," said Tulfar. "I took the liberty of bringing some wine."

The Elven lord entered, closing the door behind him. "Are you certain this is wise?" he asked. "If they learn of this, they will accuse us of plotting against the Earls Council."

"That's because we are." The Dwarf sat before he poured some wine for his guest. "We are at a crossroads, Lord Parvan, and we hold the key to the future of Weldwyn."

"In what way?"

"Tivilton and Mirstone are the only cities of consequence that the enemy never occupied."

"Agreed, though it was not for want of trying. However, I am unable to see how that helps either of us."

"You and I are in the same mine."

"I am afraid you will have to explain that to me."

"Let me put this another way—we are the only non-Humans to wield any power in Weldwyn. Don't you think it's time we had a little more say in the running of the kingdom?"

"If I understand you correctly, you are suggesting we have seats on the Earls Council."

"I am," said Tulfar.

"But we are not earls."

"But we could be."

"Our respective populations suggest otherwise," said Lord Parvan.

"Perhaps, but our reserves of gold say different."

"Are you suggesting we withhold coins from the Crown when they need it most?"

"Not at all. What I'm suggesting is we give them their due without reservation. After that, we'll offer them even more funds in exchange for representation."

"And you believe they will agree to this?"

"Alric will. I'm sure of it. As king, he'll need that gold to rebuild the country."

"He is not king yet," said Lord Parvan. "And if the rumours are true, they may not set him upon the Throne."

"You know there's no better candidate. He's Leofric's son, for Gundar's sake. Who else would they pick?"

"I see you are unfamiliar with the rules regarding Royal Succession in Weldwyn. If they are not happy with Alric, they may force a marriage on Althea, thus making her husband king."

"Althea doesn't want the Crown," said Tulfar. "And I know for certain she wouldn't willfully submit to that."

"She will have little choice in the matter if the council proposes otherwise."

"I know the princess well and can speak with some authority on the matter. As of this moment, she is plotting something with far greater vision than wife to a king." He chuckled. "Then again, I suppose some might consider it the same thing."

"You speak in riddles."

"Aye. Perhaps I do, but the point is, she won't marry a husband chosen by the Earls Council, and I doubt her brother would allow it in any case."

"It would not be his choice."

"You forget, he's the head of the Royal Family now. Even if he's not made the king, that still gives him the right to arrange her marriage, or deny it, for that matter."

"Then it would be in our best interest to bend our influence towards confirming Prince Alric as king."

"Yes," said Tulfar, "and we would gain an ally of great power by that act."

"That does not guarantee he will grant us representation on the Earls Council."

"No, but in Merceria, our people have a seat on the Nobles Council. I'm guessing he wouldn't oppose the idea here in Weldwyn."

"You think him that influenced by the Mercerians?"

"Aye. He's married to their queen, and we all know how persuasive she can be."

"Do not remind me," said Parvan. "Her actions led to my self-imposed exile from the court of King Leofric." He stared at the Dwarf, ignoring the drink before him. "You honestly believe this will work?"

"I do," said Tulfar.

"What do you want me to do?"

"Nothing, save permit me to use your name alongside my own. If we stand together, we have a better chance of success."

"Then so be it." Parvan rose. "Good day, Lord Tulfar. I wish you well in this. I shall return to Tivilton, but you can reach me there if you find it necessary." He turned abruptly and left, leaving his host alone.

Tulfar looked at the cup of wine. "No use in wasting that." He grabbed it, downing its contents, then let out an enormous belch. "Most satisfying," he said, talking to himself. "Now, let's see how our prince feels about all this."

SIX

Arrangements

AUTUMN 966 MC

L ochlan looked around the table. Prince Alric sat at one end, with the two princesses taking each side. As the guest, he sat at the opposite end from His Highness and couldn't help but feel they were judging him.

"I know you, Your Highness," he finally said, eyeing the prince, "and Princess Althea and I have spoken much in the past few days, but who is this young lady?"

"Edwina, my sister," said Althea. "We thought we might use the opportunity to seek her input."

"On what, precisely?"

"If we are to move forward in peace, then we must put aside our differences. One way to do that is through the union of our two lines."

The hair on the back of Lochlan's neck rose. "Are you suggesting a marriage?" His eyes locked on Edwina. "Your sister is very young."

"It is not Edwina we are suggesting you marry," replied the prince. "And in any case, her studies preclude her from being considered a member of the Royal Family."

"I'm afraid I don't understand. Are you saying you banished her?"

"Not at all. She will always be my sister, but she has taken up the call of magic. She is training as an Air Mage and, under Weldwyn law, is no longer in the line of succession."

"You must excuse my ignorance of your customs," said Lochlan, "but I understood women are not allowed to rule in Weldwyn. How does her use of magic change that?"

"It doesn't," said Edwina. "But under the laws of succession, should my siblings prematurely pass, my future husband might rule, or any sons I bear.

That possibility was removed when I discovered my affinity for magic. So, you see, I'd be ill-suited as your bride, were I old enough or not."

"How does one go about becoming a mage?"

"My magic potential was first noted by the late Tyrell Caracticus, Master of the Dome. Unfortunately, Kythelia's warriors killed him. In his place, I've been learning the rudiments of arcane lore from Lady Aubrey Brandon, a Life Mage of considerable merit."

"How does a Life Mage train mastery of the air?"

"The basics of magic are the same, regardless of which element is employed. As to learning actual Air Magic spells, let's just say it will likely prove challenging."

"I wish you well in your pursuits," said Lochlan. "You're studying at the Dome?"

"No. Hawksburg, a town in Merceria."

"I'm afraid I'm not familiar with it."

"We're getting a little off topic," said Althea.

"He's just being polite," her sister replied. "Which shows he, at least, has some manners."

"Are you suggesting I don't?"

"Calm yourselves," said Alric. "I might remind you we have a guest present."

"Am I a guest," said Lochlan, "or a prisoner? It's so hard to tell these days."

"You are free to leave whenever you like, but it would be in your best interest to stay."

"Very well. You've suggested the idea of marriage to ensure peace, and you obviously intend for me to be the husband in such an arrangement, though for the life of me, I can't understand why you didn't pick another Clan leader. Who, then, would be my bride?"

"Me," replied Althea. "Providing you agree to such an arrangement."

"You?" Lochlan said a little too loudly.

"Yes, me. Is that so hard to imagine? We are similar in age, and both from ruling houses after all."

"My pardon, Your Highness. I don't mean to offend, but why would you want to marry me?"

"Have you not been listening to this entire conversation?"

"I have, most assuredly, but the Clanholdings are a dangerous place for a woman of Weldwyn."

"She will not be alone," said the prince. "I'd send bodyguards to ensure her safety."

Lochlan, staring at Althea, noted her look of... what was it? Hope? Fear?

"I believe a marriage between the two of you would do much to calm tensions between our kingdoms," continued Prince Alric. "And the fact that Althea is of Royal Blood illustrates how seriously Weldwyn takes the matter."

"It will take a lot to mend the rift between our peoples," said Lochlan, "but if there is to be any chance of success, we must be willing to make the first step. I agree to this arrangement, providing Princess Althea does as well."

"I do," she replied, "or I wouldn't have proposed it in the first place."

"It was your idea?"

"Naturally. Who else would suggest it?"

"I thought your brother the mastermind behind it, or perhaps the Earls Council?"

Alric chuckled. "The earls know nothing about our discussions today. If they did, they'd do everything possible to prevent it."

"Why would they do that?"

"There are some who seek her hand in marriage for themselves."

"Let me guess," said Lochlan. "They see it as a path to the Throne?"

"They do."

"How do you know I won't do the same?"

"The earls would never confirm a Clansman as the King of Weldwyn, and in any case, I'm in good health and already have a son, should anything happen to me."

"I suppose it's mere coincidence that by marrying off your only eligible sister, you guarantee your own ascension to the Crown?"

"I hadn't considered that, but I suppose you make a good point. I remind you, however, Althea, not me, proposed this."

"Yes, of course. My pardon, Your Highness."

"Well?" Alric pressed. "What do you think of this idea of marriage?"

"As I said, I agree, but it will likely take some effort to convince others of its merits. I must admit, I didn't see this coming. All my life, I've been a scholar. Never, in my wildest dreams, did I ever imagine I might be required to marry to ensure peace for the people of Dungannon."

"Am I so hideous to the eye?" said Althea.

"No, not at all. Quite the reverse, in fact, yet I wonder if I am worthy of such an honour."

"You are a Clan Chief. That, alone, would suffice."

"For this marriage to be legitimate, it needs to be carried out in Dungannon, according to our traditions."

"No," said Alric. "She's a Princess of Weldwyn and must be married under the watchful eyes of Malin."

"Perhaps we might do both," said Althea. "One ceremony here, in Summersgate, and another in Dungannon, once we arrive."

"That would be an acceptable solution," said Lochlan. "Might I ask when you intend for the ceremony to occur?"

"As soon as possible," replied Prince Alric. "I'd like to see Althea wed before the earls hear of it and try to interfere."

"But you'd have to announce the wedding, surely?"

"Yes, but there is no requirement to give them any official notification."

"I think this wedding would require an immense amount of planning."

"Indeed. Thankfully, I have the Mercerians' full support in this endeavour, so there are many whom I can rely on for their discretion."

"And how will the earls react once they learn we are married?"

"At that point, it'll be too late," said Althea. "We'll be off to Dungannon under the protection of my brother."

"I assume you'll provide an escort?"

"Only to the border," said Alric. "Naturally, my sister will have her own bodyguards to keep her safe in the Clanholdings, along with riders for carrying letters."

"So, she is to spy on your behalf?"

"Not spy," said Althea, "merely report on our progress. If you take exception to that, then we can make other arrangements. What if I agree to show you all correspondence I send?"

"No," said Lochlan. "The offer is most generous, but I must decline. If you are to be my wife, I should show you trust, and I cannot, in all conscience, do that by watching your every move."

"You are a generous soul," said Althea. "I doubt any other Clan Chief would make such a promise."

"I meant every word. Now, if you will excuse me, I have some work to do."

"But you haven't even had a chance to eat?"

"Much as I would like to stay, I must take this proposition to my people. The winter snow will soon be upon us, and I want to see them settled back in their Clanholdings before they freeze to death."

"I understand," said Althea.

"Give me two days. If I can't convince them to support the marriage, I shall know by then."

"Two days it is," said Alric. "In the meantime, I'll begin preparations for your people to return home."

"Thank you, Highness." A servant escorted Lochlan from the room.

. . .

"Well?" said Alric. "What did you think?"

"He's nice," replied Edwina. "Not at all what I expected."

"Which was?"

"Some hairy beast with a thick beard and a bad temper. I also thought he'd be a lot older."

"And you?" said Alric, turning to Althea. "Are you still willing to give up your future?"

"I'm not giving up anything. In fact, you might say I'm embracing my future."

"Well," added Edwina, "you'll be embracing something!"

"Where did that sweet young sister go that I remember so well?"

"She grew up. I'm a young lady now."

"Then perhaps you might learn to talk like one."

"You're fifteen now," said Alric. "Is that any way to talk to your sister? Especially one you might not see again for quite some time?"

"No," replied Edwina. "I suppose not. Sorry."

"Apology accepted," said Althea.

"I must admit to some surprise," said Alric. "Now that you've had time to think things over, I thought you might reconsider."

"The idea of marriage to a stranger is frightening, yet, at the same time, it has a certain excitement to it. Tell me, what was it like marrying Anna?"

"It was marvellous," replied Alric.

"And did you always know you wanted to marry her?"

"Not in the least. The truth is, the first time I met her, I couldn't stand her."

"So what changed your mind?"

"I got to know her better and see her for the person she truly is."

"How long did that take?" asked Edwina.

"Close to a year, if I'm being truthful. By the time she returned to Merceria, I couldn't imagine my life without her."

"Will Althea feel the same?"

"That is for her to discover for herself."

She turned to her older sister. "Do you love him?"

"Love him?" said Althea. "I barely know the man."

"He's not without his charms."

"What are you getting at?"

"Well, for one thing, he's not the ugliest of men. You might also appreciate him for his scholarly pursuits, though I don't imagine they hold a candle to the former inhabitants of the Dome."

"You speak as if the Twelve Clans couldn't possibly have men of learning."

"Are you saying they do?"

"I am merely insinuating that we, as people of Weldwyn, have no real idea what their society is like."

"Meaning what? That you'll be living in a cave?"

"Hardly that," said Althea. "They adapted to a life of occupation easy enough. That indicates that their houses are not so different from ours."

"And if they are?"

"Then I shall have to learn to adjust."

"I must say," said Alric, "you're being very accepting of all this. I don't think I would be, were the roles reversed."

"Ah, but you weren't raised to be married off."

"Yes, I was, when you think about it. As the third son of a reigning monarch, what other choice did I have?"

"You could've spent your life as a warrior. Hold on a moment—you did precisely that!"

"So, what you're saying," said Edwina, "is that dear brother Alric got to marry the princess, lead an army, and cover himself in glory?"

"More or less, yes."

"So why are they taking so long to embrace him as king?"

"That's easy," said Althea. "Politics."

"I'm afraid I don't understand."

"Nor should you ever have to, now that you've taken up a life of magic. The truth is, we are all pawns in the game of power that surrounds the Throne."

"Queen Anna doesn't have that problem."

"Actually," said Alric, "she does. Ever since she took the Throne, people have been plotting against her."

"How does she deal with that?"

"She surrounds herself with those she trusts, as I must now do."

"You mean like Marshal Gerald?"

"That would be Marshal Matheson to you," said Alric.

"Everyone calls him Gerald," said Althea.

"In private, yes, but he is the Duke of Wincaster. As such, his proper form of address is Your Grace. That, by the way, is an important lesson."

"How?"

"When you're in Dungannon, you must learn the correct forms of address. From what I know, the Clansmen insult easily, and the last thing you want to do is get on someone's bad side."

"I shall be sure to watch my tongue. Any other advice you care to give?"

"Yes, ruling isn't so much about commanding others as reaching a consensus. If you truly want to succeed, you'll need the support of those around you."

"Except she won't have that option," said Edwina. "She'll be all alone in a foreign land."

"Well," said Althea, "not completely alone. I'll have bodyguards, not to mention a new husband. Hopefully, he'll support me in my endeavours."

"Let us pray it is so," said Alric. "Speaking of endeavours, what is it you hope to accomplish? I know we want to bring our two realms closer together, but have you thought about how you might do that?"

"I've given it considerable attention of late, but I shan't know until I'm there. My priority, naturally, will be to develop an understanding of their culture. Once I've done that, I'll better understand what's important to them."

"I don't want to speak ill of the Clansmen, but you're playing a very dangerous game here. If things go sour, it could well be the death of you."

"I shall take the greatest of care to remain safe."

"Somehow," said Alric, "I doubt that."

"Why would you say that?"

"I know of your exploits during the war to liberate Weldwyn. Not the type of thing a timid person would attempt, let alone succeed at."

"What of it? Did you not take risks in Merceria's name? You were certainly busy during the invasion of Norland?"

"I did my duty as Prince of Weldwyn, not to mention Merceria."

"As did I," said Althea. "Or are you insinuating that as a mere woman, I am not allowed to become a warrior?"

"I have too much experience in Merceria to doubt your abilities, Althea, but leading a few companies of Dwarves is not the same as marrying a Chief of the Clansmen."

"Nor do I expect it to be. I'm curious, though, that you choose to bring that matter up. I'm led to understand it's the same argument they're using to deny you your kingship."

"What would you know of such things?"

"I've learned much from the Dwarves, including their importance to the Crown's treasury. The contributions from Mirstone are the highest in the entire kingdom, yet they lack a seat on the council."

"That's because it's an Earls Council," said Alric, "not one made up of barons. Last time I checked, Lord Tulfar was a baron. Are you now trying to tell me I'm mistaken?"

"No. You are correct, but perhaps it's time that we, as a realm, had more people deciding the fate of the land. That's how they do things in Merceria, isn't it?"

"I won't deny it, but that only came about because of necessity."

"Yet the kingdom isn't any worse for it, is it?"

Alric smiled. "Sometimes you're a little too clever for your own good. I'll admit I've given it some thought, but I can do nothing till I'm king."

"And I can do little till I'm... whatever it is I'll be called."

"Clan Chief's woman?" suggested Edwina.

"I suppose that's as good a name as any."

"Perhaps he'll be accepted as High King, like his father, then you can be his queen?"

"The title matters little," said Alric. "Of more importance is the influence you might wield. Make friends in Dungannon—the more powerful and influential, the better."

"And if they don't accept me?"

"I doubt you'll have that problem. As wife to the chief, they'll see you as a way to influence him. I suspect you'll have no end of people wishing to do you favours."

She laughed. "I doubt that very much."

"Don't be hasty. Those who seek power will do anything within their means to acquire it. You must learn to distinguish between those who genuinely seek friendship and those who simply curry favour."

Althea sat back. "I see I've got a lot to learn."

"You'll get there, eventually. In the meantime, you can always count on me for advice, even if I am hundreds of miles away."

"That would be reassuring were it not for the time it will take to get a message to you."

"There's a simple answer to that," said Edwina. "You need a magic circle. Then the mages could use their recall spell to travel there instantly."

"And how would we go about obtaining one of them?"

"You'd need a master craftsman to fashion it," said Alric, "then a mage of exceptional power to empower it. Of course, even that might not be enough."

"Why would you say that?"

"Your sister here can correct me if I'm wrong, but the amount of magical energy to travel to a circle is directly related to the distance involved."

"That's correct," added Edwina. "Just travelling from Wincaster to Summersgate is a drain on even the most experienced mages."

"And what," asked Althea, "is the cost to create such a circle?"

"They're expensive, I'm afraid," said Alric.

"Well then. It appears we must rely on more traditional methods of communication for the time being."

SEVEN

Trouble

AUTUMN 966 MC

H ayley looked up from her notes. "Are you sure this is correct?"

"As far as I can tell," replied Bertram Ayles. "I checked with the Master of Heralds, and he could find no record of it."

"And this is only just coming to our attention now?"

The ranger shrugged. "It's not as if anyone had any reason to doubt his claim."

"I understand that, but the man was the Baron of Bodden for years. He even sat on the Nobles Council because of it."

"Yet was never officially sworn in, according to records."

"Could the records be missing?" asked Hayley.

"Why would they be missing?"

"I don't know; perhaps someone plots to discredit him?"

"I thought of that," said Ayles, "but it would take a lot of effort to arrange such a thing, and very few people have access to the records."

A knock on the door drew their attention.

"That'll be Sam," he said. "She was looking through some of Revi's books on the nobles of Merceria."

"To what end?"

"To see if there is some sort of law that doesn't require a swearing-in ceremony."

"Come in," called out Hayley.

The door opened, revealing the young ranger.

"Find anything?"

"Nothing useful, I'm afraid," said Sam, "though I confirmed his claim to the title was legitimate, assuming his brother was dead. Then again, I suppose that's the crux of the matter here, isn't it?"

"What we need is an eyewitness."

"Don't look at me," said Sam. "That was long before I was even born. You might check with the marshal, though. He served Lord Richard for years."

"I'm afraid that won't help." Hayley dug through her papers. "I have a statement here somewhere from Gerald. He admits someone may have borne Lord Edward from the battle."

"May have?"

"I'll agree it's mere speculation at this point. We're also dealing with events over thirty years ago, and in my experience, people seldom have perfect memories. What we need is some sort of independent corroboration."

"You mean other witnesses," said Sam. "Who else was there?"

"There are several, but the only one I recognize is an old knight by the name of Sir James. According to Gerald, he was there the night Lord Edward died."

"And where do we find Sir James?"

"He's up in Bodden. I want you and Bertram to head up there and get a statement from him."

"That's a long way to travel," said Ayles.

"Not really," replied Sam. "If she's available, Albreda could take us to the Whitewood. The keep is only a short distance from there."

Ayles shuddered. "I don't know if I like the idea of having my body flung halfway across the kingdom like that. What if something goes wrong with her spell?"

"You think Albreda could fail in her casting?" said Hayley. "You might want to reconsider that."

"Actually," added Sam, "if she did miscast, the spell simply wouldn't work."

"Oh yes?" said Ayles. "And how would you know that?"

"I travelled with Lady Aubrey once or twice."

"There," said Hayley. "Happy now?"

"Couldn't we ride there?"

"Don't be ridiculous. That would take weeks, and the queen wants this resolved as quickly as possible."

"Begging your pardon, Lady Hayley, but I don't see this ending well. Are you sure we can't just bury it?"

"Are you suggesting we hide evidence?"

"Lord Richard was a great man. Do we really want to tarnish his reputation?"

"Our job is to determine the truth, nothing more. If that happens to ruin Dame Beverly's inheritance, then I'll take no pleasure in it, but we are a kingdom of laws. Regardless of the consequences, we must see this through to the end."

Hayley looked down, talking as she wrote. "I'm drafting a request for a mage to transport you to Bodden and back. I trust that the two of you will be sufficient to conduct this investigation?"

"Yes, my lady," said Sam.

"What if they refuse to co-operate?" asked Ayles.

Both women looked at him in annoyance.

"What? Lord Richard was well-loved in Bodden. They won't be eager to see his barony given to a stranger."

"If that should prove true," said Hayley, "I would expect you to show your ranger token."

This stopped his complaining, for every ranger wore a token around their neck, identifying them as the queen's agents. Charged with keeping the peace within the borders of Merceria, a refusal to co-operate with one was considered an act of treason.

"When do you want us to leave?" asked Sam.

"As soon as possible. This afternoon even, if a mage is available." Hayley handed over the note. "Here, take this. It authorizes you to call on a mage. You'll need to check the duty roster to find out who's on call."

"Certainly."

"Oh, and one more thing. I shouldn't have to tell you this, but this investigation is of the utmost importance. Do I make myself clear?"

"Yes," they answered in unison.

"Good. Now, get out of here. I have work to do."

They exited the room, leaving Hayley alone with her thoughts. She enjoyed the role of High Ranger, but some days, the duty was distasteful and burdensome. "This would've been so much easier if you'd been sworn in as baron," she said as she glanced over her papers. "Why couldn't you have settled this properly when you were still alive?"

Kraloch reached out to feel Braedon's forehead, but the young princeling squirmed in his mother's arms, unaccustomed to an Orc's touch.

"What do you think?" asked the queen. "Is he ill?"

"I readily admit I have little experience with Human younglings, but he feels warmer than I expected. With your permission, I shall cast a spell of healing on him to be safe."

"Would that work if it was a fever?"

"Likely not, though there are other spells I can use. If you would feel more comfortable, I could call on Lady Aubrey to examine him?"

"No. I have complete faith in you, Master Kraloch. You may cast at your discretion."

"It will be easier if you could keep him steady."

"Hold on a moment," said Anna as she turned to Gerald. "Here, you take him. He always calms down when he's with his grandfather."

The marshal took the child, cradling him. Prince Braedon looked up at his grey beard and smiled.

"There," said Anna. "Now you can cast your spell."

The Orc shaman closed his eyes, digging deep within to bring forth his magic. He'd cast the spell of healing many times during his lifetime, and it became easier to call upon the arcane power each time.

His hands glowed as he placed them on the young prince's chest, letting the magic flow into him. Braedon glowed slightly, and then the light dissipated. Kraloch reached out once more, touching the child's forehead, and this time the prince simply stared back.

"That seems to have sufficed. By my reckoning, he is no longer warm."

"Thank you, Master Kraloch."

"You are most welcome, Majesty."

The door opened, admitting Evard Brenton, one of the Palace guards. He bowed deeply. "Your Majesty."

"Are you looking for me?" asked Anna.

"No, Majesty. I am here for Master Kraloch. He is required to use his magic."

"Is someone injured?" asked the Orc.

"No, but I have a request from the High Ranger for a mage to take two people to Bodden."

"I assume that means she's investigating the death of Lord Edward," said the queen. "It's the talk of the Palace at present."

"I wouldn't know, Majesty. They have told me nothing of the details."

"Very well," said Kraloch. "You may inform them I shall be along shortly."

The guardsman bowed, then left without any further words.

"Hopefully, they can soon put a rest to this farce," said Gerald.

"As long as it's done legally," said Anna. "I don't like this any more than you, but we have laws for a reason, and I shan't twist them to suit my own needs."

"I wonder how long this will take. I can't imagine Beverly is happy with any of it."

"Nor I, but it will be some time before I can make a final decision."

"What makes you say that?"

"There's only so much information they'll find in Bodden. If someone carried off Lord Edward, then the proof we need will be found in Norland."

"So, the rangers will need to go north," said Gerald. "But Norland isn't under our rule. How do we assure they'll co-operate?"

"We must rely on diplomacy."

"I can't imagine Bronwyn will like that very much."

"I think it better if she remains unaware of the investigation."

"And if she finds out?"

"Heward is still in their capital," said Anna. "If anyone can help keep the peace, it's him."

"Heward's a fine knight and one of our best commanders, but I don't see him as the kind of person who'd be good at getting to the bottom of this."

"And he shouldn't need to. In any case, the investigation is in Hayley's hands now. It's her decision as to how to proceed."

Kraloch moved to the centre of the circle. "I assume it is only the two of you?"

"It is," said Sam. "We need you to take us to the stone circle in the White-wood, the one closest to Bodden."

"And will you require me to return you to Wincaster when done?"

"Eventually, but I'm not sure how long we'll be there."

"Then I shall arrange for someone to visit Bodden in two days. If your task is still incomplete, whoever it is can arrange a further delay."

"That would be wonderful. Thank you."

She moved beside him, and then they both looked at Ayles. The fellow stood outside the circle, looking pale in the glare of the lanterns.

"Maybe I should stay here," he said. "After all, someone has to look after things in the Palace."

"We have orders to go to Bodden," insisted Sam. "Surely you're not suggesting you disobey a direct order from the High Ranger?"

He grumbled but finally moved to stand beside her. Kraloch closed his eyes, pulling forth his magic. The spell of recall was a complex ritual requiring the utmost concentration. He'd first learned it from Aubrey, who, in turn, had been taught the spell by none other than Albreda. It was to her domain they travelled now, for her lands stood adjacent to Bodden.

Every mage in Merceria learned the spell of recall, yet only a small, select group was permitted to commit the stone circles of the Whitewood to memory. All of this passed through Kraloch's mind in an instant, while another part concentrated on taming the arcane forces flowing through him.

As the surrounding air whipped around them, the runes set into the floor glowed, and then a cylinder of light encircled them, blocking their view of the walls, growing more intense until the scent of the woods drifted towards them. Kraloch took a deep breath when the cylinder fell, revealing a circle of stones. In the distance, a howl echoed off the trees.

"W-w-what was that?" asked Ayles.

"Albreda's guardians," said the Orc. "They sense when the stone circle is activated."

"Are they wolves?"

"Naturally. They are her pack. We shall see them soon enough with any luck, for we must travel through their hunting grounds to get to Bodden."

Ayles patted his chest, then ran his fingers through his hair.

"What are you doing?" said Sam.

"Making sure I arrived in one piece. This whole magic thing is just... unnatural."

"You fear it because you do not understand it," said Kraloch. "My people have harnessed magic for generations. To us, it is as ordinary as raising wolves."

"We don't raise wolves in Merceria."

"My pardon. Perhaps I should say it is as ordinary as raising Kurathian Mastiffs?"

"Or how about horses," offered Sam. "That might be a better example, and one Bertram here can easily understand."

"Which way now?" asked Ayles.

"This way," said Kraloch, heading deep into the woods.

They'd gone only a hundred or so steps when a huge wolf appeared, immediately making his way over to Sam and rubbing up against her.

"Hello, Snarl," she said, ruffling his fur. "It's been a while since I saw you last."

"You know him?" asked Kraloch.

"I do. Albreda used to visit Bodden often, and Snarl here sometimes accompanied her, though he usually remained outside the village perimeter. Ayles knows her too, don't you, Bertram?"

He nodded but made no attempt to move closer. "Can we continue on our way? I'm eager to get to Bodden before nightfall. I don't much fancy being in these woods after dark."

"You are perfectly safe here," said Kraloch, "and under the protection of Albreda."

"Last I heard, she was in Hawksburg."

"Just what is it you fear?"

"Oh, I don't know. Bears? Wildcats? Wolves?"

"Wolves will not attack you here. They are our escorts, come to see us safely to the edge of the woods."

Snarl, as if in understanding, padded off, leading them westward.

The old knight stared out from the walls of Bodden. "Are you sure?" he asked. "I don't see anyone."

"Most assuredly, Sir James," replied the sentry. "There are three in total."

"Is one perhaps Lady Aubrey?"

"I'm afraid not, sir."

The trio advanced until Sir James could finally see them. "That's the archer. What was her name again?"

"Sam."

"Funny name for a woman, that."

"It's short for Samantha, Sir James."

"Who's that with her?"

"Another ranger would be my guess, along with an Orc."

Sir James squinted, hoping it would improve his sight. "Would that I were younger. In my youth, I could've spotted a robin at two hundred yards."

"Indeed, Sir James."

The visitors came within hailing distance.

"Greetings. I am Sam of Bodden, and this is Bertram Ayles of Stilldale. We are rangers in service to the queen."

"And your companion?" called out the knight.

"Master Kraloch of the Black Arrows, whom I believe you already know."

"Ah yes, of course. I should have recognized you sooner." He paused a moment before he bellowed out orders to open the gate. As the visitors made their way in, he descended the stairs to greet them. "What brings you to Bodden, if I might ask?"

"We're here to see you," said Sam. "Along with anyone who might've witnessed what happened to Lord Edward at that siege all those years ago."

"Then we best get up to the keep. I'll send word for all surviving witnesses to gather in the map room."

"And how many would that be?"

"Only a handful, I'm afraid. Life is short on the frontier." He slowed, turning to look at her. "I knew they'd send someone, eventually, especially after that fellow showed up here."

"And by 'that fellow', I assume you mean Sir Randolf?"

The knight frowned. "Who else? I can't say I like the thought of him dragging Lord Richard's name through the mud."

"He has said nothing against the baron's character."

"But he laid claim to his lands. That, by its very nature, indicates he has no respect for the man's accomplishments." He shook his head. "I wouldn't expect you to understand; you're too young."

"I might remind you I'm a Queen's Ranger."

"I meant no offence, but one can't simply rewrite history for the glorification of an individual."

"You think he's seeking glory?"

Sir James mulled it over before replying. "No, not glory, maybe gold? Then again, Bodden was never the wealthiest of baronies. This claim, though, feels more... personal, as if he wants to pay back Lord Richard for some imagined slight."

"Still, if he has a legal claim, we must investigate it."

"You may do what you like. I shan't stand in your way. However, I need to warn you that Lord Richard was well-loved by those who served him."

"And we shall honour that. I promise you."

They entered the keep and made their way up a set of stairs. "What would you like to know?" asked Sir James.

"You're the one who informed Lord Richard of his brother's death, weren't you?"

"I was. Lord Edward was obliterated when he ignited the combustibles."

"And you saw this yourself?"

"I suppose, if I'm being honest, I didn't. As I recall, it was dark at the time. We'd been under siege for some time and knew the final assault was coming. We packed the wall with anything and everything that would burn at Lord Edward's direction."

"In a wall?" said Ayles.

"Yes. You must understand it was still under construction then, so there were lots of scaffolding and open space to pack things into. To top it off, we filled an entire barrel with lamp oil and added it to the pile."

"And how was it to be ignited?"

"The original plan was to light a fuse. To that end, we'd soaked some linen in the lamp oil, then stuffed it on top, hoping it would take a while to burn down to the barrel and ignite its contents."

"And did it work?"

"The sudden explosion seems to indicate otherwise."

"But you claim you didn't see him light it?"

"That's true. Upon seeing the wall swarming with Norlanders, Lord Edward grabbed a torch and ran towards them. I'd assumed he would touch it to the linen and run, but enemy warriors swarmed the courtyard at that precise moment. I grabbed a few men and rushed for them, then there was a gigantic explosion before we could go more than half a dozen steps."

"So, you never actually saw him die?"

"True, but you didn't see the explosion. No one could've survived that."

"Thank you," said Sam. "You've been of considerable help."

"That's it? That's all you need of me?"

"We may have a couple more questions once we interview the others, but I doubt that will take long."

EIGHT

The Tribunal Gathers

AUTUMN 966 MC

L ord Jack Marlowe, Viscount of Aynsbury, sat back in his chair. He'd returned to Summersgate only to discover he'd been appointed to a Royal Tribunal, its stated purpose to investigate and judge the involvement of Lord James Goodwin in the recent occupation.

Across from him sat Lord Tulfar Axehand, the Dwarven Baron of Mirstone, with whom he was familiar. The other individual, however, took him completely by surprise. Lady Lindsey Martindale, Viscountess Talburn, was the last person Jack expected to participate in this enquiry.

"So," he said, trying to figure out the best way to start. "It appears we have our work cut out for us. Where do you suggest we begin?"

"How about with the accused," replied Lord Tulfar.

"What do we know of him?"

"He's the son of Lord Melvin Goodwin, cousin to the Ramsays of Norwatch. His father was, by all accounts, a womanizer and spendthrift, much as his son is rumoured to be."

"You make that sound undesirable," said Jack.

The Dwarf ignored him. "Lord Melvin's marriage was arranged, and Lady Jane bore him only the one son."

"And how does that fit in with this charge of treason?"

"There's a suggestion his plotting allowed the Clansmen to enter Summersgate unopposed."

"A suggestion?" said Lady Lindsey. "Surely we need more than idle speculation to punish the fellow?"

"Indeed," replied Lord Tulfar. "That's why they've assembled this tribunal."

"Still," said Jack. "That doesn't explain why they chose us three to look into matters."

"Because we are the closest thing to nobility that the kingdom has at this point. In case you haven't heard, Brida killed most of the barons and earls during the recent occupation."

"I suppose that makes sense, then. Do we know how he let the invaders in?"

"It's said," replied Tulfar, "that someone bribed the guards to leave the west gate open when the enemy attacked."

"And are there survivors who can verify that?"

"We have a list of names to go by, but to my knowledge, no one has asked any further questions."

"Well then, it appears we have a good place to start."

The Dwarf leaned forward, resting his elbows on the table. "I do hope you're taking this seriously, Lord Jack."

"I am. Most seriously, indeed. I'm sorry if I come across as uncaring, but I'm in a little over my head on this one."

"But you are a cavalier," said Lady Lindsey. "I thought you fearless?"

"And I assure you such is the case on the battlefield, but this..." He waved his hands to indicate the table. "This is very different from leading warriors into battle."

Lord Tulfar buried his face in his fingers. "Gundar, give me strength."

"You say it was the west gate, Baron?" asked Jack.

"Aye, it was."

"Then I should like to begin there."

"And what, precisely, do you propose we do?"

"Well, we could start by obtaining a list of who manned the gate that day. From there, we'll determine who survived the occupation and, with any luck, be able to narrow down our witnesses."

"That," said Tulfar, "is a surprisingly good idea. I didn't realize you had it in you."

"I shall take that as a compliment," replied Jack.

"What about his mother, Lady Jane?" asked Lady Lindsey.

"I'm not sure what you're asking."

"Is she to be considered a suspect in this treason?"

"I suppose we must consider everyone a suspect until we learn otherwise, though I fear that will make our investigation much harder."

"In what way?" said Tulfar.

"Well, I don't know about you, but I'd certainly lie to cover it up if I committed such a heinous crime."

"Are you suggesting that nobody will tell the truth?"

"Oh, I'm sure there'll be tales aplenty coming from so-called witnesses. The problem we have is, how to tell the truth from lies. I don't suppose there's a mage with a spell that could help us?"

"You would know better than us," replied Tulfar. "You served with the Queen of Merceria."

"Correction," said Jack. "I serve His Highness, Prince Alric."

"It amounts to the same thing."

"We shall have to pry it out of them," said Lady Lindsey.

Jack paled. "Are you suggesting we torture people?"

"If need be. Why? Have you a better idea?"

"The Queen of Merceria believes such treatment only clouds matters."

"Why would she think that?"

"Because a man under torture will admit to anything to end his pain."

"Then so much the better," said Lady Lindsey. "We'll wring a confession out of the fellow and be done with it."

"But I just finished explaining why that won't work."

"All we're looking for here is someone to blame. Does it matter whom we select? Obviously, the earls believe him guilty, or they wouldn't have chosen us to sit on this tribunal."

"Be that as it may, I, for one, would like to learn the truth of the matter. What say you, Lord Tulfar?"

"I agree with you," replied the Dwarf, "but we must consider the matter carefully before making a decision. There's also the issue of whether or not he worked alone."

"You also suspect his mother was involved?"

"Anything's possible at this point, but I doubt she wields the influence needed to bribe the guards at the gate. I also get the impression Lord James is not the brightest of men."

"Are you suggesting he's simple-minded?"

"No, merely that he wasn't the one in charge. Consider the details of the invasion. To get inside Summersgate, the Clansmen coordinated their attack with the open gate. How did they accomplish that? Discovering that is even more important than blaming Lord James."

Lady Lindsey was having none of it today. "Why in the name of Malin would you say that? Surely punishing the traitor is the important thing here!"

"Is it?" pressed the Dwarf. "If we can't work out how they coordinated this whole thing, the same technique could be used again. I don't know about you, but I'm not thrilled with the idea of the city gates not being secure."

"Then I shall go to the gate myself," said Jack, "and see what I can learn."

"I would offer to accompany you," said Tulfar, "but I've got a wedding to attend."

"A wedding?"

"Yes. Didn't you hear? Princess Althea is to be married."

"To whom?"

"Lochlan, the Clan Chief of Dungannon."

"Why was I not informed?" demanded Lady Lindsey.

Jack chose to ignore her protestations. "Is Prince Alric aware of this?"

"Aye," replied the Dwarf. "'Twas he who told me of it. I'm surprised you didn't know. You are the prince's champion, aren't you?"

"Yes, but I've been down in Aynsbury dealing with my late father's passing."

"Murder, more like," grumbled Lady Lindsey. "At the hands of the Twelve Clans."

Jack refused to be sidetracked. "When did you say this wedding was to take place?"

"This very afternoon at the Dome."

"The Dome? Why in Malin's name would they hold it there?"

"With the Palace destroyed, it's the only place large enough to accommodate the expected guests."

"I suppose that makes sense."

"I'm sure His Highness would appreciate your presence. Shall I send word you'll be attending?"

"Who else is invited?"

"Quite a few of the Mercerians, some of our people, and a smattering of Clansmen. Fitting, I suppose, if you consider Lochlan's family ties."

"Why in the name of the Gods was I not invited," asked Lady Lindsey, "particularly when they thought to include you?"

"Princess Althea fought with my warriors during the invasion," said Tulfar. "Can you say the same?"

She fell silent, brooding over her snub.

"I'd be much obliged if you would see to it," said Jack. "It's not something I'd care to miss."

"I shall do so immediately, providing we're finished here?"

"For now, but I'll try to dig a little deeper into this mystery before the ceremony."

"Well, don't dig too deeply. The ceremony is to take place later this afternoon. That doesn't give you much time." Tulfar rose, gathered his notes, downed the rest of his ale, then left the room.

"He's a wily one," said Lady Lindsey. "I'm not sure I trust him."

"Why ever not?" asked Jack.

"He wants a seat on the Earls Council and will do anything to achieve his objective."

"That will prove difficult. He's not an earl."

"Not yet, but I fear he aims to change that."

"I don't understand your animosity. Or is it you see him as beneath you? After all, he's a baron, and you're a viscountess."

"True power has nothing to do with one's position in society—it's the influence one wields. He has a Royal Princess under his control, and I fear he'll use that to further his own aims."

"Under his control? You show too little faith in Princess Althea."

"Come now," she said. "You and I both know a woman of Royal Blood is no more than a puppet."

"My experience in Merceria tells me otherwise."

"Their influence has corrupted you."

Jack shook his head. "It is not corruption. I've had my eyes opened to possibilities. Weldwyn would be a much better place if we adopted some of the customs of our ally."

He noted the look of distaste on her face.

"I fail to understand your hatred of the Mercerians," he continued. "They've come to our aid twice now in the wake of Clan invasions, yet you paint them as our enemy. Why can't you accept that they want us to prosper?"

"Prosper? Is that what you think they want? I hate to disabuse you of the notion, but they seek to dominate us, if not through military might, then by their culture. Tell me, do you honestly believe they would be as friendly if we possessed a larger army than theirs?"

"Yes, I do. Queen Anna truly desires peace and prosperity, which are things that benefit us all."

"This kingdom has never been weaker," she replied. "And, while we are most vulnerable, Mercerian warriors patrol our streets."

"Only because King Leofric lost our army."

"That wouldn't have happened had it not been for our so-called alliance with Merceria."

"We had little choice," said Jack. "Had we not helped in Norland, the enemy would have overrun Merceria. Do you really think they would've stopped there?"

"I can see you won't listen to reason."

Jack chuckled.

"You find something humorous?" demanded Lady Lindsey.

"I was just about to say the same thing to you. You sit here, ranting about the evils of Merceria, yet I see no other kingdom offering us the hand of friendship. Do you?"

"An ally who seeks to rule over us is no friend."

"They do not want to rule Weldwyn."

"Yet isn't that precisely what will happen if they name Alric king?"

"What are you prattling on about?"

"It's simple. If Alric becomes King of Weldwyn, then it only follows his son will be king thereafter—a king born to a Mercerian queen. When that happens, Weldwyn will be no more."

"Why would you think that?"

"One kingdom means one set of laws," said Lady Lindsey. "Do you believe the Mercerians will accept Weldwyn laws over their own?"

"That's what this whole thing is about, isn't it? You don't want Alric to be king."

"I readily admit that, but I'm not the only one who thinks along those lines. In the coming days, you may find your master's influence has fallen significantly since the war."

"I will not stand idly by and watch someone else usurp the Throne."

"You forget yourself, or is it you find it convenient to ignore the laws of succession? Our tradition calls for the Earls of Weldwyn to select the next king. Whether or not you agree with their choice, you are bound by oath to accept their decision as a noble of the realm."

"That does not prevent me from using what influence I possess to sway their vote."

"And what, precisely, does that mean? Will you march warriors into the Earls Council and force their hand? I doubt that would go over well."

"No, of course not, but if Alric's succession is in jeopardy, I owe it to him to do all I can to help."

"And where do you draw the line?"

"I shall not raise arms against the council, if that's what you're insinuating."

"You say that now, but I know you, Jack Marlowe. You seek honour and glory to the exclusion of all else. You wouldn't hesitate to slay every last earl on the council if Alric were to ask."

"He would never do such a thing, but if he did, he would no longer be worthy of my service. You claim to know me, Lady Lindsey, but you only believe what you see. I'll always be the carefree cavalier to you, yet I've seen death aplenty, and that changes one's perceptions about many things."

He stared back, daring her to respond, but instead, she rose, making a show of straightening her dress. "I'll assume this meeting adjourned for now. That should give you and Lord Tulfar plenty of time to attend this wedding that so mocks our customs. Shall we resume discussions tomorrow at noon?"

"Most certainly."

"Then I bid you a good day, Lord Jack, and hope you take joy in the festivities this afternoon. I fear it may be some time before you have another chance to celebrate." With that, she left.

Jack sat in silence, his mind racing. Lady Lindsey's words indicated she might be conspiring against Prince Alric. She believed him unfit for the Crown, but was that because of the influence of Merceria, or was it merely a convenient excuse to advance her own agenda? She'd indicated others thought as she did, which, more than anything else, truly distressed him.

He shook his head, attempting to clear it but to little avail. He stood, downed the rest of his wine, and then tried to concentrate on other matters, but the thought remained like a burr stuck to one's boots.

A servant finally entered to clear away the table. "Is there anything you require, my lord?"

"A great deal, it would seem."

"My lord?"

"What?" Jack looked at the fellow's confused expression. "Oh, never mind. I'm merely thinking out loud."

Jack found Lord Tulfar at the Quarry, a common enough place for members of the nobility to while away their time. As soon as he entered, he spotted the baron huddled alone in a corner, nursing an ale.

"Mind if I join you?" Jack called out.

A wave of Tulfar's hand indicated he was welcome, and the cavalier took a seat, calling for an ale.

"I thought you had places to be?"

"Aye, I do," the Dwarf replied, "but not for some time yet. It appears all the preparations are taken care of. I asked about you, and you're more than welcome to attend. His Highness wasn't aware you'd returned to Summersgate, else he would've ensured you received an invitation."

"I wasn't gone all that long. They must've arranged it on short notice?"

"Very short, indeed. I only learned of it yesterday."

"Why the rush?"

"His Highness wants the Twelve Clans marching back to their own territory before the week is out."

"And they can't do that without the wedding?"

"They could, but Althea wants to show her support by marching with them as the wife of their chieftain."

"March?" said Jack. "Surely you mean ride?"

"Not at all. She intends to travel to Dungannon on foot, sharing the burden her new people must endure."

"I sincerely hope they're not expecting our escort to do the same?"

"Not at all," said Tulfar. "There shall be three companies of horsemen to escort them to the border."

"And then what? Is she to be abandoned to the Twelve Clans?"

"You needn't worry about her safety. I've taken measures to ensure it."

"Meaning?"

The Dwarf smiled. "Let's just say I've planned a little surprise for everyone." He gulped down his ale. "Now, let's get to the heart of the matter, shall we? You didn't seek me out to discuss the wedding. What has Lady Lindsey been up to?"

"What makes you believe my visit has anything to do with her?"

"Come now. I've been a baron for nigh on eighty years. Why, I remember Lady Lindsey as a little girl. It's a shame when I think about it. She had so much promise."

"You don't approve of her?"

"That's putting it mildly. She always acts in her own best interest."

"That's rather amusing. She indicated the same of you."

"No doubt she told you I wanted a seat on the Earls Council."

"She did. Said you were only supporting this marriage to curry favour with Prince Alric."

"I can see how she might assume that, but the truth is, Althea impressed me during the war. In a way, I think of her more like a daughter than a member of the Royal House."

"And you support her heading off to the Clanholdings?"

"I support her doing whatever she wishes. If that means travelling west, then so be it."

"And that has nothing to do with your desire for more power?"

"It's not power I seek, merely a voice to represent my people. You Humans rule over Weldwyn with no thought to my people or those of Lord Parvan. If there's one thing we learned from Merceria in this war, it's that it doesn't need to be that way."

Jack sat back, mulling things over while a server appeared, depositing a tankard of ale before him.

"Well?" pressed Tulfar. "What have you to say to all of that?"

"I agree with everything you said."

"Then what's the problem?"

"With you? Nothing. On the other hand, Lady Lindsey is an entirely different matter."

NINE

The Wedding

AUTUMN 966 MC

Three Holy Brothers guided Lochlan to the front of the temple, where he stood facing an altar depicting Malin, the Goddess of Wisdom, as they anointed him in holy oils.

Many well-wishers filled the Dome, but aside from a few in the Mercerian delegation, he recognized no one. A choir sang as a brother wiped the oil from Lochlan's brow, and then he turned to see Althea making her way towards him. Before her, Edwina scattered flower petals on the floor as they slowly walked down the aisle. Beside them, Prince Alric looked regal in his finest clothes.

Lochlan's eyes met those of his bride-to-be, her hair done up with garlands of flowers intertwined within her braids. Her smile lit up the room, and the guests broke into compliments on her beauty. Then, before he even realized it, she stood beside him, her brother moving to stand to one side.

The Holy Father conducting the ceremony waited until the choir finished before launching into a sermon on the sanctity of marriage in a monotonous tone, making it difficult to follow what he said. Lochlan smiled and pretended to understand, nodding his head reverently to appear to embrace the spirit the occasion demanded.

The speech finally ended, and Alric stepped forward to announce his sister worthy of the union. Moments later, a woman Lochlan didn't recognize announced the same for him. She bore a vague look of familiarity, and he thought she could be one of the mages of Weldwyn, but he wasn't sure.

"Give me your hands," intoned the Holy Father, "that I might unite thee in sacred matrimony."

Lochlan held out his right hand, palm down, Althea doing the same, their hands coming into contact, though only briefly.

"This day, I call upon all present to witness the union of Althea, Princess of Weldwyn, to Lochlan, Chief of Clan Dungannon. May they prosper in their marriage and be blessed by many children."

The Holy Father took a strip of cloth from around his neck, laying it across their wrists. "What is decreed this day let no man put asunder and guide these two in death to the Afterlife together, that they need never be parted."

As the words sank in, Lochlan felt panic rising. Was he to be held in marriage evermore? In his homeland, he'd be pledged to his wife until death, but apparently, it was more permanent here.

"It is time for the gifts," announced the Holy Father.

Alric appeared at his side, a sword in hand, buckling it around Lochlan's waist, then stood. "I give you this sword that you might protect your new bride." The prince then stepped back.

The woman he'd seen earlier moved up beside Althea. "I give you this ring of granite," she said, "to signify the resolve with which you take this man as your husband." She slipped the ring on to Althea's finger, and they turned to face the Holy Father.

"By the power invested in me by the Goddess Malin, I pronounce you husband and wife. Now face your guests so they may revel in your happiness."

Lochlan and Althea turned and everyone cheered. Music started from somewhere unseen as folk surged forward to offer congratulations. It had all been quite confusing to the Clan Chief, but there was no mistaking the genuine joy in people's hearts. They might hate the Twelve Clans, but a wedding was a time for celebration, and they embraced it with enthusiasm.

Tulfar made his way through the crowd, taking his time to allow those before him an opportunity to offer their best wishes. Finally, he stood before the newly married couple, breaking into a smile.

"Princess Althea," he began. "I offer you the very best of wishes this day, along with a gift." He turned, indicating a Dwarf standing some distance off, bearing a standard.

"A flag?" asked Lochlan.

"Not just a flag: the banner of the Dragon Company, her own personal Dwarven warriors to command."

"I thank you, Lord Tulfar," she replied. "It is a generous gift and most appreciated."

"A company of Dwarves?" said Lochlan. "Why in the name of the Gods would you need that?"

She turned to her husband. "If nothing else, they will be a shining example of what a well-disciplined company looks like. It is also a mark of prestige, for what other Clan has such a collection of veteran warriors?"

He grinned. "I suppose you make a good point."

"Who is to command them?"

"Haldrim," said Tulfar, "whom you already know."

"But Haldrim was a commander of arbalesters, was he not?"

"Indeed, Your Highness, and still is, for I armed the Dragon Company with those very same weapons."

"Then it is a most valuable gift, and I thank you for their service."

"How many are there?" asked Lochlan.

"Fifty," said Tulfar, "although I suppose it would be more if you include their leaders and such."

"I hope you'll not take this the wrong way, Lord Tulfar, but how are we to feed them?"

The Dwarf chuckled. "Not to worry, my lord. They will eat almost anything, though, for purposes of this trip, they'll be surviving on stonecakes."

"Stonecakes?"

"I'll explain all about them later," said Althea. "For now, let it suffice to say they will be providing their own sustenance on the trip. Now, if Lord Tulfar will excuse us, I believe it's time for us to dance!"

Lord Elgin, Earl of Riversend, sipped his wine, a scowl upon his face.

"Something bothering you, Lord?"

He looked up to see one of the Mercerians but struggled to place him.

"Lord…"

"Lord Gerald," the fellow replied, "though admittedly, it's not a title I use very often."

Elgin shook his head. These foreigners had no idea of the importance a title held. "Don't let me interrupt you, Lord," Elgin replied. "I'd hate to take you away from something important."

"Not at all. The truth is, I'm not one for celebrations myself. You?"

"I must admit to a little surprise at this union. Such a hasty affair leads me to wonder if they rushed it to facilitate a… how would you say it? Indiscretion?"

"Are you insinuating something was going on between Althea and Lochlan?"

"It is not beyond the realm of possibility. After all, they're both young, and we all understand the passion of youth."

"I would watch my tongue if I were you. Suggesting things like that might get you into trouble."

"What kind of nonsense is this? I am Lord Elgin Warford, Earl of Riversend! In the absence of a king, I am one of only five men who rule over Weldwyn."

"Good for you, but it still doesn't excuse your behaviour. You should take greater care with your words."

"Who are you to lecture the likes of me?"

"I'm sorry," the old man said. "Did I not introduce myself?"

"You called yourself Lord Gerald, but that means little to me."

"Well then, I'd better correct that, hadn't I? My full name is Lord Gerald Matheson, Duke of Wincaster and Marshal of Merceria. Does that name sound a little more familiar, perhaps?"

"You're the one who led the army of liberation, aren't you?"

"I am, although admittedly, the warriors under my command freed you from the Clansmen."

"And for that, I am truly thankful," said Lord Elgin, "but it gives me no pleasure to see a Clansman wed to the Royal House of Weldwyn."

"Because you wanted her for yourself?"

"Whoever told you such nonsense?"

"No one, but your face betrays you."

"Let me make myself clear. It is not that I had any particular desire to wed her myself, but better a Weldwyn noble than a savage Clansman, surely?"

"Savage," said Gerald. "That word seems to be frequently bandied about these days."

"What are you implying?"

"The Orcs were described as savages, but I've found them pleasant people to be around, far nicer than some of the nobles of Weldwyn."

Blood rushed to Lord Elgin's face. "You dare to insult me, sir?"

"Not at all, my lord. I merely point out that one should take care when speaking ill of a people. You never know who might be listening."

"My apologies, Your Grace. I didn't mean to spoil an otherwise festive occasion. I shall keep my opinions to myself in future." Elgin spotted a familiar face amongst the guests. "If you will excuse me, I must speak with Lord Julian."

Aubrey took a seat, removing her shoes to give her feet a rest.

Edwina sat down beside her. "Tired?"

"What can I say? It's been a busy day."

"You didn't have to stand in for Lord Lochlan, you know."

"Someone needed to," replied the mage, "and I didn't see any of the nobles of Weldwyn offering their services."

"Can you blame them?"

"No, I suppose not." Aubrey looked around the room. The important folk of Weldwyn bunched together, ignoring their Mercerian allies for the most part. "I can see we still have a lot of work to do."

"We'll get there," said Edwina, "but it takes time."

"Do you honestly believe your sister can guide the Twelve Clans into peaceful coexistence?"

"She's been known to have a stubborn streak from time to time, and her recent experiences with the Dwarves of Mirstone only made her more so. She'll be fine."

"And how do you feel about her travelling to the Clanholdings?"

"I imagine she'll find it challenging, but in a good way. Althea always did think best when there were obstacles to overcome. I'm more concerned about how she'll adapt to being married."

"Are you two close?"

"We were, as children, but we grew apart as we got older. Now, we'll be on opposite sides of the map: her to the west, taming the Twelve Clans and me to the east, learning magic."

"I never thought of Merceria as the east," said Aubrey, "but I suppose you make a good point. As to your training, we still have a lot of work left to get the conservatory up and running, and I need to figure out how to train an Air Mage when we have no tutors available."

"Is Air Magic truly that rare?"

"It is in these parts. Master Kraloch's made enquiries with the Orcs, but those we've located so far are too distant to be of any real use to us."

"You'll find a solution," said Edwina. "I have faith in you."

The early morning sun lay below the horizon as the Twelve Clans began moving out, the Weldwyn horsemen leading the way. Haldrim and the Dragon Company brought up the rear, their Dwarven mail glittering in the predawn light.

Althea walked beside her husband, determined to share the long march to her new home. Lochlan silently accompanied her, unsure what to say, for he'd not seen her since the ceremony. She'd been far too busy planning and preparing for this journey.

The Twelve Clans did not have a disciplined army, which was reflected in how they marched—more a mob than a collection of warriors, made even more so by the confiscation of their weapons. Lochlan and Althea were permitted swords, while others retained only their knives.

Althea concentrated on leading by example, setting out at a brisk pace, but soon slowed to avoid outpacing the others. She risked a look at Lochlan, but he seemed lost in thought, his gaze directed westward.

"Thinking of home?" she asked.

"It's your home, too," he replied. "Now that we're husband and wife. Assuming we are husband and wife?"

"What do you mean by that?"

"I'm not sure of your customs in that regard, but back home, we're not considered married until we've consummated the union."

Her cheeks turned crimson, and she looked away, unsure how to respond.

"I understand this is an arranged marriage," Lochlan continued, "but sooner or later, we'll need to produce children, if only to cement relations between our two kingdoms."

"I'm well aware of that, but we barely know each other. Let's at least wait until we've spent some time in each other's company."

"It appears we have a long trip ahead of us. Perhaps we might be well-served to put the time to good use?"

"What are you suggesting?"

"Tell me about yourself," said Lochlan. "I know little of you, save that you're Leofric's oldest daughter."

"I hope you know more than that?"

He chuckled. "Perhaps a bit."

"Then talk to me. Tell me what you think you know, and I'll correct you if you're wrong."

"Very well. Let's see, where shall I start?" He looked her over, bringing another flush to her cheeks. "Your manner indicates you're well-read, much more so than most women your age. I also know you speak Dwarf, and that's a difficult tongue to master, which shows you have the grit to over-come obstacles."

"Grit?"

"Yes, an old Clan expression. It means to have fortitude and persever-ance in the face of obstacles. Something tells me you've struggled to find your place in society."

"I'm a princess. My fate was always to be married off for political expediency."

"Then it seems you failed to avoid your fate."

"Ah, but you were a husband of my choosing, not someone pressed into service for the sole purpose of marraige."

"Pressed into service? What strange manner of speech your people have."

"The term comes by way of the southern ports."

"Oh, I'm fully aware of where it comes from, just as it proves my point."

"The point being?"

"That you're educated. I've a feeling there are not many others in Summersgate who'd be familiar with that term."

"Anything else you care to add?"

"You're very conscious of what people think of you."

"What makes you say that?"

"The fact you're walking when you could just as easily demand a carriage."

"You're wrong on that count. I didn't walk because I was worried about what others would say—I chose not to ride to show my dedication to the people of the Clanholdings. I don't do things by half measures, Lochlan, and I've committed myself to bettering your lives."

"And by that, you mean making us more like your fellow countrymen?"

"I think we can both agree," replied Althea, "neither of us knows much about the other's culture. That's something we need to change, going forward. The first step towards resolving our differences is to understand each other."

"I agree. Now it's your turn to tell me what you think you know about me."

"You're young for a Clan Chief, and you were reluctant to take on the responsibility. Deep down, you're only doing so because it's what Brida would have wanted."

"Leave my sister out of this."

"You feel guilt over her death, that much is clear, yet I don't see why? Kythelia was the one who killed her after all."

"I warned her about the Elves' treachery, but she wouldn't listen."

"Did the Dark Queen herself visit the Twelve Clans?"

"No. She sent an emissary, a fellow by the name of Lysandil, who brought greetings in Kythelia's name. His silver tongue talked the Twelve Clans into invading Weldwyn—not that it took much effort."

"You say you warned her. What made you think him untrustworthy?"

"He was too quick to promise victory, for all our previous attempts to subdue Weldwyn ended in complete disaster. Still, his words won over my sister, particularly after he showed her the might of Prince Tarak's fleet." He chuckled. "Not that it helped us much. We captured the capital, all right, but that was primarily due to the actions of a few insiders."

"Did you know of that before you marched?"

"No. Nor, do I believe, did Brida. We arrived at Summersgate expecting to siege the place. Our information was that the army of Weldwyn had been destroyed, with few men left to fight."

"Your information was right in that regard," said Althea. "And you might have held it were it not for Kythelia massacring your Clan Chiefs. It would've been a much different result had your leaders lived to organize a defence."

"That is all in the past," said Lochlan. "Now that it's over, I need to concentrate on building a future for my Clan."

"Not just yours—ours—and it's not only Clan Dungannon. If we are to succeed in this, we must include all the Clans."

"And how do you propose we do that?" He shook his head. "You don't know the Clans the way I do. They are a scattered people, each with their own ideas and ways of life. My father, Dathen, was the first High King of the Twelve Clans in living memory. Other than Brida, I doubt there'll ever be another."

"Perhaps you're right, but that doesn't mean we can't find common ground amongst them. In any case, that won't be for some time yet. Let's first concentrate on Dungannon and see where that might take us."

"We only just started this journey, and you're already set to make changes?"

She smiled. "The journey of a thousand miles begins with but a single step."

TEN

The Crypt

WINTER 966 MC

Hayley pulled her cloak tighter in a vain attempt to ward off the frigid wind swirling around her. Ahead of her, Gryph lumbered along, disappearing into the snow squall, only to reappear a moment later. They'd left the Whitewood some time ago and somehow located the road to Beaconsgate, but the drifting snow made further navigation almost impossible. She had a vague sense that the city lay to the northeast, yet the thick, white flakes blocked the sun, leaving her wondering which direction was which.

Gryph howled, putting Hayley on the alert. She slowed her horse and considered stringing her bow, but chances were any attacker would be upon her long before she had time to nock an arrow, let alone release it.

The wolf's ears flattened, his snout pointing off the road to the right, where a tiny flicker of light occasionally peeked through the flurries. She dismounted and drew her sword to be on the safe side.

Hayley crept forward, her horse on a long lead, her canine companion in stalking mode. Laughter drifted towards them, and then a few children's voices joined in. She released her pent-up breath and relaxed, for the likelihood of bandits having such company was slim.

She spotted a pair of wagons through the snow, while between them sat a roaring fire. All eyes turned towards Hayley as they noted her approach, and a tall, lanky individual picked up a makeshift club as he stood.

"Who goes there?" he called out.

"My name is Hayley Chambers," she replied. "I'm a simple traveller on my way to Beaconsgate."

The fellow eyed Gryph. "Simple, is it? Your companion says otherwise."

"Don't be alarmed. This is Gryph, and he's friendly."

"Come," called out an older woman. "Warm yourself by the fire, and tell us how you came to be in the company of a wolf."

Hayley drew closer, sheathing her sword. Three children sat by the fire, the oldest a boy of about twelve summers. His two sisters were a few years younger, maybe seven or eight, though she hadn't much experience in guessing ages.

"We're traders out of Harrowsbrook," said the man. "My name is Barden, and this is my wife, Beatrice."

"Are you hungry?" added Beatrice. "There's food to spare."

"Thank you, but no," said Hayley. "Tell me, do you travel this road often?"

"Usually twice a year," said Barden. "Typically, in spring and fall, war permitting, but we're late getting away this year. We run a general store down in Harrowsbrook."

"And what takes you to Beaconsgate?"

"We're always looking for new trade items that might interest our customers."

"Yes," added Beatrice, "and some of our local goods can fetch a high price in the city." She looked around. "Of course, the snow isn't helping."

"How much farther is it?"

"Another day, maybe two, if this weather continues. We thought we might set up camp and at least keep warm. The last thing we need is to go off the road and damage the wagons in this storm."

"I noticed the sword," said Barden. "Are you one of those Mercerian women warriors we've heard about?"

"Not a warrior so much as a ranger. We're responsible for keeping the roads safe for folk such as yourselves."

"You're a long way from home."

"True, but as I said, I'm headed to Beaconsgate."

"Might I ask what for?" said Beatrice. "It's not every day we see a Mercerian on these roads."

"You might say I'm investigating something." Hayley sat beside the fire, with Gryph curled up at her side.

Barden handed her a tin cup full of pungent wine. "Investigating, you say? That sounds awfully mysterious."

Hayley chuckled. "You might say it suits the times. Tell me, have you heard of someone named Randolf Blackburn?"

He spit on the fire. "Aye, I know the name. He was a favourite of Lord Hollis. Why do you ask?"

"He's the reason I'm here. He's made a claim on one of our baronies."

"Has he, now? That's fascinating. How does a Norlander lay claim to a Mercerian title?"

"It's a complicated tale, but in essence, he claims to be the son of one of our barons."

"And what does the baron say to that?"

"I'm afraid he's no longer with us," said Hayley. "In fact, I'm travelling to Beaconsgate to find out where he's buried."

"If he was someone important, he'd be in the crypt beneath the Temple of Saxnor."

"And if he wasn't?"

"Then he'd be in the graveyard, rotting away. How long ago did this fellow die?"

"That's a good question. We believed he died over thirty years ago, but now there are claims he survived in captivity."

"Could he still be alive?"

"Not according to the man making the claim," said Hayley. "And if he were alive, he'd be very old."

"You should talk to the Holy Father in Beaconsgate," suggested Beatrice. "He'd have a list of everyone interred there since they built it two hundred years ago."

"Thank you. I shall do precisely as you suggest."

"And if you find his burial place?" asked Barden.

"Then I'll have a better idea of his fate."

"Providing you can prove the deceased baron's identity."

"I suppose that's true," said Hayley. "I hadn't considered that."

"Well, at the very least, there'll be a birth record for the two Blackburn siblings."

"You've heard of Celia Blackburn?"

"Oh yes. In many ways, she was worse than her brother."

"How so?"

"She was ruthless," said Beatrice. "I don't know if you're familiar with this part of Norland, but Lord Hollis was a brutal ruler. He often sent his warriors to the surrounding towns to round up tribute."

"Tribute? You mean taxes?"

"No, I mean anything they could get their hands on. Hollis ruled by intimidation, and the Blackburns weren't above getting their hands dirty, especially when things took their fancy. They disappeared for a few years, and rumour was they went south, into your neck of the woods."

"That fits with what I know. They became Knights of the Sword, but then Randolf vanished after his sister's disgrace."

"How does one become a Mercerian knight when they're from Norland?"

"Also a good question," said Hayley. "I assume they lied about their place of birth."

"You say Randolf vanished?" said Barden. "That's likely when he returned to Norland and resumed his service with the earl. I'd be careful in Beaconsgate if I were you. His name still carries some weight there."

"It doesn't frighten me," said Hayley.

"It should."

Beaconsgate was small, by Mercerian reckoning, being more of a town than an actual city, but its lack of buildings didn't affect the size of its crowds.

The trader's warning was still on Hayley's mind as she made her way to the Temple of Saxnor. Gryph stayed close, wary of the crowds yet unwilling to wait outside the town while the High Ranger explored the streets. The wolf's presence was enough to keep bystanders at arm's length, leaving Hayley time to mull things over.

If Lord Edward was interred beneath the temple, how would she prove it? A body was one thing, but a corpse made little distinction between noble and commoner. How would she tell if it belonged to Edward Fitzwilliam?

She chided herself for thinking too far in advance. Step one was to see if there was a body; the actual verification of the identity could come later.

The temple was an impressive structure, easily the tallest in all of Beaconsgate, for its stone bell tower soared above the rooftops like a sign from Saxnor.

She slowed as she neared. In design, it was similar to the temples found in Merceria, not unusual considering their shared heritage. However, the dark-grey stone it was made of was unlike anything in Wincaster, giving the place a sinister look.

Hayley entered the building through the front doors, which stood wide open despite the bitter cold. Down the nave she went, her boots echoing on the marble floor. As if sensing her caution, Gryph slowed his pace, his ears on the alert for any sign of danger. Their entrance soon garnered the attention of a rotund individual.

"May I help you?" he called out, his voice higher than his stout frame suggested.

"My name is Hayley Chambers," she replied. "I'm here to talk to whoever's in charge?"

"That would be the Holy Father, but I'm afraid he's not here at this precise moment."

"A pity, as I've come rather a long way to find him."

"Is there something I can help you with?"

"And you are?"

"My apologies. I'm Brother Caldwell. I'm one of the five brothers who help the Holy Father in the performance of his duties."

"I'm given to understand there is a crypt beneath the temple holding the remains of people of import?"

"You are correct. Is there someone, in particular, you're interested in?"

"There is."

"Then come with me, and I shall check our records. As the crypt is immense and the halls dark, finding who you're looking for would be difficult without resorting to our notes."

He led her into a small office, wherein he pulled an immense tome from a shelf and placed it onto a table with great reverence. He muttered a prayer before opening it.

"Have you any idea when the individual was interred?" he asked.

"I'm afraid not. That's one of the reasons I'm here."

"Might I trouble you for a name?"

"Lord Edward Fitzwilliam."

"There's no one here by that name," he announced quickly.

"How can you be so sure?"

"The name Fitzwilliam is well known to us," said Brother Caldwell. "The late Lord Hollis despised the Baron of Bodden, and I daresay his nephew is not far from having the same opinion."

"His nephew?"

"Yes, Lord Asher, the new Earl of Beaconsgate, now that his uncle is no longer with us. Believe me, I would know if there was a Fitzwilliam interred in the crypt. Are you sure he was even here?"

"So claimed Randolf Blackburn."

Her host winced.

"Is something wrong?" she asked.

"The name is not unknown to me... to any of us here at the temple, if I'm being honest. He enforced Lord Hollis's decree that the temple pay a tithe to support the recent war. He and his minions saw fit to march in and ransack the place, carrying off many objects."

"Objects?"

"Yes, symbols of our faith: candlesticks, bowls, pretty much anything easy to convert into coins. However, I doubt he would've made off with a body from the crypt. You mentioned the name Lord Edward; is there any chance he might've been interred under another name? Fitzwilliam would've been too easily recognized."

"Quite possibly, though I don't know what he would have used. Perhaps Blackburn?"

The Holy Brother slowly flipped through the pages. "I'm afraid this may take some time."

"I'm in no hurry. I'm more than capable of searching through that book of yours by myself if you've somewhere else you need to be?"

"Much as I appreciate the offer, my superior would be furious if I allowed an outsider to handle the temple's records." He flipped through a few more pages. "You say Randolf Blackburn lays claim to the Barony of Bodden?"

"I never said it was Bodden."

"True," said Caldwell, "but you mentioned the name Fitzwilliam."

"Does that matter?"

"I'm fully aware of how the laws of succession work. He'd have to be Lord Edward's son to claim the title. If I found the record of Randolf's birth, it would give us some idea of when Lord Edward was still alive, unless you believe he impregnated a woman from the Afterlife?"

"No, of course not," said Hayley. "Please proceed however you think best."

The brother returned to the shelf, reading the spines of books until he found what he was looking for. "Here it is," he said, dropping this book down with far less reverence than the first time. "This is the record of all births in the region, at least all the births that count."

"Meaning?"

"Randolf Blackburn was a man of consequence. I very much doubt his father would've been buried in a pauper's grave."

"He did mention he couldn't use his real name, but I have no idea when he changed it."

Caldwell rubbed his hands together, revelling in the mystery. "Then let's see what we can discover, shall we?"

It was late by the time Hayley found what she was looking for, but part of her wished her search had failed. Beverly's claim to Bodden rested on her father's position as baron, yet the discovery of what appeared to be her uncle's body supported Sir Randolf's assertion.

His father supposedly died when Sir Randolf was seven, and the date of internment had, unfortunately, confirmed that claim. Still, it didn't necessarily mean Lord Edward was his true father.

The temple's records listed Edward Blackburn as the father of both Celia and Randolf, yet Hayley still held out hope the interred body was not the previous Baron of Bodden. The final proof would be the baron's ring. She hoped the body of his widow, a woman named Rosella Blackburn, might provide further clues. Randolf claimed she'd lived longer than Lord Edward, and therefore she would've inherited his possessions.

Lord Hollis was reputed to be the man responsible for saving Lord Edward, but Hayley found that difficult to believe. The two had been bitter enemies for years but had never met. How would Hollis even recognize an unconscious and wounded Baron of Bodden? It all came back to Edward's supposed wife. The temple possessed no record of her death or their marriage, but Randolf claimed otherwise. Was she still alive or buried in a pauper's grave? Clearly, there was work to be done here, both in identifying the remains in the crypt and finding out more about the enigmatic Sir Randolf Blackburn.

The High Ranger left the temple, deep in thought. There was much to consider in this case, for the more she uncovered, the more complicated things became. She began to doubt she'd ever resolve the issue, merely keep finding more threads to unravel. She was so involved in contemplating all the possibilities that she almost ran head-on into a pair of men.

"What have we here?" said a dark-haired, rough-looking fellow with a week's worth of beard. "Is this a Mercerian I see before me?"

"It must be," replied his companion, "for Norland women are much too refined to wear weapons."

Hayley looked them over. The dark-haired one appeared prone to violence, while his companion, thinner and with a shock of blond hair, had a hungry look to his eyes, like a viper waiting to strike.

"I have no quarrel with you," she finally replied. "Allow me to be on my way, and I shall trouble you no more."

"I think it's a little too late for that, don't you?"

"I have no desire to fight you. Let us put this misunderstanding behind us."

The first man, easily a head taller than Hayley, stepped closer. Gryph growled, causing the brute to glance over at the wolf. Resigned to a fight, Hayley moved in, bringing her knee into contact with the fellow's groin. Predictably, he crumpled to the ground, letting out a high-pitched screech as he fell.

His thinner companion reacted quickly, drawing forth a cudgel from his belt and charging forward, his weapon held high. In her career as a ranger, Hayley had dealt with this type of thing before. She allowed her attacker to come close, then sidestepped, extending her leg slightly to trip him.

He, too, collapsed to the ground, the wind knocked from him. Hayley knelt over him, drawing a dagger and placing it at the back of his neck, preventing him from rising.

"I say it's time to move on," she said. "What are your thoughts on the matter?"

Gryph moved closer, his bared fangs barely a finger's width from the man's face.

"Most assuredly," he gasped. "I apologize for the misunderstanding."

She was about to release him when she spotted the knife at his waist. The handle was of polished shadowbark, an expensive luxury for someone dressed as a commoner. A quick glance at his companion, still rolling around clutching his groin, confirmed he possessed an expensive-looking scabbard. She wondered if her encounter was even an accident. Was somebody trying to interfere with her investigation?

She tucked her knife away and rose, clicking her tongue to get Gryph's attention. A hand signal brought him to her side, and then she continued down the street, her senses alert for any other trouble.

The encounter rattled her, and Hayley worried if it had been wise to come here alone. All it would take was a knife in her sleep, and she'd never be heard from again. She shook her head, clearing away the dark thoughts. Gryph padded along beside her, scanning the crowd as if looking for prey. She realized he would keep her safe, and her muscles finally began to relax.

Randolf Blackburn claimed the Earl of Beaconsgate was instrumental in saving Lord Edward. If Hollis were still alive, he'd be the perfect witness to verify Randolf's story. Then again, Hollis hated Merceria, so it was unlikely he would've co-operated with her enquiries even if he were involved. She considered talking to his nephew, the new earl. There was a possibility Hollis kept records, or some of the older servants might remember events.

She bent over and scratched Gryph's head. "Well, what do you think? Shall we chance it and try visiting the earl?"

He stared back and licked his chops, eliciting a chuckle from her.

"Very well. I know when I've been out-manoeuvred. We'll do it your way —food first, visit second. Does that satisfy you?"

His ears pricked up at the mention of food. Hayley scanned the street, finally resting on a sign naming a tavern.

"How appropriate," she said. "The Black Crow. I must tell Revi they named it after Shellbreaker." She glanced once more at her wolf. "Come on, Gryph. Let's see what they've got on the menu."

ELEVEN

Accusations

WINTER 966 MC

Jack Marlowe leaned back, the mound of papers before him growing as a servant placed even more onto the pile. "Do we have to read all of these?" he asked.

"Only if you want to get to the bottom of this," said Tulfar.

"And what is it, exactly, that we're looking at?"

"Correspondence that was in Lord Godfrey Hammond's possession."

"Who is?"

"For God's sake," piped in Lady Lindsey. "Do we have to spell it out for you? Lord Godfrey stands accused of conspiring with Lord James Goodwin to allow the enemy entry into Summersgate."

"That I understand," said Jack, "but I don't see the point in reading all of this! Surely someone else can deal with the drudgery?"

"I might remind you," said Tulfar, "that a man's life hangs in the balance, possibly two, if this implicates Godfrey."

"Very well. I concede the point. Might I ask how we acquired these letters?"

"They were seized when they arrested Godfrey."

"I'm surprised he didn't see fit to destroy them."

"He tried. You'll notice some of them are charred around the edges, evidence he threw them into the fireplace. Thankfully, the man in charge of the arresting detail saw fit to rescue them."

"And what of James Goodwin? I don't suppose he has any incriminating letters?"

"Not yet," said Lady Lindsey, "but they're carrying out an extensive search of his estate. Don't worry. If there's anything to be found, we'll soon have it in our possession."

"I thought," said Jack, "you wanted this to be over? You were ready to find him guilty without any evidence whatsoever."

"That's true, but your commitment has swayed my opinion in this regard. I now believe we should weigh the evidence and deliberate on the facts before passing judgement."

"Just out of curiosity, are we to try Lord Godfrey as well?"

"I imagine we will, eventually, but Lord James is our priority at the moment. It's up to the Earls Council whether or not to give us that additional responsibility. Until then, we shall concentrate our efforts on the task at hand."

"This is all mundane stuff," said Tulfar. "Lots of letters from Lord James, mostly complaining about his mother. That's Lady Jane, isn't it?"

"It is," replied Jack, "and I tend to agree with your observation. It appears there was no love lost between them, which is a bit of a surprise."

"Why would you say that?"

"I've met Lady Jane. She's the current paramour of Lord Gerald."

"And?"

"She was most distraught to learn of her son's betrayal. It's believed he played her for a fool."

"That makes sense," said the Dwarf. "His anger and frustration in these letters are easy to see, as is his dismissal of her intellect."

"I've only met her briefly," said Lady Lindsey. "Is she, perhaps, dim-witted?"

"Not in my experience," replied Jack, "but you would know her better than I."

"Why would you think that?"

"You thrive on knowing other people's business. In your heyday, you were known as the court gossip."

"It is not gossip to speak the truth. However, I know very little about Lady Jane. She was, in a manner of speaking, mostly a reclusive individual, especially after the death of her husband. Quite frankly, I'm surprised she worked up the nerve to even talk to Lord Gerald."

"Yes... well, let's not dwell on that, shall we? Now, where were we?"

"Trying to discover some useful information," said Tulfar. "Gossip is one thing, but we need facts to determine the innocence or guilt of Lord James. Is there nothing we can find that would help in that regard?"

A knock interrupted their discussion.

"Yes?" called out Jack.

The door opened, revealing a servant. "Lord Osric is here to see you, my lord."

"To see me?"

"Well, the tribunal."

"Remind me who he is, again?"

"The Baron of Hanwick," said Tulfar. "It's a town in the northeast corner of Weldwyn, up by the Mercerian border."

"Oh yes. Now I remember." Jack returned his attention to the servant. "What does he want? We're rather busy."

"He says he is here on behalf of Lord James Goodwin, my lord."

"Does he, indeed? Well, in that case, you'd better show him in." Jack looked at Tulfar. "I wonder what this is all about?"

"We'll find out in a moment," replied the Dwarf.

Lord Osric Bloomfield was in his mid-forties. Before the war, that would've made him middle-aged, but in the wake of the invasion, he was now one of the oldest surviving nobles. Had his barony not been so close to the Mercerian border, he would likely have suffered the same fate as his contemporaries, but a bout of ill health stepped in and saved him, for he was in Almswell at the healing baths when war broke out.

"Lord Osric," said Lady Lindsey. "You grace us with your presence."

"Thank you," the old baron replied. "You honour me, my lady."

"Can I offer you a drink?" said Jack. "I always find conversation flows smoother with the help of a little wine, don't you?"

"That's most appreciated. Thank you." Osric grasped the offered cup, raising it in a toast. "To your continued good health," he said, then took a sip.

"I must say this is a bit of a surprise," said Tulfar. "We weren't expecting anyone to intercede on Lord James' behalf."

"I could not, in good conscience, stand by and allow a miscarriage of justice. Every noble deserves representation."

"So, you're a friend of Lord James?"

"Not really. I know him, of course, but we did not socialize other than those rare occasions on which all the nobles of Weldwyn gathered."

"Very well," said Jack. "I concede he has a right to be represented, but you could've simply informed us of this in writing."

"I come to you to offer myself to speak on his behalf," said Lord Osric. "But to present a defence of his actions, I need your permission to examine the evidence. I assume you have evidence?"

"We do, but to be quite honest, we're still sifting through it."

"I should also like free rein to carry out my own investigation, although I understand if you insist on guards accompanying me. I will turn over anything I find in the way of evidence, regardless of whether it bodes well or ill for Lord James."

"Very well," said Jack.

"I shall draw up a letter authorizing it," said Tulfar. "Then we three will sign it, making it official. I can have it to you by this evening, if that's convenient?"

Lord Osric bowed. "That would be fine, thank you. You can send it to me at my house in the capital."

"Anything else we can help you with?"

"Might I enquire about the actual crime you are charging him with?"

"Treason comes to mind," said Jack, "possibly even collaborating with the enemy. You should be aware that both carry a sentence of death should we find him guilty."

"And his lands?"

"Will be confiscated in the name of the Crown."

"But there is no Crown at the moment," said Lord Osric.

"True," replied Jack, "but in the absence of a king, the Earls Council is more than capable of carrying out that sentence. In any event, this tribunal is still in the early stages of its investigation. It's conceivable the list of crimes perpetrated by the accused may grow. If it does, I shall be sure to inform you."

"Would it be possible to visit Lord James? I understand he's incarcerated, but I don't know where they're holding him."

"He's in the city jail for the time being," said the Dwarf, "as the dungeons beneath the Palace are buried under debris. If you want to see him, that's your prerogative, but I must warn you he needs to be in the presence of a guard at all times when not in his cell. I can send a note allowing you access if you still wish to visit him?"

"That would be most excellent. I shall make myself scarce, as you appear to have much work to do. Good day, my lords, my lady."

Tulfar waited until the door closed behind their visitor. "What do you think? Is he telling the truth?"

"About what?" asked Jack.

"About not really knowing Lord James."

"I'm not sure what you're suggesting."

"Merely that he may be a co-conspirator of the accused, trying to cover up the villain's tracks."

"He's Baron of Hanwick, a fairly remote location. Besides, he's only now returned to Summersgate."

"Still, it's a mite convenient he wasn't here to fall prey to Brida's wrath."

"You weren't here either," said Jack, "yet no one is questioning your loyalty."

"True," said the Dwarf, "but then again, I sent warriors to help fight against the enemy. Where was Lord Osric during all of this?"

"He was ill," replied Lady Lindsey. "He's suffered from poor health for much of his life and frequently seeks treatment in Almswell."

"I'll concede the point, but he still could've provided aid in the form of warriors."

"And what would he have sent? Leofric snapped up all the warriors in Hanwick on his march into Norland, and now they're all rotting corpses littering a field in the middle of nowhere."

"Actually," said Jack. "Kythelia enslaved them as spirits, but you made your point."

"Leofric was a fool," said Tulfar. "He marched off to war and left the realm undefended. No wonder the Twelve Clans invaded. Now, we need to get back to the entire reason for this gathering, the examination of all these documents." He paused as a thought struck him, turning to Jack. "Weren't you heading to the west gate?"

"I was, but news of the wedding interfered with my plans."

"You still could've gone later in the day."

"And risk disappointing all those women? My lord, I have my faults, but depriving the fairer sex of my company is not one of them."

"You're not amongst the fairer sex now," said Lady Lindsey. "And before you claim otherwise, know that I am old and therefore immune to your charms."

"I would disagree," said Jack, "but in this case, I'll accept your judgement." He stood. "Very well. I shall head out to the west gate to put matters to rest. Do we have the list of who was on duty that night?"

"Yes," said Tulfar. "Hold on a moment." He dug through his papers. "Ah, here it is." He held it up triumphantly.

Jack crossed the floor, snatching it from the Dwarf's hands. "Thank you, my lord. I'm sure this will prove most illuminating."

"Remember," said Lady Lindsey. "You're looking for the guards on duty that night, not the bottom of a tankard."

"You wound me with your accusations, my lady. I might be a notorious flirt, but I know how to go about my business when the occasion demands."

"I'm sure you do, providing your business involves either women or drink."

"Hah," said Lord Tulfar. "She's got you there."

"I'm not sure whether to be insulted or amused."

"You can be both if you like, providing you come back with some answers."

"That I shall do with all speed."

At the west gate of Summersgate, merchants hurried from the capital, eager to get their goods to distant cities before the heavier snows of winter descended. The city's liberation had restored trade, but the delay brought on by the occupation took a heavy toll. Now, there was an explosion of activity as people sought to increase their profits while demand was at an all-time high. Jack tried to picture what it must've been like the night the Twelve Clans entered the city, but the surrounding noise distracted him.

The guards were so preoccupied, they mistook him for a simple traveller. It wasn't until he introduced himself that they noted his presence.

"My pardon, Lord," said the one in charge. "We weren't expecting visitors."

"That's quite all right," replied Jack. "I see you're busy today."

"Aye, it's been like this all week." He waved forward one of his guards to inspect a wagon before turning his full attention to Jack. "Is there something I can do for you, my lord?"

"Yes. I'm investigating the events leading up to the capture of Summersgate." He glanced at the paper he carried. "I have a list of those on duty that night. I wondered if any of them are here today?" He handed over the note.

The guardsman scanned through its contents. "Mallory is dead," he said, "and Bradford has been ill for some time."

"And Walsh?"

The guard swept his gaze over the press of people. "That's him over there, on the back of that wagon."

Jack followed his arm to spot a thin, red-headed fellow poking some bundles of hay with a spear. "What's he doing?"

"Looking for contraband."

"In a wagon full of hay?"

"You'd be surprised what we find, my lord. It wouldn't be the first time a criminal tried to escape the law by hiding in the back of a wagon."

"Would you be so kind as to inform Walsh I'd like to speak with him?"

"Of course, Lord."

Jack waited as the guard called the fellow over. Moments later, the man stood before him, wearing a bemused grin. "You wanted to see me, Lord?"

"Indeed, I did, or rather, I do. I understand you were on duty the night we lost the gate?"

"Yes, Lord."

"Can you tell me, in your own words, what transpired?"

"Not exactly."

"What do you mean by that?"

"Well, I didn't see anything."

"But you were on duty that night?"

"Aye, I was, but it was my turn up in the tower, keeping a lookout. If you want to know what happened below, you'd need to speak to Bradford."

"Still, I'd like to hear your version of events. You said you were up in the tower. When did you first suspect something untoward was happening?"

"That's easy. The enemy came close to the gate. Not their entire army, mind you, only twenty or so warriors. When I saw them coming, I called out to those below, then sent an arrow or two down into the group of them. By that time, they'd already reached the door, and the sounds of fighting drifted up to me. In that instant, I knew they'd somehow gained entrance."

"But you didn't see them actually enter?"

"I'm afraid not. Though, come to think of it, I heard Mallory speaking with someone right before that."

"To whom was he talking?"

"I don't know—a noble of some sort."

"Why would you assume that?"

"He called whoever it was 'my lord'."

"So, it was a man?"

"Not to be rude, but who else would he call 'my lord'?"

"Was it an old voice or a young one?"

"I really couldn't say," replied Walsh. "They weren't talking very loudly."

"Yet you claim to have heard the conversation!"

"Only in that he referred to the fellow as 'my lord'. I'm sorry I couldn't be of much use to you."

"Unfortunately, your friend Mallory is no longer with us."

"Have you talked to Bradford yet?"

"No. This is my first stop. Might you know where I can find the fellow?"

"Certainly, Lord. You know the Amber Shard?"

"Indeed. They serve some of the finest ale in all of Summersgate."

"There's a carpenter across from it—that's his father's business. He has a room on the top floor, overlooking the street."

"I was told he's ill."

"Ill? Well, I suppose some might see it that way."

"Are you suggesting he's not?" asked Jack.

"To be honest, many folks hereabouts are angry about how things turned out that night, and they blame us."

"So, you're suggesting he's pretending to be ill to avoid the accusations?"

"It drove Mallory to take his own life, or at least that's the accusation."

"Mallory killed himself?"

"You didn't know?"

"I assumed he died in the war. Hang on a moment. What do you mean by accusation? Are you suggesting there's another explanation?"

"It's rather convenient, don't you think? Him dying before anyone can get his side of the story?"

"You believe he was murdered?"

Walsh looked around nervously. "I'm not suggesting anything of the sort, merely that it's a strange coincidence."

"Is that why you're so nervous?"

"You would be, too, if you were in my boots."

Jack shook his head. "This is getting ridiculous."

"Lord?"

"The more I dig, the more complicated this gets. It's no reflection on you, Walsh, but I'm beginning to suspect someone wants this entire affair covered up."

TWELVE

Dungannon

WINTER 966 MC

A bitter wind blew in from the west, chilling Althea to the bone, but she refused to reveal her discomfort, turning instead to Lochlan as a distraction. "How much farther, do you reckon?"

The young Clan Chief smiled. "We shall be there before nightfall."

"And is it always this windy?"

"This is a calm day. Wait until the winter storms hit, then we'll be buried in snow."

They'd crossed the river days ago, passing through a wide plain before moving into some hills. Their escort had turned back as they entered Clan territory, but the Dragon Company was still there to protect them in this dangerous region.

"Are there no roads in the Clanholdings?"

"There are streets within the towns, but none out here in the wilderness."

"Then how do you trade goods with the other Clans?"

"By boat. Two main rivers run through our land, and the easternmost one, the White River, cuts straight through Dungannon territory. If you followed it to the sea, you'd be in the port of Windbourne."

"And how many boats does the Clan Chief of Dungannon own?"

"None," replied Lochlan. "The boatholders control all the traffic on the river."

"Who are they?"

"Families who hold the secrets of constructing and operating boats. They keep a tight rein on who's allowed to build or use the river to ship goods. Supposedly, they do that to ensure efficient trade, but I believe it's more about controlling the flow of coins."

"And how many are in Dungannon?" asked Althea.

"We have three, but more are scattered throughout the Clans."

"You have only three boats?"

Lochlan laughed. "No. Sorry, I thought you were asking about the boatholder families, not the vessels themselves. There are ten boats, or at least there were when I left Dungannon."

Althea looked behind them to where the bulk of the Clansmen followed in their wake. "And what of them? Less than a tenth are from Dungannon."

"No doubt they'll rest here a day or two before continuing on their way to their respective villages, assuming there are enough boats to take them."

"You just said there were only ten. That's nowhere near enough to take all of them."

"And if we depended on our boats alone, I would agree, but there are likely some from other Clans bringing trade goods."

Lochlan halted as they topped a rise, pointing to the west. "There it is," he said. "Your new home."

From this distance, she could see Dungannon spread out on the eastern side of the White River's crystal-clear water. It was a sprawling town, but not what she expected, for no wall protected them in this dangerous land, although there were several watchtowers. The largest structures appeared to be a cluster of granaries, but this time of year, the fields lay barren.

"Strange," she said. "I expected a bridge over the river."

"Whatever for? It's not as if there's anything worth seeing on the western bank."

He left the rise, heading for Dungannon, forcing her to hurry to catch up. As they approached, a call came from the nearest watchtower, and then a small group appeared, cheering the return of their fellow Clansmen.

Althea held back, unsure of the welcome she might receive. The townsfolk mixed in with their returning kin, but sorrow soon replaced their glee as people learned of the losses.

A group of older warriors pushed their way to the front, spears and shields at the ready, a clear response to the approach of the Dwarves who'd stayed back.

"Fear not," said Lochlan. "They are friendly."

One of the warriors stepped in front of the others, his wrinkled countenance revealing his age. "So, it's true?" he said. "Brida is dead?"

"She is, but I've returned to take her place." He turned to Althea. "This is Daragh, senior oathman to the Clan Chief of Dungannon."

"Oathman?"

"Yes, a warrior sworn to serve the chief."

"That being the case, why was he not in Weldwyn?"

"I wanted to be," replied Daragh, "but we needed someone to remain behind and take charge of the town's defence."

"And how have things been since we left?" asked Lochlan.

"Quiet, my chief, as one would expect with everyone off fighting a war." He eyed the Dwarves. "What has brought the mountain folk to Dungannon?"

"This is the Dragon Company, a band of Dwarven warriors responsible for keeping my new bride safe."

The townsfolk erupted into chatter, for this was news indeed.

"Bride?" said Daragh.

"Yes." He paused a moment. "She's a Princess of Weldwyn."

Althea waited, expecting anger, but they looked at her with only interest. Surprisingly, the thought of a bride for their chief overcame any loathing of their traditional enemy.

Althea took a moment to look around at the buildings. They were not too different in design from those in the countryside of Weldwyn, with thatched roofs and wattle-and-daub construction, but something struck her as odd. After they'd gone a block or two, she finally realized what appeared so out of place—few of the buildings were more than a single floor. It was a striking difference, especially when compared to Summersgate, for almost all the houses in the Weldwyn capital were two stories, with some even taller.

The procession slowed, and then Lochlan, whom she'd lost sight of, reappeared. "Come," he said. "I've arranged for your lodging."

"Am I not going to live with you?"

"Not yet. You're to be the wife of a Clan Chief. It's a tradition that we don't share a bed until after we are married in the manner of the Twelve Clans. Until then, you'll stay with my cousin Mirala."

Haldrim appeared at her side.

"Yes, Captain?" said Althea.

"I was wondering where you'd like the company to set up, Highness?"

She turned to Lochlan. "Where is your cousin's house?"

He pointed at a small, squat structure surrounded by what looked like weeds. A short woman in her thirties with wild, unkempt hair stood out front, watching them as they talked. Lochlan waved her over, and Althea noted her limp as she approached.

"Greetings," said the woman, turning her attention to the newcomer. "And who do we have here?"

"This is Althea, Princess of Weldwyn. She is to be my bride."

"Bride? Can it be my young cousin has finally deigned to notice a woman? And a beautiful one at that!" She cackled in delight, and then her face grew sombre. "Did you say she was a princess?"

"I am," said Althea. "My father was King Leofric."

Mirala looked askance at her cousin. "Is this some sort of trick?"

Lochlan stood up straighter. "I can assure you it is not."

"Ours was an arranged marriage," explained Althea. "My brother believed such a union might bring peace between our two realms."

"Peace?" Mirala shook her head. "There can be no peace here in the Clanholdings. If we're not fighting your people, we're fighting amongst ourselves. It's our way of life."

"Then perhaps it's about time we saw fit to change things?"

Lochlan's cousin smiled, then turned her attention to the Clan Chief. "I like her, but if you two are to marry, we've much work to do." She grabbed Althea by the arm, pulling her away.

Haldrim sighed, then followed along in their wake, still trying to decide where the company should set up camp.

Mirala's house was close to the southern end of Dungannon, downriver from the centre of the town. The weeds Althea had noticed earlier turned out to be a small garden blocked off with a dilapidated fence, presumably to keep people from trampling her plants. Not that anyone seemed to bother the poor woman, for everyone they passed gave her a wide berth.

Althea waved Haldrim over as they approached the front door. "You can camp to the west, along the river's edge for now, although I imagine you'll eventually want to dig into those hills to the east."

"The hills?" said Mirala.

"The mountain folk prefer living underground. I'm surprised you're not more familiar with them."

"Such folk have never graced Dungannon with their presence, but the same cannot be said about other Clans. Their trade goods are muchly prized, particularly their ironwork. How many accompanied you?"

"One company," said Haldrim, "though we have extras."

"Extras?"

"Yes: smiths, delvers, bakers. You know, the usual sorts when you're looking to establish a garrison."

"You brought your own bakers?"

"Of course. Someone has to make the stonecakes."

Mirala shook her head. "I have no idea what that is, but never mind. Let's get you inside, Princess, and see that you're cleaned up."

"What about Brogar?"

"What's a 'Brogar'?"

"My bodyguard," said Althea "Or rather, one of them."

Mirala glanced at her home. "I have little room for visitors."

The princess turned to Haldrim. "Have Brogar stand watch out here."

The Dwarf captain bowed his head. "Yes, Highness."

"Come," said Mirala as she took the steps leading to her front door.

Althea thought the house was short, but it turned out half of it was dug into the ground. The rough-cut wooden door opened easily to the touch. Inside was a single room, circular in shape, with a slightly raised fire in the centre surrounded by stones bearing pictograms. Off to one side was a pile of furs, while on the opposite stood a work table containing many different dried plants.

"You're an herbalist, aren't you?" said the princess.

"Amongst other things. Now, come. Sit by the fire, and let me see what I have to work with."

Althea sat as Mirala walked around her. "I don't believe I've ever seen anyone with hair quite like yours." She ran her fingers through it. "It's so soft." Next, she felt Althea's arms, nodding approvingly. "I was afraid you'd be one of those stick women, but it appears you have some muscle."

"The results of wielding a sword," replied Althea. "You can thank the Dwarves for that."

The older woman leaned in close, staring into her eyes. "Now, tell me the truth, Princess. Have you ever lain with a man?"

Althea blushed slightly but stared back at her. "No, why? Is that important?"

"It is when you're marrying a Clan Chief. The last thing we want is someone showing up claiming you're carrying his child."

"I can assure you I tell the truth."

"Not even on the long walk back to Dungannon?"

"Hundreds of men surrounded us!"

The old woman chuckled. "That seldom matters amongst the Clans."

"Well, it does in Weldwyn." Althea took a deep breath, steadying her nerves. The question unsettled her, but she should've expected it. She chastised herself, then noticed her host staring at her. "Anything else you'd like to know?"

Mirala sat. "Tell me, and be truthful now, whose idea was it for you two to wed?"

"Why does that matter?"

"I'm not a fool, despite what others say. I know my cousin, and he's not the type to come up with something like this."

"I proposed the idea."

"Why?"

"To ensure peace for future generations."

"A very noble sentiment, but I have a hard time believing it. Was it perhaps that you sought to dominate us?"

"I can assure you that is not the case. It comes from an honest desire to better the lives of our respective peoples."

"I believe you." Mirala sat back, letting out a long breath.

"What else do we need to prepare?" asked Althea.

"To be honest, nothing save for keeping you in seclusion until the ceremony begins. I imagine my home pales compared to what you're used to."

"I like the looks of this place. It feels... comfortable."

Her host chuckled.

"Something wrong?"

"No," said Mirala, a touch of sadness in her voice. "It's just that I'm not the sort to garner compliments unless people want something."

"You mean your herbs?"

"Aye. Old Mirala is the crazy lady they come crawling to when they're sick."

"But you're not that old, are you?"

"Not by the reckoning of the seasons, but they see the old as a drain on resources. It's their way of implying I have no real value."

"Yet you heal people."

"As I said, their attitude changes when they come seeking help."

"Then we must strive to change that."

"And how do you propose we go about that, Highness?"

"Well, you can start by calling me Althea."

"And then?"

Althea looked around the room, letting her gaze rest on her host. "Let's begin with your hair, shall we? Do you own a brush by any chance?"

Two days later, Althea and Mirala emerged into the frosty morning air to see the townsfolk standing in two lines, creating a path for the bride to walk down. Althea's appearance garnered many nods of appreciation, but they were all surprised by the sight of Mirala. Instead of her usual nest of hair, Althea had brushed out the knots and tied it back into an elaborate braid.

The custom was for the bride to walk down the path, followed by her benefactor—in this case, Mirala. However, Althea walked with her host by her side, defying the custom. There was a good chance the locals might take umbrage at such a flagrant flouting of the rules, but as it turned out, no one objected.

As the path led through the village, those they passed fell in behind them, resulting in a large gathering by the time they reached the meeting hall. A warrior announced her arrival, and then Lochlan came out, looking resplendent in a tunic of white and silver.

He moved to stand before her, his breath frosting in the cold as he bowed his head in recognition. Next, he took her right hand, guiding her to where a man wearing a bearskin stood waiting. On his chest hung a medallion bearing a familiar-looking symbol.

Althea struggled to remember where she'd seen it, then realized it was the mark of Tauril, Goddess of the Woods, generally associated with the Elves.

The Holy Father, if that's what he was, waited for the rest of the Clan to join them before raising his arms and calling on the Gods to bless the union. All present went quiet as she and Lochlan placed their hands out front, palms up.

Althea concentrated, trying to ignore the cold seeping into her limbs, but to little effect. When she shivered, Lochlan looked at her, mistaking its meaning.

"Nervous?" he whispered.

"No, cold. Are all your ceremonies held outside?"

A wry smile crossed his lips, but the Holy Father shushed him, then laid a wooden stick across their hands.

"I give you this branch from the sacred grove," said the Holy Father, "to sanctify your union. Just as it bends without breaking, so, too, will your life together." He reached around behind him and then produced an acorn. "Just as this holds the promise of a great tree, so your union signifies the growth of a family. Go forth and plant the seed that your love may grow."

Althea looked at Lochlan, fearful they were expected to consummate their marriage before others, but he whispered to her, "He means the acorn."

The crowd clapped, and she looked around, unsure of what to do next. Lochlan took her hand and gently tugged her towards the river.

"Come," he said. "We'll follow the water upstream and find a place to plant it."

"And then?"

"Then we shall be husband and wife."

"You realize the ground is frozen?"

"I do. Don't worry. We're only picking out a location. The actual planting won't come until spring."

"So, we're not married until winter's over?"

He laughed. "That's only a formality. Under our customs, we are married whether we plant the acorn or not. Now, let's get this over and done with so we can celebrate."

The crowd roared, lifting their tankards in salute. Althea glanced at Lochlan, who was grinning like a fox as they chanted his name. The food had been plentiful, the drink strong, and the folk of Dungannon had thrown their arms wide open towards their chief's new bride.

She looked around the room as a chant started. They were calling for something, but the echo in the hall made the words difficult to understand. Once more, they raised their cups, staring expectantly at the newly wedded couple.

"What are they doing?" she asked.

"They want us to kiss."

"Here? In front of everyone? That would be most improper—such is not the custom in Weldwyn."

"This is your home now, Althea. You said you wanted to learn our ways, or was that all bluster?"

She wanted to argue the point, but he had the truth of it. She was the wife of a chief now, not a Weldwyn princess. "Very well," she said. "Let us not disappoint the people of Dungannon."

He leaned closer, and their lips met. The kiss was tender, unexpectedly so, and his lips lingered on hers. When he finally withdrew, she craved more. She wanted to say something to him, but the oathmen of Dungannon lifted her chair into the air. They paraded her around the hall as the towns-folk broke into song, and all she could do was hold on tight while she strained to see Lochlan, their eyes meeting in an unspoken moment of understanding.

When they finally lowered her chair, someone placed a tankard in her hands and called for everyone to toast the new bride.

Then the dancing began.

Althea awoke to the sound of crackling flames. She reached out to Lochlan, but the bed lay empty beside her.

The Clan Chief's home was one of the largest buildings in town, with a master bedroom bigger than the other rooms. She rose, donning a cloak to ward off the early morning chill and pulled the door open a crack to spot Lochlan stoking the fireplace. He was concentrating on the flames, the side of his face illuminated by the flickering light. She struggled with her emotions, unwilling to disturb his solitude, while at the same time, seeking his company.

She'd chosen to come west, yet nothing was as she'd expected. She'd always believed the Twelve Clans were barbarians, but her experience thus far proved precisely the opposite. These people lived in homes, not hovels, grew crops, and helped their neighbours. She straightened her back, and her head complained, causing her to curse.

"Althea?" said Lochlan. "Is that you?"

She stepped out from behind the door. "Was that mead we drank last night?"

"Let me guess; it feels like a goblin is hammering on your skull?"

"Goblin?"

"Yes, small green folk that…" His voice trailed off as he noted her look of confusion. "An old wives' tale, nothing that need concern you."

She moved closer to the fire, her eyes meeting his. "Last night," she said. "Did we…?"

"Enjoy each other's company? Yes. If you're asking if we were intimate, then no, not in the physical sense. I have too much respect for you to take advantage like that."

"Like what?"

"You passed out from all the drink. It took both Mirala and I to carry you in here and put you to bed."

"Where did you sleep?"

"Beside you. Don't worry. I stayed above the blankets."

"Surely you froze?"

"I was fine. I had a covering of my own."

"That was silly of you. We are married now. That obliges us to produce an heir."

"There's no hurry," said Lochlan, "and when we do finally consummate our marriage, I want it to be by mutual agreement."

She moved closer, feeling the warmth of the flames. "I didn't want to disturb you earlier."

He smiled. "You're my wife, now. You may disturb me anytime you wish."

"I shall try not to take advantage of that."

He finally looked at her. "Tell me, do you read much?"

"You know I read. We've talked of this before."

"Then let me put it another way. Do you enjoy reading?"

"It's a necessary part of being a royal."

"That doesn't answer my question. I want to know whether or not you take pleasure in it?"

"Reading is for disseminating information to others."

"Is that what you believe? Had you no children's tales?"

"Naturally," said Althea, "but they were designed to teach us how to read."

He shook his head. "You surprise me."

"In what way?"

"You had all the gifts that royalty confers, yet you failed to appreciate them. Reading is a gift, Althea, and one that shouldn't be wasted."

She stared back in confusion while he moved across the room, selecting a book from a small pile. He returned, placing it in her hands.

"What's this?" she asked.

"A book."

"Clearly, but what is its significance?"

"I want you to read it."

"Why?"

"One of my ancestors wrote it. It tells of the formation of the Twelve Clans and their attempts to tame this wild land."

"Attempts?"

"Our ancestors had high hopes, but in the end, little has changed since their time."

"Are there many Clansmen who read and write?"

"It's not a common skill, but a few, like myself, have taken it upon themselves to pass down such knowledge. I only wish there were more."

She glanced at his collection of books. "Then that's a place to start. Have you any in that pile suitable for children?"

He laughed. "No, but I know where I could lay my hands on some. There's a scholar down in Glanfraydon by the name of Camrath. He has the largest collection of written works in all the Clanholdings. We must visit him sometime."

"Or," said Althea, "we could bring him here, to Dungannon."

"To what end?"

"Knowledge is power. Build him a great library, and those books will be within easy reach."

He smiled. "I like the idea."

"Then there you have it. Consider it a wedding present for me."

"Oh? And what do I get as a present?"

"Access to all those books!"

"You have a keener mind than I," said Lochlan.

"Not keener, simply different, but that only stands to reason, considering our upbringing."

"And with whom do we start this noble quest for literacy?"

"Mirala."

"Surely you jest?"

"Why? Because you see her as having little value? She has a great mind, Lochlan. Who else knows so much about herbs and remedies?"

"Very well. Mirala, it is. Now, how do we create a place to store books?"

"You mean a library," corrected Althea. "Let's leave that for discussion another day, shall we?"

"Why? Have we something else that needs doing?"

She smiled. "I am no longer suffering the after-effects of last night's celebration."

"And?"

She stood, holding her hand out to him. "It's time we did our duty."

He grinned. "Are you suggesting what I think you are?"

"Unless you know another way to consummate our marriage, then yes!"

THIRTEEN

The Past

Gorath trudged through the snow-covered Glowan Hills, but the morning sun was so warm the Orc opened his cape to cool himself off. It wasn't long before he entered the town of Burrstoke and was sitting before the fire at a local tavern. If the locals objected to the presence of an Orc, they kept it to themselves as talk of local events filled the room. He finished his tankard of ale as the server returned.

"Another?" she asked.

"No, thank you. I am looking for someone. A knight by the name of Sir Randolf of Burrstoke. Do you know him?"

"I know OF him, though he doesn't frequent this establishment. What business is he of yours?"

Gorath showed her the medallion hanging from his neck. Every Queen's Ranger wore one—the symbol of the rangers on the front and a number denoting their seniority on the back. His bore a stylish number two, and by the server's reaction, she obviously understood the implication.

"I am not here to arrest him," he explained. "Merely to ask him a few questions about something that happened long ago."

"He keeps to himself these days," she replied. "Mostly on account of ill health. They say that's why he came back to Burrstoke."

"I assume that means you know where I can find him?"

"Go out the door and turn left, head down the street three blocks, and then you'll come to a two-storey house—that's his."

"Thank you. You have been most helpful." He rose, depositing some coins on the table.

"Rangers don't pay for their food and drink."

"They do now," said Gorath. "It is not our place to bring hardship on others."

He threw on his cloak and left the tavern. Finding Sir Randolf's house was easy enough; getting him to answer the door proved a little more difficult, for even after a couple of knocks, no one answered. The thought suddenly struck him that the fellow might be out and about, but then he heard footsteps within. He knocked one more time.

"Go away!" came a voice.

"Open up in the queen's name."

"The queen, is it? And who are you to demand things in the queen's name?"

"I am Gorath, a Queen's Ranger!"

"Well then," grumbled the voice. "Why didn't you say so?" The latch was thrown back, and then an old man peered through the crack in the door, his thin beard snowy white. "An Orc?"

"Yes. Would you like to see my ranger medallion?"

"No, of course not. You took me by surprise, that's all." The man threw open the door. "Come in, come in. Take a seat by the fire."

Gorath entered, closing the door behind him. "I am truly sorry to intrude, but I have come a long way to see you."

"Have you, now? From Wincaster, I suppose?"

"Yes. The High Ranger, Lady Hayley Chambers, sent me."

"I'm fully aware of who the High Ranger is. I'm old, not out of my wits." He paused a moment as Gorath sat. "Can I offer you a drink? Some ale, perhaps?"

"That will not be necessary, although I thank you for the offer."

The old knight dragged another chair before the fire and sat. "To what do I owe this visit? I'm not in trouble, I hope?"

"Not at all. I am here on a matter concerning Bodden. No doubt you heard of Lord Richard Fitzwilliam's death?"

"I'm sorry to say I have. He was a great man and will be sorely missed."

"Another has come claiming his title."

"But that is Lady Beverly's, surely?"

"The one making the claim asserts he is the son of Lord Edward Fitzwilliam."

"Impossible," said the knight. "He died in an explosion."

"There is some evidence they carried him off to Norland, where he recovered."

"Astounding! But what has that to do with me?"

"You served under Lord Edward, did you not?"

"You know I did—else you wouldn't be here."

"Yes," said Gorath. "Of course, pardon my manners. Can you relate to me the events of the evening to the best of your recollection?"

"Saxnor's beard, that was decades ago. Let me think. If I recall, we were under siege. Lord Edward considered surrendering—did you know that?"

"I did not. Might I ask what changed his mind?"

Sir Randolf barked out a laugh. "Nothing! Lord Richard took it upon himself to destroy the enemy's siege engines. I imagine the marshal gave you all the details?"

"Of the raid, yes, but I am more interested in the events leading up to Lord Edward's death. When was the last time you saw him?"

"Let's see, now. After the meeting, I was sent to the new wall to oversee the stockpiling of combustibles. The idea was to blow up the wall as they assaulted. It wouldn't win us the battle, but the prevailing belief was that they might be open to a negotiated surrender if we bloodied them."

"What was the nature of these combustibles?"

"Pieces of wood soaked in oil, mostly, but anything else that would burn. We even packed the cavity with odd bits of metal."

"Meaning?"

"Nails, horseshoes, even cutlery, if you can imagine. The idea was to send bits of metal flying when it exploded."

"I assume you completed the task?"

"I did before I took up my position with the other knights. Lord Edward had formed a reserve, ready to rush into the fray should something go wrong. That is to say, if the combustibles didn't have the desired effect."

"How many other knights were with you?"

"Seven, but I'm afraid they'll do you little good now."

"Why is that?"

"They were Knights of the Sword, and six of them died during the civil war."

"And the seventh?"

"Died when the wall exploded. As luck would have it, he was hit in the head by a piece of flying rock."

"No helmet?"

"Oh, he had a helmet, but it was crushed beneath the weight of the stone."

"Did you see the explosion yourself?"

"I did. I was there, but I don't recall seeing Lord Edward. Someone called out that he was about to light it, but it was dark, and the torch blinded me."

"I assume, by that, you mean you saw a person running with a torch but could not identify him?"

"That's correct, though I believe Sir James witnessed everything."

"We already have his account of the night's events."

"Then why did you need mine?"

"Merely to corroborate some details."

"Might I ask a question?"

"Most certainly," said Gorath. "What would you like to know?"

"This knight claiming the title, how does he explain Lord Edward surviving the explosion?"

"He states that men under the command of Lord Hollis bore the baron's body away."

Sir Randolf shook his head. "To think he might've been alive all these years. It's too much to take in."

"I understand you knew him well?"

"Whoever told you that?"

"I am given to believe you and he were close friends?"

The knight laughed. "Whatever gave you that idea? I despised the man, although I still followed his orders. I looked up to Lord Richard. Now, that was a real baron."

Gorath stared back for a moment, mulling things over. "Just to be sure there is no mistake on my part, are you saying you and Lord Edward were not friends?"

"That is correct. I was his liege man, for I was bound to his service by order of King Andred, but aside from my duty as a member of the garrison, I rarely spoke to the baron."

"Thank you. You've been most helpful."

"I have? I fail to see how?"

"I suspect you revealed the... what is the expression? Ah yes. The weak link in his armour? Do I have that right?"

Sir Randolf chuckled. "Assuming you mean you found a flaw in this fellow's story, then close enough. I'm glad I could help."

Gorath stood. "I shall compose a statement of our discussion, and then you can sign it, providing you have no objection?"

"Of course not."

The Orc dug into his pack, pulling forth some rolled parchment and a small box containing ink and quills.

"I have a table over here if you like," offered Sir Randolf. He waited as Gorath took a seat and began writing. He occasionally clarified things, even crossing out a line and replacing it when the old knight offered more details. Eventually, he sat back, handing the knight the quill.

"Does this guarantee Lady Beverly's claim to Bodden?" asked Randolf.

"I cannot say this will be enough, but it's certainly a good start."

"In that case, where do I sign?"

. . .

Hayley looked up at the massive structure the Earl of Beaconsgate called home. It wasn't as big as the Royal Palace in Wincaster, but it wasn't far off. The most significant difference was the surrounding area, for while the Palace was situated in the heart of the Mercerian capital, the earl had built on the outskirts of the city. She'd seen it over a year ago when the queen sent her to retrieve Bronwyn, but this was the first time she approached from the front.

She dismounted, passing the reins off to a waiting stable hand. Gryph, meanwhile, kept his distance, wary of the great structure. "You best wait here," she called out.

"Madam?" replied the stable hand.

"Sorry. I was speaking to Gryph."

"Who is?"

"The wolf over yonder?" She pointed.

The fellow's face grew pale, and he hurried off to the stables with her horse.

Another servant stood by the front door, waiting for her. "His Lordship is expecting you, madam."

Something in his tone irritated her. "That's 'my lady'. I'm the Baroness of Queenston."

He shot a look of annoyance her way before quickly suppressing it. "Of course. My apologies, my lady."

Hayley forced a smile. It was a minor victory yet satisfying to know she'd put the man in his place. It served him right for being so righteous. She was about to say so but then realized she was no better, lording a title over the fellow. Had she changed so much from the poacher of her youth? Her father would be disappointed.

She put aside such thoughts as she followed him into the palatial home. The servant said nothing, simply led her through a maze of hallways to eventually arrive at a large room bare of furnishings, save for a few small tables lining one wall. The opposite side featured an impressively large window looking out into a massive grass field.

Hayley moved closer to get a better view. There was no denying the grounds were well-kept, but something about the well-ordered bushes and trees bothered her. It was as if the lords of Norland were trying to control nature itself. She'd seen this type of thing before, the Royal Gardens in Wincaster being a prime example. There, however, the groundskeepers went to great efforts to ensure the scene looked natural. Here, on the other hand, it just felt… wrong.

"How do you like the gardens?"

She wheeled around to see a man unlike most of his countrymen, for he was clean-shaven with his hair styled short but somehow seemed older than his years might indicate.

He moved to stand beside her but focused his attention on the gardens. "My aunt arranged all of this, though sadly, she is no longer here to appreciate it. Beautiful, isn't it?"

Hayley considered her answer. She suspected compliments were likely to be more effective than the truth. "Yes," she finally replied. "I don't believe I've ever seen its like."

"When I became earl, I swore to undo all the wrongs my uncle committed, but I didn't have the heart to tarnish the memory of Aunt Sidonia." Lord Asher turned to face Hayley. "But you didn't come all the way here to discuss the garden."

"No, I didn't. I'm here looking for something."

"You intrigue me. What, exactly, is it you hope to find?"

"The truth."

The earl smiled. "Even more interesting. Would you care to elaborate?"

"I'm here investigating rumours that Lord Edward Fitzwilliam survived the siege of Bodden."

"Ah. Now we get to the crux of the matter. What is it you believe I can do to help?"

"From what we've determined, he was brought here to Beaconsgate to recover from his injuries."

"I was very young at the time and living elsewhere, but I heard the rumours. That, however, does little to help you in your investigation."

"My understanding is he lived here for some time. Years, in fact. That said, he may have left evidence of his presence behind."

"Such as?"

"A ring bearing his coat of arms. He used it to seal official correspondence."

"And you believe it's here somewhere?"

"I do."

"What leads you to that conclusion?"

"I know it wasn't buried with him, and it's not the type of thing that would be carelessly tossed aside."

He stared back but held his tongue.

"Is it here?"

"That," he finally replied, "is a difficult question to answer. My uncle left several interesting artifacts, but I've yet to make a full inventory of them."

"Would it be possible to look?"

"How do I know you're not here to steal something?"

"I seek only Lord Edward's ring."

"A ring given into the care of my uncle. That now makes it my possession."

"So you admit the ring does exist?"

He smiled. "Clever. Very well, you tricked me into revealing its existence. The least I can do is let you examine it. However, I will not allow you to remove it from these premises. Agree to that condition, and I'll take you to it."

"I agree," said Hayley, "and you have my word I shall not attempt to reclaim it."

"You mean steal."

"It matters little what you call it. I only seek to restore it to its rightful owner."

"Do you?" said Lord Asher. "It seems to me the rightful owner should be Randolf Blackburn."

"That has yet to be determined."

"We have a saying in Norland that ownership is proven by possession."

"And what of thieves?"

He chuckled. "A thief, by virtue of his skill, becomes the owner of that which he steals."

"So, you're justifying taking what you want?"

"Is that not how nature works? The strong rule the weak. The victims show their weakness by allowing their possessions to be taken. On the other hand, the thief proves their superiority in accomplishing the theft."

"I'm sure you'd feel different if something of yours was stolen."

"Ah, but I possess the means to recover stolen goods, so you see, I am one of the strong."

"It's a fascinating concept," said Hayley, "but a little too distracting to my purpose in being here. You claim to have the ring. May I see it now?"

"But of course. Come with me, and I'll take you to it."

He led her through the estate to a small room attached to his study, where the shelves were littered with all sorts of strange objects, everything from a stuffed squirrel to a small glass globe containing what looked like a Human eye.

"My curios," said Lord Asher. "My uncle started the collection, but I've added several things since the war." He lifted a dagger. "See this? It's an Elven blade made from the finest steel."

Hayley looked at it, but it didn't impress her. It was no more of Elven steel than her own blade, but she wasn't about to correct the earl.

"And the ring?" she prompted.

"Ah, yes. Now, let's see. Where did I put it?" He rummaged through a shelf, shifting objects to determine what lay beneath. "Here it is." He held it up to the window, the better to view it.

Hayley moved closer. The ring was made of gold and bore a coat of arms, but she could not discern much detail from her current angle.

"May I?" she asked.

He handed it over. The plain band was large, as rings go, most likely to fit over a glove should it prove necessary. To her mind, this was typical of what a baron might possess, but the important thing was the coat of arms. At first glance, it looked similar to Beverly's coat of arms, not surprising, considering she was a Fitzwilliam, but there were differences. Each baron typically adopted their own coat of arms, changing it slightly when they took over the responsibility of running the barony. Beverly's, for example, would include the addition of a rose, a tribute to her mother. This one was plainer, a simplified version of the Fitzwilliam coat of arms, likely making it easier to recognize on a wax seal.

"Well?" asked the earl. "What do you think? Did it belong to Lord Edward or not?"

"It's certainly a possibility. Might I take an imprint of it?"

"Of course. Let me fetch you some wax." He dug through another shelf, retrieving a small stick, which he held above a candle before pressing it onto a piece of paper. Hayley placed the ring face down and pushed against it for a moment.

"I hope this helps," said the earl.

She removed the ring, taking care to hand it back to him. Lifting the paper, she returned to the window to ensure she had a clear imprint of the ring's coat of arms.

"Perfect," she said at last. "Thank you, Lord Asher. You've been most helpful."

He offered her a slight bow. "I'm glad I could be of assistance. Just out of curiosity, do you believe this strengthens Sir Randolf's claim?"

"This ring answers many questions, and it certainly seems to verify his claims that Lord Edward was taken to Beaconsgate."

"But?"

"The presence of this ring alone proves nothing. Someone could've found it on the battlefield."

"You must admit the likelihood of finding something like that is remote. How often does one randomly find jewellery on the battlefield that isn't on a body?"

"Perhaps you answered your own question?" replied Hayley. "Who's to say it wasn't taken from Lord Edward's corpse?"

"Ah, but think of what you're suggesting. Your version of events has Lord Edward blown to bits. Surely, you're not now implying his body remained intact after such an explosion?"

"True, that's unlikely, but I prefer to deal in facts. This ring is one piece of the puzzle, but there are many other threads to unravel."

"I trust you'll keep me informed of your progress?"

"I do not report to you, Lord Asher, but to my queen. However, you may rest assured all will be revealed once a final decision is made."

FOURTEEN

Investigation

L ord Osric looked up as the guard escorted the prisoner into the room, his shackles dragging on the stone floor.

"Lord James," he said by way of greeting. "I trust you are doing well since we last spoke?"

"Well? I'm rotting away in a cell while they plan my execution. I would hardly call that well!"

"Of course. Sorry. Now come, sit. There is much for us to discuss."

James looked at the guard. "Is he staying?"

His host looked at the fellow. "Would you do us the courtesy of remaining outside the door?"

The warrior nodded, then left the room.

"There. Satisfied?"

"Immeasurably."

"Good," said Osric. "Let's get down to business, shall we?"

James grunted something noncommittal.

"The case against you is strong," continued Osric. "I can't help but feel the results are somewhat of a foregone conclusion. They mean to execute you, my lord, and there is precious little I can do about it without your help."

"You agreed to represent me. Are you now backing down from that promise?"

"Not in the least. I committed myself and intend to see it through, but if I am to help, I must know the truth of the matter."

"Truth?" said James. "The nobles of Weldwyn aren't interested in the truth. All they seek is a confession!"

"Look here, I understand this is hard on you, but such complaints will do little to save your life. When we last met, you refused to tell me anything, for you wanted me to discover what they knew. Now, you must at least give me something to work with."

"Very well. If you must know, it was my mother's idea. She had contacts amongst the Twelve Clans, and though I'm reluctant to admit it, the treachery at the gate sprang from her mind."

Osric sat back. "You're lying."

"Why would I lie?"

"I've known your mother for years, and she's not the type of person to betray her king."

"Ah, but she did, didn't she? After all, she was caught spying against the Mercerians. You might want to mention that to this so-called tribunal."

"She's made a complete and thorough confession of her transgressions, and the tribunal accepted her innocence in this matter."

"Convenient," said James, "but placing the blame on her still represents my best hope for a dismissal of all charges."

"Is that you speaking, or Godfrey? You realize you would never be in this situation were it not for that fellow. He's a snake, my lord. He'll turn on you at the first opportunity, if it means saving his own neck."

"No, you're wrong. Godfrey would never betray me." James leaned forward, lowering his voice. "Now listen to me, Lord Osric. There is only one path to take. I must insist you blame it all on Mother!"

"I will not make unsubstantiated claims against Lady Jane! If you persist in making such a demand, I must withdraw my assistance." He waited a moment. "Well? What have you to say for yourself?"

"I will not allow my name to be besmirched in this manner. My mother was the mastermind behind this. I swear."

"Then we are done. Guard!"

The escort returned, taking hold of the chains and pulling the prisoner towards the door.

"Good day, Lord James," said Osric. "We shan't meet again. I pray you find solace before your execution."

James Goodwin threw himself onto his bed, the sound rattling off the walls of his tiny cell. "Bad news, I'm afraid," he said. "I'm beginning to wonder if it might be better to come clean?"

"Now is not the time to succumb to mere suspicion," replied Lord Godfrey. He stood in the cell opposite, pressed against the iron grating, the better for his co-conspirator to hear him. "If you confess, you'll condemn us both to death."

"Yes, but at least it would be quick."

"You don't know that."

"I've read my history. Traitors suffer gruesome punishment, the kind of death that takes forever."

"That, my friend, is utter nonsense. Besides, what little evidence they possess is nothing more than hearsay."

"How can you say that?" said Lord James. "You told me they took all your correspondence."

"And they were welcome to it. The truth is, nothing in there is incriminating. I'm not a fool."

"Yet you talked me into helping you in this treasonous act!"

"Ah. So, it's all my fault now, is it? I might trouble you to remember you were just as eager to gain power as I was."

James fell silent, if only for a moment. "This all went bad so quickly. What did we do wrong?"

"It might be easier to explain what went right."

"But it was foolproof!"

"Hardly that. Even the best-laid plans have flaws; in our case, we failed to account for the duplicitous actions of Kythelia. We would still be amongst the city's elite if she hadn't killed Brida. Not that those Mercerians helped much."

"Yet here we are, under sentence of death."

"Not death," said Godfrey. "At least not yet. You forget, as nobles, albeit low-ranking ones, we are still allowed our day in court."

"I doubt that will serve us well."

"You might be surprised."

"What in the name of the Gods are you talking about?"

"This affair is not the first time I've dipped my toes into politics. Let's just say several people owe me favours."

"I doubt they'd come to your aid now, not with a charge of treason hanging over your head."

"The thing you need to understand about people," said Lord Godfrey, "is that everyone has secrets. Learn whatever those are, and you possess the power to control them."

"Are you suggesting you can blackmail your way to freedom?"

"You say blackmail. I, on the other hand, prefer the word persuade. It sounds much more civilized."

"Enough to make them drop the charge of treason?" asked James.

"I can't answer that yet, but I've spent years collecting information about a good many things, including people others saw as relatively unimportant. Since the war, many of those same individuals now find themselves in positions of authority."

"And how many of these individuals are the tribunal that will pass judgement on us?"

Lord Godfrey smiled. "Not all of them, but I think one shall be sufficient. After all, they only have to cast the seeds of doubt."

"But we're guilty."

"I believe that's more a point of view, don't you?"

"We conspired to rule under the invaders."

"No. We chose to spare our countrymen the burden of being ruled over by foreigners—that's a big difference."

"So say you."

"And so, too, will my ally on the tribunal. Trust me, James. I have no doubt this trial will be onerous, but in the end, we'll win through. I promise you."

"How can you be so sure?"

"The Twelve Clans gutted the nobility of Weldwyn. Many titles sit unclaimed, leading to a shortage of nobility. Finding us guilty would only make things worse, don't you see?"

Lord James shook his head. "I wish I was as comfortable with this as you."

"Then set your mind at ease. We've done nothing you need feel ashamed of."

"I helped the Twelve Clans round up the nobles of Weldwyn."

"True, but that's something they could've easily done without your assistance. All you did was help ease the pain of their arrest. Imagine how things would've gone had you not been there. Why, there would've been blood running in the streets. Yes, you gave up a few barons, but in doing so, you allowed their families to be spared. Had you not intervened, the entire kingdom would now be bereft of heirs!"

"It would be an easier burden to bear if we knew the extent of the tribunal's evidence."

"True. Yet, despite the lack thereof, we are still in reasonably good health. At the very least, we should be thankful they haven't executed us out of hand. I believe that's what the Mercerians wanted."

"They are barbarians," said James. "Unfit to be our allies."

"I tend to agree. Unfortunately, they've corrupted Prince Alric."

"What are you inferring?"

"Only that we will see more Mercerian customs adopted, moving forward."

"Assuming we survive all of this."

"As I said before," said Lord Godfrey. "I have friends, or at least people, who will help."

"I admire your conviction, but what's to stop them from keeping silent and watching us hang?"

"I took steps to ensure my notes would be released upon my death. If they're hoping to shut me up, my demise will do precisely the opposite. I also made sure they're all aware of that fact. So, you see, I have everything under control."

"There could still be witnesses."

"People often misinterpret what they observe. I've also found that such folk sometimes end up dying prematurely, thus sealing their lips forever. I suppose what I'm trying to say is you shouldn't worry about such things."

"Is all this truly necessary, Jack?" said Gerald. "I already submitted my account in writing."

"You have?" replied the cavalier. "Does that go for Lady Jane as well?"

"Lady Jane? What does she have to do with Lord Edward's death?"

"I'm afraid there's some confusion over why I'm here. I'm part of the tribunal investigating Lord James Goodwin!"

"Oh, my apologies. I thought this was something else."

"I'm sorry for the mix-up, but I'm not here to see you, Marshal. I'm here for Lady Jane.

The woman to Gerald's right sat up. "Me? Whatever for? Surely, you're not suggesting I'm to be put on trial?"

"Not at all, my lady. It's only that I read your account of events during the occupation of Summersgate and wanted to clear up a few things."

Jane squeezed Gerald's hand. "Very well. You may ask your questions, but I doubt it will add anything to what I've already said."

Jack consulted his notes. "You mentioned Lord Godfrey was a frequent companion of your son. Can you be more precise?"

"They used to spend a lot of time together."

"Doing what, may I ask?"

"I always assumed they were spending time in the company of women, but the truth is, I can't really say for sure what they got up to."

"And how often did they leave your estate?"

"Technically, the estate was my son's, not mine. My late husband's will specified it became the possession of James. I was merely a guest."

"Would you say you got along with your son?"

"I would've said yes if you'd asked me before I left Summersgate. Recent events, however, would seem to indicate otherwise."

"Was it his idea for you to live at the estate?"

"No. It was a stipulation of my late husband's will."

"How did your son feel about that?"

"James could be moody at times," continued Lady Jane. "One might even say rude, but he was under immense pressure, particularly after the death of King Leofric."

"I'm not sure I understand," said Jack.

"After the king died, Weldwyn was in a panic. People were sick with fear and turned to the nobility for guidance. James tried to provide that help, but I fear he wasn't up to it. Once the Twelve Clans invaded us, things only got worse. As you are no doubt aware, Brida rounded up most of the nobles, and then the executions began. My son was fearful he, too, might be caught up in the frenzy."

Jack closed his eyes, thinking things through. He had no wish to antagonize the woman, but something felt like it had been left unsaid. Could he coax it from her?

"Is everything all right?" asked Gerald.

The cavalier's eyes snapped open. "Yes. Why?"

"You appear to be in some discomfort. A headache, perhaps?"

"It's this tribunal. I feel the Earls Council expects us to reach a quick decision. They appear more interested in a scapegoat than the truth."

"And your opinion is?"

"I'd much prefer to know the truth," said Jack, "no matter how long it takes to dig it up."

"Then you must continue with your line of enquiry. What else would you like to know?"

The cavalier turned his attention once more to Lady Jane. "You said earlier you thought you got along well with your son before you left the capital. Has your opinion now changed?"

Her jaw tightened. Gerald took her hand, squeezing it slightly, causing her to glance at the marshal. She soon softened her gaze.

"It has," she finally replied. "Though I am loathe to admit it."

"Might I ask what changed your mind?" asked Jack.

"My son convinced me to spy on the Mercerians to avoid his arrest. Looking back on it, it was an outrageous request, for what do I know of armies?"

"Bearing that in mind, why do you suspect he sent you out of Summersgate? Was it to protect you, perhaps?"

"I could well believe that had he sent me to safety, but to spy? What could be more dangerous? Clearly, he had another motive in mind."

"That motive being?"

"H-h-he wanted me dead," squeaked Lady Jane.

"Surely there would be simpler ways to do that. He could've turned you over to the Twelve Clans, for example."

"When I left, James provided me with a letter allowing me to leave the city. I did not recognize the seal, but when the guard at the gate saw it, he let me proceed on my way."

"Do you still possess this letter?" asked Jack.

"I'm afraid not. I was travelling on foot, and a downpour thoroughly soaked me, destroying it. I'm sorry."

"You have nothing to be sorry for, my lady."

"Are you quite finished?" asked Gerald.

"Not yet, Your Grace. There's still the matter of his associate." Jack looked at Lady Jane. "How familiar are you with Lord Godfrey Hammond?"

"I know him, of course," she replied. "As I said earlier, my son spent much time in his company. He was a frequent guest in our home, but typically not when I was present."

"Would you care to expand on that?"

"James said my presence was an embarrassment. When such arrangements were made, I either ate in my room or went out and partook of a meal elsewhere."

"Did he say why?"

"No. As I said earlier, at the time, I suspected he was bringing women home for entertainment. Certainly not something a man would wish his mother to be aware of. I suppose, looking back, that was not what he was doing, but a parent tends to be blind to their child's faults."

"How would you describe Lord Godfrey's manner on the few occasions you did interact with him?"

"He was well-spoken and polite, but I don't recall him saying much of anything to me except for the usual pleasantries when one enters another's home."

"And you never saw him, outside of his visits to your son?"

"Not at all, but then again, I was not one to socialize. I tended to keep to myself."

"She's a very private person," added Gerald. "Is there anything else you need to know, or are we done?"

"I have all I require," replied Jack. "Thank you, and sorry for any discomfort I may have caused. I know this couldn't have been easy for you."

"What will happen to my son?" asked Lady Jane.

"That largely depends on what we find. He's charged with treason—a very serious crime, and his guilt would surely result in a death sentence. Unfortunately, the manner of death for a traitor is quite... how shall I put this—"

"Excruciating?" offered Gerald

"Yes, and not quick by any measure."

"Then perhaps it's time they changed the law?"

"I couldn't agree more," said Jack, "but such things are out of my control. Prince Alric will wield the power to do so once he's king, but I'm afraid even that's in doubt at the moment."

"Surely they'll make him king now that Althea is married? Who else do they have to choose from?"

"Who indeed? Unfortunately, the council has fallen silent on the matter."

"Can you not press them for an answer?"

"They claim that matters of state are keeping them far too busy to render a decision."

"Matters of state?" said Gerald. "What can possibly be more important than naming a king?"

"I'm not privy to that information. I would suggest your own queen make some enquiries, but under the circumstances, I fear that might only make matters worse."

"How could it be worse? You have no king!"

"True, but a foreign queen pushing for her husband to be crowned would likely be seen as interference."

"I hate to admit it, but your argument makes sense. In any case, Queen Anna is far too busy trying to keep neutral in this whole Bodden affair."

"How is Dame Beverly holding up?"

"About as well as can be expected," said Gerald.

"But surely the queen will grant her a title elsewhere?"

"No doubt, but Bodden is her home. How would you feel if someone usurped your claim to Aynsbury?"

"I'd fight it tooth and nail. Quite frankly, I'm surprised Beverly hasn't done so herself."

"She has a strong sense of duty to the Crown, but I fear, if things don't go in her favour, it may well cause a fracture in her relationship with the queen."

"So where does that leave Sir Randolf's claim?"

"In the High Ranger's hands."

.   .   .

Lord Elgin slammed his fist onto the table. "This is intolerable! Am I to be thwarted at every turn?"

"We must have patience," said Lord Beric. "We'll eventually win the others over to our way of thinking."

"You haven't grasped the enormity of the situation. Without Althea as my bride, I cannot claim the Throne."

"You might as well face facts, my friend. It's impossible for you to marry your way to the Throne." He fell silent as if a thought just occurred to him.

"What is it?" prompted Elgin.

Beric waved him off. "Oh, nothing. Ignore me."

"Come now. Something crossed your mind. I can see it on your face."

"It occurred to me Edwina is still unmarried."

"She is, but the recent discovery of her magic eliminates her from the line of succession."

"Then perhaps you could exploit a flaw in that law?"

"What are you suggesting?" asked Elgin.

"She might not be able to rule, but if I understand our laws correctly, she could still wed, and nothing precludes her husband from making a claim."

"True, but that would put that Clansman's claim above my own."

"Then that's where we should expend our energies."

"I thought you were against the idea of me ruling?"

Beric shrugged. "I'm always looking for ways to increase my own influence. If that means removing an impediment to make an ally more powerful, then so be it."

"Are you suggesting we try to annul the marriage?"

"No, but the Clanholdings are a dangerous place. What if that husband of hers were to die?"

A hint of a smile graced Lord Elgin's lips. "Yes. I see what you're getting at. I could then swoop in and console the poor widow."

"There's only one small problem with that," said Lord Beric. "Or rather, two."

"Which are?"

"First, we'd need to arrange a fatal accident for Lochlan. That, in and of itself, is no small feat."

"And second?" pressed Elgin.

"As a widow, Althea would have the choice of whom she marries. Prince Alric wouldn't control her future anymore."

"I hadn't thought of that. There's also the matter of timing. If I am to be king, I must act soon. To do otherwise will only cement Alric's claim. I have contacts amongst the Twelve Clans, but I need Lord Godfrey to take advantage of them."

"Lord Godfrey is in the dungeons."

"True, but surely, as members of the Earls Council, we have the authority to commute his sentence?"

"Ordinarily, yes," said Lord Beric, "but he has yet to face trial. You can't dismiss what hasn't been rendered."

"What if we arranged his release until trial? After all, he's a noble of Weldwyn. Surely we can accept his pledge that he won't flee?"

Lord Beric nodded. "Very well, providing you can give me your personal guarantee he has the connections you need amongst the Twelve Clans?"

"He does. You may rest assured that between my wealth and his connections, that Clansman is as good as dead."

"How long do you believe such arrangements would take?"

"Until spring, at least. Can we stall the council till then?"

"We must," said Beric. "Especially if that's all we've got, but might I ask why so long?"

"We want this to appear as an accident. That means whoever does the job will need to get into Lochlan's confidence, which can't be done on short notice without arousing suspicion."

"And you're sure you can find someone to do this?"

"If there's one thing I've learned about dealing with the Twelve Clans, it's that you can find someone to do anything with enough gold!"

FIFTEEN

A Meeting of Clan Chiefs

SPRING 967 MC

Althea watched as the first boats of spring headed up the river. "What we need," she said, "is a road. Then we wouldn't be dependent on the boatholders' schedules."

"I agree," said Lochlan, "but wanting to build a road is a long way from actually constructing it."

"I don't know about that. If you think about it, it's not so difficult. We mark off a trail and then clear away any debris that blocks it."

"Debris?"

"Yes, you know—trees, large rocks, that sort of thing."

"Surely you're not suggesting we cut our way through a forest?"

She chuckled. "No. The road can weave to avoid the larger trees, but we'd have to remove some of the undergrowth. That and the smaller trees."

"You make it all sound so easy."

"The trick," said Althea, "is keeping it from wandering off into the middle of nowhere, but if we stay close to the river, I doubt that will be a problem."

"There are other things to consider," he replied.

"Such as?"

"This is dangerous countryside. All manner of wild beasts roam the region."

"Then we ensure warriors are present to keep the workers safe."

"And what workers are those?"

"Surely there must be some here willing to do the work?"

"Of chopping down trees and digging up rocks? You overestimate the zeal of the Clans."

"Then we'll pay them," said Althea. "I have yet to see one of your countrymen who could resist gold."

Lochlan laughed. "Yes, I suppose that's true, but gold doesn't exactly grow on trees in these parts, and I doubt the boatholders would be keen to see their customers contributing to a road."

"Even for the benefit of all?"

"That's precisely why they'd object. Look at this from their perspective. They control the river traffic, thus ensuring they receive a tithe from everything coming in or going out of Dungannon."

"Then it's time that changed, isn't it?"

"I agree with you, but it's difficult to compete with a full purse."

"Are you not the Clan Chieftain?"

"I am, but that means little against the might of the boatholders."

"You mean their coins?"

"Exactly, and they can afford to pay off anyone who doesn't agree with them."

"Then we must build this road without their knowledge."

"Impossible," said Lochlan. "You can't hire workers without everyone in town knowing we're up to something."

"So that's it, then? We give up on everything?"

"I'm not quite ready to do that. What you say has merit, but we've yet to determine how to proceed. In the meantime, I suggest we take a trip to Banburn."

"Is that our nearest neighbour?" asked Althea.

"It is. It lies a couple of days upriver. As I see it, the problem is we need the boats to get there."

"Why can't we march overland?"

"As I mentioned earlier, there are plenty of dangerous creatures in the area."

"So you say, but I have yet to see any. In any case, we can take the Dragon Company—they'll keep us safe."

"The intent was to visit Banburn, not capture it."

"Then they'll wait outside the town while we meet their chief. Who rules there?"

"Last I heard, a fellow going by the name of Raurig."

"The last you heard? Did he not take part in the invasion of Weldwyn?"

"He sent warriors but chose to sit out the war at home. I can understand why—Prince Tarak murdered his father to ensure my sister's ascension to High Queen. And he wasn't the only one, either."

"How old is Raurig?"

"By the standards of the Twelve Clans, ancient. Why, he must be almost forty by now." He tried to keep a straight face, but she saw right through him.

"Forty, indeed. Next, I suppose you'll tell me his father was only a year older?"

"No. Raurig, the elder, was almost sixty."

"Is that the common tradition here, being named after your father?"

"It's not unusual."

"Yet you weren't named after King Dathen?"

"Ah, but I was never considered for the role of chieftain while he lived."

"I'm afraid you'll have to explain that one to me. Is the position of chieftain not hereditary?"

"Oh, it is, but typically the first-born is the heir, and that was Brida."

"So, it's not unusual for a woman to become chieftain?"

"No, it's not. At the time of the Weldwyn invasion, we numbered three women chieftains amongst our people."

"And now?"

"Just one, as far as I'm aware—the daughter of Warnoch, late chieftain of Drakewell, but her domain is way up in the mountains, far from here."

"How many chiefs died under Kythelia's hands?"

"Almost all of them," said Lochlan. "Only those who remained here in the Clanholdings survived."

"But you survived. Was that because she didn't see you as a threat?"

"The truth is, once I learned of Brida's fate, I left Summersgate as quickly as I could. I suppose some might see me as a coward for abandoning my people."

"You did what you needed to survive," said Althea. "And had it not been for your timely arrival in the Mercerian camp, Kythelia would likely still be alive. Do not think so little of your accomplishments."

"Easy for you to say; you didn't flee at the first sign of trouble. Instead, you found your courage and brought the Dwarves to the battle. Would that I had been so resourceful."

"Each of us must tread our own path, Lochlan, and I'll not compare my journey to yours. Whether we are both here at this point by the will of the Gods, or merely happenstance is for others to debate. What's clear is your people need guidance. How about it, Lochlan? Will you let your people continue to live in squalor, or will you give them a better life, as they deserve?"

"I never thought to hear those words from one of Weldwyn."

"I am no longer a Princess of Weldwyn. I am the wife of the Chief of

Dungannon. A role I gladly accepted, and I'll not sit idly by and see the people of this Clan suffer needlessly. We can make a better life for them, but you must be willing to put away the past and embrace the future."

He still looked uncertain, so she pressed him further. "You consider yourself a scholar, yes?"

"I do."

"Think of Dungannon as a living book whose final chapter is yet to be written. Do you want future generations to read of your failure or your success?"

"I'm beginning to wonder if the Twelve Clans have a future."

"All the more reason to act now, before all is lost. Your people... our people, need guidance. Give them something to occupy their minds, a goal to achieve, and you will have given them a future."

He set his jaw. "You're right. Moping achieves nothing. Very well. Let's make arrangements to travel to Banburn and meet Raurig. Perhaps between us, we can find a way to free ourselves from the shackles of the boatholders."

Lochlan, Althea, and her escort of Dwarves set out the next day, keeping to the east side of the river as they travelled north, not deigning to inform the villagers of where they were heading. If anyone pressed Mirala, she would reveal that they were on a Dwarven quest, a lie chosen to keep questions to a minimum, for the townsfolk of Dungannon knew very little about the mountain folk.

The first part of their journey was easy enough, as the terrain north of the hills of Dungannon was primarily flat. Rain proved their biggest enemy, for spring in the Clanholdings was a wet season, swelling the river.

Lochlan had never visited Banburn but knew it sat near the river's source, an underground spring that bubbled to the surface, sending steam into the air year-round. These waters were said to have healing qualities, but Lochlan was not the sort who believed in such things.

By the end of the week, Banburn came into view, sitting before a huge forest that protected it from the elements. The bubbling pool was not in the centre of the town, as expected, but just one of several water sources feeding into the White River.

The town stretched on for some distance but was mainly along the riverbanks. Like Dungannon, most buildings were single-storey, but here and there, a taller one poked above the rest. The largest of these contained a tower rising above the town in a position of dominance, leading Lochlan to stare.

"What is it?" asked Althea, noting the object of his attention.

"That building," he replied. "I've not seen its like in the Clanholdings before. They must've used thick timbers to support that tower's weight."

"I imagine so. We use something similar in Weldwyn to hold church bells. The tower is there to elevate them so they can be heard from far away."

Lochlan shook his head. "It is not our way to worship the Gods in such a place. We hold our ceremonies out in the open, where the Gods can see us, not hidden beneath a rooftop."

"Then perhaps it's just a bell tower to warn the townsfolk of danger?"

"Quite possibly. Still, it illustrates how similar our cultures are in some ways."

"But you just denied the possibility of it being a place of worship?"

"I meant in terms of building design. We have, I believe, much more to learn about each of our people's ways."

"You'll get no argument from me."

Lochlan halted, prompting the rest of their party to follow his example. "I think we best leave the Dragon Company here, don't you? I shouldn't want Banburn to fear we mean to attack."

"Is that likely?"

He chuckled. "It's not as rare as you might imagine. Our history is full of conflict, and not so long ago, raids were common in these parts."

Althea turned to Haldrim. "You may rest the company here, Captain. We shall journey the rest of the way unaccompanied."

"As you will, Highness, but I don't imagine Brogar will find that palatable."

She looked at her bodyguard, then at her husband. "Is it permitted to have a personal guard?"

"Certainly," said Lochlan. "In fact, it's quite common. You might even say it confers a certain status on a person. After all, only the most important need protecting."

"Come with us," said Althea, waving at Brogar.

They continued northward along the river's bank and soon spotted some men coming towards them.

"Don't worry," said Lochlan. "They're only here to ensure we mean them no harm."

An older warrior with greying hair stepped in front of his companions. "Who are you that comes to Banburn?"

"I am Lochlan, Clan Chief of Dungannon, and this is my wife, Althea, and her bodyguard."

The man stepped closer but didn't draw any weapons. "Aye, I recognize you, Lochlan of Dungannon."

"Have we met?"

"We have, though it was before the war. I was at the gathering of the Twelve Clans when the Elf convinced us to join his cause."

"Not our best decision," said Lochlan.

"Agreed. It led to misery and death. Are you here to speak with Raurig?"

"We are. Will he agree to see us?"

"Undoubtedly. If you'll come along, I'll take you to him."

They finally entered Banburn proper and passed by several homes. The construction here was much like that of Dungannon, but the timber frames looked more solid, likely because of the large forest nearby that provided an abundance of wood.

The great hall stood at the end of a road, its tall, arched ceiling and ornately carved pillars within, leaving Lochlan impressed, while Althea felt confined despite its height. To her mind, the pillars obstructed not only the view but caused visitors to bunch together, making it difficult to manoeuvre. Then again, perhaps it was meant to do precisely that.

Raurig sat by the hearth, a drink in hand, but he stood as his visitors entered, tossing his cup aside.

"Is this Lochlan, Chief of Dungannon, I see before me?"

"It is, indeed."

Their host swept his gaze over Althea. "And who is this enchanting beauty?"

"My wife, Althea, Princess of Weldwyn."

"Princess, is it? Now, that comes as a bit of a surprise. We'd heard rumours to that effect, but you know how people talk. I thought it a jest, yet here you stand before me. And you, you rogue, married at last? Whoever would've thought you'd one day be Clan Chief?"

"Do you insult my husband, my lord?"

The man sobered. "Not at all. You must forgive an old man his manners, Lady. We are not used to such august company. Speaking of manners, please, come and sit." He turned slightly, indicating some chairs arranged before the fireplace. "More drink!" he bellowed.

"What brings you to Banburn?" asked Raurig.

"We have something to discuss with you," replied Lochlan. "Something we believe might benefit both our Clans."

"You have my attention."

"You and I both know what a stranglehold the boatholders maintain over trade."

"Are you proposing we build our own boats? If so, I'll stop you right there. The families who control that kind of thing are wealthy, not the sort you want to annoy."

"Actually," said Althea. "We have no objection to that. What we propose is the building of a road between here and Dungannon."

"Hear her out," said Lochlan. "Her argument makes a good deal of sense."

"I'll listen," replied Raurig, "but I have my doubts."

Althea steeled herself. "The boatholders control all traffic on the rivers, but the real issue isn't that—it's the high tariffs they charge. They also maintain the right to refuse goods, leaving those who wish to ship such items in a difficult position."

"And you believe a road would solve that?"

"In Weldwyn, the roads spurred commerce, and with commerce came better prices and a flourishing of its people. And before you complain about it, the other kingdoms found the same thing. Roads allow merchants to carry their goods from town to town, buying and selling as they see fit. To do that by boat would cost a fortune."

"And what would be involved in creating this road you speak of?"

"A road is little more than a path," explained Althea. "It requires us to clear away trees and underbrush, maybe even make a few small bridges over streams, that sort of thing. None of it needs skilled labour but would require a group of warriors to keep the workers safe in the wilderness and patrol it once it's complete."

Raurig nodded. "I'm no scholar, but I agree with you on the benefits. I've often felt the boatholders demand too much for their services. Perhaps the mere threat of a road will force them to lower their prices?"

"We must follow through. Even if they cut the tariffs, they'd likely raise them again if it became clear we weren't going to proceed with the construction."

"What sort of numbers are we looking at regarding workers?"

"The more, the better," replied Lochlan, "but if we both contribute twenty, we'll have close to what we need. Naturally, we should coordinate our efforts, or else we might find ourselves working at cross purposes."

"When would you like to start?"

"We need to stock up on tools, but I suggest we pick a route now while it's still relatively cool. Once the warmer weather comes, we should be well on our way."

"And if no one uses this new road?"

"The history of Weldwyn shows us they will," said Althea, "but even if it fails, what has it cost you? A little gold and time? Hardly the sort of thing that would bankrupt a Clan of your standing."

Raurig sat up straighter, pleased with the compliment. "I shall give it some thought, but I cannot guarantee you an answer today."

"And if you see the merit in this idea?" asked Lochlan.

"Then I will send word. Actually, ignore that. I'll send word whether I end up supporting the road or not. If there's to be co-operation between our respective Clans, then we should be plain-spoken."

"In that case, I look forward to hearing from you."

SIXTEEN

Pressure

SPRING 967 MC

B everly could feel her father's presence as she stood in the highest room of Bodden Keep, the one her father referred to as his map room. The view, as always, was magnificent, yet today she found little to cheer her. Bodden was her home, had been for her entire life, yet there was a very real chance it would be taken away from her.

Footsteps approached, and then Aubrey appeared at the door. "I hope I'm not disturbing you?"

Beverly forced a smile. "Just taking a last look around."

Her cousin entered the room, moving beside the knight who stared out over the countryside. "It's a marvellous view."

"Even more so once the roses bloom. I shall miss this place."

"You haven't lost it yet, and there's a good chance you won't."

"Easy to say, but the evidence indicates otherwise."

"What evidence?" said Aubrey.

"I've been going over my father's records."

"And?"

Beverly turned to face her cousin. "Are you aware he was never sworn in as baron?"

"But he was the baron for decades!"

"He acted as baron, but as far as ceremonies go, he was never in truth given the title."

"Why ever not?"

"The nobles of Merceria must be sworn in by the ruling monarch in Wincaster. I can only assume he was needed here in Bodden."

"I suppose Norland raided a lot in those days, but the fact he sat on the Nobles Council should prove the king held him in high regard."

"Regard is one thing, but the courts will insist on facts."

"Then listen to this, Cousin. Your father, my uncle, was the General of the Mercerian Army and a great man. He supported the queen when she fought for the Crown and was a key strategist during the conquest of Norland. No one, save yourself, has done more to further the queen's cause."

"Not true. What about Gerald?"

Aubrey laughed. "All right, I'll admit Gerald might have done more, but it doesn't change the fact that Uncle Richard was one of her strongest supporters."

"All true, yet I wonder if it will be enough. We are living in different times than my father's. Merceria is now a kingdom of laws, not one controlled by wealthy nobles. The privilege of the past is no longer a guarantee of success."

"I understand you miss your father, but if he were here, he'd be the first to tell you that you must endure. He was the very best of us, Beverly, the noblest of nobles, which is something that carries on in you."

"You're just saying that to cheer me up."

"Am I?" said Aubrey. "Is it working?"

Beverly smiled, this time genuinely. "It's hard to be in a bad mood when you're around, Aubrey."

"I'll take that as a compliment."

"Did you come here for that reason alone, or is there something you needed?"

"I came here to see when you wanted to return to Wincaster."

"I must fetch Aldwin first."

"Already done. He's gathering his tools, just in case he won't be coming back. He said he'd meet us down in the great hall."

"And Sir Preston?"

"Ready to assume command of Bodden when you leave. Personally, I think you should have held on to this place as tightly as possible."

"It was the queen's idea that Bodden is managed by a neutral third party, the better to ensure a smooth transition should it prove necessary."

"What will you do once you're back in the capital?"

Beverly shrugged. "I have my duties as the Commander of Horse to keep me busy, not to mention my position as Knight Commander of the Order of the Hound."

"You're also the queen's champion."

"And your point is?"

"Simply that you have a lot in your favour. You'll get through this, Cousin. I promise you."

"I wish I had your enthusiasm."

"Look at this another way. Who's handling the investigation?"

"Hayley."

"See? One of your closest friends and a fellow Knight of the Hound. Surely that accounts for something?"

"This wouldn't be so bad if it weren't dragging out for so long. At least if a decision was made, the wait would be over."

"Perhaps we should return to the old ways," said Aubrey, "where the ruler could pass a summary judgement based on their opinion?"

"No, not after all we've been through to get where we are today. Very well, you made me realize I'm just being petulant. If I am to lose Bodden, then so be it, but I won't simply stand around waiting for the hammer to drop."

Aubrey smiled. "Another smith's expression. Have you no shame?"

"Come. Let us find that husband of mine and return to Wincaster."

"Are you sure this is entirely necessary?" asked Gerald. "I only just returned from Summersgate."

"I must make a decision concerning Bodden," replied Anna. "Sir Randolf surfaced months ago, and we have yet to determine what we are to do."

"You're the queen."

"Yes, and you, my closest friend, not to mention advisor."

"So?"

"So, advise!"

"Let's hold off until Hayley tells us what she's discovered, shall we? Speaking of which, shouldn't we bring her in?"

"Yes, of course." The queen nodded to one of her servants, who then opened the door, revealing the High Ranger.

"Your Majesty," said Hayley, bowing deeply.

"Enough of the theatrics," said Anna. "Come. Sit down and tell us what you make of this whole sordid affair."

"Sordid?"

"Of course, unless you have evidence that Lord Edward was legally married in a ceremony conducted by a Holy Father of Saxnor?"

"I have found no evidence of that, Your Majesty."

"Then what did you find?" asked Gerald. "Anything that could put this matter to rest?"

"Yes, and no," replied Hayley. "Let me explain."

"I think you'd better," said the queen. "The last I heard, you travelled to Norland."

"I did indeed. There I found the purported remains of Lord Edward. That is to say, I found a body in a crypt but had no way of verifying it belonged to Lord Edward. He was officially listed as Edward Blackburn, but Sir Randolf claims it was to protect his true identity."

"Is there any way to verify this claim?"

"Not directly, no, for I could find no witnesses to the baron's death. However, I did visit Lord Asher, the new Earl of Beaconsgate. He possessed a ring bearing Lord Edward's seal."

"A ring, you say? Did you bring it back with you?"

"I did not. The earl refused my request, though I did take an impression of it."

"Refused your request?"

"Indeed, Majesty," said Hayley. "He claimed it was his property, and unfortunately, my position of High Ranger carries no weight in Norland."

"It seems," said Gerald, "that your findings support Sir Randolf's claim."

"They do, yet I met with some… opposition."

"Meaning?"

"I felt like someone was watching me. There was even a slight altercation on the streets of Beaconsgate, though nothing came of it."

"You believe they were trying to warn you off?"

"Possibly," replied Hayley. "Although I can't dismiss the possibility it was simple resentment at the presence of a Mercerian in their town."

The queen shifted in her seat. "You say the new earl co-operated?"

"Yes. I detected no deception on his part."

"Yet, you've not seen fit to end your enquiries. Is there a reason for that?"

"There is, Majesty. As you might expect, we've gathered statements from witnesses, not that there are many left to find after all these years. Unfortunately, none of them witnessed the baron's death first-hand. The stories all support each other, allowing for minor differences in details, but the gist of it's all the same. The entire garrison believed Lord Edward dead."

"That still doesn't explain your hesitation."

"Permit me to ask a question, Your Majesty. It's pertinent to the matter, I assure you."

"Go ahead."

"I'm told after Sir Randolf announced his claim in the great hall, you retired to the map room of Bodden, where you discussed the matter in more privacy."

"We did, but that scarcely qualifies as a question."

"According to some statements, Sir Randolf explained how he got his name. Do you remember it?"

"I do," said Gerald. "He claimed to be named after Sir Randolf of Burrstoke."

"Yes, he did," added the queen. "Do you think it's pertinent?"

"I sent Gorath to talk to Sir Randolf of Burrstoke in person, hoping he might provide more details about Lord Edward's death."

"And?"

"He essentially corroborated everyone else's version of events. It was only in passing that he happened to mention something a little more curious. I hoped Gerald might provide some insight."

"What did he say?" asked Gerald.

"He claims he and Lord Edward were not on the best of terms, a far cry from close friends. Hardly the type of association that leads someone to name their son after him."

"I hadn't thought of that, but now you mention it, it does seem strange."

"Could Lord Edward have thought otherwise?" asked Anna.

"Lord Edward was not one to make friends of his subordinates," said Gerald. "I hate to speak ill of the dead, but let's just say he didn't have Lord Richard's easy-going manner."

"If that's true, then this entire claim could be nothing more than a fabrication."

"Do any of our mages know a spell that can determine when someone is lying?"

"I wish they did," said the queen. "It would make the Nobles Council so much easier to deal with. Your thoughts, Hayley?"

"If this is all a lie, then it begs the question, why?"

"That's easy," said Gerald. "Power. Well, power and wealth—the two tend to go hand in hand." He leaned back but then suddenly sat up again. "Hang on a moment. What if this is all about revenge?"

"In what way?"

"This could all be an elaborate plot to punish Beverly."

"That makes sense," said Anna. "It was Randolf's sister, Celia, who tried to kill Beverly in Norwatch."

"That's a long time to plan revenge," said Hayley.

"Not really," said Gerald. "We already know Celia was plotting with Norlanders. In hindsight, it's probably safe to assume that meant Lord Hollis."

"Yes," agreed the queen, warming to the subject. "And once we returned, we were embroiled in a civil war, hardly the time or place for Randolf to avenge his sister's death."

"And then they invaded us."

"That's right! Randolf was likely promised Bodden as his reward for serving Hollis, but that all went up in smoke when we defeated them in the war."

"That doesn't necessarily invalidate his claim," said Hayley. "There's also the possibility that Sir Randolf simply believes what he's been told."

"Good point," said Gerald. "It sounds like Lord Edward died long before Randolf was aware of his true identity."

"There's still the matter of the ring. If someone fabricated all this, then how did they get hold of Bodden's seal?"

The queen chuckled. "It seems the more we learn, the more questions arise. I can see now why it's taken you so long to reach a decision."

"What would you like me to do, Majesty?"

"It appears we need to dig deeper. You said you have an imprint of the ring?"

"I do."

"I should very much like to examine it."

"To what end?" asked Gerald.

"I have an eye for detail. There might be something about it that explains its presence in Norland."

"Are you suggesting they stole it?"

"At this point, anything's possible."

"I shall have it brought to you this afternoon," said Hayley. "In the meantime, I'll consult with my senior rangers and see if we can't come up with a way of flushing out the truth."

Revi Bloom looked across the table. "Why am I here again?"

"Because you're my lucky charm," said Hayley.

"I thought you were mine?"

"Can't it work both ways?"

He smiled. "Of course, but I wonder what I can add to the discussion."

"You're a mage and possibly the smartest person I know. At the very least, you could listen to our discussion and chime in should you think of something relevant?"

"Of course." He waited as the others filed in. Gorath, her adjutant, sat to Hayley's right, with Sam and Bertram Ayles taking up seats on either side of the Life Mage.

"I called you here," began the High Ranger, "to determine if we can't come to a consensus on how to proceed."

"You mean we're not done with all of this?" asked Bertram. "Isn't the investigation over?"

"Far from it. In fact, the more we discover about this entire enterprise, the more we find it needs further investigation."

"So what is it now?"

"I can answer that," said Gorath. "The claim that Sir Randolf was named after Sir Randolf of Burrstoke is likely a lie."

"And that affects us, how?"

"It reveals a crack in their story," said Hayley. "It's up to us now to discover what else is a lie."

"I hate to be the bearer of bad news," said Bertram, "but many people become forgetful in their old age."

"True, and if it were only Sir Randolf, I'd agree, but according to the marshal, it's an accurate statement. Lord Edward had few friends amongst the garrison of Bodden."

"That's sad," said Sam, "but not surprising, based on his reputation."

"Which is?"

"He ruled Bodden long before I got there, but word amongst the older soldiers was that he was an obstinate man, much like his father."

"And Lord Richard?"

"Quite the opposite."

"Can you be more specific?" asked Gorath.

"With Lord Richard, you always knew he'd do his best to bring you back alive. On the other hand, they said Lord Edward was dismissive of his men."

"Are you suggesting they hated him?"

"Perhaps not so much hated as disliked."

"This is interesting," said Hayley. "I wonder if someone in the Bodden garrison might have conspired to get that signet ring into the hands of Lord Hollis?"

"I don't see how," said Sam. "Any Norlander in Bodden would've stuck out like a sore thumb."

"Not necessarily," said Ayles. "The truth is, they're not so different from our own people. After all, we do share a common ancestry. Now, I'm not saying a Norlander wandered in and stole the ring, but there's also the possibility someone in the garrison took advantage of the siege to steal what wasn't theirs."

"Yes, but the baron's seal? Surely that would've been noticed?"

"What if they took it after the baron's death?" asked Sam. "I imagine things were pretty chaotic in the wake of the explosion."

"I have another option," said Gorath. "What if the baron died as we origi-nally thought, and someone happened upon his ring?"

"That bears considering," said Hayley.

"And the ring could've been stolen anytime after that," added Sam. "If I understand correctly, a new ring would have been made for his successor, so it's unlikely anyone missed the old one."

"Also, a good point, but I'm afraid that leaves us in a difficult position. We know that ring somehow got into the hands of Lord Hollis. Aside from the question of how it got there, we must look at possible motives."

"Lord Hollis is dead," said Gorath, "and thus, has nothing to gain."

"Ah, but Lord Asher does," said Hayley. "Think what it would mean to him to have an ally in Bodden?"

"I'm just wondering," said Ayles, "if the actions of Randolf's sister could affect his claim to the barony? She was, after all, an admitted traitor."

"No. By that reckoning, the queen herself would be subject to punishment for the actions of her brother King Henry."

"This is all far too complicated. Couldn't we hang the man and be done with it?"

"And break our oath to uphold the law?"

"So, what now?" said Sam.

"You and Ayles return to Bodden. Sir Preston is the acting custodian, so be sure to be forthright with him. I want you to search through any documentation that might help explain Lord Edward's behaviour. You should also keep your eyes out for his ring."

"Don't we have his ring?"

"We do, or rather we know where it is, but one can never be certain. Remember, you're looking for any evidence that might verify or disprove Lord Edward's relationship to Sir Randolf of Burrstoke. I'll admit it's unlikely to come to light now, but we must make absolute certainty of our facts."

"What about other warriors?" asked Gorath. "I know we questioned all the knights and such, but there is a good chance that one or two of the footmen might have seen something."

"That's right," said Revi, surprising everyone. "You should seek out a man named Edgar Greenfield. He served in Bodden years ago but is a queen's courier now. Assuming he's not dead, of course. Gerald likely knows more about the fellow, or the queen, as he was in her service for a long time."

"And what of Norland?" asked Gorath. "Do we return to Beaconsgate in an attempt to find out more about Lord Edward?"

"I think it better that you concentrate on Sir Randolf for the present," replied Hayley. "We know so little about him. See what you can discover about his background but be discreet."

"I am an Orc. I can hardly be discreet."

"True. Perhaps I'll go myself."

"It is dangerous," said Gorath. "You told me you had a run-in with a couple of men while in town."

"That's a good point. Maybe that will allow us to learn more about what's happening there."

"So, you mean to return, regardless of the danger?"

"Not right away," she replied, "and not without gaining some allies first."

"Meaning?" asked Sam.

"It's time I used a little diplomacy."

SEVENTEEN

Witness

SPRING 967 MC

L ord Tulfar looked up at the sign. "Are you sure that's correct? This is a carpenter's shop. Isn't the man we're looking for a guard?"

"He is," replied Jack. "His father owns the business. Apparently, Bradford lives above it."

"Well then, we'd best get a move on before he disappears."

"You think that likely?"

"No offence to you, Lord Jack, but if there's one thing I've learned when dealing with Humans, it's that they like to cover up their mistakes."

"Bradford's colleague was of a similar opinion."

The Dwarf looked up and down the street. "You don't suppose he's in danger, do you?"

"That's very likely the case," replied Jack.

"I'll stay here and keep an eye on things. Call out if you need help."

"You're not coming up?"

"Why would I? You're more than capable of taking his statement by yourself."

"And you intend to stand out here on the street?"

"I thought I might have a chat with his father. You can learn much about a person from their parents."

"Very well," said Jack. "Now, let's see, how do I get up there?"

"Down that alleyway is a set of stairs," said Tulfar. "I imagine those will take you to his front door... or would we call that a side door? You know, this would be a lot easier if Humans lived underground like sensible folk."

"You mean like the Dwarves?"

Lord Tulfar smiled. "Of course."

Jack moved into the alleyway, his senses alert. He half expected someone to be lurking there, ready to pounce, but all he saw was a rat, and even that quickly skittered away.

He took the stairs two at a time, arriving at a weather-beaten door. "Hello?" he called out. "Is anyone home?"

He knocked after waiting a moment for a reply, then looked around. This side of the building had no windows, leaving him little in the way of options. It was early morning, far too early for a supposedly ill guardsman to be wandering the streets.

"Curse me for a fool," he muttered under his breath. "I should've come here right away, not wasted my time talking to others." He turned, ready to descend the steps, when he heard something falling inside, perhaps a bowl or tankard. He pressed his ear to the door, trying to hear more.

A rhythmic tapping, as if someone was tapping wood, drew his attention. Jack braced himself, then kicked the door, but it resisted his efforts. He tried again, and the door flew open this time, revealing a cramped room with light filtering in through the shutters on the front of the building and a man lying on the floor. By all appearances, he'd fallen from the bed and couldn't move anything but his right hand, which held a shoe he kept banging on the floor.

Jack crossed to the fellow's side and rolled him over. Spittle bubbled from the man's mouth, and a foul odour met his nose, causing him to gag. He felt for a pulse. The poor soul, presumably Bradford, was still alive but weak. Jack moved to the window, throwing open the shutters, flooding the area with light and fresh air.

The stench quickly cleared as he scanned the room, looking for any signs of what had transpired. A tankard lay on the floor, its contents splashed onto the floorboards. However, of greater interest was where the liquid had evaporated, leaving a thin white film.

"Don't struggle," said Jack. "I'm going to try to get you to a healer."

It took him a few tries to lift Bradford, and then he staggered to the door, kicking it aside to move outside. As he descended the stairs, he called for help. Tulfar was soon there, ready to lend assistance.

"Bradford?" asked the Dwarf.

"I assume so. I think he's been poisoned—we need to get him to a healer."

"We have no healers left in Weldwyn. The war saw to that!"

"Then we'll take him to the Dome. With any luck, one of the Mercerians will be able to summon help."

Lord Tulfar commandeered a hand cart, dumping out its load of apples. The vendor complained, but a gift of coins silenced him. Jack dropped Bradford into the cart, then pushed it down the street, Lord Tulfar leading the way.

Kraloch stooped over the old tome, scanning its contents.

"I didn't know Orcs could read." said a voice from behind him.

"Most cannot," he replied, "but Lady Aubrey taught me."

Osbourne Megantis moved closer, then gazed down at the ancient text. "I must warn you; I've read this one, and it's far more likely to put you to sleep than tell you anything of interest."

"It is merely something to pass the time."

"Tell me, do the Orcs have their own written language?"

"We did, many generations ago, but it has been lost to history. The Mercerians devised a way to spell out our words using their own language."

"Why in the name of Malin would they do that?"

"We use it for written communication within the Army of Merceria. In that way, any intercepted messages are incomprehensible to the enemy."

"Clever," said the Fire Mage, "but then every commander must understand your language."

"Or have an Orc to translate," said Kraloch.

"One that can read, obviously."

The Orc shaman nodded. "It is so, yes."

"You Orcs amaze me," said the Fire Mage. "I thought you'd be more useful employing your magic in battle."

"I am a shaman dedicated to healing others."

"Yet you do have elementalists, don't you?"

"Only a few in these parts, and even then, only masters of earth."

"No fire, then?"

"I am afraid not."

"Too bad," said Osbourne. "It would've been interesting to compare notes."

"Notes?"

"Yes, written observations. It is a term we often use at the Dome, or at least we did before the invasion."

"I am led to believe you are the sole wielder of Fire Magic in Weldwyn. Is that not so?"

Osbourne drew himself up to his full height. "That's true. It also makes me the senior mage at the Dome, now that Master Tyrell is no longer with us."

A heavy footfall drew their attention, and then one of the Dome's few remaining students threw open the door. "Master Osbourne, you must come quickly!"

"Why?" replied the Fire Mage. "What's happened?"

"A pair of nobles demand your attention!"

"Calm yourself. You're a messenger, not a herald. Now, who are these nobles?"

"I recognize only one, Master. Jack Marlowe, the cavalier. The other is a Dwarf."

"And why, pray tell, do they wish to see me?"

"They asked for the person in charge, presumably to help them with the injured fellow."

"Injured?" said Kraloch. "Why did you not begin with that?"

The student shrugged. "I didn't think it important."

"Lead on," said Osbourne, "and let us get to the bottom of this."

They made their way through the Dome, emerging to find their visitors on the front steps. Kraloch moved to the injured man's side, looking him over."

"What have we here?" he asked.

"I think he's been poisoned," said Jack. "I found him on the floor."

"Any sign of what did this?"

"Something in his drink, I suspect, but I thought it best to get him to help as quickly as possible. Can you do anything for him?"

"I shall certainly try," said Kraloch. The shaman closed his eyes before he called forth his power. His hands glowed with a pale-blue light, and then he laid them on his patient, where the light faded into the poor soul, racing through his veins and briefly causing his stomach to glow. His breathing slowly eased.

"Bring him inside. I shall need to treat him further."

"You mean you didn't cure him?" asked Jack.

"Were I able to identify the toxin, I would have a better idea. I used my magic to neutralize toxins, but whatever caused this may still be within him."

"I'm not sure I understand?"

"Think of it this way. If you ate something poisonous, such as a poison-berry, it would sit in your stomach, releasing its toxin slowly. The spell I cast removed the poison from his blood, but it does not affect the poisonberry."

"So, it will just sit there, releasing yet more poison?"

"In time, it will pass through his system, as all food does, but we must watch him for any recurrence of his symptoms."

"I saw some sort of white powder," said Jack.

"Where?"

"On the floor. He'd knocked over his cup, spilling the contents."

The Orc nodded. "That is good. It means there is likely little of it left within him."

Osbourne beckoned some students who tried to lift Bradford. The poor fool tried to stand, but his legs were having none of it.

"You must carry him!" snapped the Fire Mage. He watched them struggle, then finally they got hold of him and bore him inside. "Fools!" he shouted. "If there's one thing I cannot stand, it's incompetence."

"They are students," said Kraloch. "Can you say you were any different at their age?"

Osbourne scowled but refused to answer. Instead, he turned his attention to their visitors. "Might I ask, Lord Jack, why you thought this man warranted our attention?"

"He is a key witness," the cavalier replied. "His testimony could well put a traitor into the hangman's noose."

"And how is that of import to me?"

Lord Jack simply stared back.

"Are you saying," said Lord Tulfar, "that you only treat patients you deem worthy?"

"I am no healer," said Osbourne.

"But I am," said Kraloch. "And I will refuse treatment to no one. I suggest you come inside, gentlemen. That is the correct term of address, is it not?"

"Close enough," said Tulfar, smiling. He gave Osbourne a stern look before following their witness.

"Thank you, Master Kraloch, for your assistance," said Jack. "As for you, Master Osbourne, I shall remember this day well."

Bradford's eyes fluttered open. Above him, a green face stared back, causing his pulse to quicken. Were they under attack? He struggled to remember where he was until the room came into focus, and he realized he was lying on a bed.

The Orc nodded before moving away. "He has recovered."

Another face appeared, but this one he recognized. "Lord Jack?" said Bradford. "What are you doing here?" He let his gaze wander. "Where exactly am I?"

"At the Dome," came the reply. "I found you on the floor in your home. We believe someone poisoned you. What do you remember?"

"I... I'm not sure. I seem to recall being beaten."

"That is consistent with his wounds," said the Orc. "There was a lot of bruising on his chest and abdomen, along with some on his arms, leading me to suspect someone forced him to drink the contents of that cup you mentioned."

"Yes, that's it," said Bradford. "Somebody came asking questions, said they were from the tribunal. Who are all of you?"

Jack chuckled. "Me, you clearly know. This is Master Kraloch, the one responsible for saving your life, and this"—he nodded towards the Dwarf—"is Lord Tulfar Axehand, Baron of Mirstone. Can you tell us more about these visitors? You said they identified themselves as members of the tribunal?"

"Yes. There were three of them."

"All Human?"

"That's a strange thing to ask," said Bradford. "Of course they were Human. What else would they be?"

"Can you describe them?"

"One was well-spoken and of average height, with dark-brown hair, perhaps even black, and a clean-shaven face."

"Was he young, old?"

"He was, in age, much like yourself, Lord."

"And the other two?"

"Similar in height but dressed in plain clothing. They didn't speak much, but I gathered they were of common birth."

"Did they ask anything of you?"

"Only to remain silent, but they didn't say why. When I tried asking them questions, they beat me."

"And when was this?"

"After dark, Lord. Though I can't, in all truth, tell you how long ago that was. I don't even know how long I've been here."

"We came to see you this very morning." Jack looked at the Orc.

"I suspect they administered the poison last night. Whatever they gave him was likely watered down too much to take immediate effect."

"So they bungled it?" said Lord Tulfar.

"Very likely, yes."

"This has serious repercussions."

"I agree," said Jack. "Someone is claiming to represent the tribunal."

"Yes, and going around trying to kill witnesses. Speaking of which, I shall send word for some of my warriors to come here and guard him."

"Is that necessary?" asked Bradford.

"You tell me," said Lord Jack. "Your life's in jeopardy, not mine. They already tried to kill you once. If they learn you survived, they're likely to try again."

Lord Godfrey smiled as they opened the cell door. "Thank you, gentlemen. Your service is duly noted. I know the way from here."

The jailer and his assistant wandered off down the hall, leaving Godfrey to stroll over to Lord James.

"I'm sorry I couldn't get you out as well," Godfrey said, "but there are limitations to what my associates can accomplish. Do not fear, though. I shall spare no effort to ensure they dismiss the charges against you."

"Easy for you to say while I'm still imprisoned. How did you arrange your release, if I may ask?"

Godfrey chuckled. "You may ask, but I'm afraid I can't reveal my sources. It would put them in too much danger. As I said earlier, I still have some powerful friends."

"What will you do now? Flee Weldwyn?"

"I considered that, but no. Flight is not the answer for me—there's too much here I enjoy. In any case, where would I go? It's not as if Merceria would grant me leave to live as I like in their land."

"There are always the Twelve Clans?" said James.

"And be forced to live as a barbarian? I think not."

"Then Norland?"

"That might've been a good choice in years past, but these days, it's firmly under Merceria's thumb. I suppose I could travel to the Continent, but who knows what that's like. No, I'm afraid I must remain here in Weldwyn for the time being."

"Do you not realize the fate hanging over your head? You are under sentence of death!"

"Ah, but they can't execute me for treason without proof, and therein lies the difficulty. They need witnesses, yet it appears none are willing to come forth."

"That you know of."

"Few were aware of our efforts before the city fell, and I arranged for those who do know to remain silent."

"And how did you accomplish that?"

"Coins, for the most part, though some required a more permanent solution."

"Are you suggesting you had people murdered?"

"Murdered is such a coarse word. I prefer silenced."

"Have you no shame?"

"Shame? I don't know the meaning of the word, and quite frankly, neither should you. Politics is a filthy business, James, which means, on occasion, we must get our hands dirty."

"By murdering people?"

"Come now. People die all the time. What difference do one or two deaths make in the grand scheme of things? It's not as if they are of any real consequence. You and I are meant for greatness, and if that means pushing people aside from time to time, then so be it."

"I'd argue the point," said James, "but I can't help but agree with you."

"There, that's the spirit. Now, don't worry. I'll take care of everything." Godfrey turned to leave but then thought better of it. Instead, he drew closer until he was up against the cell bars. "I shall free you," he said. "You have my word."

"See that you do." Lord James forced a smile. "Now, get out there and take care of those witnesses before they start preparing the noose."

"You know full well it won't be a rope that they use. They'll scoop out your stomach and watch you bleed to death, likely in front of a crowd."

"All the more reason you should fight for my freedom. I'll not willingly go down without a fight, but if you abandon me, I will reveal your part in all this."

"I wouldn't blame you for that, but as I said, I'll do all I can to secure your release." He paused, pondering their situation. "Before I go, there is one more thing."

"Which is?" said James.

"I was just thinking of your mother. You don't suppose she knows anything, do you?"

"My mother? Never! The woman can barely string two sentences together."

"That does not preclude the possibility she may have overheard something."

"If she has, she certainly hasn't revealed it."

"Why would you say that?"

"Simple," said James. "I'm still here, alive in this cell. If she possessed any evidence, I'd already be dead."

"Not if she's protecting you."

"And why would she do that?"

"Like it or not, you're still her son—her only son, to be precise. Of course, we can't preclude the possibility she wants you dead after all you did to her."

"I thought you were trying to cheer me up?"

"I am, James. I am."

"By suggesting my own mother might betray me?"

Godfrey simply smiled. "I'd best be on my way. I have things to do." He walked down the corridor without looking back.

EIGHTEEN

The Scholar

SPRING 967 MC

A n unexpected traveller leading a donkey approached the fields of Dungannon, causing the oathmen in the towers to send word to the Clan Chief, for almost all visitors came by riverboat. As he drew closer, it soon became clear the cart the donkey pulled was laden with chests and sacks.

Alerted to the visitor's arrival, Lochlan and Althea came to discover who it was. They'd only gone a few steps when Lochlan broke into a grin. "Camrath!" he called out.

The visitor smiled, revealing a decent set of teeth for one of such advanced years.

"It is good to see you," the old man replied. "Or perhaps you'd like me to address you as Lord, now that you are the chief?"

"It's good to see you, too, my friend," said Lochlan, grasping his mentor's hand.

"But who is this that joins us? Could it be that the young scholar has captured a prize?"

"This is my wife, Althea, daughter of King Leofric."

"Leofric, you say? These are strange times, indeed."

"I'm happy to see you," said Lochlan, "but the last time we met, you were down in Glanfraydon."

"And so I was, but it appears the new Clan Chief has no place for men of learning. I hoped you might see wisdom where he only saw waste?"

"You are most welcome." Lochlan peered at the cart. "And what is all that?"

"Why, my books, along with other assorted notes and scrolls."

"Your entire collection?"

"Indeed, though it pains me to say so. Much of it is delicate in nature, and I fear they may not all have survived the journey." He looked at Althea. "Do you read, my dear?"

"Of course. Reading was considered an essential skill at court. I can also read a bit of the mountain folks's tongue, though I don't expect to be fully proficient for some time yet."

"You surprise me," said Camrath. "I did not anticipate the wife of Lochlan being so well-educated."

"Literacy is common amongst the people of Weldwyn, at least in the merchant class and nobility."

"I'm afraid you'll find it considerably less so here in the Clanholdings."

"Come," said Lochlan. "You must be starving after the day's travel. Let us bring you inside and see you fed."

"I need to look after my books first."

"I'll see to that," said Haldrim, appearing out of nowhere.

His arrival made Camrath jump, which, in turn, caused Lochlan to laugh out loud.

"You consider that funny, Lord?"

"Only in the purest way, I assure you. Your books are in safe hands, Master Camrath. Now, come. Let's get you inside."

Althea set down her cup. They'd gathered around the fireplace after eating. "My husband tells me you're the most revered scholar in all the Clanholdings."

"I must admit it's true," replied Camrath. "Yet, at the same time, few truly care. Young Lochlan here is the only other scholar I'm aware of, possibly with the exception of yourself."

"I'm no scholar."

"You're well-educated by Clan standards. That, alone, makes you a valuable asset. I would guess you're likely better read than myself, although not as steeped in lore."

"And you would be right," she replied. "Much of my reading concerned matters of Weldwyn law. Well, that and my more recent study of the Dwarves of Mirstone."

"She has a company of them," added Lochlan.

"Of books?" said Camrath.

"No, Dwarves. Warriors she brought with her from Weldwyn. They were a wedding gift."

"They enslave Dwarves?"

"No," said Althea, chuckling. "They are paid for their service."

"Interesting. I wonder if I might visit them at some point in time?"

"I don't see why not," said Lochlan. "They're here in Dungannon."

Camrath shook his head. "My, how times have changed. It wasn't so long ago you came to me, desperate to learn about Elves."

"That didn't go so well for the Twelve Clans."

"So I heard, but if I recall, you bore reservations from the beginning. It's too bad your sister didn't heed your warnings."

"No one could've foreseen Kythelia's treachery."

"So, it was the same Elf after all?"

"It was," said Lochlan. "She butchered Brida, along with most of the Clan chiefs."

"Yet you still managed to return to us."

"That was Althea's doing."

The old scholar turned to Althea. "Was it, now? And why would you send your enemies home? Not that I dislike what you did, but wouldn't it make more sense to kill them?"

"If there is to be a lasting peace, then we must learn to trust one another."

"A scholar and a diplomat—you are blessed, indeed. Was it also your idea to wed young Lochlan here?"

"It was."

His gaze swivelled to the Clan Chief. "And you agreed to this?"

"I did. I felt it the best way to serve my people."

Camrath sighed. "Well, I suppose it isn't all bad. She's certainly not hard to look at."

"Excuse me?" said Althea. "I am a princess of Weldwyn, not a toy for your amusement."

"I meant no offence, my dear. Forgive an old man his outburst; I beg of you. I see others so rarely these days, particularly those of your gender."

"Tell me, Master Camrath, have you always been a scholar?"

"I first took to reading in my youth. I had the honour of serving the Clan Chief of Glanfraydon, and he ordered me to assist his scholar in that capacity. She taught me to read and write. The library became my responsibility upon her death. I added to it over the years when I could, but such things are rare amongst our people."

"Then where did these other books come from?"

"Mostly from merchant ships visiting our shores. The docks of Windbourne see much traffic, particularly from the Kurathian Isles, and word quickly spread that I would pay for any books they might bring me."

"Anything new and intriguing?" asked Lochlan.

"As a matter of fact, yes. I came across a book that might pique your interest, especially after all you've gone through in Weldwyn. It's a treatise on dragons, a translation of a Kurathian tome. It purports to have all sorts of information about the creatures."

"Such as?"

"Their breeding habits, diet, that sort of thing. There's a particularly interesting section about the various breeds they've identified, and the methods used to keep them in line."

"In line?" said Althea. "You mean servitude!"

"Is it servitude to keep a hound?" Camrath shook his head. "You people of Weldwyn have such strange ideas."

"Dragons are intelligent creatures, many capable of speech."

"Absolute nonsense! They are beasts, nothing more."

"Melethandil would tell you otherwise."

"Melethandil?"

"Yes, the dragon who helped us liberate Summersgate. I couldn't talk to her myself, but I can assure you some did."

"I am at a loss for words," said Camrath. "Unfortunately, my knowledge comes from books like those I brought with me, and the opinions of the authors can taint them." A faraway look came to his eyes. "It would be marvellous to see such a creature."

"It's said there are many of them in the Kurathian Isles," said Lochlan.

"Yes, I know, but I am far too old to travel such a distance. In any case, they said the climate there is sweltering, and I doubt my constitution could handle it."

"Are you suggesting you're ill?"

"Ill? No, merely old and worn out."

"What will you do now?" asked Althea. "You're welcome to remain here, though there is likely little to occupy your time."

"If I'm being honest, I hadn't given it that much thought. When it became clear my time in Glanfraydon was over, I packed up what I could and headed north. I only thought of coming here after I was on my way."

"Yet you didn't travel by boat," said Lochlan. "That was a dangerous choice, my friend. You could've been killed by all manner of beasts."

"Yet here I am," said Camrath. "Safe and sound. I know how dangerous everyone says the wilderness is, but I saw no hint of it along the way."

"Thank the Gods for that."

"What if you could spend your last years in comfort, surrounded by books?" asked Althea.

"I'm not sure I understand what you're suggesting?"

"The Dome in Summersgate has a vast library."

"Wasn't it destroyed?"

"The Weldwyn mages sent much of it to Merceria for safekeeping, but they have since returned it."

"I doubt the mages of the Dome would welcome one such as me."

"Nonsense. I could write a letter on your behalf. In Weldwyn, we prize our knowledge. Scholars are people to be looked up to, regardless of where they're from."

"And you would do this for me?"

"Of course."

"Very well. I shall take you up on that offer, providing you agree to keep my collection here in one piece."

"Of course," said Lochlan. "We'll build a place precisely for that purpose."

"Yes," agreed Althea. "And we shall call it the Library of Camrath, in your honour."

A tear came to the old scholar's eye. "I thank you most kindly, Lady. You overwhelm me with your generosity, so much so, I am worn out from all the excitement. With your permission, I shall retire for the evening."

"By all means," said Lochlan. He waited until their visitor left before continuing. "That was quite a gift you gave him."

"He was your mentor. Without him, you wouldn't be the man you are today."

Over the next few days, Dungannon was a beehive of activity. Raurig, the Chief of Banburn, had sent word his Clan supported constructing the road, necessitating the employment of scouts to mark off the route to Banburn.

They intended it to parallel the White River, but there were spots where water overflowed the banks in spring. Added to this was the difficulty in clearing rocks and trees that would make the road easier to use for wagons.

The timber frames for the library went up within days of Camrath's arrival, but Lochlan had the misfortune to come down with a cold, forcing him to leave the bulk of the supervision to Althea while he nursed a nasty cough. At Mirala's suggestion, he confined himself to bed, occupying his time by perusing the treatise on dragons that Camrath had gifted him.

As it turned out, the road construction proved a great source of wood, with many of the trees felled to clear the path providing the wood necessary to build the library.

Althea came up with the idea of a wooden roof instead of one of thatch, believing it better able to withstand the rain. Luckily, a member of the Dragon Company was familiar with making shingles and was willing to pass on his knowledge. Progress was swift, and although Lochlan wasn't there to see it in person, they hefted the roof framing into place by the end of the week.

The people of Dungannon, unused to such construction, spent much of their time watching, many joining in and lending what aid they could.

A real sense of community grew out of the work. Before long, the Dwarves became an intrinsic part of the village. The road to Banburn was well underway when Camrath announced it was time for him to leave.

Lochlan was sad to be losing the scholar's company after so short a time but insisted on dragging himself out of his sickbed to see his friend off.

"I shall miss you," he said. "Are you sure you won't stay?"

"I thank you," said Camrath, "but I insist on leaving before I outstay my welcome." He let his gaze wander to the three dispatch riders Althea had ordered to escort him. "I shall send word once I reach Summersgate. I promise you." He chuckled. "I must admit, I'm looking forward to it. Whoever thought that poor, old Camrath would set foot in the infamous Dome?"

"Goodbye," added Lochlan. "And enjoy yourself. You've earned it!"

Lochlan watched as the riders headed off on the long trek eastward.

"Will they be safe?" Althea asked.

"There is little danger between here and the border," he replied, "and he is well-guarded."

He coughed, automatically covering his mouth.

Althea, expecting him to say more, turned to see him staring at his fingers, shocked. "What is it?" she asked.

He lowered his hand, revealing a blood-spattered palm. Moments later, his eyes rolled up in his head, and he collapsed.

Camrath headed east, his escort skirting the north end of the hills bordering Dungannon. The countryside flattened the farther east they travelled until, a few days later, they came across the great Loran River that demarked the border of Weldwyn.

"How shall we cross?" asked the scholar.

"There's a ford," replied the Weldwyn captain. "We merely need to travel upriver a little to find it."

They turned north, sticking to the western bank. The river here was wide and deep, ideal for seaborne traders who wished to travel to the great city of Loranguard.

Camrath had spent his life in this land, and although he'd seen Kurathian ships in Windbourne, he'd never left the territory claimed by the

Twelve Clans. The future promised great things, and he imagined living a life of splendour amongst the wealthy of Summersgate.

They finally crossed the river at noon. With talk of a ford, he'd expected shallow water, but it was, in fact, quite deep, requiring the mounts to swim for a short distance. He briefly wondered how the Clansmen had crossed on their return home. No doubt they swam or came across on rafts. They climbed up the eastern bank and rested the horses, dropping to the ground to lie under the cloudless sky and dry off.

Camrath was restless. After only a moment, he rose, moving to stand at the river's edge, staring westward. He was leaving his home, and while the prospect of visiting the Weldwyn capital excited him, he knew he could never return.

He'd betrayed Lochlan and, by so doing, sealed his own fate. Was his soul doomed to wander the Underworld? Long ago, Camrath had given up his worship of the Gods, but now he was conflicted and wanted their guidance. He'd done the unthinkable: killed the only man who'd ever looked up to him, and for what? Gold?

A great sadness crept over him, his heart aching at the memory of what he'd done, but it was too late to make amends. He'd cast his lot and must now live with the consequences.

His thoughts turned to the promised reward, and his mood brightened. Camrath had spent his entire life in relative poverty, his survival dependent upon the charity of others. It served him well for years, but with the loss of his sponsor came his dismissal and, ultimately, his exile from Glanfraydon. Setting this plan in motion had been difficult, but he was confident no one would suspect how he'd carried it out. Lochlan would die—of that, he had no doubt—but nobody would ever connect his death with the tome of dragons.

The thought made him chuckle, rousing the interest of his escort. They spared him a glance, then simply shook their heads before returning to their own conversation.

The book—it all came down to the book. The unique tome was a translation, that much was true, but Camrath himself had done the work, even going so far as to add his own fascinating details. The tricky part was making the ink. Well, that and writing without poisoning himself.

He stared down at his ink-stained fingers. Even if they discovered the ink was poisoned, what chance was there they would connect it to him? Camrath was clever, attributing the book to an entirely fictitious name, yet part of him feared discovery. He tried to put such thoughts out of his head, but they kept returning. The plan was to kill Lochlan, not Althea, and all of a sudden, he feared the Princess of Weldwyn might take an interest in the book. All it would take was for her to peruse the pages, to touch the finely drawn illustrations, and then her fate would be sealed!

Panic threatened to overwhelm him. If she died, his new employer would be furious! He looked around, desperate to find a way out of his misfortune. Logic took hold once more, and he calmed himself. They were days out of Dungannon, and even if Althea died, he'd be in Summersgate long before word reached there. Once the remaining gold was in his possession, Camrath could disappear and live a life of luxury under an assumed name. Never again would he be reliant on others to survive.

What did it matter if he betrayed one person to secure his future? He consoled himself with the thought that people died every day. Lochlan could just have easily slipped from his horse and hit his head. All Camrath had done was help him along the way, sparing him the agony of a prolonged death. His escort called out, and he turned to see them remounting.

"It's time to move on," said the captain.

"Indeed it is," replied the scholar, his conscience now clear.

NINETEEN

Complications

SPRING 967 MC

Aldwin set down the tankard. "Come," he said. "Have some mead."

"I'm not in the mood," said Beverly. "First Bodden, and now he lays claim to the Wincaster estate. Am I to lose everything of my father's?"

"You will always have the memory of him. They can never take that away from you."

She grabbed the tankard. "You're right, of course. It's just that I feel so helpless. When I was born, my father promised Bodden would be mine one day. I was too young to remember, of course, but he told me again when I was older."

A soft knock came at the door, soon opening to reveal a servant. "My lady? The High Ranger is here to see you."

"Please send her in," said Beverly.

Moments later, Hayley entered. "This is not an official visit," she said. "In fact, if anyone asks, I wasn't here at all."

"Then what brings you?"

"I wanted to tell you how things were going, Bev, at least in an unofficial capacity."

"Is it good news or bad?"

"That's still up in the air. Some doubts are creeping in about Sir Randolf's claims, but from a legal point of view, nothing that negates his claim to Bodden. Were you aware the king never swore in your father as baron?"

"I thought as much. I looked in Bodden but could find no evidence of it. Why?"

"I've had people searching through the archives here in Wincaster, and they couldn't find any record either. The earliest reference to him as Baron of Bodden appears in a dispatch a month after Lord Edward's supposed death."

"From the king?"

"Yes."

"Wouldn't that constitute proof the king accepted him as baron?"

"That's one way of looking at it, but they believed Lord Edward dead at the time. Randolf's entire claim rests on the story of his survival."

"And did you find any proof that he survived?"

"We found his ring. That's about as much proof as I expect we'll ever see. There's a body they claim is his, but how does one prove that? Even Aubrey doesn't know that kind of magic."

"Wait a moment," said Aldwin. "Aubrey can talk with ancestors. Couldn't she simply communicate with Lord Edward?"

"I wish she could," said Beverly. "Unfortunately, her magic doesn't work like that."

"Yes," said Hayley. "She can cast the spell, but there's no control over who answers it. Revi explained it all to me."

"Revi? Is he talking to spirits now?"

The ranger chuckled. "No. He's far too busy researching the Saurian Gates. Don't worry. He's taking precautions, and once a month, he has Aubrey and Kraloch ensure there's no permanent damage."

"Damage?" said Aldwin. "What type of damage?"

"Apparently, close proximity to the gates induces a buildup of a sort of miasma of the mind, if you will. It's what originally drove him mad."

"And he's still studying it?"

"There's no danger. Aubrey and Kraloch came up with a cure. Besides, it takes weeks of exposure to build up."

Aldwin shook his head. "I'm never comfortable around mages."

"You like Aubrey," said Beverly.

"Yes, but she's family now."

"And what about Albreda?"

"I can see I'm being out-manoeuvred here. Perhaps it's best if I remain silent."

"You said something about a ring?" said Beverly, returning her attention to Hayley.

"Yes. I visited Lord Asher, the Earl of Beaconsgate. He has a ring that appears to be the property of Lord Edward."

"Do you have this ring on you?"

"Unfortunately, no. He insisted on keeping it, claimed it was a gift from a dying man."

"Convenient."

"Have you your father's ring?"

"I do. Would you like to see it?"

"If I may."

Beverly removed the ring from her hand and passed it over.

"Might I ask how you came by it?"

"Albreda brought it to me shortly after my father's death. Why? Are you now telling me it's not mine to keep?"

"Not at all. This signet ring was your father's property. I've no doubt he wanted you to have it. While it indicates he left Bodden for you, it does not prove your father's claim to the barony was legitimate."

"And what was my father to do in his brother's absence? Allow Bodden to remain leaderless?"

"I'm not your enemy, Bev. I'm only trying to explain how the law works."

"You're right. I'm sorry. I didn't mean to direct my anger at you. It's just that this whole situation has dragged on for far too long."

"Agreed, and far longer than should be necessary, but we are a kingdom of laws now, and we must see justice done."

"Tell me," said Aldwin, "and be honest now, what will happen if Randolf's claim is recognized?"

"The title of baron would be awarded to him, along with any land and belongings in the baron's name. It's good you're already married, or he'd have a say in who you wed."

"Surely you jest?"

"It's true," said Beverly. "As a single woman, I'd be under his protection, which means he could arrange a marriage. I suppose he could always contest our marriage, couldn't he?"

"No," said Hayley. "The queen would never allow that. Your smithy would be gone unless you wish to take up your trade in Randolf's service?"

"I'd sooner feed pigs for a living. Not that there's anything wrong with doing an honest day's work."

"That's my husband," said Beverly. "Even when he's insulting someone, he has to be polite about it."

"Look," said Hayley. "I know this has been difficult, but we'll get to the bottom of this, eventually."

"Have you any good news?"

"The queen won't consider the issue of who owns this estate until the title is settled. There's also a case to be made that Lord Edward never stayed here, whereas your father did. That alone might be enough to let you keep it should things turn out for the worst. I'm sorry I couldn't have brought better news, but at least you have some idea now where the investigation stands."

"Is there anything we can do?" asked Aldwin.

"I'm afraid not. Any involvement on your part could be construed as interference."

The servant reappeared.

"Yes?" snapped Beverly. "What is it?"

"I'm afraid you have more visitors, my lady."

"Who is it this time?"

"The marshal, madam, along with the Dwarven smith."

"You mean Herdwin?"

"Yes, that's the one."

"Then you'd best show them in. Sorry for yelling at you."

"Quite understandable, my lady. These are trying times." He disappeared into the hallway.

"I'd best be off," said Hayley. "I have lots to do." She held out the ring.

"You'd better hang on to it for now," said Beverly. "You might need it."

"I'll take good care of it. I promise."

She turned to leave just as Gerald and Herdwin entered the room.

"Hayley?" said Gerald. "What are you doing here?"

"I'm not here," the ranger replied, "and you never saw me. You either, Herdwin." She brushed past them, heading for the front door.

"What strange customs you people have," said Herdwin.

"What's wrong?" asked Beverly.

"What makes you suggest something's wrong?" replied Gerald. "Can't I visit one of my commanders from time to time?"

"You're not the type to drop by unannounced."

The Dwarf laughed. "Hah. She's got you there!"

"Perhaps you'd best sit," said Aldwin. "I get the impression this will take a while."

"So?" said Beverly.

Gerald sighed. "I'll admit you have the right of it. We have a potential problem brewing in the east."

"The east? You mean north, don't you? I assume you're referring to Ironcliff?"

"No," said Herdwin. "Stonecastle. You remember last autumn when Kasri and I told you we were to be forged?"

"Is that why you're here? Have you set a date?"

"That would hardly be construed as a problem in the east," said Gerald.

"Yes, of course. Is this somehow related?"

"Aye, it is," continued Herdwin, "but I think I'd best start at the beginning."

"That would be appreciated."

"As you're aware, Kasri and I travelled to Stonecastle to see if the smith's guild would reinstate me."

"Yes," said Aldwin. "Although I still don't understand why you felt the need."

"Kasri is the designated successor to Ironcliff, and I'm a smith without a guild. Dwarven society frowns upon such a union. In any event, we travelled there and met with King Khazad. Unfortunately, he could not sway the guild, but while we were there, we learned one of his watchtowers ran into a bit of trouble. Kasri and I went there, only to discover the Halvarians had captured it, the very same people threatening Ironcliff."

"I remember," said Beverly. "You said you destroyed a bridge to stop their advance."

"Aye. I did, though it nearly cost me my life."

"But you destroyed it. That must be the end of it, surely?"

"I very much doubt it," said Herdwin. "We had a chance to talk to several of them, and I didn't like what I heard."

"Meaning?"

"They're fanatics, and they're determined to move west. The bridge might slow them, but it won't stop them."

"And Stonecastle?"

"If attacked, they'll withdraw under the mountain. They can hold off an attacker for years if needed, but it won't stop the Halvarians from moving into Merceria."

"What do you need me to do?"

Gerald's eyes bore into her. "I need you to march troops to their aid, General."

"General?"

"Yes. You've more than earned it. Your father's advisors are there for you, but you're more than welcome to recruit your own if you wish."

"When do I march?"

Gerald smiled. "That's the spirit. Herdwin will brief you on what you can expect regarding the terrain. After that, you'll need to decide what companies to take and how many. I'd like to see you on your way before the end of the month, if at all possible."

"And the Elves of the Darkwood?"

"Lord Greycloak will be expecting you. We'll arrange for you to rendezvous with him at the Last Hope Inn. You remember it, of course?"

"I do."

"Good. As for me, I must return to the Palace. If you have any questions, feel free to drop by. Let me know once you decide how many men you want to take."

"I'll be going with you," said Herdwin.

"And Kasri?"

"She's been busy up in Ironcliff, but I'm hoping she'll join us before we march."

Gerald returned to the Palace to find Anna sitting at a table, examining a piece of paper.

"What have you got there?" he asked.

She looked up and smiled. "Oh, I didn't see you there. How did things go at Beverly's?"

"As well as it could, given the circumstances."

"Did she like her new promotion?"

"I believe so, but this business with her inheritance is wearing on her."

"I know," said Anna. "I'd like it all to be over too. If it were within my power, I'd simply grant Bodden to her, but then I'd be giving up on the entire idea of a kingdom ruled by laws. I'm beginning to think the whole thing is a colossal waste of time."

"Bringing law to Merceria is not a waste of time, Anna. You did that to protect future generations from people like King Andred."

"And what use is that if I must sit back and watch my closest friends suffer?"

"Hayley will sort it all out."

"I certainly hope so. Sir Randolf is becoming unbearable."

"In what way?" asked Gerald.

"Sophie told me he's been buying rounds at the Queen's Arms and regaling everyone with his impending appointment as the baron."

"Can we arrest him for that?"

"No, of course not. For Saxnor's sake, if I could do that, half the Nobles Council would be in irons."

"Who is it this time?"

"The Duke of Colbridge. He's pushing for the council to recognize Sir Randolf's claim."

"Why would he do that?"

"To punish me for not marrying him."

"That was years ago," said Gerald. "Surely he's over it by now?"

"You'd think so, but His Grace, the duke, is not quite done with the idea of matrimony. He has proposed I arrange a marriage between him and Aubrey."

"Good luck with that. Aubrey would never agree to it."

"Yet under Mercerian custom, it's within a monarch's rights to arrange such things, even demand them."

"You're not seriously entertaining the thought?"

"No, of course not," said Anna, "but that doesn't stop him from deluging me with requests to consider it."

"You make it sound like he's flooded you with letters."

"He has. Five in the last two weeks, not to mention the veiled suggestions coming in from other nobles of the realm who insist that it's past time Aubrey was married. They think it only proper that Hawksburg has an heir, someone to carry on should Aubrey meet with an unfortunate accident."

"Have you talked to Aubrey about this?"

"Not as yet. I thought it better to shield her from all this nonsense."

"And what of Randolf's nonsense?"

"The council is pushing me to resolve it sooner rather than later."

"They have a point," said Gerald. "Bodden's an important stronghold against Norland aggression."

"Norland is hardly in a position to threaten us these days."

"Why not put the matter to the Nobles Council?"

"I would if I believed we had enough votes to support Beverly's claim. Unfortunately, while we were liberating Weldwyn, the storm clouds were gathering at home."

"Meaning?"

"Opposition to my rule."

"I thought that would've stopped with the arrest of Stanton."

"So did I. We all believed he was behind the growing discontent against the Orcs, but it appears he was only one of the actors in this travesty of a play. Hayley was looking into it, but with all this nonsense over Bodden, I'm afraid she's had no time to dig deeper."

"Perhaps it's time to call in the experts?"

"You mean Arnim and Nikki? I was just thinking the same thing."

"I'll send word down to Haverston immediately."

"Good. Tell them I expect to see them by month's end."

"Shall I inform them of what you have in mind?"

"No details, but tell them it's a matter of great importance to the security of Merceria. That ought to pique their interest. And ensure you send a trusted messenger. I don't want word of this getting out."

"You could always send one of your couriers?"

Anna smiled. She'd hired retired warriors to carry messages and gather information when she was only a child. Originally, she'd intended to use them to broaden her understanding of the land and its people, but as the years went by, she relied on them more and more for accurate and timely information. "Very well," she said at last. "Find me Edgar Greenfield."

"I saw him recently," said Gerald. "He was drinking down at the Weasel."

"The Weasel? That doesn't sound like your usual haunt."

He chuckled. "It's not. I was there to talk to Sergeant Gardner."

"Oh? About what?"

"With Beverly moving up to fill her father's boots, I decided to make Captain Carlson's temporary position as commander more permanent."

"And you want Gardner to take over as Captain of the Wincaster Light Horse. Is that it?"

"It is."

"I believe him to be a good choice. The sergeant has always been a loyal servant of the Crown. He's also served under Beverly before."

"Yes, on multiple occasions," said Gerald. "And he certainly has the battle experience."

"Speaking of promotions, who do you want to take over Beverly's position as Commander of Horse?"

"That's easy—Lanaka."

"A bold choice," said Anna. "I doubt the Nobles Council will take kindly to the idea of a Kurathian leading our cavalry."

"Ah, but he's not Kurathian anymore, is he? You granted them land here, which makes them Mercerians now. He's also the new Earl of Tewsbury, so I doubt his fellow nobles would speak ill of him to his face. Besides, he's an outstanding choice to command our cavalry."

"I thought you'd pick Sir Heward or perhaps Sir Preston?"

"Both fine knights, I agree, but we need them to lead our heavier companies. Our light horsemen require the most attention right now, and Lanaka's best suited to undertake that responsibility."

"Then the Nobles Council can complain all they like. You're the Marshal of Merceria; it's entirely up to you who commands. Let me deal with any complaints from the nobles."

"Speaking of the council," said Gerald. "What have they been up to of late?"

"Very little, if I'm being honest. With the war finally over, most returned to their estates, the better to oversee their domains. That will all change soon enough, though. Once the spring planting is done, they'll all make their way back to Wincaster. Then, the real work begins."

He noted the look on her face and chuckled. "Come on, now. You relish it, don't you?"

"Honestly? Some days I'm more sympathetic to how things were under my predecessors." She paused a moment. "I don't mean that, of course. I'm just frustrated at our lack of progress."

"On what, Bodden?"

"Not only that. It seems as if we defeated Kythelia, and then everything just came to a halt. What I'd like to do is get to work making changes here in Merceria. We still have loads of archaic laws to rewrite, not to mention your army reforms."

"We'll get there in time," said Gerald. "You just have to be patient."

"Is that your advice for your queen?"

"No, for an old friend."

She smiled. "Then I shall take it to heart."

TWENTY

Proof

SPRING 967 MC

J ack Marlowe stared down at the document. "Are you absolutely certain about this?"

"I am," said Tulfar. "I took Bradford's statement myself. He confirmed Lord Godfrey ordered Mallory to open the gate. The Orc shaman, Kraloch, bore witness to the confession."

"This is pretty condemning. It could easily result in Godfrey's death."

"It's clear to me he deserves it. The only problem, as far as I see, is it doesn't do much to convict Lord James. He was, if you remember, our primary duty."

"I'm well aware," said Jack, "but we cannot overlook this evidence simply because it's outside our purview."

"What do you want to do about it?"

"Is Lord Godfrey still in our care?"

"I'm afraid not," said the Dwarf. "Arrangements were made for his release."

"And you allowed it?"

"I could hardly refuse! The Earls Council signed the letter authorizing his release."

"This gets more complicated by the day," said Jack.

"Perhaps we should've listened to Lady Lindsey and rendered a guilty verdict?"

"It's fine to say that now, but there was no actual proof of his crimes at the time. Ultimately, the Earls Council must bear the responsibility for Godfrey's release."

"They appointed us as members of the tribunal. Surely that grants us the authority to place him back into confinement?"

"Ordinarily, I'd agree," said Jack, "but it seems of late the council is more interested in their own gain than dealing out justice."

"You don't trust them?" asked Tulfar.

"No. In fact, I hate to admit it, but there's a real chance they'll end up pardoning him. Assuming they can't just hush up the entire story."

"You believe they'd do that?"

"Call it a gut instinct if you want, but I feel our new earls are eager to establish their authority."

"How well do you know them?" asked Tulfar.

"That's just it, I don't," replied Jack. "I've heard of them, but if you placed us all in the same room, I wouldn't be able to pick them out. You?"

"I spend most of my time back in Mirstone. It's only recently I've become more involved in the politics of Weldwyn."

"May I ask you a question?"

"Certainly," said the Dwarf.

"Do you support Alric's claim to the Throne?"

"Of course. Who else could possibly rule Weldwyn?"

"I'm with you on that," said Jack, "but others feel his youth is an obstacle."

"Nonsense. His Highness has extensive military experience, and his association with the Mercerians has helped him hone his diplomacy skills. He's well-suited to be king."

"If only all the earls saw him that way."

"I fear they're more interested in expanding their wealth and power instead of working for the kingdom's good."

"They're earls," said Jack. "The accumulation of wealth and power is precisely what keeps them going."

"I'm not arguing against that, but does that need to be done to the detriment of the realm?"

"Look. Even if Prince Alric becomes king, he'll still be required to deal with the earls."

"What if there was a better way?" said Tulfar. "What if all the nobles made up the council like they do in Merceria?"

"That would certainly complicate matters."

"Yes, but then we'd all have a say in how things are run."

Jack shook his head. "This isn't Merceria. The men of Weldwyn would never stand for it."

"And what about the Dwarves of Weldwyn, or the Elves, for that matter? Do we not get a say in how this land is ruled?" The Dwarf paused for a moment. "Think of yourself, Jack. Wouldn't you like to have a voice? Malin knows you fought enough for king and country to earn one."

"Our laws have stood for almost a thousand years."

"Then perhaps it's time they changed with the times. We don't live in villages anymore, Jack. We live in cities and send ships across the Sea of Storms. It's time to put the past behind us and move forward."

"And you believe granting all the nobles a voice on the Earls Council would do that?"

"I do," insisted Tulfar. "Look at it this way. You're close to Prince Alric. If he becomes king, you'd have his ear. Does that not amount to influence?"

"Yes, but I fail to see why that's a problem. A good king always surrounds himself with advisors."

"But shouldn't his subjects have a say? What if the Earls Council tripled the taxes on us Dwarves?"

"They would never do that," said Jack. "They need your mines."

"That's true of Alric, but no one can predict the future. What if, down the line, we get a king who loses his wits?"

"Then the Earls Council will remove him."

"Not if they benefit from his madness."

"What are you trying to suggest?"

"The earls could control a mad king. They would, in effect, become rulers of Weldwyn."

"But they're ruling now?"

"Precisely," said Tulfar. "Hence their need to avoid naming Alric the king."

"So, you're saying they're refusing to crown him just to hold on to power?"

"Exactly!"

"I suppose," said Jack, "a larger council would make it more difficult for a select few to seize power."

"That is precisely the point I was trying to make. Do you think His Highness would view it that way?"

"He's seen enough of the Mercerian court to understand the benefits. The only problem I can see is the earls' refusal to name him king."

"Will he fight them for the Crown?"

"That would mean civil war. I doubt he'd condone that."

"It wouldn't be much of a fight. The entire army stands behind him, and I'm sure the Mercerians would support his claim."

"They might," said Jack, "but let's hope it doesn't come to that. I'm not keen to witness the bloodshed a civil war would deliver upon our people, nor do I think he would."

"So that's it, then? We continue on the same way as we have for centuries?"

"I shall bring your concerns to His Highness, but I won't make any promises."

Tulfar nodded. "I can live with that. Thank you, Jack, for at least hearing me out."

"You're more than welcome. Now, let's get that warrant written out for the arrest of Godfrey Hammond, shall we?"

Lord Elgin slammed the door, then moved across the room, throwing himself into a chair.

"Problems, Your Grace?"

The voice startled him. "For Malin's sake, Godfrey, you almost scared the wits right out of me. What in the name of the Gods are you doing here? Don't you realize there's a warrant out for your arrest?"

"Oh, I know. That's why I came here. You and I are inextricably linked, Your Grace. If my head rolls, yours won't be far behind."

"Don't be ridiculous. I've done nothing treasonous, unlike yourself!"

"Haven't you? Might I remind you that YOU contacted me! Or had you forgotten you wanted Lochlan of Dungannon—how shall I put it? Oh yes. You wanted him to meet with an unfortunate accident. Something that I, with my contacts, was able to arrange."

"He's dead, then?"

"I have reports that say he was poisoned. Don't worry. It's untraceable."

"And the princess?"

"There is a slight chance that she, too, might succumb to the poison, but I doubt it'll come to that. I expect news of Lochlan's death will reach us any day now. It shouldn't take much longer for Princess Althea to return home after that."

"I paid your fee in full. What more can you possibly want?"

"I would see these charges against me dismissed."

"That is beyond my means. Perhaps you should try appealing to the tribunal?"

"Don't give me that," said Godfrey. "I'm a desperate man, Elgin, and desperate men do desperate things. If you can't clear my name, then you can at least get me to safety."

"And why would I do that?"

"Because if they catch me, I'll tell them everything."

"Everything? Who would believe you—a condemned traitor?"

"You might be surprised, especially when others can confirm my accusations."

The blood drained from Elgin's face. "What others?"

Lord Godfrey smiled. "Do you honestly believe I'd tell you? That would put them all in danger. Suffice it to say, if I'm brought to trial, all manner of trouble will come your way. The name of Lord Elgin Warford, Earl of Riversend, will forever be associated with treasonous acts."

"You wouldn't dare!"

"Wouldn't I? What have I got to lose? I'm already facing the death penalty, and an unpleasant one at that." He calmed his voice. "I have no desire to be drawn and quartered, Your Grace. Neither, I gather, do you? We've worked together in the past. Let us now forge a new alliance going forward?"

"I can't," said Elgin. "Not now, after all this treachery has been brought to light. It would be the end of me."

"The end of you? What about me? I'm the one facing an excruciating death. You, on the other hand, plotted murder. I suppose that means you'd get a quick beheading. Then again, your target was a royal by marriage, so perhaps it's treason after all?"

"Very well. I'll see you taken to safety."

Godfrey bowed. "There. That wasn't so hard, was it?"

"Where do you want me to send you?"

"Now that, my good fellow, is a very interesting question. Where, indeed? I thought of remaining in Weldwyn, but it's no longer safe for me here. To tell the truth, I doubt even the Mercerians would offer me a welcome."

"How about the Twelve Clans?"

"When I arranged the death of one of their chieftains? I think not!"

"Norland, then? Or a ship could take you to the Continent?"

"The Continent is likely to be far too foreign for the likes of me, but Norland has potential."

"You'd have to watch out for the Mercerians. They still maintain a large presence there."

Godfrey smiled. "Then I shall be sure to avoid the major cities. They might know my name, but I highly doubt anyone there knows my face."

"Then it's settled. I'll arrange a horse and supplies to see you on your way."

"I shall also require a purse to grow accustomed to a new lifestyle."

Elgin scowled. "Will a thousand crowns be sufficient?"

"Five might be better, but I'll settle for three."

"Three thousand crowns? Are you mad? I can't produce that amount out of thin air."

"That's not my concern. Give two-thirds of it to me in trade goods, if that's easier, but I won't flee Weldwyn empty-handed."

"Trade goods? I suppose you'll need a wagon as well?"

"Or a pack mule. Ideally, I'd like to take a boat upriver from Falford or, better yet, Almswell. There's less chance of discovery there."

"And then you'll leave me alone?"

"You have my word you'll hear no more of me once I'm safely ensconced in Norland."

"Very well. I shall do all within my power to make suitable arrangements. How can I contact you?"

"You won't," said Godfrey. "I'll contact you. Less chance of discovery that way. Oh, and that reminds me. You might be approached by an old Clansman named Camrath."

"To what end?"

"Why, for payment, of course. I promised him one thousand pieces of gold for the murder of Lochlan, the Clan Chief. By the way, don't even think about taking that out of my share."

"He's coming here?"

"Well, to the Amber Shard—that's where we were to rendezvous. I expect he'll be there sometime this week."

"And he is to wait there every day until I show up?"

"No, that would be ludicrous. I arranged to meet him at noon, so you need one of your men to visit the place each day at that time."

"How do you know I won't just kill the fellow?"

Godfrey shrugged. "If you want to eliminate him, then go ahead. It matters little to me."

Lord Dryden Wentworth, the new Earl of Loranguard, took his seat. "Good morning, gentlemen. I'm sorry I took so long to get here, but Loranguard was still reeling from the Clan invasion. I understand there are several matters requiring our immediate attention?"

"There are, indeed," said Lord Elgin. "Chief amongst them is the selection of the next king."

"But Prince Alric is to be crowned, surely?"

"Some of us feel he is not the best candidate?"

"Oh?" said Dryden.

"Do not mistake my concern for criticism. Alric is a fine warrior, but it takes more than battlefield prowess to rule over a kingdom."

"And by that, you mean?"

Elgin looked at his ally, Lord Beric, for support.

"Merely that he lacks courtly experience," added Beric.

"What absolute nonsense. He's been married to a queen for how long now?"

"Almost three years," offered Lord Oliver. "More than enough time to learn his way around a court. I'll say it again, Elgin; your argument has no merit."

"I would tend to agree," said Dryden, "but I'd like to hear Lord Julian's opinion on the matter."

"I support Alric's claim," said Julian. "Furthermore, I suggest we approve it immediately."

"Why the rush?" asked Elgin. "Surely another few weeks would make little difference?"

"I see no further reason for the delay," said Dryden. "Weldwyn is like a great ship, and it feels like no one is at the rudder. Without a king at the helm, gentlemen, we are wandering around aimlessly."

"Hardly that," said Elgin. "We are merely being cautious."

"You call it cautious," said Oliver. "I prefer the term stupid."

"Can we not act like civilized men?" said Dryden. "We're all here for the good of the kingdom. Let us put aside our differences and see what we can accomplish."

"Fine with me," said Lord Beric. "I shall be more than happy to accept the majority's decision."

"Coward," accused Elgin.

"How dare you!" shouted Beric.

"You gave me your word!"

"That was before the majority agreed to make a decision. You can't sit on the fence forever."

Elgin grew desperate. "You can't make Alric king."

"Why ever not?" asked Dryden.

"He is under the control of the Mercerians."

"We've heard all these arguments before," said Oliver. "Alric fought to liberate Weldwyn—he's his own man. Besides, who else has a claim to the Throne? The only other surviving members of the Royal Family are Althea and Edwina. One is married, and the other, a mage, excluding her from the line of succession. Unless you're suggesting Leofric begat a child out of wedlock? It wouldn't be the first time a king sired a bastard."

"No," said Elgin, "it wouldn't, but that's beside the point. Leofric has no bastards, as you are well aware. I have no doubt the man was an absolute paragon of faithfulness, but I recently came across news that might change everything."

"Come on, then," said Dryden. "Spit it out."

"I recently learned Lochlan, the Clan Chief of Dungannon, has died. That would make his widow, Princess Althea, available to be wed."

"But she cannot rule. She's a woman."

"True, but her husband could."

"You just told us her husband's dead. Surely you're not suggesting he will somehow come back to life?"

"Not at all," said Elgin, "but she can remarry."

"That would still make her husband second in line after Alric."

"Not if this august body believed her next husband was a more suitable choice for king."

"This is ridiculous," said Oliver. "Now you're just making things up to delay us even further. Tell me, what is it you're hoping to achieve?"

"I only suggest we not be hasty. The crowning of a king is a relatively rare event, and it behooves us to select the best possible candidate for the position."

"And we have," said Dryden. "But, for the sake of your peace of mind, let us now take a vote. All those in favour of Prince Alric as our new king?" He looked around the room.

Lords Julian and Oliver put their hands up right away. Lord Beric, initially opposed, raised his after a moment, along with Lord Dryden. Only Elgin's hand remained down.

"I'm sorry," said Dryden, "but the will of this council is that Alric, Prince of Weldwyn, shall be the next king."

Elgin rose. "You haven't heard the last of this."

"No. I don't suppose we have, but it's the end of any discussion on the matter for the moment. Now, how do we proceed?"

Lord Elgin stormed from the room.

"Typical," said Oliver. "Elgin doesn't like to lose."

"Ignore him," said Beric. "He'll come around to our way of thinking soon enough. Time to move on to other subjects."

"I couldn't agree more, but the next logical step is to inform His Highness of our decision."

"Very well. Let us do so immediately."

"May I have that honour?" asked Julian.

Dryden looked around the table. All nodded, save for the absent Elgin. "The majority of the council approves."

"Then I shall be off with all haste, the council permitting?"

Once more, they all nodded. Lord Julian rose with all the solemness he could manage, straightened his clothes, and then strode from the room, his head held high.

Dryden turned his attention to Beric. "You know Elgin best. Will he be a problem?"

"I hope not, but one can never be entirely sure what he's thinking."

TWENTY-ONE

Dragonweed

SPRING 967 MC

Lochlan squirmed, the sweat pouring off him in rivulets, soaking the bed, evidence of the battle raging inside his body.

Althea mopped his brow. "Lochlan?" she called out. "Listen to me. You must fight this."

"It's no use," said Mirala. "He can't hear you. Whatever is inside him is ravaging his mind and body."

"Is there nothing you can do?"

"I've done all I can to give him comfort, but without knowing the cause of it, there is little hope of a cure."

The older woman moved closer, taking the cloth. "I shall tend to him for a while. You need a break."

Althea left, stepping outside for a breath of fresh air. Spring was in full bloom, and summer would soon be upon them, but would Lochlan even live to see it?

Brogar appeared at her side. "Any improvement?"

"No," she replied. "He's been stuck in bed for days now, and still no sign of recovery."

"And Mirala?"

"Powerless unless we can determine the cause."

"I suspect he's been poisoned."

"Why would you think that?"

"In the short time I've known him, I've come to appreciate his sense of order."

"Meaning?"

"He has little variety in his diet and keeps to a daily schedule. He's disciplined in that way, a rare trait amongst the Clansfolk, or so I'm led to believe."

"How does that suggest poison?"

"I'm just saying, a man of regular habits is easy to poison. Everyone knows when he takes his meals."

"But we eat what Mirala prepares for us. Surely you're not suggesting she's responsible?"

"Then we must look elsewhere. What else did he spend his days doing?"

"You know that as well as I. Before he caught a cold, he was either overseeing the construction of the road or the building of the new library."

"Neither one of those suggests poison of any sort. Have you looked for marks on him? Perhaps a bite of some sort?"

"He displays none, and in any event, Mirala assures me there is nothing in these parts that has a venomous bite."

"We must be missing something," said Brogar. "What else does he do?"

"Read? But I have yet to hear of a poison administered by sight alone."

The Dwarf snapped his fingers. "That's it! Don't you see? He'd have to touch a book to turn the pages. Perhaps something in a book made him ill. A contact poison of some sort?"

"Is that even possible?" The colour fled from her face as everything fell into place. "The book of dragons. Camrath gave it to him as a gift. Malin's locks, Camrath must have poisoned him! But why?"

"Perhaps he was unaware of the poison?" suggested Brogar.

"He would've had to handle the book. How would he not also fall ill unless he knew and took precautions?"

"At this point, it's merely speculation. We don't know for sure that it's the book."

"True, but it's at least worth looking into."

"If it is the book, then we should take care handling it. Where is it?"

"Lochlan had it, but I put it back with the others as he grew sicker." She rushed off to the partially constructed library, her Dwarven bodyguard struggling to keep pace.

They'd packed Camrath's collection in crates, then covered them in oiled skins to keep them dry as the construction proceeded. Althea now tossed these aside, seeking her goal.

She soon found it, a hefty tome with an ornate depiction of a dragon carved into its leather-bound cover. She didn't touch it, merely stared at it as if it might give up its secrets. She grabbed one of the smaller skins, wrapped it around her hand, then lifted the book from its place of rest.

"Over here," said Brogar, moving a small crate to act as a table.

Althea laid it down, bending close to examine the cover. Satisfied nothing was amiss, she lifted a corner and opened the book, revealing the parchment pages within. "Camrath said it was a new translation."

"These pages indicate as much. They don't look nearly as old and worn as others I've seen." Brogar pulled out his dagger and handed it to her. "Here. Use this to flip the pages."

She turned three pages, then stopped. Before her lay a colourful image of a dragon, brightly inked in red, green, and blue. Of more interest, however, was the smear where someone, presumably Lochlan, had run his fingers over the scales depicted on the beast's back. "This must be it."

"This supports the idea of poison ink, but that still doesn't tell us what the poison is."

"No," said Althea, "but if Camrath created it, he must have got the idea from somewhere."

"Yes, but where?"

She cast her gaze around the room, finally settling on the crates. "Unless I miss my guess, I'd say the answer is likely in one of these books."

"Surely you're not suggesting we search them all?"

"Why not? Have you something better to do? Besides, the vast majority will have nothing to do with poisons." She moved closer, removing a lid and withdrawing a volume. "This one's called *A History of Sea Trade*. I doubt it has what we're looking for."

Brogar moved closer. "There are a lot of books in here. I suggest we start by making a list, and then we can divide them up and have people search through them."

"What people?" said Althea. "Most Clansfolk can't read."

"Aye, but you forget the Dwarves. Us mountain folk can all read. I suppose it comes from having such long lives compared to Humans."

"Yes, but can they all read the common tongue of Humans?"

"Of course. Our own language is used only for ceremonies. Most of us are also fluent in Orc."

"I find that surprising," said Althea.

"It shouldn't be. The Elder Races used to speak one language, but as the centuries passed, we each developed our own dialects. Dwarf and Orc changed the least, but Elvish... well, that's another matter entirely."

"You're saying I could learn Orcish?"

"Most certainly. I can teach you if you'd like."

"And Elvish?"

"I'm afraid that's not one I've mastered. Haldrim might be able to help you with that, although from what I recall, some intricacies of the language are difficult to master." He shook his head. "Who but the Elves would have twenty-seven words to describe a leaf?"

"But the same can be said of Dwarves," said Althea. "Take the word 'stone' for example?"

"Aye, that's true; I'll not deny it. I suppose it only makes sense, considering where we live. In any case, we're getting off topic. The important thing here is to take a tally of all these books."

"Yes, we'll organize them into piles, based on their subject matter. Once that's done, we'll hand out the books and have your people read through them, looking for anything that might help us." She chuckled. "I suppose we'll have to call it a book club."

Brogar frowned. "Why would you make a weapon out of a book?"

"No, the word 'club' refers to a group of people who gather, in this case, to discuss books. You see..." Her words trailed off, for the Dwarf was missing the point. "Never mind. It's not important."

Althea and the Dwarves spent hours searching through the books, but it soon looked like a colossal waste of time. She was almost ready to give up when Brogar called her over.

"I found it," said the Dwarf. "Or at least, I think I have." He waited until she stood over him before continuing. "There's a reference here to something called dragonweed."

"Never heard of it."

"Nor have I, but according to this description, it's so toxic it burns the skin on contact. It even describes how to boil it down to produce a lethal powder."

"Does it say what it looks like?"

"It has a red stem with leaves resembling the wings of dragons. Oh, I suppose that's why they call it dragonweed."

"Does it list a cure?"

"No," said Brogar.

"We should take this to Mirala—she knows plants. Perhaps she'll be more familiar with it?"

They rushed to Lochlan's side, where his cousin tended to the Clan Chief.

"We found it," said Althea, "or at least, we think we have. Are you familiar with something called dragonweed?"

"I am," she replied. "It grows all over the Clanholdings, but we teach our children to give it a wide berth."

"Why not burn it out?" asked Brogar.

"We tried that," said Mirala, "but the smoke from such a fire is noxious, even deadly."

Brogar held up the book. "According to this, you can turn it into a powder. A powder, I might add, that makes for a very lethal poison."

"That makes sense; if I recall, the symptoms match those of Lochlan's."

"And you never thought to mention this earlier?"

"Do you know how many plants there are in the Clanholdings? I can't remember them all!"

"Sorry. Nobody's blaming you for this," said Althea. "What we need to know, though, is whether you can cure him?"

Mirala's eyes flicked to Lochlan. "If dragonweed is the cause, it must be a weak dose."

"Camrath would have had to mix it with ink."

"That would explain it."

"Can you brew a cure?"

"I can certainly try. Keep an eye on him, Althea. I must go and find some plants."

"I'll help," said Brogar, "but you need to tell me what we're looking for."

They left in a hurry, leaving Althea alone with Lochlan. She picked up a ladle and brought water to his lips, dribbling it into his mouth. He lay there, thin and malnourished, clear evidence of his extended infirmity. She wondered if he would last long enough to benefit from Mirala's remedy.

Brogar watched as Mirala poured the mixture into a cup. She'd been at it all night, boiling a collection of weeds and flowers to produce a pasty mixture with a decidedly unpleasant odour. She added this to a weak tea and stirred it, checking every so often.

"I smell mint," said the Dwarf.

"That's the numbleaf in the tea."

"Numbleaf?"

"Yes."

"I thought that was for pain?"

"And so it is," said Mirala. "Dragonweed burns."

"But surely he has none left in him by now?"

"Dragonweed coats the stomach; that's why it's so effective as a poison. If we are to cure him, we must remove that residue."

"Remove it?"

"Yes. This concoction causes his stomach to revolt, pushing the contents upward, but it will burn along the way. The numbleaf is there to ease his pain."

"And that will cure him?"

"It will remove the toxins that imperil his life. After that, his body can mend itself."

"But he's so weak," warned the Dwarf.

"He has survived this long, which shows a remarkable will to live. With the dragonweed removed, there's nothing left to threaten his life."

"When will it be ready?"

Mirala lifted the spoon and examined it. "The paste is dissolved."

"Meaning?"

"It is complete." She lifted the cup. "Open that door for me, will you? I don't want to risk spilling any of this. It took me far too long to brew it."

Brogar rushed to open the door, then held it as Mirala made her way out into the cool night air. As soon as she passed, he rushed ahead to open the door to the Clan Chief's home.

Althea looked up as they entered, worry in her eyes.

"We have it," said Mirala. "Let us hope it isn't too late." She moved to stand over Lochlan. "Tilt his head up."

Brogar moved closer, using his strength to bring the patient into a sitting position, then Althea lifted his head. Mirala poured the brew down Lochlan's throat, pinching his nose to force him to swallow. Lochlan choked and sputtered, but Mirala kept at it until the cup was empty.

He started coughing in spasms, each louder and longer than the last, until a caustic, red bile spewed from his mouth, covering the bed and splattering onto Althea's clothing.

"Sorry," said Mirala. "I should have warned you about that."

"It matters not, so long as he recovers."

Brogar wrinkled his nose. "It stinks," he said, staring at the red discharge.

Mirala looked at Althea. "You need to be careful handling those clothes. Dragonweed can be very dangerous, even after it's been ingested."

"Should I burn them?"

"No!" said Brogar and Mirala at the same time.

"Bury them," added Mirala, "and bury them deep."

Althea returned from her errand just in time to see her husband coming around. Lochlan opened his eyes, struggling to focus. "Althea, is that you?"

"I'm here," she replied.

"What happened? Where am I?"

"You were poisoned, but Mirala found a cure."

"Poisoned?"

"Yes, by Camrath."

"No. It can't be!" He struggled to say more, but the strength left him. His eyes closed, and then his head went slack.

"He's exhausted," said Mirala. "Let him rest. I suspect he'll make a full recovery, but it will likely be a week or more before he's up and about again."

"That long?" said Althea.

"The poison no longer pains him, but he's weak. I suggest we start him on a weak broth and then work him up to solid food over the next few days."

"I can't thank you enough."

"Don't thank me. Your people identified the poison."

"Yes, but without your skills, it would have all been for naught. I shall not forget what you've done, nor will Lochlan, I'm sure."

Camrath nursed his ale. He'd arrived in Summersgate virtually unchallenged, save for a brief nod from the guards at the gate. Now he sat in the Amber Shard, waiting for his contact to arrive.

It was frustrating, for this was the third day in a row he'd sat here while the bells tolled noon. Three days in which he could've been enjoying the wonders of this magnificent city!

His eyes dropped to his ale. The dark-hued drink was a wonder to behold and far tastier than anything the Twelve Clans ever offered. He would enjoy life in the Weldwyn capital, of that he was sure, but if he didn't get the rest of his reward soon, he'd run out of funds.

The Amber Shard was quiet this time of day; aside from himself, there were only three other patrons. He wondered how such a place could survive but decided it must grow busier later in the day.

A clean-shaven man with close-cropped hair entered, halting in the doorway to scan the room before moving towards one of the tables, where he said something Camrath couldn't hear. Plainly, the answer wasn't to the fellow's liking, for he moved farther into the room, drawing closer to the scholar. Could this be the contact he'd been waiting for?

"Are you Camrath?" the fellow asked.

"Aye, that's me. And you are?"

The stranger grinned. "It's better for you if you don't know. Tell me, was your affair in the Clanholdings carried through to a successful conclusion?"

"It most certainly was. Have you my payment?"

The man looked around the room before meeting Camrath's gaze. "May I sit?"

"Of course."

The fellow sat, then lowered his voice. "The payment is here," he said, patting his vest, "but it would be better to pass it along somewhere more private, where prying eyes can't see us. You understand?"

"I do. I do, indeed." Camrath scanned the room, his gaze settling on a door opposite the entrance. "Might I suggest the alleyway out back?"

"An excellent idea."

They both stood, the scholar leading the way. He pulled open the door and stepped into the alleyway, turning to face his new acquaintance.

"I'm afraid this is all new to me," said Camrath. "Is this how you normally conduct such business?"

"It is. Don't worry. I have your reward, but if someone in there had seen me give you a large purse, you would, no doubt, be set upon by thieves as soon as you left the place."

The scholar's eyes widened at the thought of so many coins, but then his common sense took hold. "Here, now. You couldn't possibly be carrying that much."

The fellow merely smiled, then the dagger went deep, not from the front, as Camrath had feared, but from behind. He'd been so concerned that this man was out to double-cross him that he'd completely neglected to consider he might have an accomplice!

The old Clansman crumpled to the ground. The clean-shaven man moved to stand over the body, watching the growing pool of blood with fascination. "That was neatly done."

"Thank you," replied the knife wielder. "I pride myself on being professional."

"And now?"

"Search him."

"What for?"

"For anything of value."

"He looks to have little of any worth."

"True," replied the assassin, "but we want to make it look like a mugging gone bad. If we leave him with anything, it will look suspicious."

"And a dead body won't?"

"You worry too much, my friend. Take a good look at him, and tell me what you see?"

"And old man, nothing more."

"Then you're blind."

"Pardon me?"

"Here lies the body of a Clansman, and an old one at that. Do you imagine anyone will take any interest in a dead foreigner?"

"No. I suppose not."

"Good. Now, let's go get a drink, shall we? I've worked up a mighty thirst."

TWENTY-TWO

Discovery

SPRING 967 MC

G erald speared a sausage and was about to bite off the end when Anna entered the room.

"It's just as I suspected!" she exclaimed before throwing herself into a seat, with a triumphant look.

"What is?" he replied.

"The ring that was supposed to belong to Lord Edward."

"Supposed to? Whatever do you mean?"

"It's a forgery, though admittedly, a clever one."

"What makes you say that?"

"I went to the archives," said Anna. "Saxnor knows there are enough of Lord Edward's messages down there to find a good example of his seal."

"So that's where you've been. What made you think of that?"

"I was reflecting on what Hayley said. If Sir Randolf lied about his namesake, it stands to reason everything else is a falsehood."

"Sir Randolf of Burrstoke is very old," said Gerald. "Perhaps his memory is simply failing?"

"Nonsense," she replied. "He's only slightly older than you." She grinned. "Unless you're admitting to forgetting things as well?"

"No, of course not."

"Well then, I'll take the word of a Mercerian knight over a foreigner any day."

"But Randolf is a Knight of the Sword."

"Which Randolf?"

"Both," said Gerald.

"Yes, but our pretender spent a lot of time in Norland. I'm beginning to think this was all a plot from Lord Hollis."

"But he died in the war."

"Yes, but I believe he put all these pieces into motion."

"Just out of curiosity, what leads you to think the ring is a forgery?"

"The last few letters from Lord Edward showed a flaw in his ring, as if it had been damaged. Here, let me show you." She produced a scroll she'd tucked up her sleeve, laying it out on the table, then using some cups to weigh down the corners. "Look at the seal and tell me what you see."

Gerald leaned in close. "My eyes aren't what they used to be, but I'd say it's a coat of arms."

"It is," said Anna, "but around it is the shape of a shield, yes?"

"Yes, what of it? From what I've seen, it's a common enough affectation."

"Yes, but note the edges of the shield. See how there's a slight cut through the one side?"

"What does that mean?"

"It means the seal was damaged slightly."

"How?"

"I don't know," said Anna. "Perhaps it was an accident, but it doesn't matter." She pulled forth another parchment, this time from her other sleeve. "Now, look at this and tell me what you think?"

Gerald bent to the task, drawing a candle closer to see more clearly. "There's no damage."

"Precisely. Now, that stamp is from what I'll call the Norland ring. This other," she said, pointing at the original document, "was written only two days before his death. The forgery is a good one, I'll give you that, but as far as I know, there's no such thing as a self-repairing ring!"

"So that proves the ring is a fake. Will that be enough to convince a court?"

"I hope so, but it still doesn't prove Lord Edward wasn't in Beaconsgate."

"You said the forgery was good," said Gerald. "What I'd like to know is how they pulled it off. Wouldn't they have needed access to his ring to copy it?"

"Yes, or any letter he sealed over the years. They could have created the ring after the fact, even years after his death."

"So, someone had to secure access to the royal archives?"

"One would presume so. We now limit access to those records, but my predecessors took no such precautions."

"Could Randolf have been the one to do it? We know he was made a Knight of the Sword during Andred's reign."

"It's possible," she replied. "But it's just as likely Sir Randolf is being used by others, in which case there's something else going on."

"What are you suggesting? That he's not the villain in this?"

"Consider this," said Anna. "Lord Hollis hated the Fitzwilliams for years, decades, even. Eventually, he learns of Lord Edward's death, specifically how he died. Knowing the body could never be recovered, he sets out to cause as much distress to the family as he can. He concocts a story about Lord Edward surviving, then finds a woman somewhere who can claim Lord Edward fathered her children. Maybe the woman was in on it, and maybe she wasn't."

"Hold on a moment," said Gerald. "How could a woman not know who fathered her children?"

"Ah, but he was supposedly using an assumed name, don't you see? According to Hayley, the body belonged to someone named Edward Blackburn. I imagine Lord Hollis employed him."

"But Randolf said Lord Edward eventually succumbed to his wounds, didn't he?"

"That's the story, but we don't know that's the truth. What if Hollis had the man murdered? Randolf was only a child at the time, so he wouldn't remember much."

"I suppose the mother could've been in on it too," offered Gerald. "But Dame Celia claimed Bodden was hers, so she must have known."

"There's also the matter of Randolf appearing shortly after the death of Lord Richard."

"Yes. How do you account for that?"

"I think he was waiting."

"Waiting? But we didn't even know Fitz was ill?"

"True, but he was old, and unlike you, he didn't have a Life Mage using a spell of regeneration on him from time to time."

"So Randolf waited for word of Fitz's death?"

"I imagine he was already in Bodden," said Anna. "Ever since we opened up the Queenston road, trade has been booming. It would've been easy enough for him to enter Bodden without being recognized."

"But Fitz knew everyone."

"Correction. He used to know everyone, but in the last year or so before his death, Bodden almost doubled in size. Even a man of his calibre can't keep track of everybody, and truthfully, during the war, he spent more time in Wincaster than Bodden."

"Your argument makes sense," said Gerald. "And if Randolf was in Bodden all that time, somebody has had to have seen him. What troubles me, though, is who's behind this entire endeavour. Hollis might have started it, but then someone would've had to take over after his death. Lord Asher, perhaps?"

"I don't favour Asher," said Anna. "He might be involved, but he's too young to be the mastermind behind this."

"Then who?"

"I fear it'll be some time before we can answer that."

Gerald scowled. "Not more of Kythelia's work?"

"No. At least, I don't believe so. Elves look at the long-term. This feels a little more rushed."

"Rushed? It's been thirty years!"

"Yes, but they think in centuries."

"Then the Twelve Clans?"

"I doubt it. We're far too distant to be a threat to them."

"We did help defeat them."

"Yes," said Anna, "but somebody put this plot in motion years ago, and it had to be someone familiar with the situation in Bodden. I know everything points at Hollis, but I can't quite believe it was his idea. His men raided Bodden for years, even sieged it, proving he preferred a blunter approach."

"Perhaps we'd be better served to consider who would benefit the most from this situation. Norland, perhaps?"

"No, not after we defeated them. The earls who survived were allied with us, not against us. We even let them select their queen, despite our own misgivings."

"Well, it certainly wouldn't be Weldwyn; that only leaves the Twelve Clans."

"Not quite."

"What are you suggesting?" asked Gerald.

"You just gave orders sending Beverly east."

"That's right, to face down the Halvarians. Surely you don't believe they're behind all this?"

"It's a distinct possibility. By now, they probably realize we're allied with the Dwarves of Ironcliff, not to mention Stonecastle. They likely see us as a threat."

"I can understand that," said Gerald, "but this whole Bodden affair has been in the works for years? Are you suggesting they've had agents in Merceria all along?"

"Think about this from their point of view," said Anna. "From the Dwarves of Ironcliff, we know Halvaria is expansionist. Herdwin and Kasri's experience only confirms it."

"Yes, but they stopped them in the passes."

"Also true, yet it's in their best interests to keep Merceria busy with internal matters."

"Not another civil war?"

"I doubt it would come to that," said Anna, "but consider all the troubles we've had of late. We thought Lord Alexander orchestrated the backlash against the Orcs, but removing him from power has changed nothing."

"But he confessed to his part in it."

"He did, and I have no doubt he encouraged it, if only to act in opposition to my rule, but whoever is behind this has far more resources than him."

"What makes you say that?"

"The unease is growing. Every city in Merceria now has people clamouring for the Orcs to leave, save for Hawksburg."

"How do we fight that?"

"That's the problem, isn't it? King Andred would have sent warriors to keep the peace, and I suspect that was the intention behind all this."

"Yes," said Gerald. "Effectively spreading our army out over the countryside instead of letting us mass it to repel an attack. But where would an attack come from? They can't come through the passes near Stonecastle. They tried that already."

"They'll attack near Ironcliff, either that or by sea."

"By sea?"

"If they're as large as I believe they are, they're on the Sea of Storms. And if the Kurathians can sail from their islands to invade Weldwyn, I doubt the Halvarians will be scared off."

"Well," said Gerald. "If they do attack from the sea, there's only one place for them to land."

"Yes, Trollden. I feel it prudent to dispatch additional warriors, don't you?"

"Most definitely. I'll write the orders this very day." He sighed. "You know, it would've been nice to have some peace and quiet for a change. It feels like all we've done the last few years is fight war after war."

"I know what you mean," said Anna. "I hoped Kythelia's death would end such strife, but it appears we are not so lucky."

"You should let Alric know. If a seaborne invasion is possible, then Weldwyn is at risk, perhaps even more so than us. Have you any word regarding his ascension to the Throne?"

"Not as yet," she replied, "but I expect the Earls Council to make an announcement any day now. I arranged for a mage to always be present at the Dome, so we can get word back here as quickly as possible, but it's stretching us thin."

"Agreed. We need Aubrey to get her conservatory up and running as soon as possible. Any news on that front?"

"It's ongoing."

"Well," said Edwina. "It looks like this place has seen better days."

Aubrey surveyed the old Royal Estate, located northwest of Hawksburg, astride the Wickfield road. "Looks can be deceiving," she replied. "The outside may be a little rough around the edges, but I assure you the inside has been the object of much attention these last few months."

"And this is yours?"

"It was a gift from the queen. She was born here, you know."

"Really?" said Edwina. "I assumed she was born in Wincaster."

"The estate used to be a favourite of her mother."

"Yet the exterior leads one to believe it has been dormant for some time. Any idea why?"

"I'm afraid not."

"It's haunted," offered Clara.

Aubrey regarded her newest student. "Why in the name of Saxnor would you say that?"

The young woman shrugged. "Everyone knows the stories." She looked at her companions, seeking their support, but Durwin chose that moment to stare off into nothingness rather than add to her claim, and the two Orcs, Kurzak and Gurza, had no idea what she was talking about.

"I can assure you, it's not," said Aubrey. "I spent my entire childhood in Hawksburg. I would've known about it if there were ghosts here."

Clara looked at her feet. "I was only repeating what I heard."

"Which is?" She noticed her student's reticence. "Come now. You'll never make a decent mage if you can't speak up for yourself."

"The old folks say, years ago, the ghost of an old woman roamed these parts."

"How many years ago?"

"I'm not sure, but the man I heard it from was ancient, and he claimed his father witnessed the ghost first-hand."

"Ancient?"

"Yes. At least as old as the Marshal of Merceria."

The young woman's statement made Aubrey pause. Her great-grandmother had been a Life Mage, and she must have learned to walk amongst spirits because the spell was in her book of magic. Aubrey remembered the first time she cast the spell in the queen's presence. On that occasion, her dog, Tempus, reacted as if he could see them. Could the same be said of some Humans? A cough brought her attention back to her students.

"Is that important?" said Clara.

"Sorry. My mind was elsewhere. What were you saying?"

"That the person relating the tale was old."

"Oh yes. This is, however, a discussion best left for another day."

Durwin chose this moment to speak up. "Are you suggesting that ghosts are real? I thought you said they weren't?"

"I said no such thing," replied Aubrey. "I merely indicated there were no ghosts here, at the estate."

"So ghosts ARE real?"

"A ghost is nothing more than a spirit, and we know Orc shamans communicate regularly with them."

Durwin face went white. "I wish I'd known that before I took up the life of a mage."

"What are you complaining about?" said Clara. "You're to be trained as an Earth Mage, hardly the sort of thing that involves ghosts."

"We have visitors," said Edwina, nodding towards the gate.

Aubrey smiled. "It's Albreda."

"Greetings," called out the Druid. "I hope you don't mind, but I brought Aldus Hearn with me. I thought we might be of use."

Her companion cleared his throat. "Are these the new students?"

"They are, indeed," said Aubrey. "Shall I introduce them?"

"If you would be so kind."

"This is Edwina," she began. "She possesses the potential to learn Air Magic, though how we are to accomplish that is beyond me."

"Ah yes," said Albreda. "The Princess of Weldwyn. I've heard all about you."

"Nothing bad, I hope?" said Edwina.

The Mistress of the Whitewood said nothing, favouring her with a slight smile.

"This is Clara," continued Aubrey. "She'll eventually learn Life Magic, but we must get her through the basics first."

"And this one?" asked Aldus.

"Durwin. According to my spell, he should prove capable of using the magic of the earth."

"Indeed? I would never have guessed that. You appear to be more of a city dweller."

"I am," said Durwin. "I was born and raised in Wincaster."

"Wincaster, you say? How curious." Hearn turned to Aubrey. "How in Saxnor's name did you find him?"

"He was serving in the garrison here at Hawksburg."

"That's right," he added. "I joined the army when Norland invaded. When Lady Aubrey cast her spell, I just happened to be close by."

"How convenient," said Albreda. "And these other two?"

"This is Kurzak," replied Aubrey. "An Orc of the Black Arrows. His tribe's been helping rebuild Hawksburg since the civil war. I believe he'll be able to use Fire Magic. Finally, we have Gurza—she's a member of the Black Ravens and shows strong potential to be an Earth Mage."

"The Black Ravens, you say? I'm surprised you didn't learn from Kharzug. He is, after all, a master of earth."

"He is too busy," replied Gurza, "and already has a student."

Albreda returned her attention to Aubrey. "And you're absolutely sure they all have the potential to use magic?"

"Yes. I developed a spell I call 'detect magical potential.'"

"I'm glad you've expanded your capabilities, but you might want to reconsider the name. It lacks a certain finesse."

"Would you care for a demonstration?"

"No," said Albreda. "Your word is good enough for me."

"How are we to begin training these people?" asked Hearn. "Have you a course of study in mind? It seems to me having them learn the magical alphabet is the most logical method."

"Actually," said Albreda. "I think we should adopt a more pragmatic approach."

"Here we go," said Hearn. "Pushing back against the established methods again."

"Hush now. Let me finish. I suggest we use the methods favoured by the Orcs."

"Which are?"

"We teach them a basic spell right from the start—the orb of light, for example. It only requires a short incantation: two words, to be exact."

"Nonsense," said Hearn. "They need the discipline of a traditional approach."

"That would take years. Why, I wager I could have Gurza casting magic by week's end."

"That is a dangerous approach."

"Yet the Orcs have been doing it for generations. Of course, it's entirely up to Aubrey. After all, it is her conservatory—"

"Hold on!" said Aubrey, interrupting their argument. "You two clearly have strong opinions on the matter, but I've already decided how to proceed. I've had quite a few discussions with Kraloch on the matter, and we both agreed the best way to do so is just as Albreda suggests. And since the orb of light is a universal spell, we can teach it to all students simultaneously."

"There," said Albreda. "A most sensible approach. Is Master Kraloch to join us?"

"Eventually, but he's needed in Summersgate for now. The queen wants a mage on call there at all times for relaying important messages."

"I'm surprised she didn't use Aegryth. She is, after all, from Weldwyn."

"She did, but Aegryth is in Wincaster at the moment, ready to travel in the other direction as needed."

"I can see we need a lot more mages," said Hearn. "Especially with all these magic circles the queen has planned. What about Master Bloom?"

"Revi arrives this evening, along with some additional staff, to help run the place."

"Staff?"

"Yes. Servants, not instructors. I thought it best the students concentrate on their studies, especially considering our urgent need."

"And how many instructors can we count on, long-term?"

"Apart from us? There's Kraloch and Revi, of course, and Osbourne Megantis, the Weldwyn Fire Mage, has agreed to lend his expertise in a limited capacity, as has Aegryth."

"What of Gretchen Harwell and that Kurathian fellow?"

"You mean Kiren-Jool? They're both Enchanters and are willing to help, but until we find someone capable of using enchantments, they'll be of limited use."

"And what of our young Air Mage here?" said Albreda. "Who is to train her?"

"We'll teach her the universal spells."

"And the Air Magic?"

"I'm working on it."

"Which means?" asked Hearn.

"Kraloch contacted several Orc shamans and located a master of air named Rotuk, but he's far to the east. He has, however, agreed to act as an advisor, though obviously a distant one."

"Excellent," said Albreda. "When do we start?"

TWENTY-THREE

The Prince

SPRING 967 MC

L ord Julian stood perfectly still as the Orc, Kraloch, called forth his magic power. The Dome's casting circle glowed, and then a cylinder of light shot upward, blocking the view of the room. Moments later, it dropped, revealing a completely different chamber.

"We are here," said Kraloch. "Within the walls of the Royal Palace in Wincaster." He moved to the door, opening it to reveal a pair of well-armed guards. "I bring Lord Julian Lanford, Earl of Falford, to see His Highness, Prince Alric." The guards nodded, then returned to their posts beside the door.

Surprised by the Orc's easy manner with the Royal Guards, Lord Julian followed along, unsure of what to make of things. They went down several hallways before arriving at a doorway, where another pair of guards, bearing the Royal Coat of Arms of Weldwyn, stood.

The one on the right opened the door and peered in. "Lord Julian to see you, Highness."

"Show him in," came the reply.

The earl entered, bowing deeply, then noted the Mercerian marshal's presence.

"Is there a reason for your visit, Your Grace?" asked Alric.

"My pardon, Highness. I bring news from Summersgate."

"Ah, finally. What is it?"

Lord Julian eyed Gerald.

"For Malin's sake, out with it, man," said Alric. "You can trust the marshal."

"The Earls Council has rendered its decision. I am honoured to inform you we've officially recognized your claim to the Throne of Weldwyn."

Alric turned to the marshal. "Typical. I spend months in Summersgate waiting for a decision, and the moment I leave, they make up their minds!"

"When is the ceremony to be held?" asked Gerald.

"That's an excellent question." The prince looked at the earl. "Well?"

"The Earls Council formally requests the presence of Your Highness in Summersgate so we can make the necessary arrangements. There are also legal matters to attend to."

"Such as?"

"Naming of your heir, the status to be confirmed upon your wife, that sort of thing."

"My wife is already a queen."

"Of Merceria, yes, but her status in Weldwyn has yet to be determined. It is, admittedly, a complex situation in which we find ourselves. Never before has a King of Weldwyn married a foreign queen."

"Thankfully, this will be the last time we need to worry about that."

"Why would you say that?" asked the earl.

"My son, Braedon, will eventually become king of both Weldwyn and Merceria."

The earl paled. "Oh dear. I hadn't considered that."

"You make it sound like a bad thing. I always believed it was a good thing. How about you, Gerald?"

"I'm in complete agreement with you, Highness, although I can see where that might cause some difficulties, at least in the beginning. After all, the laws of Weldwyn and Merceria differ considerably in many areas."

Lord Julian fumbled for a response. "Surely you're not suggesting we adopt the ways of Merceria?"

"That will be my son's decision," said Alric, "not mine. In any case, I'm looking forward to growing old, so that won't be for some years yet."

The earl breathed a sigh of relief. "Might I ask, Highness, when would you be able to return to Summersgate?"

"I have several matters to attend to here, first."

"I thought you'd wish to return as soon as possible?"

"As I said, there are things requiring my attention. However, once Master Kraloch recovers, he can return you to Summersgate." He looked at the Orc. "I trust you'll be fully recovered by morning?"

"I will."

"Good. In that case, I'll have someone see you to the guest quarters, Lord Julian. May we expect you at dinner? I'm sure my wife, the queen, would like to pay her respects?"

The earl bowed. "It would be my pleasure, Your Highness."

"Nash!" bellowed the prince.

The door opened, revealing one of the guards. "Yes, Highness?"

"Escort Lord Julian to the guest quarters, will you? And then inform Her Majesty the earl will be joining us for dinner."

"Yes, Highness." The guard locked eyes with the earl. "This way, Your Grace."

Alric turned to Gerald. "You'll join us, of course."

"I assume I can bring Lady Jane?"

"Of course. The more, the merrier." He suddenly froze. "Oh dear."

"Is there a problem?"

"It just occurred to me they've charged Lady Jane's son with treason. I wonder how Lord Julian will take her presence at dinner?"

"Perhaps I shouldn't invite her?" said Gerald.

"No, don't be ridiculous. In any case, I'm sure Anna would prefer the two of you there rather than Lord Julian. He can always leave if he disapproves of her presence."

"I don't want to get you into trouble with the Earls Council. Saxnor knows they've given you enough trouble already."

"You leave the Earls Council to me."

"Speaking of which," said Gerald. "I heard the Dwarves were pushing for representation."

"They were."

"And?"

"And what? It wouldn't be the first time someone asked to sit on the council, and I very much doubt it will be the last."

"So, you mean to ignore them?"

"Not at all," said Alric. "But there's little I can do until I'm crowned."

"And then?"

The prince merely smiled. "Let's take this one day at a time, shall we?"

Gerald reached out and stabbed a slice of meat, placing it on his plate, an action drawing the attention of Lord Julian, who managed little more than an incredulous stare.

"He certainly likes his beef," said the queen. "Have you tried any yourself, Your Grace?"

"I'll admit it's a little rare for my taste. The duck, however, is magnificent. Wherever did your cook come up with the idea for this delicious sauce?"

The queen smiled. "It's a Norland recipe."

"Yes," added Gerald. "They smother everything in sauce up there. It's quite nice once you get used to it. Alric was telling me this is your first time outside of Weldwyn. How do you like it so far?"

"I'll admit it takes a little getting used to, but for the most part, the people I've met are not so different from those back home. One thing I do find confusing, however, is the difference in courtly etiquette."

"How so?" asked the queen.

"The Weldwyn court is much stricter. That is to say, more methodical."

"He means stuffy," offered Alric. "I'd been complaining about that exact thing to my father for years, but he wouldn't listen."

"We have our moments," said Anna, "but by and large, we're far less formal unless the occasion demands it. Did King Leofric not eat with his family?"

"Rarely, as far as I know," said the earl. "Although His Highness might be able to shed more light on the matter."

Alric, caught with a mouthful of food, struggled to swallow. He took a sip of wine to wash it down, then turned his attention to his wife. "It's true, for the most part. He ensured we ate together at least once a week, sometimes more if he could arrange it, but he was a very busy man. He was usually up long before me and had already eaten by the time Mother woke up."

"And did he eat by himself?"

"Most of the time, though Lord Weldridge occasionally accompanied him. Those two were thick as thieves."

The earl cheeks grew red. "I hardly consider that term appropriate to a member of the Royal Household, Your Highness. Do you?"

"I meant no disrespect to my father." Alric turned to Anna. "Would it offend you if I said you and Gerald were thick as thieves?"

She chuckled. "No, of course not. Then again, I know you say it with good intentions."

"As I do in my father's case. So, you see, Lord Julian, I am not suggesting anything unsavoury."

"Of course, Highness. My apologies if I misunderstood."

"Just out of curiosity, how close was the vote?"

"The vote?"

"Yes, to offer me the Crown. I suspect it was not unanimous."

"I regret to say you have the truth of it," said the earl. "In fact, until Lord Dryden claimed his seat, it was split right down the middle. It wasn't that we don't respect you, Your Highness, but some felt you lacked experience at court."

"But you weren't amongst them, Lord Julian?"

"I'm pleased to say I was not. I was in favour of your immediate assumption of the Crown. I regret it took us so long to decide the matter, but Lord Elgin refused to budge. Lord Beric was just as bad, but in the end, he finally came round to our way of thinking."

"And Lord Elgin?"

"I hate to admit it, but he's not happy with our decision. At least it's all over and done now."

"He still believes me too young?"

"I don't wish to speak ill of the man, but I believe he coveted the Throne for himself."

"I don't really know Lord Elgin," said Alric. "I never saw him at court while I was there."

"Lord Elgin is the second son of Lord Thomas of Riversend. He only assumed the title after the death of his brother at the hands of the Twelve Clans. As such, he spent most of his time at his father's estate."

"Tell me what you make of the fellow?"

"I'm not sure I'm the best person to speak of such things."

"I'll be leaning heavily on the Earls Council in the future and need to know who I'm working with."

Lord Julian nodded. "Yes, I suppose that's true. Very well. I'll give you my impression, though I must warn you it's purely from a political point of view."

"I would have it no other way."

"Lord Elgin believes it's important to maintain our customs and history."

"Meaning he doesn't like the idea of change?"

"Precisely. He's also a man who enjoys his creature comforts."

"There's nothing inherently wrong with that," offered Gerald. "I like to put my feet up every once in a while."

"I think he means to the exclusion of others," said Alric. "Did I get that right?"

"Indeed, Highness," said the earl. "He is also unforgiving where others are concerned."

"Unforgiving? Are you trying to tell me he bears a grudge?"

"That's a polite way of putting it, yes. He was quite upset that he and I didn't see eye to eye where the matter of the Crown was concerned. In fact, he stormed out of the meeting when we decided to offer you the Throne."

"So, he now stands in direct opposition to my rule?"

"I'm sure he'll come around eventually," said Lord Julian.

A servant entered, moving directly to whisper in the queen's ear.

"Are you sure?" she asked.

"Yes, Majesty. She's waiting outside."

"Then send her in." The queen turned to her guests. "You must excuse the interruption, gentlemen, but Aegryth has come on a matter of great importance."

"Aegryth?" said Gerald. "But I thought she returned to the Dome to take the place of Kraloch."

"She did, but she carries news she says can't wait."

The Earth Mage entered, bowing to the queen. "My pardon for the interruption, Majesty, but I come bearing important news for His Highness."

"Then speak," said Alric.

"We've received word Lochlan's been poisoned, Highness."

"And my sister?"

"Is well. She dispatched riders after her husband took ill."

"Is he dead?"

"We await further details, but it sounds bad. The Twelve Clans are not known for having healers."

"That's strange," said Lord Julian. "Elgin said he'd heard a rumour that Lochlan was dead.

"And you didn't see fit to tell me?" Alric's knuckles turned white as he clenched his knife.

"We took it for idle gossip, Highness, but maybe there's some truth to it after all?"

"I must go to her," said Alric.

"If Lochlan has been poisoned," replied Aegryth, "there is little we can do about it now."

"I cannot leave my sister amongst the Twelve Clans. Without Lochlan, her influence over them collapses. Are you sure there are no further communications?"

"I'm afraid not," said Aegryth. "Word was sent back to Dungannon requesting more information, but it will be some time, likely weeks, before we know more."

Alric slammed his fist on the table. "I knew it was a bad idea to let her go west. Now her life is in danger!"

"She has the Dragon Company to protect her," soothed Anna.

"Against poison?"

"I doubt she was the intended target. From what I've learned of the Twelve Clans, they often fight amongst themselves, but I doubt they're foolish enough to hurt Althea. That would mean war with Weldwyn, and they haven't had enough time to recover from the last one."

"A good point," said Gerald. "I would also remind you Althea sent the message in the first place. Had she been injured in any way, I'm sure the messenger would have relayed that information."

"Yes," said Alric. "You're right. I should have thought of that."

"You're upset," offered the queen, "and I doubt I would've acted any different, given the circumstances. What if we send one of our mages to Dungannon? They could at least use the spell of recall to bring Althea back?"

"A good idea, although perhaps I should wait until we receive further news. I'd hate to send someone there only to find everything's fine."

"If someone poisoned Lochlan, they could be trying to cause friction between Weldwyn and the Twelve Clans."

"I doubt the death of a Clan Chief would cause a war," said Alric. "And in any case, the Clans are hardly in a position to attack us after the drubbing they took."

"What would you like me to do?" asked Aegryth. "Should I return to Summersgate or remain here in Wincaster?"

"Stay here for the moment. Rest up tonight, and you can recall back to the Dome in the morning. Kraloch will remain here, but I expect to see you if there's any news regarding my sister."

"Of course, Your Highness," replied the mage. "With your permission, I shall retire for the evening to recover my strength."

"By all means," said the prince.

Lord Julian waited for Aegryth to leave before turning to his future king. "And when will you be joining us to plan your coronation, Highness?"

"Alric," said the queen, "would you like some assistance with that?"

"You have far too much to do here, my dear. Don't worry. We'll send word once we're in planning mode for the coronation."

"We will?" said Lord Julian.

"Of course. As my wife and the future Queen of Weldwyn, she'll be an important part of the ceremony. She's also the most capable planner I know."

Gerald laughed.

The earl stared at him in disbelief. "You find something amusing, Your Grace?"

"I've yet to see Anna refuse the chance to plan something."

"You mean Her Majesty, surely?"

"Gerald is permitted to use my given name in private," said the queen. "And I consider this dinner a family affair."

Lord Julian shook his head. "Please don't take this the wrong way, but you Mercerians have such strange customs."

. . .

Later that evening, Gerald sat by the fire, warming his feet as he was wont to do most nights. Jane entered, bringing a smile to his face.

"I thought you might like something to drink," she said, handing over a tankard.

"Thank you. That was very kind of you. Won't you join me?"

"That depends. Are you in a good mood or sour?"

He chuckled. "Good, for the most part. Why? Is there something I should be upset about?"

"I just received word the Viscount of Aynsbury wishes to speak with me."

"Again? I thought he'd wrung every bit of the story out of you last time."

"It appears there's been a bit of a development. Lord Godfrey has disappeared."

"Wasn't he in custody?" asked Gerald.

"And so he was, but somehow he arranged his release based on the promise he'd remain in Summersgate. They now believe he's attempting to flee the country."

"Well, he'll find no sanctuary here. What has this to do with you?"

"Lord Jack feels I may have some idea where Godfrey might go."

"Why would he suggest that?"

"He was a close confidant of my son."

"Then why doesn't he talk to James?"

"I imagine he already has," said Jane.

"I think he's clutching at straws."

"Likely, but I must do my part to bring him to justice."

"Why? You owe him nothing."

"To assuage the guilt darkening my soul. My son is a traitor, Gerald, and if it hadn't been for you, I would be rotting away in a dungeon with a sentence of death hanging over my head too."

He reached out and took her hand. "What can I do to help?"

"I must travel to Summersgate and do all I can to locate Lord Godfrey."

"He's likely long gone by now."

"Nevertheless, I must try."

"Very well. I shall come with you."

"You're far too busy here. What about your responsibilities as the marshal?"

"I have others to look after things during my absence."

"Who? Lord Richard is no longer with us, and you sent Beverly east."

"Let me worry about that. In the meantime, I suggest you pack your things. We're likely to be in Summersgate for some time. Do you need a place to stay?"

"No," said Jane. "With my son locked away, I have access to the estate. I'm assuming you wish to stay with me?"

He smiled. "Most assuredly. I know Aegryth is leaving for the Dome first thing tomorrow. Can you be ready by then?"

"Yes, but you're the one who needs to make arrangements. Are you sure one night is all you need?"

"It will have to be. I can't very well let you travel to Summersgate alone!"

"I hope this is important," grumbled Arnim.

"The queen summoned us," replied Nikki. "She would hardly do that if our presence wasn't essential."

The door opened, allowing them access. Queen Anna sat at a desk littered with correspondence.

"Your Majesty," said Arnim, bowing deeply. "You honour us with your summons."

"Come now," she replied. "We all know I didn't bring you here just to chat."

"I assume something requires our attention?" said Nikki.

"It does, indeed. No doubt you are aware of the unrest spreading throughout the kingdom?"

"We were under the impression Lord Alexander was behind it? I overheard him plotting to spread more rumours."

"That was our belief, but it appears he's not the one pulling the strings."

"Then who is?"

"That's where you two come in."

"Have you any suspicions?" asked Arnim.

"I do, but I prefer not to colour your investigation with my own ideas."

"Where would you like us to start?"

"Confer with Hayley. She's had her rangers looking into this for some time now. After that, you're free to travel wherever your enquiries lead you. The Crown will, of course, cover all expenses." She pushed a sack of coins forward. "This should be more than enough to get you started."

Nikki moved closer, picking up the purse. "We'll consult with the High Ranger, as you suggest, but the most logical place to begin is to visit Lord Alexander's estate in Tewsbury."

"Commander Lanaka is the new earl, so I'm sure he'll have no objections to letting you look around the place. He's currently here in Wincaster. I suggest you visit him before you go."

TWENTY-FOUR

A Plea For Help

SPRING 967 MC

Lochlan sat in his chair, letting the sun warm him. His strength had returned for the most part, yet he still found himself tiring easily.

Today, he watched them putting the finishing touches on the new library, which the townsfolk had started calling Lochlan's Whimsy. He didn't mind, for he knew what a valuable gift he was giving future generations.

One of the workers on the roof had just finished with the shingling and was preparing to descend when he called out.

A lone rider approached from the west—a wild country full of danger. They watched as he crossed the river, his horse swimming through the deeper parts.

Lochlan rose, making his way down to the bank. Althea soon appeared at his side, watching with interest as the stranger exited the water and came to a halt.

"Greetings," the fellow began. "My name is Kendrick. I come from Drakewell seeking your chief."

"Then you've found him. I am Lochlan, Chief of Dungannon, and this is my wife, Althea. What can I do for you, Kendrick?"

The man dismounted, then fell to his knees. "I come seeking help, Lord. A great calamity has befallen us."

"What type of calamity?"

"A dragon, Lord. It came upon us from the mountains, setting fire to much of the town."

"This dragon," said Althea. "Can you describe it? Was it large?"

"Yes, it was, my lady. Its wingspan was longer than the chieftain's house."

Lochlan turned to his wife. "What are you thinking?"

"There were three dragons at Summersgate. Melethandil killed the larger of them, but the smaller one was wounded by bolts and withdrew. I suspect it fled west, finding a home in the mountains."

"That makes sense. They are said to favour such terrain. Tell me, Kendrick, why have you come to Dungannon? Surely Galchrest or Lanton would've been a better place to seek aid?"

"Aye, and Meadmont, but they all refused. I was ready to return home in defeat, but then I remembered how you saved us after the war. Without your intervention, Weldwyn would have executed all our warriors."

"What you ask is no small favour."

"I know, Lord, and my chief knows it too. Help us in our time of need, and there shall be everlasting friendship between our Clans."

"I doubt our arrows could penetrate a dragon's hide," said Lochlan.

"True," added Althea, "but the Dwarves' arbalests are more than capable of doing so. In fact, their bolts injured it in the first place."

"Can we reason with it like Melethandil?"

"You tell me—you read that book on dragons."

"You mean the one that poisoned me?"

Kendrick looked on in shock. "You were poisoned, Lord?"

"I was, but I've since recovered."

"So, you'll help?"

"We will, although it will take some time to get there. Will you march with us, or do you wish to return to bring word of our assistance?"

"With your permission, I shall return."

"Tell me one thing before you go."

"If I can."

"Warnoch was Clan Chief at the time of the invasion, but he died in Summersgate. I know he had a daughter, but I'm afraid her name escapes me?"

"Indeed, Lord. Neasa now rules Drakewell."

"Rest your horse, and we'll see you fed. You can start your way back in the morning."

"And you, Lord? When will you march to our aid?"

Lochlan looked at Althea.

"The Dwarves," she replied, "will need a few days to bake enough stonecakes, but we can be on the way by week's end."

Kendrick shook his head. "I never expected to see the mountain folk in these parts."

"I was under the impression Dwarves were living in your mountains," said Lochlan.

"They were, but that was many years ago. They've long since abandoned their mine."

"A mine, you say?"

"Yes, an iron mine, if the stories are to be believed."

"Why was it abandoned?" asked Althea.

"You'd have to ask Neasa," said Kendrick. "She's more familiar with the stories than I, although her sister, Derdra, might know more."

"Her sister?"

"Aye. She's the Clan's keeper of knowledge."

"So, a scholar, then?"

"Not a scholar so much as a teller of tales," replied Lochlan. "Most Clan history is oral, not written."

"Then perhaps, while we visit," said Althea, "I might commit her stories to paper to preserve them."

"You may do as you wish, but let's deal with the dragon first, shall we? How about you speak with Haldrim and inform him we'll be marching."

"And what will you be doing?"

"Familiarizing myself with the route to Drakewell."

"You have maps?"

"No," said Lochlan, "but I have notes on the Clanholdings that have been compiled over the years."

"And that will get us to Drakewell?"

He laughed. "Not quite. The Clanholdings consist of two great rivers running north and south. We are on the White River, while Drakewell is, if I recall, at the very source of the great Redwater River. In theory, all we need do is march west until we find that river, then follow it until we reach Drakewell."

"In theory?"

"Yes. The route will take us past Meadmont, Lanton, and then Galchrest, but there's no guarantee they'll give us leave to move through their lands."

"Could we take boats?"

"Ever since we began building the road, the boatholders have been trying to hire away all our workers. I doubt they'd be willing to take us anywhere."

A few days later, with Lochlan leading the way and Althea at his side, the Dragon Company crossed the White River and began their westward trek. They travelled on foot while Brogar led a pack mule carrying food for the Clan Chief and his wife.

The terrain to the west of Dungannon was flat, and though they saw birds of prey in the distance, no creature threatened their progress. Each night they followed the Dwarven custom and camped under the stars. The weather held, and by the end of the third day, Lochlan was quite pleased with their progress.

That evening, as they made camp, they heard roars off to the south, evidence of the dangerous creatures said to inhabit the area. Haldrim posted extra sentries, to be safe, but nothing threatened them.

Althea bid good night to Lochlan, but sleep eluded her. As the moon reached its height, she lay awake, thoughts racing through her mind. She'd seen the dragon at Summersgate but struggled to remember all the details.

It attacked by swooping down and breathing fire until Elven arrows and Dwarven bolts brought it down. Even without its flight, it had wreaked terrible damage, and the sight of it snapping a Dwarf in two still haunted her. Ultimately, the dragon climbed into the air, making its way westward, and escaping its fate. What chance did a single company of Dwarves stand against such a beast?

She tried imagining how they could carry out an attack, but for the life of her, she couldn't devise a plan. In frustration, she shifted her attention to their destination, hoping it might provide some insight. Althea pictured what Drakewell might look like, but just as it began to take shape in her mind, a sound disturbed her.

She was instantly on alert. She looked across the dying fire where Lochlan lay fast asleep. Moving towards him, making no sound as far as she could tell, was a figure cloaked in the darkness.

Althea's thoughts immediately went to the Dwarven mace Lord Tulfar had gifted to her from the armouries of Mirstone. She reached out and grabbed it, rising as quietly as possible, but her movement caught the interloper's attention. He rushed towards her, his sword glinting in the light of the dying fire. Althea blocked the swing with her mace.

"Alarm!" she cried out. "We are under attack!" Another swing caught the head of her mace, and then she counterattacked, her weapon smashing into her foe's left shoulder, the arm beneath going limp.

Behind her, a horn sounded, and then Brogar was there, driving his axe into the would-be murderer's back. The fellow fell forward into Althea, the weight of his body forcing her to the ground.

She heard the distinctive click of an arbalest trigger releasing a bolt, then a thud as it sank into flesh. With Brogar's help, she pushed the body from atop her and sat up, scanning the camp. A group of her warriors gathered around another prone figure, a bolt protruding from their back.

"We got him," called back Haldrim.

"Any more?" Brogar yelled.

"No. Only the two of them, it would seem. How's the commander?"

"She's uninjured, just a little shaken up." Brogar knelt, then turned Althea's assailant over to look at his face. "I don't recognize him," said the Dwarf.

"Nor do I," she replied, "but I've yet to meet everyone who lives in Dungannon." She got to her feet. "Perhaps his associate might prove more easily recognizable?"

Lochlan appeared beside her. "What in the name of the Gods happened here? One moment I was asleep, the next, a blaring horn woke me."

"Someone tried to kill me," said Althea, "and I suspect his partner was sent to murder you. Do you recognize him?"

Lochlan knelt. "Bring a torch, and I'll tell you. It's far too dark to make out his features."

A Dwarf held a torch over the body.

"I know this man," said Lochlan. "His uncle's a boatholder. I see they've finally taken more direct action to stop us."

"What do we do about this?" asked Brogar. "We can't let this go unopposed."

"Don't worry. We won't, but it's more important to get to Drakewell and deal with this dragon."

"They may believe you dead."

"I doubt it. Both of these would-be assassins are dead, which means no one will be able to get word back to their masters on what happened."

"Is that good or bad?"

"I'm not sure," said Lochlan, "but at the very least, it'll keep them wondering."

"What do we do with the bodies?" asked Althea.

"Leave them. By this time tomorrow night, they'll be gone."

"Really?" said Brogar. "What kind of creature carries off dead bodies?"

"I don't know," replied Lochlan, "nor do I care to find out. Accounts speak of it frequently enough for me to believe something out there does precisely that."

"We should strip them first."

"Are you that short of coins?"

"No, but there may be something on them that might prove who hired them."

"A question to which I already know the answer. Very well. Search the bodies if you feel so inclined, but we'll give such men no prayers, for they've proven themselves unworthy."

"You'll get no argument from me."

. . .

There was little sleep to be had in what remained of the night, and by sunrise, Althea stared west through bleary eyes. "How much farther, do you think?"

"Another day, maybe two, and the Redwater River will be in sight. After that, we head north, following its course, although that part of our journey will be much longer. It will likely be summer by the time we reach Drakewell."

They left the two assailants' bodies lying in the sun. Before they'd even gone a mile, birds were circling the area.

"Vultures," said Brogar. "They'll strip the bodies clean in no time."

"And the bones?" asked Althea.

"They'll either be carried away or left in the sun to crumble. In ancient times, our forebearers used to place the dead on platforms high in the mountains to be picked clean."

"And now?" asked Lochlan.

"Now they're either entombed in stone or reduced to ash, depending on their wishes."

"Reduced to ash? Are you telling me they burn the bodies?"

"Is that so strange?" said Brogar. "I'm told it's sometimes done in Merceria."

"Is that the custom here?" asked Althea.

Lochlan's face betrayed his disgust even before he spoke. "It most certainly is not. How can the Gods guide a person to the Afterlife if their flesh is reduced to ash?"

"The body is but a mortal vessel, while the Gods take the soul. At least that's our belief."

"And do your people still believe in the Afterlife?"

"Most do," said Althea.

"And what of the Dwarves, Master Brogar? Do your people believe in such things?"

"We do," said the Dwarf. "Our ancient lore tells much of the Afterlife, although where they got the knowledge from is beyond my understanding. Perhaps from the Orcs? They use magic to talk to their Ancestors."

"Are you suggesting they communicate with the dead?"

"It's a well-known fact. Why, I saw Master Kraloch do precisely that at the Siege of Summersgate. Now, you must understand, the dead they speak of... well, they linger, if you will."

"I'm not sure I understand what you mean," said Lochlan.

"They believe Orcs, too, travel to the Afterlife when they die, but those of strong will sometimes linger in a state between life and death, and it's these spirits they contact."

"And how long do these spirits linger?"

"I have no idea. It's definitely not the Dwarven custom."

"The Orcs have shamans," said Althea, "yet I saw none amongst the Dwarves of Mirstone. Do Dwarves even have such things?"

"There are Dwarf holdings with Life Mages, although we prefer the term healers. The last of ours died more than two centuries ago, but our records indicate they used to be common amongst our people."

"Weldwyn was also gifted with healers, but I'm afraid Roxanne Fortuna was the last of them."

"Strange name that," said Lochlan.

"It's the custom of Weldwyn mages to choose their name once they complete their training. I believe the same was true for Merceria, but it seems to have fallen out of favour under Queen Anna's rule."

"We have no tradition of magic in the Twelve Clans."

"Didn't your father have a Fire Mage when he invaded back in sixty-one?"

"He did. A fellow by the name of Carmus, but he was the only one I knew of."

"And where did he learn his magic?"

"There are rumours he travelled to the Kurathian Isles," said Lochlan, "but to be honest, I didn't take much interest in such things."

"Yet you consider yourself a scholar," said Althea. "I would think that is just the thing to inspire you."

"To be honest, I find the entire notion of magic to be a little unsettling."

"How so?"

"The fact they can manipulate some unseen force is very uncomfortable. Are we surrounded by some strange miasma they draw upon?"

Althea laughed. "No. The power of a mage comes from within."

"And do all of us have this power?"

"That's a good question, but I'm afraid I don't have an answer for you. I know mages tap into that energy, but as to others? I doubt anyone has the answer to that."

Lochlan nodded. "I can accept that. But what of you? Your sister has magic within her; couldn't you as well?"

"I suppose anything's possible, but I've felt no affinity for the elements, and I'd hardly make a good healer."

"Affinity?"

"Yes. Those capable of wielding magic often display some attraction to the element in question. A Fire Mage, for example, might develop an attraction to flame, a Water Mage to water, and so on. In the case of my sister, she could predict the weather. I suppose you might call it a feeling."

"And you've experienced no such feeling yourself?"

"No. Then again, ever since I met Queen Anna, all I wanted was to become a warrior princess."

"And now you are one, albeit at the head of a Dwarven company rather than one of Humans."

"Do my dispatch riders not count?"

"True," he said with a grin. "Your riders are men of Weldwyn, but we see so little of them. They're constantly travelling back and forth with messages."

"And what of you?" she asked. "Have you always aspired to be a man of learning?"

"I have, and had Kythelia not lured us into invading Weldwyn, I would've been quite happy studying dusty old tomes."

"And now?"

"The burden of leading Dungannon weighs heavily on my shoulders."

"You do not bear that burden alone." She reached out, taking his hand.

"I thank you for that," he replied. "Your presence at my side is a great comfort."

"So, you're not regretting our marriage?"

He paused for a moment before answering. "No. I'll admit it felt rushed, and I hardly knew you when we first married, but I've come to appreciate your qualities."

"Which are?"

"You are compassionate, something I wouldn't have expected from a Weldwyn princess. You're also very intelligent, a fitting consort to a chieftain."

"You speak as if I'm a prize to be paraded in front of the Clan."

"You're much more than that." He stared into her eyes. "I've come to value your friendship more than I thought possible. In some ways, you've become part of me."

"I thank you for the compliment," said Althea. "I, too, appreciate the friendship that has developed between us, and I would be lying if I said I didn't feel the same."

TWENTY-FIVE

Chasing Rumours

SPRING 967 MC

Arnim swept his gaze over the room. The Lucky Duck was a typical tavern as far as such things went, although more suited to the lower classes than what he'd become accustomed to of late. Today, patrons filled the place, all here to listen to one man speak.

"Well?" he grumbled. "Where is he?"

"Hush now," said Nikki. "He's probably waiting until everyone's here, to make a grand entrance."

"And you're sure this Draven is the one we're looking for?"

"You doubt me?"

"No, of course not. Only, I'd be happier if there weren't so many people around. Trying to take him into custody in this crowd could prove difficult."

"Then it's good we're not here to arrest him."

Arnim looked at her in surprise. "I thought that's exactly why we're here?"

"By all accounts, Draven is a local. We need to find out where the coins are coming from, and to do that, we must determine who he's working for."

The room fell quiet as a bear of a man came down the stairs. His thick, black beard and the scar on his cheek gave the impression he knew his way around a brawl. Draven halted halfway down the steps, giving him a commanding view of the room.

"My friends," he began. "We come here today not out of malice but concern for our families. A danger threatens them—threatens us all, and it's time we did something about it."

A few murmurs of approval came from the audience, but the big man wasn't done.

"For too long, the greenskins have wandered the streets of Merceria, and for what—to keep the peace? Our ancestors didn't need them, and neither do we!"

Cheers this time, with a little more volume. Arnim scanned the crowd once more. A few patrons had stood upon Draven's entrance, the better to see him, while a weaselly-looking man with slicked-back hair handed out coins to many of those who remained seated.

Draven continued. "Do we just sit back and do nothing?"

"No!" came a shout.

"Then what do we do?"

"Fight!" shouted the same voice. "Fight! Fight! Fight!"

The crowd picked up the chant, with Draven encouraging them by cupping his hand to his ear as if hard of hearing. Over and over came the chorus, and then he used his hands to silence them.

"You have spoken loud and clear," he continued. "They've had their way for too long. I say enough!"

Another cheer, this time from the entire tavern.

"Let us march forth and drive the greenskins from Kingsford. Take back what is rightfully ours!"

The chanting grew to a roar, and then Draven pointed at the door and descended the remaining steps. Fortified by ale and coins, the mob surged towards the doorway as each patron fought to be the first one through.

Arnim kept his eyes on Draven. The man smiled, his eyes glued to the crowd. His associate, the weasel, made his way to the stairs, whispering into his master's ear. Draven looked at Arnim and Nikki, then made his way over to their table.

"I don't believe I've seen you here before," he said.

"We're new to Kingsford," replied Arnim.

"And what brings you to the Duck?"

"You. We have the same problem back in Haverston, and word is, you have a solution."

"Haverston, you say? If memory serves, that's small compared to Kingsford. How is it you have greenskins?"

"It's the rangers," said Nikki. "No doubt you've heard how they employ the savages."

"I have, indeed. They are a blight on our kingdom."

"I'm curious how you intend to deal with them. After all, they're in service to the queen. You can't simply kill them."

The smirk on his face sent a shiver up Nikki's spine. "Ah, but we can make it known we will no longer tolerate their presence."

"I can't help but notice," added Arnim, "you sent your people out into the streets while you remain here."

"An excellent observation. I see you're a man who understands leadership," said Draven. "At the same time, I wonder about your true motives."

"As I said earlier, we have a similar problem in Haverston."

"Then why didn't you leave with the others to see first-hand how we deal with the greenskins?"

"I'm more interested in how you recruit others to your cause. I noticed your accomplice handing out coins, and I understand their usefulness, but I'm not a wealthy man. I would soon find myself a beggar if I did the same back home."

"There are plenty of coins for those who know where to find them."

"Now you speak in riddles," said Nikki. "Are you a mage who can produce gold from the very air?"

Draven chuckled. "Hardly. I'm a facilitator at heart. A man who specializes in encouraging others, and I'm well-paid for such work."

"I'm surprised you told us that," said Arnim. "Wouldn't you prefer to be known as the leader of this movement to banish the Orcs?"

"Leader? I suppose that has its virtues. While there is prestige in commanding others, the true power is often wielded by those whose faces are never seen. I'd love to chat more, but my people need me." With that, he left, joining the mob waiting outside.

"What do you make of that?" asked Arnim.

"I don't believe he trusts us."

"Would you, given the circumstances?"

"No," said Nikki. "I suppose not, but he slipped up when he spoke of power. Clearly, someone is financing this, and I believe I know how we can find out."

"Very well, I'll bite. How do we do that?"

"Step one consists of us joining the mob out there."

"And step two?"

"I haven't quite figured that out yet," said Nikki, "but step three is shadowing Draven until he makes contact with his backer, whoever that is."

"Any ideas on that score? A criminal mastermind, perhaps?"

"I suspect we'll find an outside influence."

"What leads you to suggest that?"

"Draven's accent was noticeably bland. I don't think he's from around here."

Arnim stared back, working over the details in his head. "He certainly doesn't sound like he's from Weldwyn. You're not suggesting he's Kurathian, are you? Saxnor knows they have good reason to hate us."

"I don't think so. Hundreds of Kurathians serve the Crown, but none of them sound like Draven. He's also very well-spoken."

"I noticed that," said Arnim. "He seems well-educated, far more than he pretends to be. Do you think he might be a mage? Maybe he even used magic to influence the crowd. It's not beyond the realm of possibility."

"Not likely. We've been around enough mages to know when someone's casting a spell, and I heard no words of power."

"So, we have a well-educated foreigner, which excludes both Norland and the Twelve Clans. And if his lack of accent is any indication, he's definitely not from Weldwyn. What does that leave us with?"

"Didn't the Dwarves of Ironcliff have problems with their neighbour to the east?"

"Yes. A kingdom they called Halvaria. Do you suppose they might be behind all this?"

"It's a possibility, but far from the only one. We know very little about the rest of the Continent, so there is the potential that someone else has taken an interest in our affairs."

"An interesting observation, but if we're to get to the bottom of this, we should join that crowd before Draven gets away from us."

Farther to the northwest, in Falford, Gerald and Lady Jane sat at a table in a similar establishment, this time a tavern called the River Snake. They'd come searching for Lord Godfrey on the off chance the fugitive was here seeking a ship to bear him to safety.

Gerald looked across at Jane, noting the dark circles under her eyes. She hadn't slept well in weeks, her desire to prove her loyalty driving her obsession. It saddened him to think her guilt might consume her, and he reached out, placing his hand upon hers.

His action startled her. "I'm sorry," she said. "I've been so distracted of late."

"That's understandable, given the circumstances. Don't you think?"

Jane cast her gaze downward. "I'm sorry. I've wasted my time and yours. We've sat here for three days in a row, and still no sign of him."

"Stop apologizing," said Gerald. "Time spent with you is not wasted, regardless of what we're doing... or not doing, in this case."

"You're sweet to say so. That's one of the things I love about you."

"I wonder, however, why you suspected he might be in Falford?"

"Do you know Lord Osric?"

"Can't say I do. Why? Who is he?"

"The Baron of Hanwick, which lies north of here."

"And?"

"I ran into him while we were in Summersgate. He told me he'd taken it upon himself to represent my son."

"That still doesn't explain our presence here. Wait, did you say he had 'taken it'? As in, changed his mind?"

"So it seems. He believed Lord Godfrey had a contact amongst the smugglers of Falford."

"And so, you thought he might hire them to take him out of the kingdom?"

"Precisely."

"A sound idea, yet we've found no sign of him. What is it we do now? Keep returning to the River Snake, day after day, or return to Summersgate?"

She was about to answer when a lone figure wearing a hooded cloak entered the tavern. Something about his manner suggested a man of import, and Jane stiffened.

Gerald kept his voice low. "Is that him?"

"I'm not sure. His face is covered."

The newcomer scanned the room, and Gerald saw his gaze drawing near. In desperation, he reached out and pulled Jane closer, kissing her to keep their faces hidden. He held her longer than necessary before finally releasing her.

She stared back, love in her eyes. "Oh, Gerald. That was most unexpected."

He chuckled. "It's not as if we haven't kissed before."

"Yes, but here? In public?"

He nodded towards the new arrival. "I had to make sure he didn't recognize you."

"Of course."

"That doesn't mean I didn't enjoy it, though."

She smiled. "You're such a gentleman. How is it you're not married at your age?"

"I was waiting for the right person."

"And now?"

His smile warmed her heart. "I believe you know the answer to that." From the corner of his eye, he spied the new arrival taking a seat. "Take a good look, and tell me if you think that's him."

Jane turned her head and stared. The man sat with his side to her, but his hood prevented any view of his features. "I still can't tell."

Gerald waved over the serving girl.

"Another round?" she asked.

"Actually, I wondered if you'd like to earn a few coins?"

She huffed with indignation. "I'll have you know I'm happily married!"

Gerald turned red, much to Jane's amusement. "That's not what I was suggesting."

"Oh, sorry. What is it you want, then?"

"Do you see that man over there? The one with the hooded cloak?"

"Yes."

"He's an old friend of mine, and I'd like to play a prank on him."

"What kind of prank? I don't want to get into any trouble."

"What if I gave you a golden sovereign to walk past him and pull back his hood?"

"A gold sovereign?"

"Yes." Gerald reached into his belt and pulled out a coin, placing it on the table. "He's a vain man, you see, and doesn't enjoy showing his face. He believes it adds an air of mystery to him. Needless to say, we delight in showing him how full of himself he truly is."

"Will he not be upset?"

"Oh, he will, of that I have no doubt, but he's also notoriously cheap, so it's not as if you'd be missing out on any real profit."

She scooped up the coin. "Very well."

"Try to make it look like an accident if you can, and whatever you do, don't tell him I put you up to it."

"That's a huge ask."

"Agreed. How about I throw in another sovereign if you're successful?"

"You're a strange man," replied the serving girl, turning to Jane. "I'd watch him if I were you."

"Oh, I will. I promise," said Jane.

The girl wandered over to another table, snatched up some empty tankards, and then began winding her way back to the kitchen, her route taking her past the new arrival. To her credit, she only paused long enough to tug the back of the visitor's hood.

He quickly replaced it, but not before Jane recognized him. She turned to Gerald, her pulse quickening. "That's him," she whispered.

"Are you sure?"

"Absolutely. I'd know that face anywhere. What do we do now?"

"You tell me. You're the one who brought us to Falford."

"I must admit I hadn't properly thought this through. What would you suggest?"

"I suppose I could confront him?"

"Wouldn't that be dangerous?"

"What other choice do we have? If we go and summon help, he'll simply disappear, and I doubt we'd be lucky enough to find him a second time."

"But if you try to arrest him, might he not attempt to flee? I hate to mention it, Gerald, but you're not the young man you used to be."

"I'd take that as an insult from anyone else, but you're right. Perhaps there's a better way."

"What have you got in mind?"

"Here's what we'll do..."

~

Lord Godfrey Hammond sipped his ale. He'd come to this wretched tavern seeking to hire a ship, but the captain was nowhere to be found. If he couldn't arrange transport, he'd need to travel overland, and the thought of all the extra effort it required annoyed him to no end.

A woman brushed past his table, then halted, causing him to look up. Staring back at him was none other than Lady Jane Goodwin! What in the name of Malin was she doing here? Panic threatened to overwhelm him. He thought of reaching out with his dagger and killing her before she raised the alarm, but a murder here, with witnesses, was the last thing he could afford.

He rushed to stand, sending his chair careening behind him. Lady Jane looked like she was ready to say something, but he ignored her, instead running towards the tavern entrance in a bid to escape. He threw open the door, rushing into the midday sun, only to trip over something and fall to the ground, knocking the wind from himself.

"My pardon," said a voice.

Godfrey started to rise but felt a sword tip at the back of his neck. "I wouldn't if I were you, Lord Godfrey. I'd hate to have to kill you."

"Who are you?"

"Let's just say I'm a friend of Weldwyn."

Godfrey was not about to give up without a fight. He slumped forward as if in surrender, then quickly rolled to the side. Not expecting such a move, his opponent backed up to avoid a possible counterattack.

Lord Godfrey was soon on his feet, his hand going to the hilt of his sword. Before him, stood an old man easily twice his age, perhaps even more.

"Who are you?" Godfrey said. "I would know the man I'm about to kill."

The older man had a relaxed manner to him despite the imminent danger. "With what? That sword of yours? You're more than welcome to try."

"Enough of this! Run away, you fool. I have no wish to see the death of you." Godfrey drew his sword and prepared to attack.

His opponent held up his weapon, a battered piece of steel that had seen better days. Godfrey sneered at the fool, lunging forward, but the stranger effortlessly parried, then retaliated, hitting Godfrey's arm with the flat of his blade. Godfrey stepped back and prepared for another attack.

Lady Jane's voice drifted towards him. "I'd give up if I were you."

"Give up? You think me a coward? I've trained for years with the sword. I'm not afraid of some old man."

She looked at his opponent, who simply shrugged. Godfrey was missing something here, but for the life of him, he couldn't figure out what.

"Time to end this once and for all," said the old man. He attacked with a simple slash, easily parried, yet there was a surprising amount of strength behind it.

"Surrender, Lord Godfrey. I have no wish to kill you."

"Who are you to think you can threaten one of your superiors?"

"Superiors?" said Lady Jane. "Have you no idea who you're talking to?"

Godfrey glanced at her to see if this was some ruse, but she appeared earnest.

"This is Gerald Matheson, Marshal of the Mercerian Army," she continued. "You couldn't have picked a more worthy adversary if you tried."

Panic rose within Godfrey once more. Everyone of import had heard of the Mercerian, yet his reputation was one of leadership and cunning. That did not necessarily mean he was a master swordsman. A calm settled over him.

"Come," he said. "Let us see an end to this." He lunged forward, whipping his sword around in a frenzy. He had the satisfaction of striking the old man's arm, but the damned fool was wearing mail! Godfrey expected the marshal to back up and give himself some space, but the seasoned warrior stepped into the attack, smashing the hilt of his sword into Godfrey's face.

The blow instantly broke his nose, blood streaming out as pain lanced through his skull. Godfrey lost his balance, falling hard onto his back. Before he even raised his head, his foe held a blade to his throat.

"Now," said Gerald. "Will you surrender, or shall I finish you off?"

Lady Jane appeared beside him. "Perhaps it's better this way—a quick death for a traitor?"

Gerald looked down at Lord Godfrey, thinking hard about finishing him. It would certainly save the cost of a court case, but he knew, in his heart, it was the wrong thing to do.

The fight, despite its short duration, had drawn a crowd. Two warriors, armed with swords, pushed their way through the townsfolk.

"What's going on here?" the elder one called out.

"My name is Gerald Matheson, Marshal of Merceria, and this man"—he gestured at his opponent—"is Lord Godfrey Hammond, a fugitive of Weldwyn."

"How do we know you're not making all this up?"

"Simple. Arrest us both, and let your captain sort it out."

The guards moved closer. "Hand over your weapon, and we shall do precisely that."

Gerald passed over his sword, then watched as they pulled Godfrey to his feet.

"This man is a liar," said Godfrey. "Look at his clothing, for Malin's sake. He's nothing but a common thug. I demand you release me immediately."

"These men are both nobles," said Lady Jane. "As such, you must let His Grace Lord Julian decide on a course of action. He's the earl here, is he not?"

The guard ignored her question. "And who might you be?"

"Lady Jane Goodwin."

"And you recognize both these men?"

"I do, indeed. This is the Marshal of Merceria, as he claimed."

"And the other?"

"A criminal and a traitor whose arrest the Earls Council has ordered. If you check with your captain, I'm sure he is aware of the warrant."

The guard bowed. "My apologies, my lady." He released Gerald's arm. "You are free to go, my lord."

"Thank you," replied Gerald. "I assume you'll take him to the local jail?"

"Indeed."

"Then I shall follow. I must make arrangements to transport the prisoner back to Summersgate. This may well lead to a promotion for you, my good man. You have Lady Jane to thank for it."

TWENTY-SIX

Preparations

SUMMER 967 MC

"Your Highness honours us," said Lord Oliver. "We haven't seen you in some time."

"If I recall, this council asked to speak to me. Perhaps we might save some time if we got to the heart of the matter?"

"We seek to know your wishes regarding your rule," said Lord Julian.

"I am to be king. What more is there to say?"

"Ah, but we live in unusual times," offered Lord Dryden. "You are married to a foreign monarch, and the only other eligible heir has chosen to wed a Clansman."

"And?"

Lord Julian leaned forward, leaning on the table. "We are not here to argue the point, merely to clarify things. There is no precedent for these circumstances, thus, we are forced to make choices. Choices, I might add, that could have long-lasting effects on the Royal House of Weldwyn."

"Very well," said Alric. "Then ask your questions, and let's be done with it."

Lord Elgin cleared his throat. "Let us deal with the matter of succession first. Prince Braedon will be your heir, but if he should die before taking the Crown, who would be your alternate?"

"Yes," added Beric. "And should the Gods choose to take you before he is of age, who would act as regent?"

"I should think his mother," said Alric. "Would that not be normal under our laws?"

"Not at all, Highness. I'm surprised you weren't aware of such things. We can't have a woman ruling the kingdom."

"Why not? It doesn't appear to have hurt Merceria."

Beric shook his head. "Their ways are not ours, Your Highness."

"In other words, you want me to pick a regent who is from Weldwyn?"

"That would be best," said Lord Julian. "But whoever you choose must be approved by the Earls Council."

"Who was my father's regent?"

"That no longer matters," said Elgin. "He was never called upon to fulfill that particular obligation."

"Still, if what you say is true, he must have named someone?"

"He did. Lord Edwin Weldridge, Earl of Faltingham."

"Then I name Lord Jack Marlowe, Viscount of Aynsbury, to be my regent, should it prove necessary."

"Come now. The man is but a cavalier, hardly the sort to be trusted with your children's future. Surely you can think of someone better?"

Alric sat back. "You appear to hold strong opinions about such things. Why don't you suggest a name, and I'll tell you what I think?"

Lord Elgin swept his arm to indicate the rest of the earls. "Perhaps one of us?"

"You'd like that, wouldn't you?" Alric paused a moment, thinking things through. "I assume you want someone of a high station?"

"Naturally. Only fitting, don't you think, considering they might one day rule the kingdom?"

"Let me finish," said the prince. "From your refusal of Lord Jack, I assume you want someone of a higher standing than a mere viscount?"

"Naturally."

"Then I choose His Grace Gerald Matheson, Duke of Wincaster."

Elgin's mouth fell open. "Surely you jest? He's not even from Weldwyn!"

"Then perhaps you'd prefer to reconsider Jack Marlowe?"

Lord Julian barked out a laugh. "He's got you there!"

"Let's move on to another topic, shall we?" suggested Dryden.

"By all means," said Alric. "What would you like to discuss next?"

"Your wife."

"You mean Her Majesty, the Queen of Merceria."

"Yes, of course. What is to be her status once you're crowned?"

"She will be Queen of Weldwyn."

"Impossible!" said Elgin.

"Was my mother not queen?"

"That was entirely different, and you know it."

"Do I? You presume a lot, Lord Elgin. I doubt my father would have approved of such behaviour."

"With all due respect, Your Highness, no one ever expected you to ascend to the Throne. Your father, may he live on in the Afterlife, did not adequately prepare you for such things."

"You forget yourself, Elgin. I've spent most of the last four years at the Mercerian court. That more than prepares me to rule."

Elgin's face grew flush. "I'm not suggesting you're not, merely that you need guidance in certain matters."

"And what matters would those be? Dealing with foreigners? I did that in Wincaster. Leading armies? I've done that as well. Shall I go on?"

"Now, now," said Julian. "Let us all calm down. We're not here to get into arguments, merely to ascertain your wishes, Highness. I will note here that your chosen regent is Lord Jack Marlowe, should it become necessary. As to your wife, I see no impediment to naming her queen."

He looked around the room. The other earls, save for Elgin, nodded their agreement.

"There," Lord Julian continued. "Now, let's move on to other things, shall we? I assume you'd like the Mercerians to participate in the ceremony?"

"Yes, if possible. I thought we might allow a small contingent to accompany the queen."

"Of course. And what of your own escort?"

"I have my companies, which I took to Merceria. I'd like them to perform that honour."

"A perfectly reasonable request."

"Tell me," said Lord Elgin. "Will your wife take the oath? It's tradition, though I can't imagine she'll like it."

"Why is that?" asked Alric.

"Are you truly so clueless? Your queen has to swear an oath to serve you, Highness. That would put her in direct conflict with her pledge to the people of Merceria."

"Then we shall change the oath."

"Change the oath? Centuries of tradition are behind those words. You can't just casually toss them aside!"

"Can't I? Says who?"

In desperation, Lord Elgin looked at his fellow earls, but they avoided direct eye contact.

Julian cleared his throat. "I'll send you a copy of the current oath so you can make the necessary amendments, Highness."

"Thank you."

"Circumstances also necessitated some changes in the day's events. The custom was to muster the escort in the parade grounds, march them through town, then circle around to arrive at the Palace. Given that the Palace is in ruins, we need an alternate location."

The prince shook his head. "Could we not simply return to the same place we started?"

"A marvellous idea," said Lord Oliver. "Would we hold the feast outside as well? It would be quite the spectacle!"

"There will be no feast. Let us instead partake of a simple meal that recognizes the suffering the people of Weldwyn have experienced."

"But you are to be king, Highness. Surely that warrants a bigger celebration?"

"I've learned much during my time in Merceria, and what stands out above all else is my obligation to my people. I will not gorge myself while others starve, or carry on a lavish celebration while others suffer. I want my coronation to bring hope to the people of Weldwyn. My own actions must demonstrate I understand their needs."

Elgin threw his hands up into the air. "I give up. His Highness intends to upend centuries of tradition. What's next, I ask? Are we to bow before the Queen of Merceria?"

"You've gone too far," said Lord Julian. "I suggest you remove yourself before you are charged with treason."

"You haven't the stomach for it!"

"Haven't I? You made it clear from the start you covet the Crown for yourself, but the truth is, you're not suited for it. You're an earl, for Malin's sake. It's about time you started acting like one!"

"Come, my lords," soothed Alric. "Perhaps we should adjourn until cooler heads prevail?"

"You'll get no argument from me," said Lord Dryden. "This meeting is now dismissed. We shall reconvene on the morrow."

Alric walked down the street, his guards close at hand. It would be nice to wander through the city unhindered by others as he did when he was a boy, but his role as the future King of Weldwyn made it necessary. The arrival of Jack Marlowe interrupted his thoughts.

"Highness," he called out. "I bring news."

The prince smiled. "Something good, I hope? I've had enough of troubles these last few days."

"Good, indeed. They've apprehended Lord Godfrey."

"Finally, a reason to celebrate. Tell me, where did they find him?"

"In Falford, if you can believe it. Tracked down by none other than Lady Jane herself."

"We must be sure to congratulate her. That's quite an accomplishment. I assume he'll be brought back to Summersgate?"

"I imagine he's already on his way. His trial will commence as soon as he arrives."

"I thought your interest lay in Lord James?"

"It does, but I suspect Godfrey will give him up in favour of leniency."

"And by leniency, you mean…"

"A lifetime of imprisonment, or even a more humane method of execution. Not that I feel the rogue deserves it."

"But wasn't his trial to be held after that of Lord James?"

"It was, but his escape garnered too much attention." Jack lowered his voice. "There are some who want a speedy trial followed by a hasty execution. Methinks someone wants to hide something."

"Methinks? Are you taking up the life of a poet now, Jack?"

"Sorry. I couldn't resist. In any case, I suspect he'll reveal everything to save his own skin. The trick will be keeping him alive long enough to learn what he knows."

"You fear for his safety that much?"

"He was in the thick of it," said Jack. "He had contacts amongst the nobles of Weldwyn and the Twelve Clans. If anyone can put together an accurate account of events leading up to the fall of Summersgate, it's him."

"Who's escorting him to Summersgate?"

"A captain out of Falford. I don't recall his name."

"Is he someone we can trust?"

"As far as I know, not that it matters. The Marshal of Merceria is also travelling with them."

"Gerald is with the prisoner?"

"Of course. As I said, Lady Jane found the fellow, and where she goes… well, you can work out the rest."

Alric halted, then lowered his voice. "I need you to do me a favour, Jack, a very big favour."

"Sounds interesting. Am I to kill someone?"

"No, of course not. I want you to take one of my companies and meet Godfrey's escort on the Falford road."

"Surely you're not suggesting someone will try to have him killed?"

"You're the one who said somebody wanted to hide something. What better way than to kill Godfrey before he can speak?"

"I'll leave this very afternoon."

"Excellent. Let me know immediately if you find anything amiss."

"I shall. I promise."

"Good. Now go, and may Malin guide you."

. . .

Lord Julian waited while the server refilled his cup. Only once the woman was out of hearing, did he continue. "What did you make of Lord Elgin's behaviour today?"

"As opposed to any other day?" replied Lord Oliver. "I suppose he was a little more contrary than normal. Why?"

"I think something has rattled his cage."

"You mean apart from the idea of Alric becoming king?"

"No," said Julian. "It's more than that. I noticed it when he arrived. He looked nervous, as though his shadow was about to jump out and bite him."

"I hardly call that unexpected. After all, he's spent the last few months directly opposing the prince. I don't imagine he liked being in the same room with his adversary."

"I can't help but feel there's more to this."

"Then ask yourself this," said Oliver. "What else has happened of late? A death in the family, perhaps?"

"We did receive some news today," said Julian. "Someone's finally found Lord Godfrey. You don't suppose that's it, do you?"

"I could hardly imagine the arrest of Godfrey would leave Elgin nervous…" His words trailed off.

"What is it?" asked Julian.

"When did we receive word of Godfrey's arrest?"

"Early this morning. Why?"

"Do you suppose Elgin heard of it before the meeting?"

"It's certainly a possibility," said Julian. "Do you think that's why he was upset?"

"I can't say for certain."

"Are you sure there's nothing else we missed in terms of news?"

"Absolutely, but that being the case, wouldn't it hint at some sort of connection between the two of them?"

"It seems to me there are far too many coincidences of late," noted Julian.

"Malin's tears, what are you talking about?"

"We know Godfrey worked with the Twelve Clans."

"And?" pressed Oliver.

"Elgin wished to make himself king by marrying Princess Althea. How curious there would be an attempt on the life of her husband. Thankfully, we have word he survived, else we'd have more troubles with the Twelve Clans."

"Are you suggesting Elgin arranged all this?"

"It stands to reason, doesn't it? Who else but a Clansman could get close enough to a chieftain to attempt a poisoning?"

"That's nothing more than idle speculation."

"True," said Julian, "but if I'm right, it would be in Elgin's best interests to see Godfrey executed as soon as possible."

"Or murdered," suggested Lord Oliver. "If Elgin does know of Godfrey's arrest, he's likely to do something to save his own hide. I suggest keeping a close eye on the fellow for the next few days."

"Come now. He's an earl. I understand him manipulating things to his advantage, but murder? I believe you overestimate his zeal."

"It's not zeal—it's desperation. Godfrey's testimony could well put a noose around Elgin's neck."

"We don't hang nobles," said Lord Julian. "They're beheaded using a sword."

"Now is not the time to argue specifics. The point I'm trying to make is desperate men will often resort to desperate measures."

"Yes, but murder?"

"He'd never wield the knife himself, but I wouldn't put it past him to hire someone to do the dirty work."

Gerald looked up at the sun. "A clear sky," he mused. "A good sign of things to come."

"You always look on the bright side of things," replied Jane, riding beside him. She glanced over her shoulder, an action he didn't miss.

"He's not going anywhere," said Gerald. "He's safely under lock and key."

"It wouldn't be the first time he's slipped away. Someone arranged for his release after his initial incarceration. There's no telling what lengths they might go to again."

"I'll admit he has powerful friends, but even so, his rescuers would have to kill quite a few guards to get to him. An unlikely scenario at best."

"But not impossible?"

"I suppose anything is possible, given enough resources," he replied, "but they'd need a good deal of warriors to cleave through that lot." He used his thumb to indicate those behind him. "In any case, if there were a rescue attempt, it wouldn't be here."

"Why not?"

"The terrain is too open, and we'd see any large group of men approaching."

"Then where would they strike?"

"If I had to guess, I'd say Kinsley. It would be easier for them to get close while we pass through the town."

"Can we avoid it?"

"I'm afraid not. If you remember, the fields in this part of the country-side are not exactly the terrain you want to bring a wagon through. We tried doing that during the war, and most of them got bogged down. Poor drainage, you see, which makes for muddy fields. Don't worry, though. We'll take precautions."

"This must seem like such a backwards land after your experiences in Merceria."

"Not at all. Merceria has only one decent road, which runs from Kings-ford to Wincaster. Everything else is little more than trails. If anything, I'd say the roads of Weldwyn are superior to ours."

"Do you miss being home?"

"Not when I'm with you," said Gerald, "but that leads me to an important question."

"Which is?"

"Once this is all over, what will you do?"

She shrugged. "I'm not sure. I suppose, to a large extent, it all depends on what happens to James. The Crown will seize his possessions if they find him guilty of treason, leaving me penniless and without a home."

"You could always come and live with me," said Gerald, then blushed profusely.

"But you live at the Palace now. Would I not be imposing on the queen?"

"I doubt she would mind. In fact, I know she wouldn't."

"What makes you so certain?"

"She knows your presence brings me happiness. So, what do you think? Would you take me up on the offer?"

"I'll consider it, but there is much to do in the meantime."

"You found Lord Godfrey. What else is there?"

"I need to ensure James pays for his crimes."

"But he's your son. Are you sure that's what you want?"

"It's taken me a long time to realize it, but he hasn't been my son for years. He takes after his father in so many ways, not least is his indifference to my well-being. It wasn't until I met you that I realized there was more to life than doing my duty to a faithless husband. I suppose I've decided it's time I start living my own life for once, and the best way I can do that is to rid myself of my son's presence for good."

TWENTY-SEVEN

Drakewell

SUMMER 967 MC

Lochlan's expedition followed along the Redwater River into the hills. The march thus far had proved tiring, even by Dwarven standards, but the knowledge that their destination was close drove them onward. When they took a short break by the water, Althea threw herself to the ground while Brogar wandered over to the river to fill his waterskin.

"Not the cleanest of water," he grumbled.

Lochlan chuckled as he sat beside his wife. "It's the iron," he said. "These hills are full of it, or so I'm led to believe. That's how the Redwater got its name."

"Do they still mine for iron?" she asked.

"I think so, though not to the extent they did years ago."

"And why is that?"

"Believe it or not," said Lochlan, "there's not a strong demand for iron in these parts."

"Do they not make pots and pans?"

"Of course, but they last forever. Not exactly the type of thing that makes for useful trade goods."

"I would suggest precisely the opposite. Back in Weldwyn, there's a constant demand for iron. If it's not used for weapons, then certainly for armour. Do they not wear iron armour amongst the Clans?"

"You know they do, but it's an expensive and time-consuming process to dig it out."

Brogar sat down beside them. "What's expensive?"

"Mining iron," explained Althea.

"Whoever gave you that idea?"

She looked at Lochlan, who shrugged his shoulders. "Perhaps I'm mistaken, but I thought I read—"

"There's your problem," said the Dwarf. "You read too much. You can use iron for a great many things, even simple ones like nails. Find yourself an iron mine, and you're set for generations."

"Apparently, that hasn't been the experience in Drakewell."

"Then they're doing it wrong."

"I suppose you have a better idea of how they are to make it easier to mine?"

"I'm no miner," said Brogar, "but I've seen the great mines of Mirstone. The trick is digging deep rather than just scratching the surface."

"I'm beginning to see the problem," said Lochlan. "My fellow countrymen don't like the idea of working underground."

"Why ever not? Surely, the expected profits would spur them on?"

"I'm sure they would," said Althea, "but I imagine they lack the expertise. After all, it's not just a simple matter of digging."

"It isn't?" asked Lochlan.

"No. You don't just dig out the ore; you have to worry about smelting it and then converting it into usable ingots. Typically, you need a very hot furnace for that sort of thing."

"Don't all furnaces burn at the same heat?"

Brogar shook his head. "You obviously know nothing of such things."

"My husband is a leader, not a smith."

"Nor am I," said the Dwarf, "but I still possess a working knowledge of mining. If you want to remain as chieftain, I suggest you learn more about whatever it is your people do."

"And I shall," said Lochlan, "but Dungannon is not the source of iron— Drakewell is. Are you now proposing I learn about every town in the Twelve Clans?"

"I hate to interrupt," said Haldrim, "but our sentries report movement in the hills."

"Likely scouts out of Drakewell. I imagine they're trying to determine who we are."

"With all due respect, Lord, I don't think it's Clansmen."

"Then who?"

"That remains to be seen. In the meantime, I'd like to box you two up."

Lochlan stared back, not quite sure what to make of the request.

"He means," said Althea, "the Dragon Company will form up around us to keep us safe."

"Very well," replied Lochlan. "If you insist."

Haldrim ordered the Dragon Company into position. The overall formation was that of a hollow square, but the warriors all faced the direction of march. They proceeded in this fashion, following the course of the Redwater.

They marched for half the afternoon, their progress slowed by the necessity of staying in formation. Althea was beginning to wonder if Haldrim had overreacted, when a shout drew her attention. Small stones fell from the sky, sounding like hail as they struck helmets and shields. Upon Haldrim's command, the formation halted, each warrior turning to face the outside of the square.

"What was that?" asked Lochlan.

Brogar picked up a stone. It was smooth, yet someone had gone to great lengths to scratch a stylized star on one side. "I should've known better," he said.

"Why? What does it mean?"

"It means we're about to come under attack."

More stones hit them, rattling off helmets.

"Where are those coming from?" asked Lochlan.

"From just over the top of that hill, unless I miss my guess."

"Surely whoever is doing it must realize the futility of it? Not a single warrior has fallen."

"Nor will one, but they have accomplished what they set out to do."

"Which is?"

"Make us halt in our tracks," said Brogar.

"Why would they want that?"

"We'll find out momentarily."

A distant drum echoed off the hills. "Here they come," said Haldrim.

Lochlan peered over their guards. The river was on their left, and beyond it, more hills. A mob of small, green-skinned creatures burst forth, scampering across the terrain carrying spears with wicked-looking tips. Brogar pushed one of his fellow Dwarves aside for a quick look, then spat on the ground.

"Just our luck," he said. "Goblins!"

"How many?" asked Althea.

"Enough to cause us some headaches."

The creatures raced to the riverbank and began yelling at the Dwarves.

"I have no idea what they're saying," said Brogar, "but it doesn't sound good."

Haldrim barked out a command, and his warriors began loading their arbalests.

"Wait," said Althea. "Can't we try talking to them?"

"And who'll do the talking?" asked Brogar. "Do you speak Goblin?"

"There must be a better option than fighting?"

"Taking care of those things won't be much of a fight."

"We're on our way to fight a dragon," she persisted. "We can't afford to lose even one warrior."

Brogar pointed. "Tell that to them!"

Another stone rattled off a helmet. Althea noted the presence of several Goblins carrying strange staffs with slings attached.

"Enough of this," she said, pushing her way out of the formation.

The chattering on the far bank subsided at the sight of her approach. She moved closer to the riverbank before calling across. "We mean you no harm."

A lone figure pushed his way from the crowd to stand opposite her. He was quite short, being only slightly taller than her waist. His leather garment reminded her of a smith's apron, and she realized it must be some sort of crude armour.

Althea held her arms out on either side and stepped into the water, advancing until it was ankle-deep. Her opponent, clutching a spiked club, did likewise. Locking eyes with her, he tossed his weapon behind him.

She motioned towards the Dwarves and then upriver, hoping to get across her meaning. In reply, the Goblin pointed skyward, then put his thumbs together and waved his hands. It didn't take her long to understand what he meant.

"They know about the dragon," she called out.

"Good for them," Haldrim yelled back. "Now, tell them to get out of here and leave us in peace!"

Althea pointed at the Goblin, then at the hills behind his people. In reply, the creature once more made the flapping motion with his hands, then pointed upstream. This was followed by him gesturing to the Dwarves and then to the hills off to the right.

"I believe he's trying to warn us."

"Hurling stones is a funny way to warn people."

Unsure of how to respond, Althea merely bowed, then returned to the company of Dwarves.

"Orders?" asked Haldrim. "Do we attack?"

Althea glanced at the river. The Goblins had pulled back, clearly in no mood for a fight. She heard a screeching noise in the distance, and her blood ran cold.

"That way," she said, pointing to the hills off to her right. "We'll avoid the river and hopefully any sign of that dragon."

"You mean the one we're here to kill?"

"We are in unfamiliar terrain, and our first priority is to reach Drakewell and see how we can be of assistance."

Haldrim obviously harboured objections but was too good of a captain to argue the point. "Very well, my lady. We shall do as you wish. I would recommend, however, that we move into a more open formation, making us less of a target should the dragon appear."

"A wise precaution and one I wholeheartedly support."

Instead of following the river, which now ran mainly west, they headed into the hills to the north. They heard no more of the dragon that day, although sentries called out the alarm several times during the night, the result of fear of the unknown.

By noon the next day, they stood on a hilltop overlooking the distant town of Drakewell, situated between two hills, astride a pool of water fed by three mountain streams. They found no further signs of the Goblins but kept their guard up nonetheless, the better to avoid any surprise attacks.

Even from this distance, they could see the damage the town had suffered. All that remained of several buildings were burnt-out shells, while scorch marks told the story of the beast's attack, leaving black streaks across the rooftops where it rained down its deadly fire.

Drakewell possessed no walls, but they wouldn't have done anything to help against an airborne menace. Althea wondered if there were any archers amongst the Clan's warriors, but then she remembered it had taken the Elves' bows to penetrate the beast's thick hide back at the Siege of Summersgate.

No one welcomed them as they entered the town, and it wasn't until they were amongst its streets that the locals came out of hiding to greet them. Even then, many looked skyward, the fear in their eyes easy to see.

"Greetings," came a woman's voice. "I am Neasa, Chief of Clan Drakewell. I assume you are Lochlan of Dungannon?"

"I am. And this is my wife, Althea of Weldwyn."

The woman looked at the princess, but her eyes held no surprise, only exhaustion. "I'm glad you're here, both of you. We'd almost given up hope." She leaned to the side, looking past them to stare at the Dwarves. "The mountain folk? We are truly blessed for them to come to our rescue. Perhaps they can drive the vile creature from its lair."

"How did this happen?" asked Lochlan.

"The creature made its lair in the mine."

"Excuse me," said Brogar. "Did you say mine? What mine? I assumed you dug the iron out from the hills?"

"Your assumption would be correct; we do, but the mine belonged to your people, and they abandoned it years ago."

"Abandoned? Are you sure they weren't driven out?"

"I'm afraid I cannot say for sure; that was well before my time. The stories indicate they stopped trading with us without warning. When we went to investigate, the Dwarves were gone."

"Did your people explore the mine?"

"None would dare go into that place of darkness. It's been abandoned ever since."

"When did the dragon first appear?" asked Althea.

"This last winter. There were reports of a flying creature to the west, but none knew what it was."

"And its first attack?"

"Once spring arrived, the hunting parties made their first forays of the season into the hills in search of game." She paused, wiping a tear from her eye. "It came from the west," she continued, her voice breaking slightly, "and never a more fearsome creature was ever seen. It flew low, scraping its talons along rooftops as it spat fire. The air choked us, the heat seared our skin, and many were caught in the avalanche of rubble when the buildings collapsed. It was horrible."

She fought to control her emotions. "Over twenty people died in that first attack, but that wasn't the end. Soon after, we learned it had set upon our hunting parties as well. In those two alone, we lost close to fifty souls."

"Are you saying it came back?"

"It did, and with just as deadly consequences."

"How many times has it returned?" asked Althea.

"Six, so far. There is no pattern to the frequency of its attacks, making it impossible to predict when next it will descend upon us. We tried scattering to the hills this last time, but the creature swooped down and bore away two of our townsfolk in its talons. I can still hear their screams."

"Something brought it here," said Brogar. "I've never heard of a dragon hunting people before, not without someone to guide it."

"Perhaps it's seeking vengeance," said Althea. "After all, it took significant wounds at the siege. It may have mistaken the townsfolk for the people who hurt it."

"Then we must teach it to keep its distance," said Lochlan. "Have you any defences?"

"None that have proven effective against a dragon," replied Neasa. "Only a few of our buildings are stone, and even they couldn't stand up to its talons. Our archers tried loosing arrows, but its hide proved impervious. How do you fight a creature like that?"

"You don't," said Haldrim. "At least not here."

"What are you suggesting?"

"The creature can fly, and we lack enough arbalests to bring it down with one volley. We need to neutralize its advantage."

"And how do we do that?" asked Lochlan.

"By finding its lair."

The colour fled from Neasa's face. "You can't be serious? That would be suicidal!"

"Yet it seems to be our best course of action. Dragons lair in caves, the one place where they cannot use their ability to fly. I'm afraid that's the only advantage we're likely to get."

"Wouldn't a cave make it easier to burn us all?" asked Althea.

"It would, but you can tell when a dragon is going to breathe fire."

"How do you know all this?"

"Let's just say I took a strong interest in them after witnessing the destruction they wrought at the Siege of Summersgate."

"And you didn't think to mention this earlier?" said Lochlan.

Haldrim shrugged. "It never came up."

"Why do you suppose it waited until now to attack?"

"I can answer that," said Althea. "We badly wounded it at the siege. After finding refuge in these mountains, it likely lay dormant, recovering from its wounds."

"And now it's hungry?"

"Precisely."

"Fair enough," said Haldrim, "but we still need to find out where this thing has made its lair. This mine you spoke of earlier. Can someone take us there?"

"Are you proposing we march directly into the dragon's breath?" asked Neasa.

"No. I propose we send a small scouting party who can use stealth to spy it out. We can't very well plan an attack if we don't even know what the place looks like."

"My sister, Derdra, can show you the way."

"Is she a hunter?"

"No, our keeper of knowledge. She is also well-versed in the history of our people, including what little we know about the abandoned mine."

"I should very much like to talk to her," said Haldrim.

"Then I shall take you to her."

.   .   .

Derdra's house was small compared to the rest of Drakewell. From outside, it looked like little more than a single room. Upon entering, however, they found something quite unexpected—a spiral staircase carved out of rock that led into a pit.

"You will find her somewhere below," said Neasa. On one side sat a small gong. The chieftain drew her dagger and used its hilt to produce a sound that echoed down the stairwell.

"What is this place?" asked Lochlan.

"The place of knowledge. Below resides the collective wisdom of past generations."

"And here I thought all our people disliked being underground."

Footsteps echoed up from the stairwell before Neasa could answer, and then a woman appeared, the spitting image of the Clan Chief.

"Who do we have here?" she asked.

"This is Lochlan, Clan Chief of Dungannon," said Neasa. "He came to help us."

"And these other two?"

"Althea, wife to Lochlan, and Haldrim of the mountain folk."

"Pleased to meet you. No doubt my sister has already told you my name. Is there something in particular you came here to find? Or are you just being polite?"

"We're interested in learning more about the Dwarven mine," said Haldrim.

"What would you like to know?"

"Dwarves rarely abandon mines without reason. I want to know what happened to them."

"Then come," said Derdra. "I cannot guarantee you'll find the answers you seek below, but I have several records left by your people that I've been unable to translate." She began descending the stairs.

"I shall catch up with you later," said Neasa.

"You're not coming with us?" asked Lochlan.

"There are other things that need my attention. Find me when you're finished, and we'll make the necessary plans."

Althea peered down into the stairwell. "It's well-lit."

"Then we'd best not keep Derdra waiting," said Lochlan.

The circular stairs were carved into the side of the shaft, with a rope strung through metal rings, acting as a safety line. Derdra and Haldrim ignored it, but Althea, feeling a little dizzy when staring down into the pit, kept a firm grip. They'd descended about the height of two men when the first hall came into view.

"That," explained their guide, "is where we store the tallies."

"Tallies?" said Lochlan.

"Yes, records of each year's hunt and harvest. We use these numbers as an indication of our progress. Over the years, we've relied less on hunting and more on growing our own food, but I'm afraid the dragon's attack has destroyed many of our crops."

She continued, talking as she descended farther down the stairs. "The next room contains a listing of all who came before."

"I'm surprised," said Lochlan. "I didn't know any of the Twelve Clans kept such detailed written records."

"We began doing so three hundred years ago. Our chieftain at the time was a man of great wisdom and wished to preserve our history for future generations. He was the one who started the construction of this underground library."

"Why underground?" asked Althea.

"To protect the records from the elements. It also allows us to expand the archives without taking up more space above."

"How many levels are there?"

"Six, at present, although a seventh is planned."

"And how deep are we going?" asked Haldrim.

"To level six, where we moved the oldest records."

"And you live here?"

"No. I live in a separate building, but I spend most of my days here. Some of us took refuge here during the last dragon attack, but it's not designed to house people."

"You surprise me," said Haldrim. "A place like this would be more than suitable for Dwarves."

"Unfortunately, as we descend to the lower levels, the air gets fouler. It became quite a problem for those seeking to escape the dragon's flames."

"You need an air shaft and some bellows."

"Perhaps that's a discussion best left for another day," suggested Lochlan.

"Ah," said Derdra. "Here we are." She led them into a short side tunnel that opened into a larger chamber.

"This looks natural," said the Dwarf.

"It is. It's one of the reasons they built the archives here."

Alcoves were dug into the walls, turning them into shelves, with books piled in some, while the vast majority held rolled-up parchments.

"This place is amazing," said Lochlan. "I could spend weeks down here. Not that we have that much time to spare."

"The records I spoke of are over here," said Derdra. She walked to the far end, where large, leather-bound books were stacked on the floor.

"Where did you get those?" asked Haldrim.

"They were recovered from the mine many years ago."

"I thought none dared enter it?"

"I was young and foolish at the time."

"You retrieved them?"

"Yes," said Derdra. "Does that surprise you?"

"I took you for an academic."

"And so I am these days, but I was full of adventure and mischief in my youth. I suppose that's why I became our keeper of knowledge. I always wanted to know more about everything." She nodded at the books. "Well? What do you think? Can you translate them?"

Haldrim moved closer and knelt, examining the marks on the book spines. "These are Dwarven runes, but it'll take me some time to read through this lot."

"Then you'd best get to work," said Lochlan. "We need to know as much as possible about the layout of that mine if we're going to defeat this dragon."

TWENTY-EIGHT

Advice

SUMMER 967 MC

Revi let the cylinder of light drop, revealing the casting circle in Galburn's Ridge. He took a deep breath, letting it out slowly.

"Tired?" asked Hayley.

"Casting always drains a mage," he replied, "and recall uses more energy than other spells. I need a moment to catch my breath."

Two guards dressed in the Mercerian livery entered the room.

"Please inform Sir Heward we're here," said Hayley.

"You mean Lord Heward," corrected one. "He's the Baron of Redridge now."

"Yes, of course. My apologies."

"If you come this way, I'll take you to him."

"Good thing you didn't bring Gryph," said Revi. "I don't imagine the Norlanders would like the idea of a wolf in amongst them."

"They kept their distance in Beaconsgate," replied Hayley, "but he's not the type to favour the city life."

"I hope I will suffice as your bodyguard?"

"Oh, you're much more than that!" Her wicked grin spoke volumes.

The guard cleared his throat. "This way, Lady Hayley, Lord Revi."

"That's Master Revi. Mages don't use the titles of nobles."

"Lady Aubrey does, my lord."

"Hah!" said Hayley. "He's got you there."

"You forget, she's a baroness, but this is not the place to argue such things. Lead on, my good man."

The guard led them from the circle into a large courtyard, where a company of Norland footmen marched past. Recent recruits, from the look of them, but something about their tunics caused Hayley to halt.

"What's the matter?" asked Revi.

"Those men—whose colours do they wear?"

"The queen's," answered their guide.

"But aren't all the warriors of Norland sworn to the earls?"

"And so they were, but Queen Bronwyn has different ideas on the matter."

"Meaning?"

"Better to have her own guards keeping her safe than someone else's."

"That makes sense, I suppose. They just look so... young."

"We're not much older ourselves," said Revi.

"Yes, you're right. Tell me, did we look that young when we first began serving the queen?"

He chuckled. "You mean the princess, don't you? She wasn't queen back in those days."

"You know full well what I mean."

"If you'd asked me that in the old days, I would've said no, but then again, we were young and full of spirit."

"Well," said Hayley, "full of something. I seem to recall Merceria's warriors as being older."

"That's because they are. You must remember, soldiering is an honoured profession back home. They don't practice the same traditions here in Norland."

"But they're descended from Mercerians."

"They are, but their customs have changed over the centuries, and not always for the better."

The guard cleared his throat again. "Are you two finished? Because His Lordship won't wait all day."

Hayley resumed walking.

"Someone's in a mood," said Revi, keeping his voice low.

"Hush now. He's probably just having a bad day."

They crossed the courtyard, entered one of the inner buildings, then weaved their way through a series of corridors.

"Here we are," said their guide, arriving at a stout wooden door. Revi reached out to grab the handle, but at that precise moment, the door opened all by itself, revealing a startled warrior of Merceria, a captain, if his sash was any indication.

"My pardon," he mumbled, then pushed past.

"I must say," came Heward's voice. "This is a surprise. What brings you two to Galburn's Ridge?"

"I come seeking an audience with the queen," said Hayley.

"And Master Bloom?"

The mage smiled. "I am merely the transportation."

"Somehow, I doubt that."

"How are things in Norland of late?" asked Hayley.

"Quiet, for the most part. To all outward appearances, Bronwyn has settled into the role of queen, but I sense she's struggling."

"How so?"

"The earls keep pressuring her to make concessions."

"What kinds of concessions?"

"They want more say over the governing of the realm. Here in Norland, the monarch has always been more of a puppet, but Bronwyn's determined not to let that happen again."

"She needs a husband," said Revi.

"Why would you say that?" asked Hayley. "Don't you believe a woman can rule?"

"Queen Anna has proven that's not the case, but look at this from Norland's point of view. Women hold no power here: at least, they didn't until they crowned Bronwyn. I think that's one of the reasons she struggles to control her subjects."

"That likely accounts for the recruits we saw out in the courtyard. Was that your idea, Lord Heward?"

"It was," replied the warrior. "Though I wish some of them had a few more seasons under their belt."

"Then why not recruit older, more experienced warriors?" asked Revi.

"Easier said than done. Don't get me wrong; there are plenty to be found, but they all come with old loyalties, which is exactly the opposite of what she wants. It'll take some time to whip them into shape, but she's smart enough to know it's a long-term investment."

"And in the meantime?"

"She relies a lot on the current Mercerian garrison. Eventually, we'll move our men back to Wincaster and let her recruits take over the role of guarding this place, but if we left now, it would likely end in disaster."

"It's that volatile?" asked Hayley.

"I might be exaggerating a little," said Heward, "but I doubt the peace would hold for more than a month or two before open warfare broke out once again. There's still a lot of animosity left over from the war."

"What are you suggesting?" said Revi. "That they hate us?"

"Not us, each other. The victors are not in a forgiving mood, and the vanquished dislike the idea of their loss being held over their heads."

"Just how many warriors is Bronwyn raising?" asked Hayley.

"The plan calls for a total of ten companies. Some of those served her during the war, but the vast majority are recent recruits like you saw outside."

"And how is she paying for all of this?"

"That's her biggest problem and where the earls come in. They're with-holding their financial support until they get what they want."

"And what is it they want, precisely?"

"Positions of power and influence. Royal Treasurer is the most sought-after since that would give them access to the realm's coffers."

"You mean the very coins they choose to withhold?"

Heward shrugged. "I never claimed it made a lot of sense."

"Actually," said Revi, "it makes perfect sense if you look at the long-term picture. Eventually, Norland's economy will recover, and now that there's peace with Merceria, there'll be many more coins to spare."

"I suppose that makes sense. You, however, didn't come all this way to talk Norland politics."

"What makes you say that?"

Heward chuckled. "You claimed to be only the transportation, remem-ber? And I'm sure the High Ranger is far too busy to visit us on a whim."

"You're right," said Hayley. "I need Bronwyn's help."

"Truly? I can't imagine with what."

"It has to do with Randolf's claim to Bodden."

"Oh? What claim is that?"

"Haven't you heard? Sir Randolf alleges he is the son of Lord Edward Fitzwilliam."

"Ridiculous!"

"Is it? I would have believed so, too, but his story is compelling, as was the initial evidence."

"Was?"

"Yes. I managed to poke a few holes in his tale, but not enough to dismiss the claim altogether."

"What can I do to help?"

"You can start by getting us an audience with Bronwyn."

"Consider it done. Anything else?"

"We may need some of the queen's new soldiers down in Beaconsgate."

"Expecting trouble?"

"You might say that. The last time I was there, I was attacked."

"By whom?"

"That has yet to be determined, but I can't rule out the possibility Lord Asher ordered it."

"The earl? But he's only just taken on the role. Do you think that likely?"

"It's only a hunch at the moment," said Hayley, "but recent discoveries indicate he's hiding something."

"Then I'd best get you that audience sooner rather than later."

"How long do you believe it would take?" asked Revi.

"That depends."

"On?"

"How long it takes me to find her. Unless I'm wrong, you'll get your audience sometime this very afternoon."

"Thank you," said Hayley. "I appreciate the assistance."

"Don't mention it." He turned to leave but then thought better of it. "I don't imagine Beverly likes the notion of losing Bodden. How's she taking all of this?"

"About as well as can be expected. Thankfully, she's been kept busy with events in the east."

"Why?" asked Heward. "What's happened?"

"There are reports of a new enemy causing problems for the Dwarves of Stonecastle. Gerald gave Beverly command of a brigade and sent her to aid them."

"You know, it'd be helpful if someone could send this sort of news here in a timely manner."

"I'll be sure to mention it to Queen Anna."

"It's not her fault," said Revi. "We might have magic circles all over the place, but without the mages to employ them, it limits us in their use."

"Then you should train more," said Heward.

"That's exactly what we're trying to do, but it's a little difficult to teach classes when one constantly needs to cast the spell of recall. Don't worry. We'll get there eventually, just not as fast as we'd like."

Queen Bronwyn of Norland looked regal as she sat on the throne despite her relatively young age. Today, the room was empty, save for a few people who'd come to plead for the queen's judgement on several minor matters.

Hayley and Revi took their place at the end of the line, but when Bronwyn noticed their entrance, she waved them forward.

"Master Revi, Lady Hayley. To what do I owe the pleasure?"

"I come in my capacity as High Ranger," said Hayley. "I seek your assistance on a matter of import to the Crown of Merceria."

"Have you, indeed? You must tell me more."

They moved closer, bowing as they halted before her.

"Your Majesty," Hayley continued. "Lord Richard Fitzwilliam, Baron of Bodden, has died."

"He was old, was he not? And in any case, he was a Mercerian baron. Of what consequence is that to me?"

"A Norlander has laid claim to the barony. A man by the name of Randolf Blackburn."

Bronwyn shifted forward on the throne, her hands coming together to intertwine her fingers. "Now, that is fascinating. On what basis does he make this assertion?"

"That he is the son of Lord Edward Fitzwilliam, elder brother to Lord Richard."

"I can't imagine Dame Beverly is too happy about that."

Hayley ignored the comment. "We are here seeking information concerning the circumstances of Randolf's birth."

"That is of little concern to me, and truth be told, if that's what you're looking for, you're in the wrong place. They record such things in the city where the birth occurred, not the capital. Where is Randolf Blackburn from?"

"Beaconsgate, or so he claims."

"You have reason to doubt him?"

"He is a Knight of the Sword, Your Highness, or at least he was. At the time of his knighting, he claimed he lived in Merceria, yet we found no evidence to support that. He now says he was born in Beaconsgate to a woman of Norland descent who bore Lord Edward's children."

"Children? So, there was more than one?"

"Yes," said Hayley. "Two, to be precise. His older sister, Celia Blackburn, died when she attempted to murder Dame Beverly some years ago."

"An intriguing tale. Would you like my help in obtaining answers in Beaconsgate?"

"Indeed, Majesty. During my last visit there, I ran into some opposition. I fear there are those who are actively working to hide the truth."

"And what do I get in return?"

Hayley stared back, not sure how to respond. The question was entirely unexpected and took her by surprise.

Thankfully, Revi stepped in. "What would Your Majesty desire?"

"That depends," said Bronwyn. "How important is this to your queen? Come now, don't make light of it. I know she favours Dame Beverly, or she wouldn't have made her champion."

"Your aid with this would be seen as a great assistance and would help strengthen the bonds between our people."

"Spoken like a true diplomat, although it does little to explain what I would receive in exchange."

"Then name your price," said Revi, "and I will judge if it's equal to the task."

"An alliance with the Crown of Norland."

"And alliance, Majesty? But you no longer have enemies on your borders?"

"It's not external enemies I fear, it's internal ones."

"You fear a return to civil war?"

"Not so much a war as a Palace overthrow." Bronwyn lowered her voice. "The earls of Norland are not above such things, and my people have heard many rumours over the last few months."

"Surely Lord Heward's presence is sufficient to safeguard the Throne?"

"Perhaps, but they can't stay here forever. Even Lord Heward has a home, and I'm sure he's eager to see how his new barony is faring, now the war is over."

"I cannot speak to an alliance," said Revi. "Although I can promise to speak with Her Majesty about it upon my return. In the meantime, what about other arrangements? A more permanent garrison, perhaps?"

"Or," suggested Hayley, "some funds to help you raise and equip your own soldiers? I'm sure Merceria would be willing to lend you the expertise to train them?"

"That is acceptable. Now, assuming you can arrange that, what is it that I can do for you? Perhaps a captain and a few guards to represent my interests?"

"That is most appreciated, Your Majesty."

"Good. I shall arrange a suitable escort pending your own queen's acceptance of my request."

"I'll recall to Wincaster first thing in the morning," said Revi. "I expect to have an answer for you in a day or two. However, it will take longer for the actual arrangements to be made."

"Of course," said Bronwyn. "I know I can trust your word when it comes to such things, but in the meantime, Lady Hayley will remain here as my honoured guest."

Beverly peered over the ridge. "Is that the bridge?"

"Aye," said Herdwin. "Kharzun's Folly, we call it, or maybe I should say 'called' it since it's now destroyed."

"And you did that all by yourself?"

"I had help to weaken the centre span, but yes, I struck the final blow, almost killing myself in the process."

"It's a miracle you survived. How deep is that gorge?"

"You know, I didn't feel inclined to measure it as I was falling. Lucky for me, there's a stream at the bottom, likely the only thing that saved me."

"They look like they've done something to that tower. Did it always have a wooden roof?"

"No," replied the Dwarf. "It used to have a large metal bowl on top serving as a signal fire. They must have melted it down for all the iron."

"It looks like they've started trying to rebuild the bridge."

"They can try all they want, but with my cousin Gelion here with his arbalesters, they'll have a hard time of it."

"I'm not sure what I can do to help," said Beverly. "I brought three hundred men here to assist, but there's little they can do unless the enemy figures out a way to cross that gap."

"Your presence here is more political than military in nature. King Khazad has more than enough companies to stop them from crossing, but the support of Mercerian troops shows everyone in Stonecastle you're trusted allies."

"I'm glad we could be of help." Beverly scanned the surrounding mountains. "Tell me, is there any other way to get across? Could a small group, for instance, scale down the gorge and come up farther downstream?"

"I don't see why not, though it would be a tough climb. Why? What are you thinking?"

"Merely that a prisoner or two might prove valuable."

"I doubt that," replied the Dwarf. "Kasri and I talked to a couple of them when we first discovered their presence."

"And?"

"They're not exactly talkative. Oh, they like to go on about how it's their God-given right to conquer in the name of their emperor or what have you, but I wouldn't say they're reasonable people. It was a little bit like talking to a stone. You can say what you want, but the stone just doesn't care."

"Can we at least get a bit closer? I'd like to see what armour and weapons they possess."

"By all means, we can go right down to what's left of this side of the bridge if you like, although I wouldn't advise setting foot on it. The last thing I want to see is the rest of it falling into that gorge."

They climbed down the ridge and then returned to the path. Leaving the Mercerian troops safely in the rear, they walked to what remained of the bridge. A couple of arrows sailed their way, but Gelion's Dwarves stood behind a newly constructed wall and sent a few arbalest bolts towards the enemy.

"You'll pardon me if I don't get too close," said Herdwin. "It's just that the last time I was here, I nearly died."

Beverly spent the better part of the afternoon watching and waiting. The enemy appeared disciplined, for only armed men approached the gorge and even then, only after archers moved into position to provide covering volleys, should it prove necessary. The enemy's side of the gorge had the beginnings of a wooden tower right at the base of the bridge, and she noted how the section facing them was covered in hides.

"It looks like a siege tower," she said, and then everything fell into place. "Unless I miss my guess, that's exactly what it is."

"How would that help them?" said Herdwin.

"The boarding ramp a normal siege tower drops is near the top. This one, though, appears to have a ramp extending all the way to its base. It's essentially a mobile drawbridge."

"But it's not tall enough to cross the gorge?"

"You're right, it's not, at least not at the moment, but what if they made it taller?"

"Even a Dwarf would have a hard time making one that tall."

"What if they used magic? At the siege of Wincaster, back in sixty-two, Albreda and Aldus Hearn animated two enormous trees to get our warriors over the wall."

"Surely you're not suggesting they'd do the same thing here? There are no trees tall enough in these mountains."

"True, but we don't know what lies beyond the mountains to the east or what kind of mages they have at their disposal. Perhaps they can meld wood in the same way Earth Mages meld stone? Or their mages can create stone? The truth is, we know so little about them."

"That being the case, what do we do about it?"

"I would start by bringing up Kasri's company to reinforce that of your cousin. If they have magic at their disposal, they could strike at any time, and we must be prepared."

"And if they get across?"

"Then we plan out a defence in depth, and make them fight for every step."

TWENTY-NINE

Traitor

SUMMER 967 MC

T he road into Kinsley was busy. Admittedly, there was a lot of trade coming from Falford, but most of those within sight looked ill-equipped to travel more than an afternoon's walk.

"I must say this is odd," said Gerald, more to himself than to his companion.

"You mean the traffic?" asked Jane. "Don't you know? It's the Midsummer Fair."

"And that means?"

"The town will be celebrating the occasion. Don't you have summer fairs back in Merceria?"

"We have fairs, but they're more about drinking, dancing, and eating. You can't possibly tell me these folks are here just to drink?"

"No, of course not. They come to participate in the games."

"Such as?"

"Bobbing for apples, tossing coins, storytelling, even swordplay, but with wooden swords. We wouldn't want anyone getting hurt."

"And they do this every summer?"

She laughed. "Of course, why else call it the Midsummer Fair? If we weren't in such a hurry, I'd suggest we stay and visit."

"It sounds intriguing, but after all the work it took to capture the rogue, I'd prefer not to waste any more time getting Godfrey back to Summersgate."

"And quite right too. There'll be plenty of time for me to show you the wonders of Weldwyn customs in the future."

Gerald slowed his horse and turned in the saddle. "Captain?" he called out.

The answer came quickly. "Yes, my lord?"

"I suggest you keep your eyes out for trouble."

"Any particular reason?"

"The streets are crowded, making it easy for someone to get close enough to attempt a rescue of your guest."

"You worry too much, Lord. I assure you I've ridden through this town plenty of times and never ran into any trouble whatsoever."

"That I can well believe, but these are extraordinary times, and Godfrey is a man of consequence, with friends who could well have an interest in seeing him freed."

"Then we shall remain alert, Lord."

Gerald returned his gaze to the road ahead, his frown growing.

"You're worried," said Jane.

"I would be less worried if I thought our good captain had some experience behind him."

"He must have served for some time to gain his rank."

"Perhaps, but he doesn't impress me as the sort with battle experience."

She chuckled. "Few could match your record, Your Grace. You should give him the benefit of the doubt."

He turned to her, ready to argue the point, but her eyes robbed him of his voice. "You're beautiful," he said instead.

Her smile lit up her face. "It's nice to know I can still turn heads, but that wasn't what you were going to say, was it?"

"Likely not, but I've forgotten what I was talking about. It's what comes from travelling in the company of a woman with such grace."

"Do you realize where we are?"

"Of course. We're entering Kinsley." He suddenly understood her meaning. "It's where we met," he quickly added. "I'll never forget the moment I first laid eyes on you. You were soaking wet; do you remember?"

"I do, and you were ever the gallant gentleman."

He pulled back on the reins as a horseman galloped past, nearly colliding with his own mount. "For Saxnor's sake," he muttered under his breath.

The traffic became even more congested as people funnelled into the narrow streets closer to the centre of town. A man with impossibly long legs meandered past, and Gerald looked on in surprise.

"Stilts," said Jane, trying to hide her amusement. "Have you never seen them before?"

"I most certainly have not. How do they stay upright on such ungainly things?"

"Years of practice, I should think."

"I don't remember this place being so busy when our army marched through."

"That's because many of the inhabitants fled. With the war over, they've returned, swelling the numbers."

"I think we took a wrong turn somewhere. Didn't we cut across the north when we marched?"

"You did, but if you recall, the rain washed away a good portion of the road."

"I would have thought they'd have repaired that by now."

"The war ended less than a year ago. I doubt they've had time to consider much other than getting their crops planted. Most of the surrounding area is taken up by farms."

"That explains all these people," said Gerald. "The population seems to have doubled, thanks to this festival."

"Fair," she corrected. "And more likely, it's tripled. Folks come from miles in every direction to participate in something like this."

"So, you've been here before? Before the war, I mean."

"No, but I've seen the same thing in other towns and villages. Who knows? Perhaps the custom will spread to Merceria?"

"I'd like that."

They entered a large, open area, a makeshift market by the look of things. The noise level increased significantly, as did the number of children rushing to and fro.

Gerald looked around in surprise. "Fascinating. I wish we had time for a proper visit."

The first sign of trouble was a shout from behind him. He glanced over his shoulder to see three men clambering onto the wagon. One had already stabbed the driver, who slumped forward, his reins falling from his hands.

His companion up front, the captain, struggled to hold off a second man wielding a knife, the attack coming so quickly that he never had a chance to draw his own weapon. As to the rest of the prisoner detail, there was no sign of them.

Gerald wheeled his horse around. "Stay here," he shouted, galloping back to where the attack was underway. He would have drawn his sword had he been in a battle, but this required an altogether different tactic. He pulled up alongside the now halted wagon and leaped from the saddle, intending to land atop one of the attackers, but he failed to take into account his aging body. Instead, he fell short, reaching out at the last moment to grab the fellow's belt before he slammed into the side of the wagon, knocking the air from his lungs. His weight did the rest, dragging his opponent from the driver's body and pulling him to the ground.

Gerald had the presence of mind to roll slightly to avoid being crushed, then kicked out, striking the fellow in the face and quieting him.

The second man struggled with the captain, but the old warrior was more concerned with where the third one had gone. He immediately thought of Lord Godfrey.

Gerald pulled himself to his feet and stumbled to the back of the wagon, his bones aching with every step. Sure enough, the villain was attempting to rescue His Lordship by smashing the padlock with a hammer. This time Gerald drew his sword.

"Give up," he shouted. "Your plan has failed."

The man snapped his head around to see the marshal approaching. He snarled, tossing the hammer at him, then jumped down from the wagon, gaining enough space to draw his own blade.

"You can't win," shouted Gerald. "Throw down your sword, and I will spare your life." He had high hopes the fellow would succumb. Indeed, it looked as if he were ready to toss his weapon aside, but then the young fool rushed forward.

His attack was easy to parry, and having spent a lifetime on the battle-field, Gerald's counterattack, when it came, was swift and lethal, slicing into his foe's neck. He stepped forward, looking down at the body.

"For Saxnor's sake," he said. "When will they ever learn?"

The wagon rolled ahead, reminding him the captain still fought for his life. He ran up front to find them locked in a life-or-death struggle.

The wagon's momentum suddenly halted with a terrible crunch, throwing the captain and his opponent from the wagon. Gerald rushed to lend a hand only to see the captain rise. The last attacker had fallen onto his own knife, which now protruded from his chest.

"Well," said Gerald. "At least we have one prisoner."

"Guess again," said the captain, pointing beneath the wagon to where his first opponent, the one he'd pulled from the driver's seat, lay. He'd remained unconscious for the remainder of the fight, but the wheel had crushed the man's skull when the wagon rolled forward.

"So much for that idea," said Gerald. The rest of the prisoner's guards pushed through the crowd.

"Where have you been?" he growled.

"Sorry, my lord. There were just too many people in the way."

. . .

Jack Marlowe slowed his horse. A large crowd had gathered in the market, impeding their progress. He ordered his men forward, and they began the time-consuming process of nudging people out of the way.

The townsfolk soon took notice of the guards and dispersed, revealing the source of their fascination. Four men lay stretched out on the ground, clearly dead, one of them with a crushed skull. Someone stood over them, placing their arms to make them look like they were sleeping. The fellow stood, turning at the sound of the horses.

"Gerald?" said Jack. "What happened here?"

"We were attacked. The man on the end was driving our wagon; the other three sought to release Lord Godfrey from custody."

"I'm sorry to have missed it." The cavalier dismounted, handing his reins over to one of his men. He stepped closer, peering down at the bodies. "It's a pity there weren't any survivors. Any idea who sent them?"

"Someone with more than enough funds to finance this, I'd wager, though I don't know whether their objective was to free him or silence him."

"You believe they wanted him dead?"

"I do." Jane pushed her way through the crowd. "Lord Godfrey has many accomplices. I suspect this attack was an attempt to silence him before he could name them."

"Then we must make doubly sure he's kept alive," said Jack. "The prince's guard will escort him the rest of the way." He paused for a moment, then smiled. "I suppose I should say the king's guard, now."

"So, it's official?" said Gerald.

"There has yet to be an actual coronation, but he is officially King Alric the First. At least, I assume he's the first. I was never one to keep up on my history."

"You are correct," added Jane. "He is also, paradoxically, destined to be the last King of Weldwyn once his son inherits the Throne."

"We have a few years before we need to worry about that. Now, where is this prisoner of yours, Marshal?"

"Over there," said Gerald, "in the wagon with the cage on the back, but I must warn you, it's slow."

"Then might I suggest we take him by horse? I'm sure we can find a suitable mount somewhere around here."

"A good idea. I shall fetch the prisoner." The old warrior wandered over to the wagon.

"You surprise me, Lady Jane," said Jack. "You're the last person I expected to see here."

"I was the one who found Godfrey."

"So I've been told. The Crown is deeply indebted to you. I'm sure His Majesty will be most pleased to reward you for your efforts."

Gerald reappeared, forcing the struggling prisoner before him. "He's a slippery fellow."

"I shall be sure to have my men keep a close eye on him." Jack turned around. "Sergeant? Take charge of the prisoner."

"I'd take it as a kindness," said Gerald, "if you would allow Lady Jane and I to accompany you back to Summersgate."

"I should be delighted to have your company."

"What do you want to do with the rest of the Falford guards?"

"I believe we can send them home, don't you? It's not as if they'll be able to keep up with the king's finest."

"Then I shall speak with the captain." Gerald wandered off once more.

"He's very dutiful," said Lady Jane.

"Indeed, he is, my lady. You have yourself quite the catch there."

A flush coloured her cheeks, causing Jack to chuckle. "I mean no disrespect, madam. He clearly thinks the world of you."

"And I, him."

"Can we expect a wedding in the future? After all, that would make you the Duchess of Wincaster?"

"I seek no title, my lord, merely his companionship."

He smiled. "Yet I sense you wouldn't refuse if he were but to ask?"

She quickly changed the subject. "What will happen to Godfrey once we return?"

"He shall be tried and then executed for treason."

"If you are so sure of his guilt, then why hold a trial?"

"We still have laws in Weldwyn, my lady, but I've seen the evidence, and it is, in a word, overwhelming. I see no way in which he might avoid death, but should he co-operate, he may have some control over the manner of it." He paused a moment, unsure of how to continue.

"You assume his words will condemn James," said Jane. "The thought has occurred to me as well, my lord, but if he is guilty of treason, as I fear he is, he deserves death."

"He is still your son, madam."

"He stopped being that when he sent me out of the city to spy for his master."

"In that case, may I offer you my condolences?"

"That would, I think, be more appropriate."

Gerald reappeared. "What are you two chatting about?"

"Oh, nothing," said Jack. "Just marriage and politics."

Jane's blush returned, which didn't escape the marshal's notice. He opened his mouth to speak, but the cavalier interrupted him. "My men found a horse for the prisoner. You'd best gather your own mounts. We'll be leaving as soon as we're able."

By week's end, Godfrey was again safely behind bars in the capital. News spread quickly of his arrest, leading Lord Elgin to call a late-night emergency meeting of the Earls Council.

Lord Beric was bleary-eyed as he took his seat. "Why in the name of Malin are we meeting now? Could this not have waited for the morning?"

"Elgin called us here," said Beric, "as is his right."

"I understand he has the power; we all do, but why at this ungodly hour?"

Lord Oliver took a sip of his wine. "I suggest we get on with whatever he'd like to discuss, although I must say he's started out on very loose footing."

Elgin cleared his throat. "No doubt you've all heard that Lord Godfrey is back in Summersgate. Having examined the case against him, I would like to recommend we dismiss the charges of treason."

"On what grounds?"

"Our evidence is thin, to say the least."

"But there are eyewitnesses to his treachery," said Oliver. "Are you suggesting they all lied?"

"Come now, gentlemen. We all know that when it comes to politics, this council determines what the truth is." He looked directly at Lord Beric. "We live in perilous times. The kingdom has suffered much of late. Would it not be better to bury this rather than open our own wounds for all to see?"

Beric stared back, suddenly wide awake. "You make an excellent point: one we should seriously consider."

Lord Julian rolled his eyes. "Come now, Beric, not you too? Godfrey is a traitor. Are you suggesting we let him go completely unpunished?"

Elgin smiled. "Hear me out, my lords, for I have considered this at great length. The people of Weldwyn look to us nobles for guidance and security. How do you think they would react should we expose the treachery of one of our own? Why, we'd never be able to regain their trust."

"I'm not sure what you're suggesting—we dismiss all charges or murder him in his sleep."

"Either would do," said Beric. "Though silence is, perhaps, a more permanent solution. It would prevent others from rallying to his cause."

"His cause?" said Lord Dryden. "He has no cause. Godfrey worked for the Twelve Clans. No one in Weldwyn would dare trust him again."

"Ah, but what of the Clans themselves?"

"Surely you're not suggesting they'd invade yet again? They haven't the men for it!"

"Not now, certainly," said Beric, "but in time, they will recover."

"Then let us hope Princess Althea succeeds in her efforts to tame them."

"It matters not," said Elgin. "The truth is any trial will reveal our weaknesses."

"And what weaknesses are those?" asked Oliver.

"Corruption. Or did you forget he paid the guards to look the other way?"

"Paid or ordered?"

"Does it matter?" said Elgin. "Either way, it exposes how vulnerable we are to such things."

Dryden shook his head. "No. It's important that justice is seen to be done."

"Justice? You dare speak of justice? We all know this won't be a fair trial. The man's guilt is already assumed."

The door opened, surprising everyone when Alric strode in with a pair of bodyguards.

"Gentlemen," he said. "I was quite shocked when I learned you'd called a meeting of the Earls Council at such a late hour. Tell me, what does this concern?"

"My apologies, Highness," said Lord Elgin, "but the business of this council is none of your concern until you are crowned."

"I'm afraid your knowledge of Weldwyn law is not as good as you think. I became king as soon as this council offered me the Crown."

"But there's been no coronation as yet."

"The coronation is but a formality. As such, this council can only be called by Royal Decree."

"You are dismissing us?" asked Beric.

"Should any of you wish to meet to discuss matters, you merely need to ask. I don't want you to think I'm taking away any of your influence." Alric's eyes met those of each of the earls in turn. "Now. I ask you once more. What does this meeting concern?"

Lord Julian was the first to answer. "Lord Elgin believes we should dismiss the charges against Lord Godfrey."

"He has his reasons," added Beric.

The king's eyes bored into Elgin. "Does he now? I'd be very much interested in hearing them."

Elgin swallowed hard, revealing his nervousness. "It's just that the kingdom's been through so much of late. Bringing this story to light will only make things worse."

"I disagree," said Alric. "The people want to know someone is to be held accountable for the pain they endured. I fear they may become more vocal in their displeasure if we brush this aside."

"Surely you're not suggesting rebellion?" said Lord Dryden.

"Is it rebellion to punish those who wronged you?"

They all stared back, none brave enough to voice any dissent.

"I thought as much," said Alric. "This council is adjourned until further notice. Do not leave the capital, gentlemen. I shall doubtless soon have further need of you."

THIRTY

History

SUMMER 967 MC

"Well?" said Lochlan. "What do you think? Will the dragon return?"

Althea looked westward, towards the distant peaks. There had been no sign of the dragon since their arrival, yet she held no doubt the beast would return. Drakewell represented nothing more than an easy food supply, and she knew hunger would eventually drive the creature to hunt once more.

"Undoubtedly," she said. "The only question is when."

"And your prediction?"

"You'd likely be more able to answer that than I."

"Me? What makes you say that?"

"You studied that book on dragons."

"You mean the one that poisoned me? I'd hardly use that as a definitive source."

"Come now," said Althea. "Surely you've read other books on the subject?"

"I have—half a dozen at least, although none of them first-hand accounts."

"What do they tell you?"

"Dragons are related to drakes and wyverns but are considerably more intelligent. At least that's the prevailing thought."

"Melethandil was capable of speech," said Althea, "but I get the impression that wasn't true of all her kind."

"I've read the same. Apparently, the larger the dragon, the more intelligent it is."

"Wouldn't size also indicate age?"

"I assume so. Human children grow more intelligent with age; it would stand to reason that so do dragons. Using that logic, the dragon in these parts is likely on the younger side."

"It's also a different colour," said Althea. "I recall its scales having a greener hue."

"So, another kind of dragon, then. Did it possess a rider?"

"Not that I'm aware, though I heard speculation the Kurathians employed mages to control their dragons."

"This gets more complicated by the day. I don't suppose we could convince the beast to move elsewhere?"

"Even if it could talk, I doubt it would listen, and why would it? From its point of view, there's plenty of food in the area."

"So we just kill it?"

"Haldrim might have a different opinion," said Althea, "but unless he suggests otherwise, I'm inclined to believe we should prepare for the worst."

"Speaking of our captain, where is he?"

"Likely back in the archives, poring over those books."

"Has he found anything that might help us with our present circumstances?"

"Not yet."

Lochlan turned his gaze to the mountains. "I doubt that dragon will stay away much longer. Didn't Derdra say it returned every couple of weeks?"

"More or less. Why? What are you thinking?"

"Merely that while it's attacking here, it won't be up at that mine."

"Are you suggesting we just sit by and watch that thing terrorize Drakewell?"

"No, of course not. We'll leave the Dragon Company here to help. If we're lucky, their bolts will drive it off."

"And if they don't?"

"Then the presence of a few more individuals will make little difference. The dragon's absence, on the other hand, is likely the only way we're going to be able to get up there and plan out how to defeat this thing."

Haldrim emerged from the archives, blinking in the noonday sun. His study of the Dwarven manuscripts had taken most of the night, and though he'd struggled to remain awake, he knew it was important to reveal his discovery to Althea.

He found her sitting in the sun, absently staring at a small waterfall trickling into the Redwater.

"I hope I'm not interrupting, my lady."

"Not at all, Captain. It's nice to see you out in the sunlight once more. I assume you found something?"

"I did, although part of me wishes I had better news."

"Go on," she urged.

"The Dwarves who built that mine had a great discovery."

"Can you be more specific?"

"Only that it was a metal unlike any discovered before. It's described as being hard as sky metal, but they claim it was found far beneath the surface."

"Are you suggesting it fell from the sky and buried itself in the mountain?"

"Not at that depth. Rather, it occurred naturally. In any case, sky metal is silver; they described this new ore as blacker than coal. They tried smelting a small sample of it but found their forges weren't hot enough."

"How did they overcome that limitation?"

"They built a hotter forge. From what I gather, they used it to forge a black metal axe."

"Black metal?" said Lochlan.

"Their name for it, not mine."

"Are you suggesting in all the thousands of years that Dwarves have mined this land, not a single one has seen such a thing?"

"I can't say for certain, but whoever wrote the account had never seen its like, nor any of the smiths employed at Tor-Maldrin."

"Tor-Maldrin?"

"Aye. Their name for the great city lying beneath the mountain."

"City?" said Lochlan. "And here we thought it only a mine! Any information about what happened to the Dwarves who lived there?"

"Very little. The book I perused predated the abandonment, though there is a reference to exploring the deep."

"Which is?"

"A network of tunnels and caves exist in the lower depths of our land, where the air is foul and strange creatures roam. In times past, great Dwarven mages could bend such creatures to their will. We call them the 'deep-ones', but you might know them as earth elementals or rock creatures."

"If the air is foul," said Lochlan, "how did they explore this 'deep'?"

"That's not specified, but I imagine they used bellows to push air down there. It would be a major feat of engineering, to be sure, but certainly not impossible, if our history is to be believed."

"Is that what they did back in Mirstone?"

"They did," said Haldrim, "but that was centuries ago. In the end, they gave up, for though it was interesting, there was little to be gained by it."

"Could one of these elementals have escaped the deep and driven away your kin?"

"I hadn't considered that possibility, although now you mention it, it explains a few things."

"So, what you're saying," said Althea, "is that there's a scarce and valuable metal down there, along with the equivalent of walking statues to guard it?"

"That would about sum it up, yes. Naturally, you'd need to add the dragon to that list."

"Could this get any more difficult?" asked Lochlan. "Perhaps it's the Gods' way of telling us to leave the area?"

"It's a bit late now," replied Althea. "The dragon would obliterate us if it caught us out in the open."

"What if we found our own refuge in the caves?"

"Won't work," said Haldrim. "They'd probably be inhabited by those Goblins we saw."

"What do you know about them?" asked Althea. "About Goblins, in general, I mean."

Haldrim frowned. "Not the sort of folk one should associate with. They tend to be vicious little brutes, keen on murder and thievery, though little else."

"Come now. There must be more to them than that."

"Like what?"

"Do they live in tribes? What weapons do they use? What tactics do they employ?"

"They're a cowardly bunch," said the Dwarf, "who run at the first sign of trouble. As such, they've never posed much of a danger to Dwarves. You saw them on the way here. They only use spears and clubs."

"And staff slings."

"That they do, but they show little knowledge of armour save for some leather skins and the odd wooden shield."

"How much of a threat do you suppose they represent?"

"For the company? None. For a group of individuals scouting out the mine, however, they'd be much more than a simple nuisance."

"Terrific," said Lochlan. "One more thing to add to the list."

"I'm not convinced of that," said Althea. "They might prove useful allies."

"Allies?" said Haldrim. "Have you lost your wits? You can't trust them!"

"Why not? It's not as if the dragon helps them in any way. They likely fear that thing as much as us. Perhaps, if we co-operate, we'll have a better chance of ridding ourselves of it?"

"With all due respect, my lady, I think trying to work with the Goblins is more dangerous than practical."

"We Humans once believed the same thing about the Orcs, yet Merceria now calls them allies."

"Orcs are a civilized race."

"And how do you know the Goblins aren't? Has anyone ever studied them? Or tried to negotiate with them?"

"You can't negotiate if you don't speak their tongue," said Haldrim. "Besides, they're barely capable of speech."

"You don't know that. You're making that assumption because they appear primitive from our perspective."

"It's dangerous even to attempt to negotiate with those things. They attacked us, remember?"

"And why wouldn't they? We were armed intruders entering their land. Would you do any different were they to show up in Dungannon?"

"No, I suppose not," said Haldrim, "but I still say it's dangerous."

"Then I shall go without you."

"At least take Brogar," said Lochlan. "I'd offer to go myself, but I'd likely make things worse."

"So be it," said Althea. "We'll leave first thing tomorrow morning."

"How will you find them?"

"I'll follow the river downstream until I reach where we originally encountered them."

"And if you don't find them?"

"Then," said Althea, "I'll come up the other bank. They're obviously familiar with the area. I doubt strangers following the river will escape their notice."

"What if they prove hostile?"

"Then it will be up to you and Haldrim to kill the dragon, but I doubt it'll come to that."

"How can you be so certain?" asked Lochlan.

"I can't. There is the chance they'll kill me on sight, but I must try something."

The two of them set out at first light, carrying little save for some stonecakes and their weapons and armour. Althea made a point of travelling in the open, the better to be seen by the Goblins. Brogar grumbled the entire way, certain they walked to their doom.

"You're more than welcome to remain in Drakewell," said Althea.

"And abandon my charge? No, thank you. I swore an oath to protect you, and that's precisely what I'll do. If that means I'll be stabbed to death by Goblins, then so be it!"

"Thank you, Brogar. I shall never forget your loyalty."

The river was simple enough to follow in theory, for all they needed do was continue along its banks. The difficulty, however, was that the riverbank was not always easy to traverse. By noon, they were moving slowly, for the ground had become rough and uneven. At some point in the distant past, it must have overflowed its banks and cut rivulets into the rock, making the footing very unstable.

Althea had only gone a few paces across this difficult ground when she heard a small rock fall off to her left. She froze, her hand automatically grasping the handle of her weapon.

Brogar, spotting her movement, immediately halted and drew his hammer, then scanned the nearby hills for any signs of trouble.

"I don't like this," he said. "They could have us surrounded."

"They likely do, yet they're not attacking. That indicates they're more interested in keeping an eye on us than killing us."

They ceased moving and waited there, watching. A small, green head appeared over the rise, and then a diminutive Goblin topped the hill, possibly the same individual Althea had encountered last time, if his spiked club was any indication. He advanced slowly, his weapon in hand but not raised in anger.

In response, Althea lifted her arms away from her own weapon. "Put your hammer away," she said. "We don't want to alarm them."

The Dwarf huffed but did as she asked. The Goblin approached, stopping within a few paces of her. He spoke but soon realized they didn't understand him. Instead, he pointed to himself. "Glisnak."

"Althea," she replied. "And this is Brogar." She pointed at the Dwarf.

"Altea," said the Goblin.

"Close enough." She pointed skyward and then put her hands together at the thumbs and flapped them as she had seen the Goblin do on their last encounter. "Dragon," she said.

Glisnak pointed upriver and nodded. "Dragon." He then cupped a hand and held it palm down while his other hand walked two fingers into it.

"What in the blazes is he trying to say?" asked the Dwarf.

"I believe he's telling us the dragon is in his cave."

"And how does that help us?"

"Hush now. Let me think." She pointed at the Goblin. "Glisnak take Althea"—she pointed at herself, then cupped her hand—"to cave?"

She saw his eyes light up. "*Wargar*," he said, then made a stabbing motion to his chest and fell to the ground. Moments later, he lifted his head, looking at the pair of them.

"I think he means danger."

"Congratulations," said Brogar. "You've mastered your first Goblin word. That being said, perhaps he's got a point? He means to indicate the dragon is dangerous. Then again, what if he's attempting to lure us to our deaths?"

"No. I don't think so. I imagine the dragon isn't particular about what it eats."

"Meaning?"

"His people likely suffered as much as ours." She raised one hand to hold out in front of her as if to stop the Goblin, then slowly drew her mace. "Althea, *wargar*, dragon," she said.

Glisnak nodded enthusiastically. He moved closer, then held out his hand.

"He wants your mace," said Brogar.

"No, I don't believe so." She tucked her mace back into her belt, then held out her own hand, palm upward, and waited.

Glisnak moved closer and grasped her hand. His was cold and clammy, yet the grip was firm, if not particularly strong. He used his other hand to point towards the hill he'd descended, then began leading her across the ground, mindful of the uneven footing.

"Just for the record," said the Dwarf. "I think this is a bad idea."

"So noted," replied Althea. "Now, come. Let's see where he's taking us."

Other Goblins soon joined them, though they kept a respectful distance. By Althea's count, there were twenty or so, but they moved around so much, it wasn't easy to get an accurate count. Each was armed with a crude spear and wore some sort of leather armour made from animal skins. They accepted the presence of Althea and Brogar quite readily, and though they didn't ignore their strange new guests, they spent more time watching the sky for signs of danger.

The distant mountains grew closer, and then the group halted. Glisnak pointed with his club, indicating a small tendril of smoke drifting up into the sky. "Dragon," he said, then made the shape of a cave. However, instead of walking his fingers into the opening, he moved them to the tip of his fingers. "*Algath.*"

"What do you suppose that means?" asked the Dwarf.

"Your guess is as good as mine, but if it means avoiding the main entrance, I'm all for it."

"That cave is still some distance to travel. It'll likely be dark by the time we get there."

She looked at Glisnak and nodded, allowing him to continue leading her. Just as the sun was settling over the mountains, they halted. The Goblins gathered sticks and lit a small fire. Most of the party lay down at this point and quickly fell asleep, but Althea and Brogar found little comfort on the hard ground.

Glisnak, perhaps sensing this, sat opposite them. He made the hand signal for mountain, then parted his fingers slightly and pointed at the gap. "*Algath.*"

"I still don't understand," said Althea.

"I think I do," said Brogar. "If the mine is Dwarven-built, as Neasa indicated, there will be vents for fresh air."

"Vents?"

"Yes. Shafts dug into the side of the mountain."

"Wouldn't that let in rain and snow?"

"They would if they opened straight up, but if it's anything like Mirstone, they'll be on an angle. There'll also be a noticeable dip at the surface to capture any water that might get in."

"So, you think Glisnak is taking us to an air vent?"

"It makes sense. I imagine someone the size of a Goblin would have little trouble climbing down a tunnel like that."

"And what about us? Would we be able to fit?"

"That's difficult to say. I've never been inside one. On the other hand, someone had to get inside the thing to shape it in the first place."

"Shape it? Are you suggesting they carved it out of solid stone?"

"More likely a master of rock and stone."

"You mean an Earth Mage?"

"Exactly. They were said to be common amongst our folk."

"And now?"

"Most of them died off without passing on their knowledge. More's the pity. We really could use one right about now."

Brogar handed her a stonecake as they sat by the fire. They'd only been there for what felt like a short time when the Goblins suddenly stood.

"It seems this was only a quick rest," said Althea.

"Aye, but I don't much fancy the idea of trying to climb the mountain in the dark."

Glisnak, as if sensing their hesitation, reached into a pouch and pulled forth something that looked like a mushroom. He mimicked eating it, then held it out to Althea.

She took it, examining it by the light of the fire.

"You can't be serious?" said Haldrim. "It could be poisonous?"

"Nonsense. If they wanted to kill us, we'd already be dead." She broke off the cap and took a bite, chewing it thoroughly. "I can't say I much like the taste."

"He likely thought you were hungry."

She stood, then reached out to steady herself against her companion. "Something's happening."

He looked up in a panic, but then she smiled.

"No, it's all right." She scanned the area. "Remarkable."

"What is?"

"I can see almost as clearly as if it were daytime."

"Let me have that." He grabbed the rest of the mushroom and shoved it into his mouth.

Althea watched as his face took on a look of wonderment.

"Well, I'll be," said the Dwarf. "I never heard tell of such a thing. I wonder how long it lasts?"

"Let's continue, shall we? We have a mine to explore!"

THIRTY-ONE

Confession

R evi knelt and patted the wolf. "This is it," he said. "Beaconsgate."

"Gryph and I were here before, remember?" said Hayley. "Though admittedly, not in the company of Norland Royal Troops."

"We shall try not to get in your way," said Captain Naran, "but at the same time, I have instructions to make our presence known to the people hereabouts. Her Majesty feels a proper show of force will remind them that she rules this land."

"Understandable," said Revi. "The question now, is how we proceed?"

"I've been thinking about that a lot of late," replied Hayley. "We've come to the end of the road in terms of trying to prove or disprove the identity of the body lying in the Temple of Saxnor. I thought we might try a different approach."

"Which is?"

"Finding evidence of Lord Edward's marriage to Randolf's mother."

"What good will that do?"

"It goes to the heart of his claim, don't you see? If there's a record of the marriage, it needs to have Lord Edward's real name on it, or it wouldn't be legal, at least not in any Mercerian court."

Revi turned to their captain. "Where would such records be kept?"

"That's easy," the warrior replied. "The Temple of Saxnor. If it's not there, then it never took place, in the eyes of the Crown."

"I suppose that's as close to any legal definition as we're going to find. Lead on, Hayley. You're the one familiar with this part of the country."

"I was only here once," she replied. "I hardly consider that as being familiar with the place."

"Still, you can find your way to the temple, can't you?"

"Of course. All we need do is head towards that big building over there. What could be simpler?" She paused a moment. "Should I leave Gryph here on the outskirts of town this time?"

"I suggest not," said Captain Naran. "In Norland, we have a legend that tells of a wolf who collects the souls of those destined for the Underworld."

"I hardly see how that helps us."

"Your companion will put the fear of death in the hearts of our enemies."

"Enemies?" said Revi. "We're here to search records, not to get into a fight."

"Yet a fight is what we may find. Lord Asher will not look kindly upon this intrusion by Royal Troops. We must be on our guard."

"And you would kill your countrymen?"

"I will do whatever is necessary to serve the Crown."

"I admire your dedication, though perhaps not your eagerness to start a fight."

"Don't be so hard on him," said Hayley. "Queen Bronwyn is a relatively young woman and must flex her muscles sometimes if she is to remain on the Throne."

"Aye," said the captain. "It's true. Never before has a woman claimed the Crown of Norland. She must prove herself ruthless if she is to survive. It is our way."

"Ruthless?" said Revi. "Our queen is beloved by all. Surely that's a better way to rule?"

"I will not speak ill of your own Royal House, but this is Norland, not Merceria. Our traditions have changed considerably since our ancestors fled your land, resulting in a series of brutal rulers fitting for such harsh surroundings. Queen Bronwyn's wish is that one day we live much as you do to the south, in a land of peace and plenty, but to get there, she must prove capable of holding the Crown against all who oppose her."

"Tell me, Captain. How did you come to command a company of the queen's guards?"

"I was amongst the first to join her cause during the war."

"And were you one of the traitors who turned against us at Galburn's Ridge?"

"I will not apologize for the actions of my queen. She did what she believed best for her people."

"I'm not sure that makes me feel safe in your company."

"Come now," said Hayley. "Let's put the past behind us. We are allies, or at least we will be once the queen informs the Nobles Council of her decision."

"There's still the matter of writing out the terms of the alliance," said Revi.

"You worry too much."

They drew closer to the town and were soon amongst its streets. The sight of Bronwyn's troops, resplendent in their yellow-and-black surcoats, caused many locals to stop and stare, but none were brave enough to approach the group. Most went out of their way to give them a wide berth, which pleased Captain Naran.

News of their arrival spread quickly, and by the time they entered Temple Square, a group of warriors in blue and black had gathered to block their entrance to the temple.

"What's this, now?" said Revi.

"Those are Lord Asher's men," said Hayley. "I recognize their colours."

"They are," said Naran. "I know their captain; I fear there shall be bloodshed after all." He halted his men and then stood between the opposing lines. "In the queen's name, I hereby order you to disperse your men."

"And I am here by order of Lord Asher," came the reply. "You are the trespassers here."

Hayley advanced to stand beside the queen's captain. "We wish only to search the records of the Temple of Saxnor. There need be no bloodshed."

"If it's bloodshed you want to avoid, then you should leave. This city falls under the dominion of Lord Asher, Earl of Beaconsgate."

"Must I remind you that your master took an oath to serve his queen?" said Naran. "Resistance here today would be considered an act of treason."

"I will not back down." Asher's captain drew his sword and stepped out before his men.

Naran, in reply, brandished his own weapon. As violence was about to erupt, Revi muttered something and pointed at the enemy leader, who let out a large yawn and then collapsed to the ground.

The queen's men surged forward, driven on by their leader's command, and within moments, the warriors of Beaconsgate threw down their weapons in surrender.

"Very well done," said Hayley, turning to Revi. "You're handy to have around."

"I do what I can. I suggest we use the opportunity to get inside before Asher's people fabricate any more lies."

"You think him behind this entire Bodden affair?"

"Perhaps not the mastermind, but he stands to gain from it, if only by disrupting things in Merceria."

They left Captain Naran to take care of the prisoners and headed inside.

Brother Caldwell, whom Hayley had met previously, was waiting for them in the main entrance hall.

"Expecting us?" said Hayley.

"One can hardly ignore the presence of so many warriors at the door. Did you come seeking further information?"

"Yes, though not about Lord Edward's body."

The brother nodded. "I feared as much."

"Feared?"

"There is an old saying that knowledge is power. The right information can enhance a ruler's reputation if presented at an opportune time. Conversely, in the wrong hands, it can also ruin it."

"You speak in riddles."

"I've had words with Elder Roswald of late."

"Who is?"

"A retired member of our order. He tends to keep to his room mostly, but when I told him of your last visit, he revealed he was deeply troubled."

"About what?"

"That, I'll let him tell you himself. If you'll come with me, I'll take you to him."

"By all means," said Hayley. "Lead on."

Their footsteps echoed on the stones as Brother Caldwell led them through the hall of worship into the living quarters, finally halting at a very worn door.

"You will find Elder Roswald within."

"You're not joining us?" asked Revi.

"No. I feel it best to give people some semblance of privacy when they bare their souls." He opened the door, revealing a small room with little furnishings save for a narrow bed, a table, and a single stool. A barred window, high up, allowed light to filter in, bathing the space in a subtle yellow hue.

"Elder Roswald?" said Hayley.

The room's occupant looked up from where he sat, squinting as he tried to focus on his guests. "Ah. It is time, then."

"May we sit?"

"By all means." He waved them over to the bed. Gryph curled up at their feet as they sat.

"I understand there's something you want to tell us about Lord Edward Fitzwilliam?"

"I do, or rather I did, or did not. Perhaps I'd better explain."

"I would appreciate that."

"No doubt," began Roswald, "by now, you realize Randolf's claim to

Bodden rests entirely on his mother's marriage to Lord Edward. I am here to tell you the entire thing is nothing more than an elaborate ruse created to discredit an old enemy."

"How do you know this?" asked Hayley.

"Rosella Blackburn was known to me long before this sham of a marriage was orchestrated."

"Perhaps you'd best start at the beginning?"

"Of course, how thoughtless of me. Let's see... Ah, yes. Rosella Blackburn. She was always a headstrong woman who dreamed of bettering her life. She became pregnant with Celia back in thirty-three, though nobody knew who the father was. I should point out that this was before the attack on Bodden that led to Lord Edward's supposed capture."

"Are you sure? I was given to understand Celia's date of birth was well after the siege."

"It is not so difficult to change dates when one puts their mind to it. In those days, I was full of life, perhaps too much so, for I broke my vow of celibacy with a young woman with whom I became enamoured. Lord Hollis somehow found out about it and threatened to expose me if I didn't co-operate, so I had no choice. I gave in and changed the date of Celia's birth to compensate for the discrepancy that an earlier date might create."

"And the birth of Randolf?"

"Never needed changing since he came along later. As for the marriage, there never was one. In fact, as far as I know, there was never a husband for her to wed."

"Then who's buried in the temple?"

The elder began a coughing fit. Revi and Hayley waited while the man got himself under control but couldn't help but notice the blood darkening the fellow's kerchief.

"You're ill," said Revi. "Let me heal you."

"You may be able to heal my body, but my soul is dying—has been for years."

"Are you saying you prefer to die?"

"I must pay the price for my misdeeds. I broke my vows, which is bad enough, but I compounded the situation by giving in to pressure from Lord Hollis. I wanted Rosella to be looked after, and the earl... well, at least he provided her and the children with food and lodging."

"Of all the people for you to care about," said Revi. "Why her?"

"I can tell you that," said Hayley. "You're the father of her child, aren't you?"

Elder Roswald's head dropped. "I am, to my everlasting shame."

Revi was not done. "But Randolf had memories of his father?"

"Is it so difficult to believe he lied? What choice had he? He was always dependent on the Earl of Beaconsgate. The offer of a barony to call his own must've been too much to resist."

"And he never knew you were Celia's father?"

"No. Never."

"If that's true," said Hayley, "then who fathered Randolf?"

"I always suspected Lord Hollis was his real father, but Rosella never confirmed it."

"What of Edward Blackburn, the man reported to be buried in the crypt?"

"Lord Hollis provided the body. There was no explanation of who he was, though admittedly, someone had dressed him in fine clothes."

"And you buried him?"

"I oversaw the burial. The earl insisted on it."

"And you entered Edward Blackburn's name?"

"Yes, though only at the insistence of Lord Hollis."

"Tell me," said Revi. "Why admit all of this now?"

"I am not long for this world," said Elder Roswald, "and I would make my peace with Saxnor before I pass to the Afterlife."

"Would you be willing to write down your statement?" asked Hayley.

He handed over a scroll. "I have already done so."

"This paper is old."

"It is. I wrote that over twenty years ago. As you can see, this has weighed heavily on my mind for a long time."

"If that's the case," said Revi. "Why not turn this over sooner?"

"To whom would I pass it? Until recently, Lord Hollis was still the Earl of Beaconsgate. He would hardly take kindly to me exposing his secret."

"Thank you," said Hayley. "This will help us immeasurably."

"I can still heal you," offered Revi. "Perhaps make you feel more comfortable, at least?"

"It matters little. If old age does not claim me, then Asher's men will finish me off. I am no fool. I know the cost of betrayal, and I'm willing to pay it to pass from this life with a clean conscience."

"We could save you, give you sanctuary in Wincaster?"

"No. I have confessed my soul. Now grant me the solitude to make peace so I might die with a pure heart."

Revi wanted to argue the point, but Hayley reached out, touching his forearm. "Let him die with dignity."

The mage turned to meet her gaze and saw the tears in her eyes. "Very well. I shall do as you ask, even though I don't agree."

They rose, making their way from the small room. Gryph, sensing their mood, padded along behind them.

"Such a waste," said Revi. "I'll never understand why someone would refuse the offer of healing."

"Healing only prolongs his suffering."

"He's giving up."

"He gave up long ago, but at least now he has atoned for his sins."

"Do you truly believe that? Can anyone ever atone for the mistakes one makes in life?"

"Are we talking about the elder or you?" asked Hayley.

"I made you sick with worry when I disappeared, and I never apologized for that."

"I'm just happy we found you."

A tear came to Revi's eye. "Be that as it may, my actions were inexcusable. How can I ever hope to make it up to you?"

She took his hand. "I can think of a few ways."

"Name them, and I will do all in my power to make them come true."

"Then let's start with marriage. How about we finally agree on a date?"

"We have waited a long time to get married, haven't we?"

"There was a war on," said Hayley. "And now I'm travelling all over the place trying to get to the bottom of this mess. That sort of thing isn't exactly conducive to planning a wedding."

He smiled. "Then let us see it done. We shall marry as soon as we return to Wincaster."

"Hold on there, Califax. It's a little more complicated than that. I thought we might begin by making a list of who to invite. We've talked about it often enough but have yet to actually put quill to parchment."

"Then let us sit down this very evening and sort out these troublesome details."

Hayley smiled. "Not that I'm complaining, but it's so unlike you, Revi. You're usually too deep in your studies to devote time to such pursuits?"

"Ah, but it relates directly to my studies, don't you see? My research is more likely to bring positive results with my lucky charm close at hand. And how much closer can two people be than husband and wife?"

They made their way outside to find Captain Naran's men guarding the prisoners.

"Everything good here?" asked Hayley.

"Indeed. We'll release the prisoners after your departure to ensure your trip is unhindered."

"What of you?" asked Revi. "Shall I use my magic to bring you and your men back to Galburn's Ridge?"

"That won't be necessary. I decided to take advantage of our present circumstances and march the men overland. It'll whip them into shape much faster than their normal training."

"But you'll need supplies, surely?"

"Her Majesty provided me with the necessary funds. Fear not, my friends. My men are in good hands."

"Then I wish the best of luck to you all," said Revi.

"When will you depart?"

Revi glanced skyward. "The weather seems fine. We might as well leave right now." He looked at Hayley, who nodded.

"Then goodbye," said the captain, "and may our paths cross again someday."

"I'm sure they will," said Hayley. She took Revi's hand and pulled him a short distance from the warriors.

Upon a nod from her, he called on his arcane power. The wind whipped up, circling them faster and faster. Gryph, recognizing the spell, ran over and stood, leaning against Hayley's legs just as a cylinder of light rose around them, blocking all view of the streets of Beaconsgate.

Moments later, the cylinder fell, revealing the casting circle in Wincaster. Gryph let out a howl that echoed off the chamber's walls.

Hayley laughed. "Yes, we're home."

THIRTY-TWO

King at Last

SUMMER 967 MC

Trumpets blared as the warriors of Weldwyn marched through the streets of Summersgate. Behind the footmen came the cavaliers, their surcoats emblazoned with colours bright enough to turn the heads of even the most stalwart of maidens.

The crowd hooted and hollered, cheering the display as the garishly dressed champions made their way towards the tournament field. People had lined the streets long before sunrise, eager for an unobstructed view of the procession. This was no ordinary parade but a celebration of the crowning of a new king!

King Alric's men, the famed King's Guard, came next, resplendent in blue and yellow. At their head rode Jack Marlowe, the Champion of Weldwyn, waving and catching roses even as he smiled at the crowd.

Pulled by six white horses, the king's open-topped carriage finally came into view. Within sat King Alric, along with his sister Edwina. The guards mounted at the back scanned the crowd as the entire procession slowly advanced.

The heavy cavalry of Merceria, their armour glistening in the morning sun, were a crowd favourite, and the Queen of Merceria, accompanied by her closest advisors, followed in their wake. The procession continued with Dwarves, Orcs and even a contingent of Saurians: small, lizard-like creatures carrying primitive-looking spears.

The Summersgate bowmen brought the parade to an end as they marched onto the tournament field, and then the great companies came to a halt, forming a long line that turned, as one, to face a platform erected for the occasion.

The king and queen exited their carriages, then waited for the honour guards to fall into place as they prepared to mount the platform.

Alric took the steps two at a time, then halted, looking over the sea of faces occupying the tournament grounds. A cheer went up, and he smiled. Never, in his wildest dreams, had he ever envisioned this day, for he'd been third in line to the Throne of Weldwyn, a youth born with little purpose. Now, he was here, ready to guide his people to a future full of possibility.

The earls of Weldwyn stood on the opposite side of the platform, watching him intently. Alric glanced behind him where Anna was climbing the steps, Gerald following her, carrying Braedon.

The Queen of Merceria reached the top, then took her place at Alric's side.

"Nervous?" she whispered.

"Not in the least."

"Liar."

"Well," he added. "Maybe a little."

A hush fell over the crowd as a man in white robes entered the platform from the rear. He carried a tall staff, topped with a blue crystal, symbolizing Malin, the favoured Goddess of Weldwyn.

The Bishop Supreme halted before a pillow and then nodded to Alric. The ceremony was about to begin.

"What do you think?" said Lord Tulfar. "Will he make a good king?"

"I believe," said Lord Parvan, "that Weldwyn has had far worse."

"What makes you say that?"

"He and I have not always seen eye to eye."

"Aye. I heard something to that effect. Care to explain?"

"It is my own fault," said the Elven lord. "I kept secrets when I should have revealed the truth. His Majesty discovered the lie when he visited me in Tivilton."

"When was this?"

"Some years ago. He was in the company of the Queen of Merceria at the time, although she was only a princess then."

"I hope this won't affect our agreement?"

"Not at all," said Parvan, "but I will need to make amends before we discuss the topic with His Majesty."

"I can live with that."

Up on the platform, the ceremony continued.

"What's he saying?" asked the Dwarf. "I can't hear a blasted thing."

"He speaks of the king's responsibility to the government and its people."

"So, nothing important, then?"

"How can you joke on such a solemn occasion?"

"My pardon," said Lord Tulfar, "but you must admit the old fool is rambling on a bit."

"He is the Bishop Supreme of Malin."

"Well, of course he is. Who else would be qualified to carry out this ceremony?"

"I can think of several individuals suited to such a responsibility."

"I wasn't really expecting an answer to that question."

"Then why did you ask it?"

"I… never mind. It's not important," said the Dwarf. "Tell me, do Elves carry on like this when they crown a new king?"

"We do not have kings, merely lords or ladies."

"But you're the Baron of Tivilton!"

"Only in the eyes of these Humans. In my own language, I am simply Parvan Luminor, Lord of Tivilton."

"Are all Elves like that?"

"I cannot answer that. I have had limited contact with others of my race these last few centuries. I believe the ruler of the Darkwood also uses the title 'my lord', but then again, their customs are not necessarily ours."

"I'm curious," said Tulfar. "You've ruled Tivilton for what, nine hundred or so years? What happens when you die?"

"You mean if I die. Another would simply assume my position."

"And how would that be done? Is someone in a different mine shaft waiting to take over, or is there a selection process your people go through?"

"My replacement was chosen more than five hundred years ago. Why? Are you planning on murdering me?"

The Dwarf stared back for a moment before breaking into a wide grin. "You had me going there. Very funny!" He was about to say more, but Lord Parvan lifted his finger to call for silence.

"The king is about to speak."

Alric rose from where he'd been kneeling, the crown of Weldwyn now resting firmly on his head. He turned to face those watching, moving closer to the platform's edge, the better for all to see him. Once more, they displayed their approval with cheers, hurrahs, and even applause.

Lord Tulfar enjoyed the experience immensely, but his companion covered his Elven ears and grimaced.

"Not enjoying this?" asked the Dwarf.

"It is a little loud for my tastes. I'd prefer to be back in the forests of Tivilton where I can hear myself think."

"Nonsense. You're needed here to give your oath to our new king." He looked past those standing before them. "Come on. It's time to go line up."

"Arise, Lord Jack, Viscount of Aynsbury, that you may serve me well," said the King of Weldwyn.

The herald announced the next noble. "Lady Lindsey Martindale, Viscountess of Talburn."

The viscountess stepped forward and curtsied while Alric held out his ring for her to kiss. "I promise by all I hold true, I will be faithful to you, my liege, and will never cause you harm or act against you in bad faith or deceit. I will rule my lands in your name, Majesty, for the greater good of the realm, the Crown, and the people of Weldwyn."

"I accept your pledge of loyalty," said Alric. "Now arise, Lady Lindsey, Viscountess of Talburn, and may you serve me well."

He looked down the line, then whispered to the herald, "How many more of these must I do?"

"Thirteen, Your Majesty."

"Are you sure you haven't miscounted? I thought there were fifteen baronies?"

"And so there are, Majesty, but two are still without heirs. You will have to name their successors at some point."

"Very well. You may continue."

The king's feast was a tradition going back centuries. All the nobles of Weldwyn were there in the Dome, along with many from Merceria, swelling the numbers. By the time the meal came, Alric's voice threatened to disappear from all the speeches.

"This is nice," said Anna. "For once, the table isn't overflowing with wasted food."

"I thought this modest meal more appropriate," said Alric. "Especially considering what the kingdom's been through."

She raised her glass to him. "Here's to the future."

He was about to respond with a toast of his own when he noted the presence of someone standing off to the other side of the table. "Is something wrong, Lord Parvan?"

The Elf stared back a moment before replying. "I am here to apologize, Your Majesty."

"Whatever for?"

"I fear some years ago, I was untruthful to you."

"You mean you lied," said Alric. "We've been over all that before."

"I wish to make amends."

"Very well. Speak."

"Shame kept me from speaking of things, the shame of what we had done. Thousands of years ago, I, like many of my people, let Kythelia's words sway me. She convinced us the Saurians were evil and desired to keep the secret of magic to themselves. Like fools, we followed her in her war to exterminate them, and then when the war ended, she turned her hatred against the Orcs. We then realized we could no longer ally ourselves with her."

"Why is this of any consequence now, Lord Parvan?"

"Ever since our disgrace, I have been leery of following others. When you and Queen Anna visited us back in sixty-one, you brought a Saurian with you, and I panicked, fearing they had arisen to seek vengeance."

"And now?"

"I realize we should not live in fear of the past. The Elves cannot make up for our previous mistakes, but we can at least contribute to a future where such things will not happen again. I wish you well in your rule, Your Majesty, and promise the Elves of Tivilton will do their part to ensure the Kingdom of Weldwyn thrives."

"Thank you," replied the king. "I know that must've been difficult for you."

Lord Parvan bowed deeply, then took a step back, revealing Lord Tulfar.

Alric chuckled. "Don't tell me the Dwarves wish to apologize as well?"

"No, Majesty, but it's come to my attention the kingdom is suffering."

"So it is, but what has that to do with you?"

"Mirstone has large reserves of gold, enough to help rebuild the kingdom."

Those within earshot quieted down, something that quickly grew to encompass the entire room.

"What is it you're proposing?" asked Alric.

Lord Tulfar looked at Lord Parvan, who nodded. "The people of Mirstone and Tivilton wish to help, that's all."

"And what would be the price of this help, Lord?"

Everyone held their breath.

"There is none," said Tulfar. "I must bow to the needs of the kingdom."

"He speaks for us both," added Lord Parvan. "The coins are yours to spend as you see fit."

"And you ask for nothing in return?"

"Nothing at all, Your Majesty."

"Then I accept your offer and extend to you the hand of friendship." Alric stood, leaning over the table to shake hands. Tulfar grasped the king's hand in both of his and shook it enthusiastically, with Parvan following suit, albeit less gregariously.

"We will not forget your contributions," said the king. "I promise you."

The two barons bowed once more, then returned to their seats.

"What was that all about?" asked Anna.

"They want representation on the Earls Council," replied Alric.

"And will you give it to them?"

"That is not my decision to make. However, I will name them both as advisors to my court." He smiled. "That's a lesson I learned from you."

"Now that I think about it, all my advisors are nobles."

"Ah, but they weren't all titled originally, were they?"

"No, I suppose not."

"Speaking of nobles, how is Beverly doing?"

"About as well as expected, all things considered. She's gone east to Stonecastle, though I must now call her back to Wincaster. The Nobles Council is due to render a verdict very soon."

"Stonecastle?" said Alric. "That's up in the mountains, isn't it? She's a long way from Wincaster."

"She is, but I sent Aubrey to fetch her. I thought the news easier to take coming from family."

"I suppose she'll use the recall spell to bring them back to the capital."

"Precisely, though I might remind you that all our mages can cast that spell, including yours."

"Mine?" said Alric.

"You are the King of Weldwyn now. That means they serve you."

"Yes, I suppose it does. It's all rather strange."

"What is?"

"I don't feel all that different from yesterday."

Anna laughed. "And why should you? You're still the same person in here." She lightly touched his forehead.

"My head feels heavy wearing this crown."

"It's the burden of responsibility. I felt the same when I first wore the warrior's crown. I think my predecessors must've all had thick necks to bear the weight of it."

He laughed. "I hadn't thought of it quite like that. Still, you have the right of it. It's good these things are uncomfortable; it reminds us why we're here, though I never expected to become king."

"Nor I, queen," said Anna. "I suppose we have that in common." She spied Lady Jane Goodwin entering the room. "Ah, Braedon must have finally fallen asleep." The queen waved. "Come, Lady Jane. We saved you a seat up here beside Lord Gerald."

"My apologies for my tardiness, Your Majesties, but the prince was fussing."

"And now?" asked Alric.

"Fast asleep, thank Malin." She looked at the queen. "Or should I say, thank Saxnor?"

"Either will do," said Anna.

Jane took her seat, sliding in beside Gerald, causing him to break out into a grin.

"She's good for him," Alric said quietly.

"Yes," said Anna. "They make a handsome couple, and it will be nice for Braedon to have two grandparents."

"It's a pity he'll never know my father," said Alric. "Though come to think of it, I spent most of my time with my mother."

"What was she like, growing up?"

"Stern. She had to be, with the five of us running rampant through the Palace." He paused a moment as a thought suddenly occurred to him.

"What is it?" she prompted.

"I was just thinking I'll have to rebuild the Palace."

"And will you restore it to its previous design?"

"Until this moment, I hadn't given it much thought."

"It will take months to clean out the debris. You've plenty of time to decide. Perhaps you'll come up with a new design? I'm sure the Dwarves would be more than willing to help."

"Why Dwarves?"

"They are talented architects and engineers, and you want something grand for a Palace."

"Do I? Or do I want something simpler? Spending large amounts on a Palace is inappropriate when the people have suffered so much."

"You forget," said Anna. "The Palace is not only your home, it's also the seat of government. The good news is we can bring architects here anytime, thanks to the magic circle here in the Dome."

"Useful things, those magic circles. I suppose I should see about building more in Weldwyn. Then again, we don't have a lot of mages left to make use of them."

"I'd lend you some of ours," said Anna, "but we haven't many to spare."

"What of Aubrey's school?"

"You mean the conservatory? She's begun training her first few students, but you knew that already, as Edwina is amongst them."

"Yes, but how long before they can cast the spell of recall?"

"You must ask her. I'm afraid their lessons keep getting interrupted every time I need Aubrey in Wincaster."

"But she has others to help her."

"Naturally, but she's the one who oversees everything."

"She gets that from you," said Alric.

"Meaning?"

"Come now. We both know how much you like to plan. Why, if you hadn't become queen, I wager you'd have ended up as an architect yourself."

"You know, at one time, Gerald and I were going to run away and live the life of commoners."

"What stopped you?"

"War, or rather, rebellion. It's strange to think I helped stop one rebellion only to lead another myself."

"History is full of strange coincidences. Perhaps Saxnor was guiding you to the Throne?"

Anna laughed. "The Gods don't intervene in our affairs, especially not Saxnor."

"Still, you must admit, your experience putting down the rebellion helped you with your own struggle to seize the Throne."

"I'll admit I learned a lot of valuable lessons, chief amongst them trusting in my friends. Without them, I would've failed."

"And that's precisely what I aim to encourage here in Weldwyn. For too long, my father kept his counsel to himself. It's time for the King of Weldwyn to heed the advice of others."

"What will be your first official act as king? Aside from appointments, that is."

"I must give some consideration to the rebuilding of the army. Thanks to my father's defeat in the north, we'll have to start from scratch."

"You have the men you commanded during the war."

"I do," said Alric, "but Weldwyn is a large kingdom. I hoped to get Gerald's opinion about a few things."

"Such as?"

"Under your reign, he's changed the rules of war. Historically, the king led our army, but you've shown that encouraging other commanders to make their own decisions makes the army much more effective."

"Correct, but to do that, you need to identify the true leaders. That's no easy task."

"Ah, but what if we created an academy to do exactly that?"

"To train commanders?"

"Why not? It works for magic, doesn't it? Imagine if Gerald, or Beverly, for that matter, could pass on their experience to younger generations?"

Anna chuckled. "You make Beverly sound like she's ancient. You do realize she's not much older than you?"

"True, but she's spent a lifetime preparing to fight, not to mention accumulating some impressive battle experience."

"And how would this academy of yours work?"

"That will require some thought. Perhaps we'd bring promising captains to Summersgate and educate them here."

"And what, precisely, would you teach them?"

He grinned. "It's only the beginning of an idea at this point. Clearly, I must give it some more thought."

"I like it. Perhaps I'll send some of our Mercerian captains once you have everything in place. We would, of course, bear the cost of their participation."

"Then I'll make that one of my first programs."

"You have others in mind?"

"Naturally, but I don't want to bore you with them right now." He plucked a grape and popped it into his mouth with a grin.

Lady Jane chuckled, and Anna looked over to see her in a whispered conversation with Gerald. She returned her attention to her husband. "Have you heard anything about the trial of Lord James?"

"We've been busy with his companion in crime, Lord Godfrey, but I suspect the evidence against Lord James is piling up."

"Why is that?"

"Godfrey is not one to go down quietly. He'll likely reveal all his contacts rather than suffer a painful death. That doesn't bode well for Lord James."

"What will happen to his estate?"

"Assuming he's found guilty, it becomes the Crown's property."

"And Lady Jane?"

"I very much doubt she'll be implicated. If anyone were to charge her for treason, it would be you."

"She's not Mercerian; thus, it wouldn't be treason. In any event, we decided not to pursue the matter."

"Because of her relationship with Gerald?"

"No. We examined the evidence, but it soon became clear she was an unwilling participant. If anything, her confession would only confirm her son's treasonous behaviour."

"Then we shall be sure to consider her story."

"Good, because my people already handed over everything we had to Jack Marlowe. Tell me, when is the trial to commence?"

"Within the week, I should think."

THIRTY-THREE

Tor-Maldrin

SUMMER 967 MC

B rogar examined the grating. "Shouldn't be too difficult to open this thing."

Glisnak elbowed past him, then grabbed the bottom and lifted it.

"Interesting," said the Dwarf. "It's hinged. Who would have guessed?" The grating was wide enough for two Humans to pass through simultaneously, but the height was a little more cramped.

"I don't see how this gets air down to the depths," said Althea.

"Normally, there would be a system of bellows to pull air into the mountain. Back in Mirstone, workers take turns operating them, but I imagine they've been silent here since they left."

"Will that give us enough fresh air to breathe?"

"That depends. Do you want to go down into the mine's deeper levels?"

"No," said Althea. "Only to where the dragon has its lair."

"Then we'll be fine. The front entrance will likely draw in more than enough air for our purposes. The problem will be getting down the vent."

Glisnak wriggled past. The small tunnel led into the mountain on a slight incline, forming a hump, then continued in an almost vertical descent. The Goblin disappeared over the hump.

Althea belly-crawled in, then halted at the peak of the rise. "I can see the shaft heading down," she said. "The walls look rough, plenty of surfaces to hold on to."

"Aye," said Brogar. "And many sharp surfaces to cut you, too, no doubt. We must take care. I hope these mushrooms don't wear out when we're halfway down."

"You should try being more optimistic. They lasted half the night, at least. You did eat yours this morning, didn't you?"

"I did, though I don't claim to like the taste."

"Come on, then. Let's get moving before we lose sight of Glisnak."

She turned herself around to go down feet first, not an easy thing to do in the close confines. "Here goes nothing," she said, then began climbing downward.

"I know I'm going to regret this," grumbled the Dwarf. He crawled in, then attempted the same manoeuvre. Moments later, he was cursing. "There's a slight problem," he called out. "I appear to be stuck."

One of the Goblins outside poked him in the leg, and his foot came free. "Never mind. I'm all sorted." He lowered his legs into the shaft and began his own descent.

The air vent was steep but not quite vertical, making it a little easier to hang on as they made their way down into the mountain's depths.

Althea lost track of time. Her limbs ached, and she began to wonder if the shaft went on forever. She looked below to spot Glisnak moving almost spider-like as he descended.

"I see something," she said, halting for a moment.

"What is it?" shouted back the Dwarf.

"I don't know—maybe a light of some sort?"

"That would be the bellows room, most likely."

"Surely all the lanterns would be out by now? How long has this place been abandoned?"

"Too long for the oil to stay burning. They're likely Dwarven lanterns."

"Which are?"

"Magically illuminated lanterns."

"I don't remember seeing those in Mirstone."

"That's because we don't have any."

"Then how do you know what they are?"

"The history of our people is full of references to such things."

Glisnak disappeared from her sight.

"I think he found the way out." She climbed down farther, where she saw an opening to one side. It took some effort to fit through the gap, but then she was inside a large room full of peculiar mechanical contraptions made of wood and iron, some with strange-toothed wheels, while others were encased in leather, much like a smith's bellows.

Brogar soon appeared at her side. "Incredible," he said. "This place puts the mine at Mirstone to shame."

"I don't understand how the bellows pull the air down," said Althea. "They're not connected to that vent."

"No, they're not, but if you look at the floor, you'll see someone dragged them out of the way. The Dwarves here must have used this very same shaft as a means of escape. I shouldn't like to think about what made them flee."

"We'd best be on our guard."

Glisnak came around from behind one of the bellows carrying a lantern and handed it to Althea.

"The light," she said. "It doesn't flicker."

"That's because it's not using a flame."

"How can that be?"

"Think of it as a glowing stone, if you like." He stepped closer. "If you look here, you'll see a shutter that rotates to shut off the opening if you want to plunge the room into darkness."

"You can't just extinguish it somehow?"

"I imagine a mage could, but then you'd no longer be able to use it."

Althea shook her head. "I shall never understand how they come up with such things."

"Your own sister is a mage now. Perhaps one day she'll make the very same thing?"

"Edwina is destined to be an Air Mage. I hardly think she'll be making lights."

"Actually," said Brogar, "I believe the orb of light is what they call a universal spell, available to all who wield magic."

"Since when have you been an expert in magic?"

"The Dwarves of Mirstone pride themselves on learning as much about the land as possible. It just so happens one of my grandmother's great-aunts was a master of rock and stone. Mind you, that was a few centuries ago. I never knew her myself."

"You, my friend, are a true fountain of knowledge. Anything else you'd like to tell me about what we can expect here?"

Brogar shrugged. "I'm afraid it's the history of my own lands I'm familiar with. As to the layout of this place, it's anyone's guess."

"Have you read anything about this place in your history?"

"Nothing at all, but that's not unusual. The mountain folk are scattered, and we seldom hear tell of other strongholds." He swung his arms around, trying to get the cramps out of them. "I must admit, I'm not made for climbing."

"Any idea which direction we should take?"

He looked at the vent to get his bearings. "That sits on the northern face of the mountain. From what I found in Derdra's records, the main entrance faces east, so we should go in that general direction." He pointed. "I should mention, however, the dragon will likely be there."

"Why is that?"

"It's the largest room by far, and you've seen the halls of Mirstone. Do you believe a dragon could fit down all those narrow corridors?"

"Likely not, but how do you know the hallways here aren't wider?"

"I don't, at least not for sure, but Dwarven engineers tend to be efficient, and we Dwarves are not as tall as you Humans. Why waste time digging away all that extra rock and stone?"

"But I remember some enormous caves."

"I'll grant you that's true, but the tunnels form the choke points. That's another reason for their narrowness."

"Is every Dwarven construction designed to withstand a siege?"

Brogar shrugged. "You know our ways. Why does that even surprise you?"

"I suppose it shouldn't." She was about to say more, but Glisnak was waving them over. "Our host appears eager to be on his way."

Althea kept the lantern aloft to avoid running into walls, for the mushrooms were only effective when there was at least a little light. In pitch darkness, they proved useless.

To her mind, they were navigating a maze, and she soon gave up trying to remember her way back to the ventilation shaft. They passed by hallways strewn with belongings, evidence of a hurried departure. Something had gone terribly wrong in this place, something that sent the Dwarves fleeing in panic.

Haldrim had mentioned the deep-ones, elementals living far beneath the mountains. Was that truly what had happened here? And if that were the case, did one linger here still, or had it returned to the depths from which it came?

A large crash echoed off in the distance, but they had no way of ascertaining its source. They all froze, hefting their weapons in case of attack, but nothing further came of it. The air grew warmer as they continued, then a slight scent of sulphur drifted towards them.

"We're close," said Brogar. "You never forget the smell of a dragon."

Glisnak waved to get their attention. "Dragon," he said, then pointed at an iron-bound door.

"This must lead to the lair," said Althea. "If this is anything like Mirstone, there'll be an armoury nearby.

"What of it? We already have weapons and armour."

"That club of his"—she nodded towards Glisnak—"won't do much against dragon hide."

"Aye, you have the right of it. I don't suppose he's strong enough to wield an axe, but a nice Dwarven dagger would serve him well."

"And you expect him to attack a dragon with nothing but a knife?"

"To be honest, I don't expect him to attack anything, but he should at least be able to defend himself. We'd best take a look before we consider any attack. That is the reason we came here after all."

Althea put her hand on Glisnak's shoulder and guided him from the door. Brogar knelt and examined the door closely. "There's no lock, so that's good. Shall we?"

She nodded, then suddenly remembered the lamp. She rotated the cover around, plunging them into darkness.

The Dwarf pressed the latch, slowly pulling the door towards himself. When it opened without making a sound, he released his pent-up breath. The room beyond was bathed in light, and it soon became apparent why, for the great doors that had once barred entry to Tor-Maldrin were thrown wide open, allowing the dragon to return at will.

"I don't see the beast," whispered Brogar, "but let me take a closer look." He moved into the room, keeping his back to the wall, only to poke his head back in a few moments later. "It must be out hunting."

Althea slipped in behind him, soon joined by Glisnak. The smell of sulphur was more pronounced here, yet the underlying stench of death was even worse, for the bodies the dragon had dragged in here littered the area. Her foot slipped on something, and she looked down and saw entrails buzzing with flies.

She fought to keep the bile down, making her way towards a nearby doorway. Above it, in Dwarven runes, was the word 'Armoury', and she thanked Malin she'd taken time to learn the mountain folk's language.

"Over here," she called out.

They stepped inside the room, finding everything in disarray, evidence its occupants fled in a hurry. Weapons lay discarded on the floor, likely tossed aside to lighten the load. Althea spotted a grey cloak with silver embroidery on its hood and sleeves. Whoever abandoned this had been more concerned with survival than material wealth.

Brogar picked up a broken spear. "What do you make of this?"

"Damaged in battle?" she replied.

"Useless now."

"Perhaps not." She took the spear. The wooden shaft was broken halfway up, making it difficult to use for a Human or Dwarf, but Althea's mind was elsewhere. She handed it to Glisnak.

"Here," she said. "This will serve you well."

The Goblin took a long look at the tip, smiling as he spied his reflection in the Dwarven metal. He then grasped the weapon in both hands and stabbed out experimentally. Looking pleased with the result, he tossed his club to the floor.

"It seems he's satisfied," she said.

"And so he should be," said Brogar. "It's not every Goblin who gets to wield such a weapon. Come to think of it, he's likely the very first."

"Is there anything else of value in here?"

"Doesn't look like it. Did you find anything?"

"Just this cloak."

"Take it," said the Dwarf. "It'll help you blend in with the rocks. Think of it as a way to conceal your location, much as a hunter might wear green to hide in the forest."

"This is a princely garment."

"Likely belonged to the watch commander."

"If that's the case," said Althea, "Tor-Maldrin must've been very profitable."

"If you recall, they found a new metal."

"Yes, that's right. Haldrim called it 'black metal.'"

"If it's as rare as it sounded, it would've been worth a fortune."

"Only if they sold it," said Althea. "And who amongst the Twelve Clans could afford such a prize?"

"I imagine they traded with more than you Humans."

"Like who? Unless you're suggesting they traded with the Goblins, no one else lives in these parts?"

"I doubt they'd do that, but who knows what lies beyond these mountains or farther north, past the reach of the Twelve Clans."

"These mountains are massive!"

"I agree, but we don't know the full extent of this place. Tor-Maldrin may go beneath the peaks to emerge on the western side of the range."

"That far? Surely that's impossible."

"Is it? We have no idea how old this mine is, only that they abandoned it. It might date back thousands of years, before even the Dwarves of Ironcliff or Stonecastle."

"If that's the case, wouldn't the entrance be larger?"

"Ah," said Brogar. "You're making the same mistake all Humans do concerning the mountain folk. Our cities don't sprawl like those of Weldwyn. Instead, they go deeper underground."

"That's not the case with Mirstone."

"No, but admittedly we don't live in the mountains. Our city grew along the lines of the veins we mine. We also have the advantage of living in relatively friendly terrain, making outdoor crops much easier to grow. Now, if you look at this place, you'd find they grow everything underground, or rather, they did. It's likely all dead by now."

"I'd love to explore further," said Althea, "but I'm afraid the dragon might return. We should probably leave while we can."

Brogar glanced around the room. "Where did Glisnak go?"

"He was here a moment ago." She, too, looked around. "This doesn't bode well."

A distant crash drew their attention, and they moved out of the armoury and back into the great entrance hall.

"No sign of him here," said Althea.

"He's probably gone and run off," said Brogar. "Goblins are not known for their bravery."

"No, wait. I heard something." She moved towards the back of the hall, where several corridors ran off from the entrance. She went to each in turn and listened.

"This way," she finally said.

The corridor sloped downward at a very shallow angle, its floor marked by two parallel depressions.

"What do you make of this?" she asked.

"I suspect carts wore down the stone. This is likely the main thoroughfare."

"Carts?"

"Dwarves don't like outside traders bringing their wagons inside. They would've transferred any trade goods to smaller carts to head below. If we follow this, it'll likely take us to the trade district."

A high-pitched scream echoed from down the corridor.

"That doesn't sound good," said Brogar.

Nor was it, for at that precise moment, Glisnak came into view, running for all he was worth.

"*Wargar!*" he screamed, barrelling past them. Behind him came a low rumble and a rhythmic thumping that shook the ground beneath their feet.

"What is it?" asked Althea.

"I'm not waiting to find out," said Brogar. "Come on. Let's get out of here."

"No, hold on. It might be something we can use."

The noise drew closer until a large, lumbering creature burst into view, its shape similar to a Human but broader, almost as if someone had stretched a man sideways. It wasn't easy to make out any other details except a faint orange light glowing from its eyes.

Althea held the lantern aloft to get a better view as it kept coming, revealing a body of what looked like stone. It slowed as it was bathed in the lantern's light, then opened its mouth and roared, a sound reminiscent of a rockfall.

"Get back," shouted Brogar. "It's a deep-one. It'll crush you if it gets close enough." He pulled her arm, desperate to get her out of harm's way.

Althea found the sight mesmerizing, but then the creature struck out, pounding the floor with its oversized fists. The entire corridor shook, a loud cracking noise erupting from the floor. She turned and fled, following the others back up the hallway.

They emerged into the entrance hall and kept running, passing through the great doors until they were out in the sun, the valley opening up before them.

Althea paused a moment to catch her breath. The deep-one appeared in the entranceway, but as the sun bled into the room, the creature held up its hands, trying to protect its eyes. After a final roar, it disappeared into the labyrinthine halls of Tor-Maldrin.

"For Gundar's sake," said Brogar. "That was close. I shouldn't like to think what those fists could do to flesh and blood."

Glisnak stared back at the mine, then stuck out his tongue.

"It appears," said Althea, "our new friend isn't enamoured of that thing either."

"That makes two of us." Brogar shook his head. "I never imagined finding myself in agreement with a Goblin." He dug out a stonecake and popped it in his mouth, waiting until it softened before continuing. "What do we do now?"

"We return to Drakewell," she replied. "It's time we finalize our plan to kill the dragon."

THIRTY-FOUR

Judgement

SUMMER 967 MC

The common folk of Wincaster packed the great hall, eager to hear the judgement of the Nobles Council. In the past, they'd held matters pertaining to the nobility of Merceria in private. However, the queen, wanting to be more open, deemed it appropriate to try the case before the people of her realm.

In his role as Duke of Wincaster, Gerald oversaw the affair, the largest gathering of the council since the recent war ended. Those nobles not already in Wincaster, had been brought here using magic lest they miss the opportunity to rule on such an important case. All were present except for Lord Herdwin and Lord Arnim, making for close quarters as they sat facing the crowd. Lady Hayley, however, sat separately as she was expected to give evidence in her capacity as High Ranger.

"If it pleases the court," she began, "the Queen's Rangers will now present their findings."

"You may proceed," said Gerald.

"As all here are no doubt aware, Sir Randolf Blackburn, Knight of the Sword, presented himself in Bodden last autumn, claiming he was the son of Lord Edward Fitzwilliam, former Baron of Bodden. He stated Lord Edward, long thought dead, had, in fact, survived the explosion that put an end to the Norland siege of nine thirty-three."

"And what steps did you take to confirm his story?" asked Lord Preston.

"We interviewed all known survivors of the events in question and found none could confirm Lord Edward's survival. Due to the unfortunate circumstances of his death—"

"Alleged death," said Sir Randolf.

"Quite so," said Lord Markham. "Would you care to expand on the circumstances of Lord Edward's disappearance, High Ranger?"

"Certainly," replied Hayley. "A Norland army marched into the baron's lands intent on capturing the keep. They laid siege that summer, attempting to reduce the walls using siege engines. By all accounts, the outlook was bleak for the defenders, and the baron was contemplating surrender."

This surprised the audience, and the entire room erupted into a mass of chattering. The Master of Heralds, theoretically in charge of maintaining the decorum of such public spectacles, banged his staff on the floor, but even this wasn't enough to calm them. It took the queen rising from her throne to finally bring the room to order.

She gave those who came to witness a stern look, then sat back down and turned to her nobles. "The council may continue."

"A point, if I may?" This came from Lord Horace, the Earl of Eastwood. "You claim Lord Edward was ready to surrender. Have you any witnesses to this?"

"I was there myself," said Gerald, "but that's irrelevant to the matter before us. Lord Edward is not on trial here. Rather, we are discussing the merits of Sir Randolf's claim. Now, let Lady Hayley continue, or we'll be here all day." He nodded at the High Ranger.

"As I was saying," continued Hayley, "the enemy was readying to assault the walls, which were still under construction. Lord Edward held the opinion that, if he could somehow blunt the attack by inflicting many casualties, he might be able to negotiate more favourable terms."

"Surely such a tactic would have the opposite effect," said Lord Heward. "It would enrage the attackers, wouldn't it? Perhaps even make them thirstier for blood?"

"I cannot speak to Lord Edward's state of mind, my lord. In any event, he decided to pack the wall with flammables, with an eye towards lighting them when the assault finally came."

"I imagine he wasn't expecting an explosion," said Lord Preston.

"Likely not. I believe he intended to bathe the wall in flames, but there's no way of knowing for sure. Lord Edward was last seen running towards the wall, torch in hand. Unfortunately, the enemy gained entry into the courtyard at that precise moment, and a wild melee ensued."

"How is that relevant?" asked Lord Markham.

"It helps explain why no one saw Lord Edward caught in the explosion."

"And his body?"

"It was never recovered," replied Hayley. "The explosion, unexpected as it was, tore a gaping hole in the wall, sending stones flying in all directions. At least ten defenders died, many burned beyond all recognition. There are no records of the number of Norlanders killed, but eyewitnesses estimate it was likely a score or more."

"So, he was killed?" said Lord Heward.

"That was the belief at the time, but several witnesses, the Duke of Wincaster amongst them, saw someone of import borne away by the Norlanders."

"They saw Lord Edward being carried off?"

"At the time, they assumed it was a Norlander."

"It was very chaotic," added Gerald.

"Now tell me," said Lord Markham. "If the keep was ready to fall, how did Bodden remain in our hands?"

"I can answer that," offered Gerald. "Lord Richard took a small group of warriors out and destroyed their catapults."

"That is correct," said Hayley, "but Lord Gerald is being modest. He was one of those warriors."

"This is all very interesting," said Markham. "Yet it still doesn't rule out the possibility the baron survived."

"My pardon, Your Grace, but I've only just begun. According to Sir Randolf's version of events, Lord Edward was borne from the field and carried to Beaconsgate, where he recovered from his injuries. At some point, he changed his name to Edward Blackburn to avoid recognition and took a wife. This so-called marriage produced two children: Celia Blackburn and, of course, Sir Randolf."

"And did you investigate these claims?"

"Yes. I travelled to Beaconsgate myself in an attempt to locate the body of Lord Edward."

"And did you find it?" asked Markham.

"I found the purported resting place of Edward Blackburn, but there was no way to prove his true identity. I then took it upon myself to locate his signet ring, which I'm led to believe he always kept on his person."

"I assume you found it?" said Preston.

"Yes. In the possession of Lord Asher, the current Earl of Beaconsgate."

"And have you this ring to present to the council as evidence?"

"I'm afraid not. His Grace refused to surrender it, claiming it was a gift from his uncle. I did, however, take an impression of it, which Her Majesty later examined and determined it was a forgery."

"Come now," said Lord Markham. "We all know Her Majesty favours Dame Beverly's claim to Bodden. How can we be sure of her findings?"

"Lord Edward signed many documents during his time as baron, but his signet ring was damaged in the days leading up to the siege. The imprint showed no sign of this."

"The fact that the ring was a forgery suggests an intent to defraud," added Gerald.

"Nonsense," said Markham. "Lord Edward could have repaired it before being captured. This is hardly proof of anything."

"Interesting," mused Lord Heward. "Tell me, was there anything else that supports the supposition this claim was nothing more than an elaborate ruse?"

"There is," said Hayley. "Sir Randolf claims to be named after Sir Randolf of Burrstoke, yet the Bodden knight revealed there was no friendship between him and the baron. In point of fact, Lord Edward's reputation was that of a most insular man, a matter others who were there at that time confirmed. This makes it very unlikely he'd name a son after someone under his command."

"As mentioned earlier," she continued, "there is no proof of Lord Edward's death or survival. However, there is also no proof he later married the woman claimed to be his wife. In fact, quite the opposite, my noble lords. I have an eyewitness account stating, without doubt, Dame Celia Blackburn was not the daughter of Lord Edward."

"Who dares make such a claim?" demanded Sir Randolf. "I have the right to face my accuser."

"I'm afraid that's impossible," said Hayley. "Since our return to Wincaster, we received word Elder Roswald has passed. However, we have in our possession a written confession from him, outlining his part in the plot to discredit the Fitzwilliams."

Hayley passed the document to Gerald, who perused it briefly before sliding it down the table.

"To summarize," she added, "Elder Roswald was the father of Celia Blackburn, and her mother was already pregnant at the time of the Siege of Bodden. He also confesses to changing the records concerning her birth date under pressure from Lord Hollis, the idea being for the dates to more closely support the new narrative."

Randolf stood up, slamming his hands on the table before him. "But someone would've noticed, surely?"

"At the time, she was in hiding, no doubt in shame after being impregnated by a man who took a vow of celibacy."

"That may prove Celia wasn't his, but it hardly counts against me."

"True," said Hayley. "Let us examine the circumstances surrounding the birth of Sir Randolf." She looked back at the knight. "You were born in Beaconsgate, were you not?"

"You know I was."

"When you were inducted into the Order of the Sword, you gave your birthplace as Mattingly."

"What of it? I could hardly admit I was a foreigner?"

"Yet you swore an oath to tell the truth. Your actions that day alone would make you guilty of lying. At the very least, we should strip you of your knighthood."

"Careful," warned Lord Markham. "We are here to evaluate his claim against Bodden, not besmirch the character of a gallant knight. Be careful what you imply, High Ranger."

"My apologies, Your Grace. Let us pass his actions off as a simple clerical error, shall we? Now, Sir Randolf, tell me about your mother."

"What is there to tell? She's no longer with us."

"Unfortunately, that is true. Otherwise, it would've been much easier to determine the truth of the matter. We discovered Lord Edward never married Rosella Blackburn, for she was born with the name Blackburn instead of acquiring it through marriage."

Hayley lifted another paper and handed it over to Gerald. "I have here a witness statement written by Holy Brother Caldwell. It attests to the fact there's no proof of a marriage involving Lord Edward, or an Edward Blackburn, for that matter. It also confirms the woman in question's name at birth was Rosella Blackburn." She turned to Sir Randolf. "Having said that, if you have proof of such a union, Sir Randolf, the Queen's Rangers would be more than willing to take a look at it."

"I knew nothing of all this," said Sir Randolf.

"I'm afraid that's not entirely true, as evidenced by your own admission stating you knew your father."

Gerald leaned forward, resting his elbows on the table. "Have you anything to say in your defence, Sir Randolf?"

"I had no knowledge of any of this," insisted the knight, "but will abide by the judgement of this council once it makes its decision."

"In that case, this court will adjourn so the Nobles Council can discuss the matter privately. With Her Majesty's permission, we shall reconvene once we've made our decision."

The queen stood, the entire room following her lead. "You have it." Anna left, escorted by her guards.

The nobles filed out next, leaving those who remained to talk amongst themselves.

"That went well," said Gorath to Hayley, "but should you not be discussing things with the Nobles Council? You are a baroness after all."

"True, but my position as High Ranger takes precedence in this case. I can hardly be expected to judge my own investigation."

"What do you think they will decide?"

"It's fair to say they'll rule in favour of Beverly."

"And what will become of Sir Randolf?"

"That's an excellent question, but I'm afraid I have no answers. It all hinges on whether or not they believe he played an active part in this deception."

"And his knighthood? Will it be stripped?"

"I can't really say. In any case, that would be up to the Knight Commander of the Sword, not the Queen's Rangers."

"And who, exactly, is the Knight Commander? Is it not Dame Beverly?"

"She only commands the Order of the Hound. I'm not sure who leads the Swords these days, not that it matters much. His membership in that order is not an issue of Mercerian law. I suppose you might say it's an internal matter."

"So what do we do now?"

"We wait for the council's judgement, just like the rest of Merceria."

"It seems simple enough," said Lord Preston. "Even if Lord Edward did survive, it's clear he never married. That makes Sir Randolf a bastard, meaning he can't inherit Bodden."

"Lord Edward could still be his father," said Lord Markham. "You must remember that before the queen's ascension to the Throne, only male heirs could inherit the title."

"What's that got to do with anything?"

"His claim predates the birth of Dame Beverly."

"But he didn't bring forth that claim until now," said Heward. "There was plenty of time for him to assert his right while Lord Richard was still baron."

"Just because he was tardy," said Marham, "doesn't mean he lacks a legitimate claim."

"You're grasping at straws," said Gerald. "The fact of the matter is Bodden wasn't up for grabs until the death of Fitz."

"That would be Lord Richard to you," said Lord Horace. "Let us not obscure the facts with sentimentality."

"Watch that tongue of yours," said Preston. "It is not your place to lecture the Duke of Wincaster."

"Well," said Markham. "Bastard or not, I still believe Sir Randolf's claim has legitimacy."

"The man is a traitor," said Heward. "He served Norland during the invasion. For that alone, he should've been stricken from the order."

"We are not here to discuss the matter of his knighthood but the fate of Bodden."

"Whether you like it or not, the law of the land passes the barony on to Dame Beverly as the only heir of Lord Richard."

"But that's just it, don't you see?" said Markham. "The entire case rests on the legitimacy of Lord Richard's claim. He could not claim the title if he was never sworn in as baron."

"That's a false assumption," said Gerald. "Even if he wasn't officially sworn in, he was still considered the ruler of Bodden. I was there when King Andred visited back in fifty-two, and he certainly treated Lord Richard as the baron. To my mind, that makes his claim legitimate."

"Actually," said Heward. "Even though I agree with Lord Gerald, it matters little. Lord Richard, baron or not, supported the queen in her bid to win the Crown. He also swore an oath of fealty to her at her coronation. So, like it or not, Lord Markham, he was officially recognized as the Baron of Bodden."

The great Troll leader, Tog, leaned forward, his head towering over all. "It is settled. Now all that remains is to inform Her Majesty of our decision."

"Not so fast," said Markham. "There's still the matter of whether or not Dame Beverly is the rightful heir."

"Fitz sired no other children," said Lord Preston. "Who else would you suggest?"

"Are there no cousins to claim the title?"

"Not in the direct line of succession."

"But she's a woman!"

The room grew uncomfortably quiet.

Gerald finally broke the silence. "It makes no difference. If you recall, the queen changed the laws of succession some time ago. This very council voted to agree with her decision, though admittedly, others occupied some of these seats then."

"This is easy enough to settle," said Lady Aubrey. "I, as Baroness of Hawksburg, move that we rule against Sir Randolf's claim."

"For what reason?" asked Lord Markham.

"On the grounds he is illegitimate."

"I second the motion," said Gerald.

Markham was persistent. "There is still much to discuss!"

"There is nothing more that needs to be said. Now, what say you all? Who is in favour of Beverly's claim?" He met the gaze of each council member in turn. The Master of Heralds, acting as record keeper, noted every vote, but it was soon apparent what the decision would be."

"By a clear majority," said Gerald, "this council declares the claim of Sir

Randolf is without merit and recognizes Lady Beverly Fitzwilliam as the rightful heir of Bodden. I shall inform Her Majesty of our decision."

The nobles filed back into the great hall, moving to stand behind their chairs as the queen entered and took her seat on the throne. She then nodded to the gathered council, who all sat, save for Lord Gerald, the Duke of Wincaster.

"It is my honour and privilege," he began, "to announce the Nobles Council of Merceria has reached a verdict, Your Majesty."

She held her reply for a moment, building tension in the room. "And what did you decide?"

"We find the claims of Sir Randolf are without merit and that Lady Beverly Fitzwilliam is the rightful heir to the Barony of Bodden."

The spectators erupted into a cacophony of cheers. The queen let the noise naturally subside before continuing.

"And was this unanimous?"

"It was not, Your Majesty, though there was a large majority."

"Very well. The Crown accepts the decision of the Nobles Council. Let it be known throughout the realm that Lady Beverly Fitzwilliam is the true heir of Bodden." She sought out Beverly who sat in the front row of spectators. "We shall make arrangements to swear you in as soon as possible. In the meantime, Lord Preston will relinquish Bodden keep to your safekeeping."

The queen rose, ending any thoughts of discussion. The nobles all stood, waiting for her to leave before they departed.

Aubrey pushed her way through the crowd to find Aldwin and Beverly embracing. "Congratulations, Cousin."

"Thank you. It's a great relief to finally put this matter to rest." She noticed the High Ranger's approach, and everyone went quiet.

"I'm sorry to have put you through this, Bev," said Hayley, "but I was under orders. I hope you'll forgive me."

"There's nothing to forgive, Hayley. You were doing your duty as I would have expected you to. In any event, it all worked out for the best."

"We should celebrate," suggested Aubrey. "And I just happen to know your newly inherited Wincaster estate has an excellent collection of wines!"

THIRTY-FIVE

Revelations

SUMMER 967 MC

T he earls stood as King Alric entered the council chamber and sat, then took their own seats.

"Let the record show," Alric began, "we are gathered here today to weigh the evidence against Lord Godfrey Hammond. Lord Dryden, would you care to begin the proceedings?"

The Earl of Wentworth stood. "Thank you, Your Majesty. I am pleased to announce the case against Lord Godfrey shall not be a drawn-out affair."

"Might I ask why?"

"He has agreed to admit to his part in the invasion provided we permit him to tell his tale to this august council. No doubt he wishes to convince us to spare him the painful death usually reserved for traitors."

"And has he enough information to warrant a merciful death?"

"That remains to be seen, Your Majesty. We agreed only to let him have his say. We've given no guarantees as to his fate."

"Then bring him in," said Alric. "It's time we get to the bottom of this."

"Are you sure that's wise?" asked Lord Elgin. "The man is a condemned traitor who'll likely say anything to save his own skin."

"Then it will be this council's task to separate the truth from the lies." The king looked at the guard standing by the door. "Bring him in, Sergeant."

The prisoner was being held in a nearby room under heavy guard, making it simple to collect him.

Alric watched the earls, trying to glean their thoughts on the matter, but each sat stone-faced, aside from Lord Elgin, who was sweating profusely. Suddenly, the man's earlier remarks about Godfrey made sense. Was Elgin himself somehow involved?

The door opened, revealing the sergeant. "The prisoner, Your Majesty."
He stepped aside as a pair of guards escorted the shackled Lord Godfrey.

"Godfrey Hammond," began Lord Dryden. "Do you understand the seri-
ousness of the charges brought against you?"

"I do."

"And you have agreed to plead guilty, have you not?"

"I have, Your Grace, providing I am allowed to speak."

Lord Julian leaned forward. "And what, may I ask, prompted this unexpected confession?"

"I wish to clear my conscience before you send me to the Afterlife."

"You mean the Underworld," said Lord Oliver. "There is no place in the
Afterlife for traitors like you."

"To others, I might be seen as a hero."

"That's quite enough of that!" snapped Elgin.

"Let him continue," said the king. "I would hear his words."

"Thank you, Majesty. I freely admit I conspired to allow enemy troops
into Summersgate. It was all part of an elaborate plan to ensure the
continued existence of Weldwyn."

"Oh, come now," said Julian. "You betray your king and then claim it's for
the good of the realm? I fail to see your logic."

"It all starts with the death of King Leofric," said Godfrey, ignoring the
outburst. "His death, or rather, the loss of the Army of Weldwyn, all but
guaranteed the Twelve Clans would defeat us. At that time, Merceria was
busy fighting in Norland, and Prince Tarak had brought a sizable army with
him from the Kurathian Isles. That's not even mentioning the part Kythelia
played. Our inevitable defeat was clear to a few of us. How, then, could we
ensure the survival of the realm?"

He paused, choosing his next words carefully. "With defeat staring down
at us, I considered it my duty to avoid as much bloodshed as possible."

"How noble of you," said Elgin. "And I imagine you saw yourself taking
on the role of protector?"

"Naturally. I say that not through any personal desire for power but
because there was no way the Twelve Clans were going to allow our own
nobles to remain in control."

"You are a noble yourself," said Beric.

"I am, yet I've never held a position of influence. My own title of 'Lord' is
a matter of social convenience brought on by my admittedly distant ties to
the Earldom of Riversend. In any case, my argument bore out when Brida
ordered the arrest of all titled nobles."

"A system of arrests you encouraged," said Julian. "Or do you deny it?"

"There was little choice," said Godfrey. "The High Queen of the Twelve

Clans had her own agenda. It was either co-operate or fall victim to the very same purge. The truth is, I was never happy with the way they treated the nobility during the occupation. That's why I left most of the footwork to Lord James."

"And what of the gate?" asked Alric. "Did you organize that?"

"I did. It was not a difficult thing to arrange. I possessed information of a... well, let's just say, I knew something compromising about those guarding the western gate."

"Are you suggesting you blackmailed them?"

"Blackmailed, threatened—it amounts to the same thing. Unlike this esteemed gathering, I clawed my way to the top. Yes, I was born into the nobility, but I've never truly been accepted. I had no source of income or family name to fall back on. So, over the years, I cultivated contacts I could use to my advantage."

"What type of contacts?" asked Lord Julian.

"Many of an unsavoury nature, but I also made some amongst the wealthy, including a member of this very council."

"This is ridiculous," said Lord Elgin. "He mocks us."

"I should very much like to hear him out," said the king. "Continue, Lord Godfrey, but I warn you, making accusations without proof will gain you nothing."

"Your Majesty is too kind. As I was saying, I made many contacts amongst the wealthy, enabling me to act as a go-between for people seeking certain services."

"What kind of services?"

"You name it: murder, mayhem, intimidation. I've arranged it all in exchange for a modest fee."

"Murder?" said the king. "Are you confessing to killing people?"

"Not me, personally. As I said, I was the middleman."

"And whose murder did you arrange?"

"What advantage would I gain by revealing that?"

"The manner of your death, for one."

"I stand here already condemned. What difference to me the method of my execution? Unless you're suggesting you would spare my life?"

"You will not be spared death!" insisted Lord Elgin. "So you might as well accept your fate."

"And I do. I promise you."

"How did you make contact with the invaders?" asked Alric.

"I was first introduced through a merchant who trades with Halsworth."

"Halsworth?" said Julian. "Where in Malin's name is that?"

"It is a Clan town on the Loran River, downstream from Loranguard. Many ships make it a habit of stopping there on their way to the coast."

"And who arranged with you to open the gate?"

"A representative of Prince Tarak."

"The Kurathian prince?"

"Yes, although he didn't see to things himself, you understand."

"And your reward for this act?" asked Lord Dryden.

"The promise of power. I intended to place myself and like-minded individuals in strategic positions where we could influence the invaders to ensure the safety of the people of Weldwyn."

"So, he offered you no payment?"

"No, and if he had, I would've refused it. You see, I did what I did out of a sense of duty: duty to the people of this fine kingdom."

"Yet you admitted to arranging murder," said Oliver. "How do you reconcile that with your duty to the people?"

"Let me be clear. I never arranged a murder lest it be in the best interest of Weldwyn. Think of how different things would be now if Lochlan had survived."

Alric sat up. "Are you saying you arranged the murder of Lochlan, Clan Chief of Dungannon?"

"I did, and rightly so. His marriage to your sister Althea was a threat to the security of this great realm. In any case, I only did as I was paid to."

"Who paid you to murder Lochlan?"

"I cannot say, for to do so guarantees my death in the most painful way imaginable."

"You're unfortunately unaware of the results of your plotting. Lochlan survived the attempt."

"Ah," said Lord Godfrey. "I'm afraid in my haste to flee Summersgate, I left my information network behind. Are you certain of this?"

"I am," said Alric, "and now, by your own words, you have admitted to plotting against the Throne, for as you know, Lochlan is husband to a Princess of Weldwyn."

"Of that, I am aware, but I am already a condemned man. All I can hope for now is a quick and merciful death."

"You have yet to offer me anything that changes the manner of your death. Reveal the name of your fellow conspirators, and I shall make your execution painless."

The prisoner considered the matter a moment, then nodded his head. "Very well. Do you know the Siren?"

"Do you mean the tavern in the western district?"

"Yes. There you'll find a woman named Jacintha. Have your men tell her Charles sent you, and she'll hand over a box, full of correspondence."

"Charles?" asked the king.

"Of course. I could hardly use my own name, now, could I?"

"And these letters reveal your contacts?"

Lord Godfrey's eyes locked with a specific earl. "Every single one of them."

"He lies!" shouted Elgin, sweat pouring down his face. "No doubt he's forged all sorts of documents to act as insurance."

"I can assure you I kept meticulous records, Your Grace, and I'm sure the Crown has sufficient means to verify my claims. I ask only that you grant me a stay of execution until you have time to evaluate my evidence."

"Very well," said the king. "Have you anything else to add?"

"Yes," added Elgin. "Perhaps you'd care to implicate the king in your treachery? That seems to be what you're inferring."

"Take him away," ordered Alric. He waited until the prisoner left the room before swivelling his gaze to Lord Elgin. "You seem nervous, Lord. Tell me, are you quite well?"

"Just a little indigestion, Your Majesty. Nothing serious, I assure you."

"Still, I believe it might be prudent to keep an eye on you all the same. Sergeant?"

"Yes, Your Majesty?"

"Please escort Lord Elgin to the guard room and hold him there."

"Is he under arrest, Majesty?"

Alric smiled. "He is our guest, but it would be bad manners for him to leave before we have a chance to chat."

"And if he attempts to leave?"

"I leave that in your capable hands, Sergeant, but I will say it would be very rude of him to attempt such a thing."

"Understood, Majesty."

The sergeant moved to stand behind Lord Elgin. "If you'll come with me, Lord?"

"A word to the wise," said Alric. "Sergeant Chapman and I fought alongside each other during the recent war. If you cross him, I have no doubt he will do his duty."

All colour drained from the The Earl of Riversend's face. "I did nothing wrong!"

"Then you have nothing to be afraid of. Take him away, Sergeant."

Chapman followed his charge through the door.

"You can't seriously believe Elgin's got a part in all of this, Majesty?" said Lord Beric.

"We shall see," replied the king. "I might also point out he may not be the only one who falls under suspicion."

"He means you," said Julian. "We all know the two of you plotted to keep the king from his Throne."

"Come now, my lord," said Beric. "I merely wanted what was best for the kingdom."

"Isn't that the same thing Godfrey said?"

"I believe it was," added Dryden. "You'd better hope your name doesn't appear in those letters, my lord."

Jack Marlowe emptied the bag onto the table. "It appears we have our work cut out for us."

"This is a lot," said Lord Tulfar. "Was there anything else?"

"The woman, Jacintha, assured me this was all she was given."

"And she didn't mind handing it over?"

"She was leery at first, but once I gave her the name Charles, she was eager to be rid of them."

"What I want to know," said Lady Lindsey, "is what will happen to those exposed by these notes?"

"I imagine it largely depends on what they're accused of doing," said Jack. "You also must realize these are the papers of Lord Godfrey, a convicted traitor, so we should treat them with some suspicion."

"Well," said the Dwarf, "at least the fellow has a clear hand when it comes to writing. I hope it won't take us too long to get through all this." He leaned forward, using his hands to scoop roughly a third of the papers towards him. "I'll take these and start reading. I suggest you two do the same."

"By all means," said Jack. "Lady Lindsey, have you a preference for which ones you'd care to peruse?"

She mimicked Lord Tulfar's movement, taking her third. "These will do nicely. Mind you, don't rush, gentlemen. We don't want to miss any important details. Oh, and if you find anything referencing anyone of import, I suggest you let the rest of us know."

Jack grabbed the remaining papers, pulling them closer to stare at them a moment. "Let's see, now. Where should I start?"

"They're all dated," said Lord Tulfar. "I suggest starting with the note with the earliest date."

"Ah, how convenient." The Viscount of Aynsbury began reading.

. . .

It was late in the evening when a servant entered, bearing a tray with food and drink for the three nobles.

Jack sat back, rubbing his eyes. "Set that on the table," he said. "We'll see to it from there."

"Is there anything more I can do for you, my lord?"

"You can inform His Majesty that we are halfway through this mess."

"Is that all, Lord?"

Jack smiled. "I think it safe to inform His Majesty that he was right in detaining Lord Elgin."

"Very well, my lord. I shall pass on the message." He quietly left the room.

Lord Tulfar lifted a tankard off the tray. "Ah," he said. "Just what I needed, a nice ale."

"Careful, my lord," said Lady Lindsey. "You don't want to spill any on these papers."

"Dwarves don't spill ale. That would be sacrilegious. Besides, our beards catch anything that falls."

Jack couldn't help but laugh. "This has been a long day. Perhaps we should reconvene in the morning?"

"I think not," said Lady Lindsey. "If you recall, several nobles are waiting to hear if any of these letters implicate them." She glanced at a neatly stacked pile of papers to her left. "We have definitely enough to condemn Lord Elgin, but others may be involved."

"I am curious about one thing," said the Dwarf. "What happens to his earldom if he's found guilty of treason? Have we any laws for that?"

"I doubt that's ever come up before," said Jack.

"Actually," corrected the viscountess. "It has—twice."

"And what did they do?"

"In the first case, they awarded the Viscountcy of Abermore to a distant relative."

"And the second?"

"Surely you remember recent history, Lord Jack? A baron brought us to the brink of war with Merceria."

"And where was I during all this?"

"Never mind him," said Tulfar. "He was busy becoming the Champion of Weldwyn."

"You were saying?" pressed the cavalier.

"They publicly executed him and gave his lands to the Lanfords, one of the most influential families in the entire realm."

Jack shook his head. "And so those with power grow even stronger. It's no wonder the Earls Council took so long to make a decision; they all seek to gain more influence."

"Influence and power are two different things," said Lady Lindsey. "Though they sometimes coincide. The Crown has always held the most power, yet, paradoxically, the heir to the Crown has to be approved by the very council they rule over."

"In that case, what does the council do when there is a king?"

"Leofric let them handle less important matters, but each ruler is different. King Alric must find his own way to deal with the earls, not to mention the rest of us nobles."

"It's true," said Lord Tulfar, "but I have high hopes for Alric. He's spent time amongst the Mercerians and understands his responsibility to his people."

"Perhaps," said Lady Lindsey, "but plenty of kings took the Throne with good intentions, while very few ever followed through."

"Why is that, do you think?" asked Jack.

"A ruler must often rely on others if they want to get things done. It is an unfortunate truth that Royal Advisors often see an opportunity to enrich their own coffers at the expense of the Crown rather than to its advantage."

"Alric is different," said Jack. "I've known him for some time now, and he has a good head on his shoulders."

"Perhaps, but the Crown is a heavy burden."

"Bah," said Lord Tulfar. "He'll be fine. We'll make sure of it."

"Yes," added Jack. "And don't forget, he's married to the Queen of Merceria, and we all know she's committed to serving her people."

"Yes," said Lady Lindsey. "Unfortunately, we do."

THIRTY-SIX

The Thing From the Deep

SUMMER 967 MC

"This creature," said Lochlan. "The thing you call the deep-one. Is it magical?"

"No," said Brogar. "But ordinarily, it lives far below the ground. That's why its flesh is like stone."

"I'm afraid I don't understand," said Althea.

"At its deepest depths, the mountain exerts great pressure. It's where you can find diamonds, and it's also exceedingly difficult to breathe down there."

Lochlan nodded. "Very interesting. Tell me, can you kill such a creature?"

"Technically, you can, but it would be difficult."

"You say it lives far underground. Why would it be wandering around the mine? You were near the surface when you saw it, weren't you?"

"I expect it got lost. The mine is very maze-like to the uninitiated."

"I would agree with that," said Althea. "I found it difficult to keep my bearings, but Glisnak found his way easily enough."

"Ah yes, the Goblin. He led you to the air shaft, didn't he?"

"He did and accompanied us as we explored. Without him, I doubt we would have found the way out."

"Althea has a plan," said Brogar.

"I'd love to hear it," said Lochlan.

Althea rubbed her hands together. "We wait until the dragon next flies out, then march the Dragon Company into the mine and take up positions in the entrance hall. When it returns, we fill it with bolts."

"A reasonable plan," said Lochlan, "but it has a fatal flaw. The dragon took many such bolts at Summersgate yet still flew here afterwards. I fear such tactics might cause it to search out another lair."

"Perhaps," said Brogar, "but then it wouldn't be our problem anymore."

"What if it flies south?" said Althea. "Would you inflict that beast on Galchrest or Lanton?"

"What else would you have us do? We need to concentrate our volleys, something difficult to do while the creature is airborne."

Lochlan smiled. "What if there were a better way? A way that didn't involve so much risk for so many people?"

"What is it you're thinking?" asked Althea.

"We start by keeping an eye on that entrance. For my idea to work, we must ensure the dragon is in its lair."

"Easy enough," said Brogar, "but what comes next?"

"We march the Dragon Company to watch the main gate. When it shows itself, they let loose with enough volleys to drive it back inside."

"How does that help?" said Althea. "We can't leave them there forever?"

"That's where the second part of my plan comes in. Using the air shaft, we'll get a small group back inside the mine."

"To what end?"

"To lure the deep-one into the dragon's lair."

Brogar's mouth fell open.

"You can't be serious?" said Althea. "Don't you realize how dangerous that thing is?"

"I imagine it's tough enough to take on a dragon. And if it's a creature of rock, as it seems to be, then I doubt a dragon's breath will do much damage to it."

"So we just let them have at it?" said the Dwarf.

"That's the idea. However, the difficulty lies in the execution. We need to somehow lure it without endangering ourselves."

"Are we to wander up and politely ask if it would like to fight a dragon?"

"No, of course not," said Lochlan, "but you said it followed you. That means we can lead it."

"And if it does destroy the dragon?"

"Then we send it back where it belongs."

"How?" asked Brogar.

"Like any lost soul, it's probably seeking a way home. If we point it in the right direction, I imagine it'll find its own path."

"And if the dragon wins the contest?" asked Althea.

"Then we move in and finish it off. At the very least, its fight with the rock creature will weaken it."

"Your plan has merit," said Brogar. "Though I'm still a little unsure about the details."

"Such as?"

"How do we lure the deep-one without getting killed?"

"I hoped we might get some help from the Goblins."

"They're poorly armed," said Althea. "How can they possibly hope to take on an elemental?"

"Simple," said Lochlan. "They won't. We want them to lure the creature to the dragon, remember? Not engage it in melee."

"I understand that but why the Goblins?"

"They're small, and if Glisnak is any indication, they possess a good sense of direction. You say he knew the way to the dragon's lair?"

"He did," said Althea, "but I still don't see how this would work."

"How many tunnels do you think lead deeper into the mine?"

"Dozens," said Brogar.

"Precisely, but we can't rely on the Dragon Company to watch them. We need them to keep the dragon from escaping, which only leaves the Goblins. We'd post them at each intersection and have them call out if they sight the deep-one."

"We can't let them go in alone," said Althea.

"I agree," added Brogar. "There's also the matter of explaining this plan to them."

Lochlan frowned. "You don't think they're up to it?"

"Honestly, they're not the sharpest axes in the armoury."

"I disagree," said Althea. "If you give them a chance, I think you'll find you've underestimated their intelligence."

"What gives you that idea?"

"Glisnak knew enough to get us into the mine. I might remind you he also navigated his way to the entrance, indicating he's very intuitive or he's been there before and remembers the path. Either way, I'd say it confirms some intelligence."

"I hate to admit it, but you're probably right. In my defence, we Dwarves were taught that Goblins are nasty folk who steal children away in the night. I know it's only an old story meant to frighten the young, but even so, I can't help but feel loathing towards them."

"I would have to agree," said Lochlan. "We have similar tales about the Goblins, and the Orcs, for that matter. Of course, it didn't help that we fought them during the invasion. If anything, it made their reputation that much worse."

"You fought Dwarves as well," said Althea. "Yet you don't look at them the same way."

"That's true, but our stories concerning the mountain folk are much different. I don't recall ever hearing tales of Dwarves stealing our young and carrying them north."

"That's interesting. Why north? What's up there?"

"I have no idea. The few maps we have lack information on the area, and the Dwarven maps I've seen reveal nothing."

"Your plan has merit," said Brogar. "But I insist on going with them. Someone familiar with Dwarven construction needs to be there."

"I'll go too," said Althea.

"No," said Lochlan. "I'll go."

"You can't. You're the Chief of Dungannon. Your life is too valuable."

"And you're my wife!"

She moved closer, taking his hands. "That is precisely why it must be me who accompanies them."

"It'll be dangerous."

"Don't worry," said Brogar. "I'll be there beside her every step of the way."

Lochlan nodded. "Very well, but don't put your lives in danger if you can avoid it."

"What's the next step?" asked Brogar.

"You've seen first-hand what we're up against. I'll need you to help Haldrim and the Dragon Company understand their role in this. While you're doing that, Althea and I will attempt to explain to Glisnak what the Goblins' role will be."

"And if you can't get the idea across?"

"Then we must abandon it and come up with something else."

Communicating with the Goblins proved harder than anyone imagined. Getting across simple ideas was easy enough, but the concept of waiting to lure a creature of the deep into the entrance proved too much for them to understand.

Instead, Althea devoted a good portion of her time trying to learn as much about their new allies as possible. They were, it appeared, a hunting party come south in search of game. From what she could understand, they had travelled for two or three days across the foothills, constantly on guard lest the dragon should appear. The monstrous creature had attacked their village, destroying much of their food, forcing them to go farther afield in their quest to replenish their stocks.

They knew little of bows other than having spied Humans using them. They were creatures more used to stealth and hiding than fighting out in the open, but their skills at wielding spears was impressive. In addition, four of them were armed with the curious sling staffs that had rattled stones off the Dragon Company's armour.

They demonstrated these weapons, surprising her with how they lobbed fist-sized stones over short distances. They would be useless against a dragon, but still, they fascinated her so much she took the opportunity to try to use one herself. After many failed attempts to hit a man-sized target, she happily returned the weapon to its rightful owner.

The day they'd set aside for the actual attack finally arrived. Under Haldrim's command, the Dragon Company would move out at dawn, their weapons ready lest the dragon be hunting in the area. It was a bold plan, for if they were caught out in the open, the beast's fire breath could well result in the death of them all.

Glisnak and his Goblins were ready to do their part, but Althea still wasn't convinced they knew what that was.

"It's strange to think of them as allies," said Lochlan. "In the past, the only foreigners to help us were the Kurathians, and then only when we paid them."

"They did not pay Prince Tarak, did they?" asked Althea.

"No, but he had his own agenda."

"Well, you're not alone anymore. Now, let's ensure enough of them survive to help out in the future."

"I'll accompany the Dragon Company," said Lochlan. "I can't have my wife going into battle without me."

"We talked about this," she replied. "You're a chieftain, not a warrior."

"True, but if I am to rule, then I need to set an example."

"This is Drakewell, not Dungannon."

"Also true, yet they are still my kin. That reminds me. I told the villagers to take refuge in the archives until we return. There's too great a risk should the dragon escape."

"A wise precaution," said Althea, "but let's hope it proves unnecessary."

The luring party, as Brogar liked to call it, was up well before first light. Glisnak led them, along with a dozen Goblins armed with crude spears. The sun had just appeared in the east when they arrived at the massive air vent leading to the mines of Tor-Maldrin.

"Sometimes it feels like we're doomed to repeat the same thing over and over again," said Brogar. He waited as Glisnak squeezed past him, then began the long climb down into the Dwarven mine.

Althea held back as the rest of the Goblins descended, then crawled in herself. The climb was tiring, but at least she knew what to expect. The Goblins were waiting when she stepped into the bellows room.

"Are we ready?" she asked.

"As ready as we'll ever be," said Brogar.

"Ready," said Glisnak, his high-pitched voice echoing off the stone walls. He led them, as before, towards the entrance hall. Once there, the idea was to seek the paths to the deep, the better to place themselves between dragon and elemental. Of course, they couldn't be everywhere at once, and there was a chance the creature was already ahead of them. If that were the case, they'd have to try to make it back to the relative safety of the bellows room.

They moved quickly, their footfalls echoing on the stone floor. Several times they heard crashing noises, leading them to speed up for short distances, but eventually, they found the door they sought. If there was any doubt the dragon lay beyond, the overwhelming stench of sulphur quickly ended it.

"All right," said Brogar. "Time to put this plan to work."

Althea sent half the Goblins with the Dwarf. The rest, along with Glisnak, would accompany her.

"Good luck," she said. "If you make contact, be sure to give a shout. We'll do no good unless we work together."

She took her group and made her way down a side corridor. At the first intersection, she designated one Goblin to stand guard and yell out should danger threaten. They then advanced, on the lookout for another crossing. Glisnak led the way, his broken Dwarf spear held ready for battle, but it proved unnecessary, for a shout came from behind them.

Althea wheeled around, readying her weapon. It had been a yell, nothing more, and she was almost ready to continue the search when the sound of thunder rumbled down the corridor.

"That's the deep-one," she called out. She began retracing her steps, ready to spring into action should it prove necessary. She moved cautiously at first, lest the creature surprise her, but sounds of fighting hurried her pace.

As they turned a corner, the deep-one was there, advancing menacingly on Brogar, who'd fallen against the wall, his leg armour crushed and mangled. At least one Goblin was down, little more than a bloody smear on the floor, and even as she watched, the elemental grabbed another by the neck as the poor thing tried to stab out with its spear.

The fist closed, and without so much as another thought, it tossed the lifeless body aside. Althea screamed out a challenge, hoping to draw its attention.

Glisnak, however, had other ideas. He advanced at a run, his Dwarf spear held in two hands, striking the creature in the stomach, causing a small pebble to slew away and reveal a glowing interior. The shock of the impact shook the Goblin, and he let go of the spear, backing up in terror.

"Glisnak," she shouted. "To me!"

The little fellow called out something in his own tongue, and then he and his companions rushed towards her. Drawn by the movement, the deep-one ignored the Dwarf and lumbered after them.

Althea waited until the Goblins ran past, then backed up as the hulking creature advanced, letting out its distinctive roar. She shook her head, feeling as though her ears would burst. Her back hit a wall, and a moment of panic threatened to overwhelm her. Something tugged her left sleeve, and she turned to see Glisnak waving at her from around the corner. His companions were nowhere to be seen, but the Goblin stayed to guide her to safety. They raced up the corridor, the footfalls of the great elemental echoing not far behind them.

Althea tried to make sense of their current position, but the sight of the creature had shaken her to her core. She thought they should turn right at the corner, but Glisnak guided her in the opposite direction.

They halted before a door, and something dripped down her face as she paused for a breath. She reached up to feel moisture leaking from her ears. Listening, she heard no sounds other than her breathing, and it wasn't until she looked at her hand and saw the blood there that she realized what had happened.

Glisnak was trying to open the door but was having difficulty. Althea grabbed the handle and pushed, but something blocked it. Nausea threatened to overwhelm her, and then her head started spinning. The smell of sulphur nearly overwhelmed her, and she staggered back down the hall just as the deep-one appeared.

Her mind raced as the absurdity of the situation came crashing home—she was literally between a deep-one and a dragon. She glanced around, desperate to find some means of escape as her death approached in the form of the elemental. In that moment of desperation, her inner voice calmed her, making peace with her fate.

She drew her dagger, handing it to Glisnak. "Here," she said. "If we are to die, you might as well go with a weapon in your hand."

He took the blade, holding it before him. They made a strange pair: a warrior princess and a Goblin armed with a dagger, yet somehow it seemed fitting.

"If this is our last battle, then we shall die with honour. Let none say the daughter of King Leofric died in fear!" She glanced at her companion, and for a brief moment, their eyes met. Both knew death was near, yet neither would shirk their duty.

Althea released a fierce scream as she moved towards the creature with slow, deliberate steps. Glisnak, seeming to understand there was no other choice, advanced at her side, the dagger held out before him like some mystical token of protection.

The deep-one roared again, and although Althea felt the vibration, she heard nothing. She was only three paces from her target when the Goblin suddenly grabbed her arm, stopping her in her tracks.

She struggled to understand why until the deep-one staggered forward and twisted around, turning its back to her, and then there was Brogar, hammer in hand, swinging wildly. His weapon struck its arm, and she heard a faint crack. Thankfully, it appeared her hearing loss was not permanent.

She grabbed Glisnak's arm and squeezed past the brute even as it smashed Brogar's shield, splitting the metal. The Dwarf cursed as he threw it to the floor. Althea was behind him now, her dizziness abated.

"This way," she shouted. "We must circle around to get to the entrance hall."

He backed up, limping slightly as he went. She released Glisnak, and they helped the Dwarf to the crossroads.

"We're almost there," she said, her voice echoing off the stone walls.

Her head pounded as sound flooded back to her. The Goblins were yelling at her, with two waving her towards another door. She knew from her last visit the entrance hall was just beyond, but now the enormity of the situation threatened to overwhelm her.

The plan was to lure the deep-one to face the dragon but to do that, they must enter its lair. Would it kill them before the elemental entered the room, or would they be able to find shelter as the two creatures fought? The only way they would know was to go through that door!

THIRTY-SEVEN

Investiture

SUMMER 967 MC

Gerald peered out from the Palace window. "There's quite a crowd gathering."

"And why wouldn't there be?" said the queen. "It's not every day a hero becomes a baron."

"Isn't it? You elevated Heward to baron, Preston as well, not to mention Lanaka, although I suppose he's technically an earl."

Anna laughed. "I concede you have the right of it. Still, none of them have Beverly's reputation. Next to you, she's my greatest ally. Speaking of which, where is she? It would be a shame for her to miss her own investiture."

"Don't worry. She'll be here. She just wants to make a good impression."

"Meaning?"

"She chose to look the part of a baroness instead of a warrior."

"You mean she's not wearing her armour?"

"To be sworn in? That would hardly be fitting."

Anna put her hands on her hips, reminding him of the little girl he met so many years ago. "Fitting? Is this Gerald Matheson I'm talking to? You're the last person I expected to worry about what she's wearing."

He shrugged. "I'm not worried—just repeating what Aubrey told me." A warrior appeared and whispered into his ear. "Very good. Thank you." He turned to Anna. "Everyone is in place. You may proceed at your leisure."

She looked out the window. "Let's start this, shall we?"

The Master of Heralds bowed, then left them to begin the ceremony.

"Any moment now," she said, and then the horns sounded. They moved to the door, where Alric waited.

"Your Majesty," said Gerald, bowing.

"Come now," replied Alric. "I'm still the same man who fought beside you during the Norland campaign."

"You are a king, and rightly so."

The King of Weldwyn shifted his feet, looking uncomfortable. "Please. I prefer if you called me Alric in private."

Gerald smiled. "I should be happy to, Majesty, but this is hardly the occasion for such familiarity."

"A valid point."

"Are you two done with all the frivolities?" said Anna. "Because I do have a ceremony to officiate."

Something brushed up against Gerald's leg, and he looked down. Storm stared up at him, his mouth dripping with drool. "It appears your dog has a poor sense of timing."

"He's still young," said Anna, "but he's grown so much these past few months. If he keeps growing at this pace, he'll soon be larger than Tempus."

"You miss him, don't you?"

"Tempus was my first real friend; he'll always be with me." She bent over and ran her hand along Storm's back. "But you're growing more like him every day, aren't you?"

"Come," said Alric. "As you said, there's a ceremony requiring your presence."

"I'll look after him," said Gerald. "You take care of things outside."

A wisp of perfume drifted his way, eliciting a wistful smile upon the marshal's face.

"I'll take him," said Jane. "You should be at the queen's side. You were, after all, one of Lord Richard's closest friends. It's only fitting you be there to welcome Beverly as the new mistress of Bodden."

Gerald picked up the end of Storm's leash and handed it to her. "He can get a little fidgety at times."

"I'm well aware. Oh, wait. Is this Storm we're talking about, or you?"

The queen laughed. "I think you've hit the centre of the target there, Lady Jane."

"Come," said Alric. "It's time."

The two royals stepped outside where the guards stood to attention. A cheer arose amongst the spectators as Gerald took a moment to adjust his tunic, then followed in their wake.

The queen chose the courtyard in front of the Palace for the ceremony, thus ensuring as many people as possible could bear witness. She'd even commissioned a sizable wooden platform erected to make it easier for all to see.

Beverly stood waiting, her husband on one side, Aubrey on the other. All three kept their eyes glued on Anna as she ascended the steps, then turned to face the crowd, which quieted in anticipation.

"We gather here this day," she began, "to recognize the claim of Dame Beverly Fitzwilliam, General of the Mercerian Army, Knight Commander of the Order of the Hound, and daughter of Lord Richard Fitzwilliam, as the rightful Baroness of Bodden."

"Dame Beverly first came into my service seven years ago and has proven a most loyal and trustworthy knight. It now gives me great honour to bestow upon her the rank that is her birthright, the Baroness of Bodden."

The queen turned to Beverly. "Dame Beverly, you are hereby ordered to present yourself before me that you might take your oath of fealty."

Beverly stepped forward and knelt, her forest-green dress folding beneath her while carefully braided red hair hung down her back. The presence of a sword at her waist brought a wry smile from the queen. Anna glanced at Gerald, who shrugged.

"Today, we invest Beverly Fitzwilliam as Baroness and grant unto her the Barony of Bodden. Do you pledge to swear fealty to the Crown and Kingdom of Merceria? To defend it against all threats and lay down your life in such service should it prove necessary?"

"I swear to serve with dignity and honour, and to serve my queen with all my strength until death takes me."

A page came forward, bearing a silver circlet upon a small pillow. The queen lifted it, then held it above Beverly's head.

"Be it known to all present that henceforth, you shall be known as Lady Beverly Fitzwilliam, Baroness of Bodden, and shall be accorded all the privileges and rights due that station." She paused a moment. "Arise, Lady Beverly Fitzwilliam, Baroness of Bodden."

The crowd roared their approval as Alric stepped forward to offer his congratulations. So enthusiastic was the response that it drowned out most attempts at talking.

Gerald moved up to be next in line. "Congratulations," he shouted, shaking her hand in a firm grip. "Your father would be proud, as would your mother had she lived to see this day."

"Thank you," said Beverly. "That means a lot to me."

Gerald stepped aside and leaned in to speak with Aldwin. "Well? Feel any different? Your good wife is no longer just a knight but a baroness now."

In reply, the smith grinned. "She has always been more than just a knight to me."

"I know, and never have I seen two people so well-suited for each other.

Congratulations to both of you."

"What happens now?" the smith asked.

Gerald steered Aldwin to one side, the better to be heard. "There's to be a celebratory dinner, providing we can get your wife away from all the adoration."

"I feel I should thank you on Beverly's behalf."

"Whatever for?"

"For always believing in her. You could have taken the easy way out when her father wished you to train her as a warrior, yet, instead, you took her dream seriously."

"If I'm being honest, I could do little else. Had I held back, I have no doubt Fitz would've learned of it."

"Still, you invested considerable energy towards her training."

"I did," said Gerald, "but her determination to succeed resulted in who she is today. Naturally, I'm pleased I could help, but you had just as much impact on her as I did, perhaps more so."

"I suppose I did," replied Aldwin, "but I couldn't have been there for her had you not rescued me all those years ago. If you and Lord Richard had not stumbled across the attack, I'd long since be buried in the ground."

"I did what I felt was right. That was a lesson I learned from Fitz. He was a gifted mentor and a great friend. Now that you and Beverly have Bodden, I must come and visit."

"You will always be welcome, as will Lady Jane, of course. Speaking of her, are you two ever going to get married?"

Gerald's cheeks grew flush. "This is hardly the time or place to speak of such things." Horns sounded. "That's my cue," he added. "I'll see you at the dinner."

Gerald quickly caught up to the queen and fell in behind her. Soon, they were back in the Palace, where Anna removed the warrior's crown.

"There," she said, stretching her neck. "That's enough ceremony for now."

Storm tore away from Lady Jane and rushed across the room to jump up and place his front paws on the queen. Anna, used to the huge mastiff, simply hugged him. A cry off to their right alerted them to the arrival of Prince Braedon, carried by his nanny.

"I'll take him," said Alric, moving to take charge of his son.

Anna smiled. "It doesn't get much better than this. The entire family all together, as it should be."

Gerald moved to the window and looked outside. "It's going to be a while before the crowd lets Beverly leave. The whole city looks to have turned out to congratulate her."

"And with good reason. Her father was beloved by all. She seems to have inherited that goodwill along with the barony."

"And what of Sir Randolf?"

"He's disappeared," replied the queen. "We suspect he's fled back to Beaconsgate, but we're not entirely certain. In any event, we've dismissed him from the Order of the Sword. We can't have a knight who serves two masters."

"Speaking of the Order of the Sword, who's their Knight Commander?"

"The marshal general previously held the position."

"You mean Valmar?" said Gerald. "But he's been dead for nigh on three years."

"Indeed. As such, it falls to me, as queen, to appoint someone to over-look the order."

"Don't look at me," said Gerald. "I've got enough on my plate being the marshal."

"Actually, I offered it to my husband."

"Yes," added Alric. "I thought I might expand it to include worthy warriors of Weldwyn. Of course, it'll take some work, for its reputation has fallen considerably from its former place of prominence."

"If anyone can repair that, it's you," said Gerald. "My congratulations to you, Your Majesty. You'll make a fine Knight Commander."

"Not Knight Commander," corrected Anna. "He'll be far too busy as King of Weldwyn to oversee things in person. Rather, he'll be the Grand Master."

Gerald grinned. "I see where this is going. Tell me, Majesty, who precisely did you have in mind for the position of Knight Commander?"

Alric couldn't help but break out into a huge smile. "Why, Jack, of course. He's more than deserving of the position."

"I'm sure it will please him to no end."

"Yes—a cavalier, a viscount, and now a knight. I don't know how the women of Weldwyn will ever be able to resist him!"

"Perhaps," said Anna, "he'll finally settle down and start a family?"

Alric thought about it for only a moment, then looked at Gerald, and the two of them broke out laughing. "Somehow, I doubt it."

"Come now. He's the viscount. He needs heirs to carry on the family name."

"I suspect he won't see it that way. Jack has always seen it as his respon-sibility to mock people who were like his father."

"People can change," said the queen. "Take Lady Nicole for an example."

"Speaking of which," said Gerald. "Where have she and Arnim been of late?"

"Last I heard, they were travelling to Kingsford."

"How long ago was that?"

"Almost five weeks now, more than enough time to make it to Kingsford and back."

"Perhaps you should send someone to look for them?" suggested Alric.

"No, it might risk exposing them. They went there to discover who was behind all this hatred against the Orcs. Let's give them some time to complete their mission."

"They could be in trouble?"

"True, but I'd hate to ruin all their hard work by bringing unwanted attention. What I will do, though, is make you a promise. I'll have Hayley look into things if I've heard nothing by the end of next week."

Arnim's head throbbed as he regained consciousness, and as soon as he tried to move, he realized his hands and feet were bound. He turned his head, feeling a wooden beam against his face as water sloshed around it. He opened his eyes, but only darkness surrounded him.

"Nikki?" he whispered. "Are you there?"

"I'm here," came the reply. "Are you injured?"

He tried to sit up, but his head protested. "Where are we?"

"What's the last thing you remember?"

"We were at the docks, watching a ship." He struggled to recall why. "We were following someone, weren't we?"

"We were—that brute Draven."

It all came rushing back. "I remember now. We've been shadowing him for weeks."

"Yes, but somebody must've noticed us because a group of thugs took us by surprise."

"Let me guess? Someone hit me on the head?"

"Exactly. At first, I feared they might have killed you, but then Draven ordered us taken aboard."

"So, this is the ship we were watching?"

"Yes, the *Fantine*, though we still don't know where she hails from."

"Well," said Arnim, "they didn't kill us outright. At least not yet."

"I doubt they will. Haven't you noticed? We're underway?"

"To be honest, my head is still reeling from the thumping I took." He finally managed to sit up.

A little light peeked through from above, revealing a rough wooden floor. Water sloshed around them, and he sensed they were in the lowest recesses of the ship.

"Ballast," said Nikki. "That's all we are at the moment."

"It stinks in here."

"That's to be expected. Even the best ships leak, and the water down here would be stagnant. At least we don't have rats to trouble us."

"I would've thought the waves would be more noticeable. They don't call it the Sea of Storms for nothing."

"The coast is more than a hundred miles from Kingsford. We must still be on the river."

"How long was I unconscious?" asked Arnim.

"It was close to midnight when they captured us."

"And now?"

"By my reckoning," she said, "it's likely late morning, but without seeing the sun, it's only a guess. Other than your head, how are you feeling?"

"Sore. They tied my hands behind my back, and it feels like the rope has rubbed my wrists raw. I don't think I have any open wounds, though. You?"

"They've also tied my hands, but aside from some bruising, I'm fine."

"I don't suppose you have a knife hidden away somewhere?"

"Unfortunately, not. They searched us both and relieved us of our belongings, including my lockpicks. It seems we are at the mercy of our captors."

"So," said Arnim, "we're prisoners aboard a foreign ship sailing for Saxnor knows where?"

"That about sums it up, yes."

"What can you tell me about our captors? Could they be Kurathians?"

"No. They spoke as we do, and their manner of dress was much the same as well."

"Then what do they want with us?"

"Information would be my guess," she replied. "They knew we were spying on them. I imagine they seek to discover who hired us."

"So, they don't know our identities?"

"It would appear not."

"Then we must ensure we keep it that way."

Footsteps echoed above them, and then what little light there was shining through moved. Moments later, a door shut, plunging them into darkness.

"It seems whoever is up there is on the move," said Nikki.

The footsteps grew fainter, and then a hatch was thrown open some distance away, letting sunlight flood into the hold. Arnim tried to focus as his eyes struggled to adjust. A man came down a steep set of stairs, holding up a lantern that revealed a face graced with patches of stubble, topped with short hair cut almost to the scalp.

"You're still alive, then?" he called out.

Arnim refused to answer.

The fellow came closer, his feet sloshing around in the water.

"Your ship's sinking," said Nikki.

The man chuckled. "That's bilge water, nothing you need worry about."

"Where are you taking us?"

"Home. Or rather, my home, to be more precise. I'm afraid that doesn't bode well for you two."

"And where is home?" asked Arnim.

"A little place we like to call Halvaria. I suppose you may know it better as the Halvarian Empire. You might as well make yourself comfortable. It'll take some time."

"Are we to starve in the meantime?"

"Not at all," their host responded. "But we'll keep you down here until we clear the coast of Merceria. I wouldn't want you to try escaping. Now that you're both awake, I'll have someone bring you some food and water."

"My associate has a head wound," said Nikki. "He needs someone to look after it."

"You mean your husband? Don't worry. He'll survive." He grinned at them, his face looking all the more menacing with the illumination of the lantern light. "We know all about you two."

"Then," said Arnim, "please enlighten us?"

The fellow squatted. "You are Lord Arnim Caster, the Viscount of... what was it again? Oh yes, Haverston. That would, I suppose, make your wife here the viscountess, although I suspect neither of you was born into the nobility. Not that I'd hold it against you, of course. In our society, there is no nobility."

"Then who rules?" asked Nikki.

"Why, the emperor, and his appointed ministers." He stared back at them a moment. "Ah, now I see it. You begin to understand."

"Halvaria is behind the unrest in Merceria," said Arnim.

"Who else could it be? The emperor has taken quite an interest in your home of late, particularly after we heard of your recent war."

"And so he sent you to spy on us?"

"Oh, we've been here for decades. Now, you're not the only kingdom we keep an eye on, but you do present us with a challenge. Never before have we seen so many races united on the field of battle. Of course, it also provided us with an opportunity to fan the flames of discontent."

"You'll never get away with this," said Arnim. "Our presence will be missed."

"I'm sure it will," replied their captor. "In fact, we're counting on it!"

THIRTY-EIGHT

Execution

SUMMER 967 MC

King Alric watched as his guards escorted the prisoner to the scaffold. Lord Elgin, stripped of his finery, looked miserable, not entirely unexpected, considering his execution was nigh.

"I don't know if I have the stomach for this," said Alric.

"This is one of the more distasteful parts of ruling," replied Anna. "There will always be those who plot against the Crown. Our duty is to see them punished."

"I have no doubt that Lord Elgin deserves death. I'm just not certain it needs to be so public. Surely a quick death would be preferable?" He looked over his shoulder. "What do you think, Gerald?"

"Justice must be seen to be done, Your Majesty. Your people need to be reminded of the punishment for traitors. Not that they're all bad, of course. Most commoners want only to get on with their lives, but it helps to know the king is looking after their interests."

"I suppose I hadn't thought of it that way."

They forced Lord Elgin to kneel while the swordsman took up a position on one side.

"It's never easy to watch the execution of a man," added Gerald. "Don't get me wrong, I've killed many on the battlefield, but it's not so personal in the heat of the moment. Far different to see a man's eyes when he knows he's about to die."

The executioner raised the sword, then looked up at his king. The sword swung at a nod from Alric, cleanly separating Elgin's head from his neck. The crowd cheered while Alric gasped with shock.

"It gets easier," said Anna, placing her hand on his knee.

"And it doesn't haunt you?" said Alric.

"You must have faith in your laws. It might be a different matter, had you any doubt concerning his guilt, but in Lord Elgin's case, the proof was easily verified."

She was about to say more, but then Gerald intervened. "Here comes Godfrey."

Godfrey Hammond was the second man facing death on this day. Unlike his predecessor, he was relaxed, casually strolling out to the scaffold, taking an interest in the clearing away of Elgin's body.

"He's calm," said Alric. "Too calm, if I'm being honest." He scanned the crowd. "Jack?"

The cavalier appeared at his side. "Yes, Majesty?"

"Keep your men alert. I fear Godfrey may have something up his sleeve."

"Understood, Majesty. I shall see to it at once."

Alric watched as Jack made his way to the scaffold, halting only briefly to say something to the guards stationed to keep the crowd at bay. Jack removed Godfrey, and then they both disappeared from sight, Jack returning without the condemned man.

"What is he doing?" asked Anna.

"Don't worry," said the king. "Godfrey will not escape his fate. Jack has merely removed the temptation for a moment while he gets his men into position."

"You truly believe they'll try something?" asked Gerald.

"The man already escaped our custody once. I'd prefer he doesn't succeed a second time."

More men appeared bearing the Royal Coat of Arms. Jack directed them to push back the crowd a few paces, then waited as they carried out his orders. Satisfied all was as it should be, he disappeared behind the scaffold and re-emerged with the prisoner in front of him.

Gerald first spied the men moving through the crowd. There were ten of them, all told, rushing towards Alric.

"Look out!" he shouted, jumping up and drawing his sword. His left hand instinctively reached out to Lady Jane, urging her to stay behind him.

Alric was on his feet in no time, but his sword somehow became entangled with his ceremonial robes. Anna stepped past him, thrusting out her Dwarven sword into the first attacker, penetrating the man's leather armour. He fell back, the life gone from his eyes even before he hit the ground.

In her rush to defend her husband, Anna overextended herself. The next one bashed her with his club, hitting her forearm and knocking the blade from her hands. He followed up with a second swing, but by this time, Alric had freed his sword and sliced into the fellow's arm. The weapon struck bone, and the man fell to one side, clutching the wound, screaming.

Gerald stepped forward, still protecting Lady Jane. A spear tip glanced off his arm, and the marshal thanked Saxnor he'd thought to wear his old mail shirt this day. His counterattack took his foe in the thigh, and he followed that with a quick slash across the throat. Blood splattered him, and he struggled to pick his next target as more men poured into the seating area. Someone's dagger scraped along his stomach, but the rings held and then he punched out with the hilt of his old Mercerian sword. His attacker pulled back, desperate to avoid damage, so Gerald pushed in close and stabbed him.

Having lost her weapon, Anna backed up, giving Alric and Gerald room to wield their weapons. Guards ran towards them, but the townsfolk, not used to such violence, tried to flee the area, desperate to get to cover, making it even worse for those attempting to help.

Alric parried a blow, but the force of it drove him back. He felt his chair against his legs and realized he had no room left to manoeuvre. In desperation, he struck out, increasing the speed of his attacks at the expense of accuracy. The renewed onslaught pushed his attackers back, and then he noted one such villain overreached as he stabbed out at Gerald. Alric took advantage of the mistake to slice through the villain's hand.

Anna, spotting her sword, tried to reach and grab it, but just as her fingertips touched it, a foot kicked the weapon away. She looked up to see a man staring down at her with an evil sneer on his face. "Time to die, Majesty!"

A metal cup struck the fellow, distracting him, and then Lady Jane pulled Anna back from the fight.

"Are you hurt?" she asked.

"I'm fine," replied Anna. "We must help!"

"What can we do?"

The queen quickly scanned the area. At the first sign of trouble, the servants had fled. Were it not for Godfrey's execution, their guards would still be in place, but they'd expected a rescue attempt, not an assault on the king's party!

Her gaze came to rest on Storm. The Kurathian Mastiff was not full grown, yet he already dwarfed most other breeds. She whistled, then called his name, causing him to rush towards her. The servant holding the other end of the leash stared in horror as he tore from his grasp.

Storm burst into the seating area, upturning chairs in his bid to come to his mistress's rescue. He had not been trained in the way of battle, yet his natural instincts were on full display. He barrelled into the fray, knocking one attacker down with his sheer bulk, then sinking his teeth into the arm of another. Such was the ferocity of his attack that it forced the enemy back.

Gerald and Alric quickly seized the initiative, surging forward to deal out death and destruction. Moments later, Jack was there, his men overwhelming the attackers who'd survived the initial onslaught.

"Malin's tears, but that was close," said the king. "I shan't make that mistake again." His gaze quickly moved to the scaffold. "The prisoner?"

"Safe, Majesty, in the care of a group of your finest," replied Jack. "I gave orders to remove him at the first sign of trouble."

"Good. Now bring him back out, and let's get on with this execution."

The cavalier looked at the new prisoners, then shook his head in disbelief. "Are you certain, Majesty? There may yet be more ready to strike?"

"The only way to end this is to remove the prize they seek. See the order carried out, Jack."

"Of course, Majesty."

Alric picked up the Dwarf blade and held it out, hilt first, for his wife. "Your weapon, my dear."

Anna took it, smiling. "Why, thank you, Your Majesty."

"You should get someone to look at your arm. You're likely to develop a nasty bruise."

"I shall have Revi see to it once this day's events are concluded."

"Shall we sit?"

"I would be delighted."

"With your permission," said Gerald. "I'd like to fetch some more men to help keep order."

"Very well," said Alric, "but it will not delay our justice. Godfrey Hammond will hang long before your return."

"Understood, Majesty."

Gerald turned to Jane. "I shall return directly."

"I look forward to it," she replied.

"Was it you who tossed the cup?" asked the queen.

"I'm afraid it was the only thing at hand."

"Well, that and Storm."

The great mastiff wandered over, resting his head on Anna's knee.

"It appears he was well-named," said Lady Jane. "He takes after his sire."

"He certainly does." Anna rubbed the dog's head, and the beast let out a howl.

"Hush now," said the queen.

"Let him be," said Alric. "He's simply celebrating a victory."

Having ordered the attackers marched off, Jack now resumed his position on the scaffold where a rope dangled from an overhead post, ready to perform its duty.

They marched Godfrey out again, but this time he appeared agitated, muttering something, but the sound didn't carry to the king. The executioner hung the rope around the prisoner's neck, then placed a stool before Godfrey, forcing him to balance atop it.

Alric's gaze wandered over the crowd, yet he could spot no signs of trouble. The townsfolk's bravery returned with the lack of further violence, and they drifted closer to the scaffold, the better to witness the spectacle unfold.

"I'm having second thoughts about being more lenient," said Alric. "If he hadn't handed over all that information, he'd have been disembowelled."

"But not Lord Elgin?" asked Lady Jane.

"He was an earl and was granted a beheading. You'll note we use a sword for nobles instead of an axe."

"And so Godfrey will be hanged?"

"He will. The executioner will carefully place the rope to snap his neck. Death will come instantly, which is far more than he deserves, given his crimes."

The executioner stood to one side, then looked at King Alric. The crowd grew quiet, and His Majesty nodded.

A boot kicked out the stool, and Godfrey Hammond began to swing, but instead of hanging limply, he choked and sputtered, his body flailing around.

"Oh dear," said Anna. "It appears your executioner has failed in his task. I've seen this thing before, during the rebellion."

Jack stepped forward and grasped Godfrey's boots, pulling down on them. The prisoner's body went limp, the sentence now carried to its completion. The crowd booed at the death, more interested in watching him struggle than meeting his end.

They lowered Godfrey, and then a physician came to examine and pronounce him dead. A pair of men bore the body from the scaffold.

"Two down, one to go," said Alric. Having realized his words, he turned to Lady Jane. "Sorry, my lady. I know this can't be easy for you."

"My son conspired with the enemy," she replied, a coldness creeping into her manner. "For that, he deserves what's coming."

They brought out James Goodwin to face his death. He, too, wore a plain linen shirt but bore none of the calm demeanour Godfrey displayed on his initial appearance.

A movement off to the side caught the king's attention, but it was only Gerald returning with more men. "We shall wait for Lord Gerald," he announced. "I shouldn't wish for Lady Jane to go through this without his presence."

They waited as the additional warriors took their places around the Royal Party. Gerald resumed his seat. "Sorry," he said. "Did I miss much?"

"Only a bungled hanging," said Anna.

He snorted. "Wouldn't be the first time I've seen that, nor I expect, will it be the last. It's not an easy task, killing a man in that manner, and Saxnor knows they don't get a lot of chances to hone their skills."

"Let's hope it remains that way," said Alric. "You may proceed!" he called out.

Once they placed the noose around James Goodwin's neck, the condemned man took his place on the stool. The executioner looked at the king, waiting.

Alric nodded, and the stool was kicked away, the rope growing taut as James fell. This time, mercifully, death was instant.

Jane buried her face in Gerald's shoulder.

"It is done," said Alric. "Let us hope it's the last time we are forced to provide such a spectacle."

The minstrels played their tunes, but there was little to lift the spirits. Executions dampened the mood of even the most gregarious of folks, and this day had seen three.

"We should've cancelled this celebration," said Alric.

"Nonsense," said Jack. "People need to know life goes on, despite attempts to thwart it. Godfrey was a villain through and through, and the others deserved their fate no less."

"Still, it's a sombre way to begin a reign."

"Look at it this way," said Jack. "Things can only improve going forward!"

"I wish I could believe that, but our recent history indicates otherwise. We are in an unprecedented time of war, Jack. There's been more fighting in the last few years than in the entire century. When will it ever end?"

"I give it another nine years, Majesty."

The king chuckled. "That's a precise number, my friend. Why nine?"

"Three years to rebuild the army, three to conquer anyone who stands in our way, and another three to impress foreign powers."

"You appear to have our future all planned out for us."

"Tell me," said Anna. "Where does Merceria fit it with this plan of yours?"

"Why, at our side," replied Jack. "As our most trusted ally."

"Remarkable, isn't it?" said Alric. "It wasn't long ago that Merceria and

Weldwyn were bitter enemies. Who would have thought we'd become the best of friends in so short a time."

"Yes, Majesty, but it's more than that. Just think, your son will eventually rule both kingdoms."

"Aye, and then the real work begins. I can't imagine how difficult it will be to devise one set of laws to govern all."

"Then perhaps," said Anna, "we should begin steering our respective realms towards a more common set of laws now?"

"That is an excellent idea, although I doubt we'll complete it by the time Braedon takes the Throne."

"Let us hope that's many years from now," said Jack. "I'd like to see the pair of you grow old together."

"Then we'll try our hardest not to disappoint you."

Alric rose, prompting those around him to stop eating and stand. "Please," he said. "Feel free to continue with your meal. I'll be back shortly."

Everyone sat down and resumed their previous topics of conversation.

"Where are you going?" asked Anna.

"Just a little business to attend to." He winked, then stepped past her to where Gerald and Lady Jane sat. "My pardon," he said, "but there is something I wish to discuss with Lady Jane Goodwin."

"Shall I leave?" asked Gerald.

"No, please stay," said Jane. "Anything concerning me can be said in your presence." She looked at the king. "Your Majesty?"

Alric cleared his throat. "As you know, my lady, upon his death, your son's estate became the property of the Crown."

"I am well aware of that, Majesty."

"Then you are also aware it is up to the king to decide what to do with it. I have it in mind to award it to you, Lady Jane, for your efforts in finding and apprehending Godfrey Hammond."

"Your Majesty is too kind, but I am undeserving of such an honour."

"Nonsense. It's the least I can do, and in any case, I am the king, and I insist you accept."

"Then I thank you, Majesty, with all my heart, although I wonder why you went to the trouble of moving from your seat to tell me?"

"Consider it a public acknowledgement of your service, my lady. Had it not been for you, we would have never again laid eyes on him, and his secrets would have lain buried forever. Your relentless determination enabled us to uncover the plots and machinations of Lord Elgin."

"What of Lord Beric?" asked Gerald. "Didn't I hear something implicated him as well?"

"Only by association, but don't worry, we'll keep a close eye on him from now on. There will be a few changes in the Earls Council in the coming weeks. I suppose, in a way, we can thank Elgin for that."

"And what of his earldom?" asked Lady Jane.

"That's an entirely different problem, one I believe will require much further consideration. In the meantime, you will always be welcome at my court—wherever that might end up being held."

"Thank you, Your Majesty."

"Not at all. It is you who I must thank, for, by your actions, you demonstrated you are truly a guardian of the Crown."

THIRTY-NINE

The Dragon

SUMMER 967 MC

A lthea stepped through the doorway into the entrance hall. Off to her right, the dragon stirred, its massive head lifting from where it lay. The rest of the Goblins ran for the nearest cover, but Glisnak stood by Brogar's side, helping the Dwarf navigate the doorway.

"Go," said Brogar. "Get yourself to the armoury."

The dragon took a deep breath, then released it, the overwhelming scent of sulphur drifting across the room. As it swivelled its head, its eyes met those of the Dwarf. Then a serpentine tongue snaked along its lips as if smelling a tasty morsel.

Brogar tried to run for the armoury, but as he took his second step, his wounded leg went out from under him, sending him crashing to the floor. A large shadow loomed over him, and he spied the dragon rising to its feet and shuffling forward.

Glisnak, no longer able to support the Dwarf's weight, ran towards the beast, his dagger held before him. He screamed at the top of his lungs, then bolted for a nearby pillar, desperate to get out of the reach of the ancient terror.

The dragon's throat began glowing, and a burning smell permeated the room. The head snapped to where the Goblin hid, and then the mouth opened, discharging a stream of fire. Glisnak ducked behind a pillar just in time to avoid a fiery death.

Althea ran to Brogar, pulling him to his feet and placing her arm around his neck, then hauling him towards safety. They crashed through the door to emerge into a crowded armoury. Surrounding them stood the remaining Goblins, each clutching a crude spear.

They struggled to breathe in the smoky air. Behind them, the entrance hall was lit up from the dragon's breath, banishing shadows.

Finally, the flames subsided, and Glisnak rushed out of his hiding place, eager to find somewhere safe. The dragon moved closer and then stretched out its long neck, attempting to snatch up the Goblin in its maw.

Althea picked up an old Dwarven spear and charged towards the beast, screaming out a challenge. Hefting the spear with all the strength she could muster, she threw it at the great monstrosity, striking it in the chest, but such was its armour that it did no apparent damage.

It hissed at her, showing its teeth in all their lethal glory. The neck glowed again, and Althea readied herself to embrace death, but before it let loose with its fiery breath, a bolt struck it, burying itself up to the head.

The glow dissipated as the creature turned to face the great double doors where Dwarves lined the entranceway, their arbalests ready. As Haldrim's command rang out loud and clear, a volley of bolts sprang forth, but then Lochlan's voice broke through, "Althea, look out. To your left!"

It was only a moment before she turned and noticed a large shape approaching from the side. The deep-one had entered the room, beating out a steady rhythm as its feet smashed against the floor."

Dozens of bolts sprang from the Dragon Company, sinking deep into the dragon, yet the creature ignored them, turning its attention to the Princess of Weldwyn.

The deep-one lumbered towards Althea. She tried backing up to get to safety, but the strange creature merely altered its course and continued heading straight for her.

The only option was to lure the deep-one closer to the dragon and hope it took the bait. She charged the ancient beast, ignoring the new threat, but a massive talon came her way as she approached. Desperate to avoid the blow, she dove to the ground, knocking the air from her lungs. As the beast's claws slashed the air above her, they snagged on her cloak, dragging her along the floor, then flinging her against the wall. Her head hit first, and although she wore a helmet, the blow nearly knocked her senseless. She struggled to rise, seeking the battle but unable to focus her eyes.

More bolts sailed forth, sinking into scales, yet still, the dragon kept moving. A deep rumble echoed off to her left, and then the deep-one shambled past, heading straight for the belly of the dragon, its fists striking out.

The dragon roared with pain, then lowered its head and grabbed the elemental between its teeth. It gnawed on its enemy, the sound like metal on stone, a high-pitched squeal that hurt the ears. Finally, it released its prey and used a claw to sweep its attacker aside.

Goblins burst from the armoury in twos, each pair bearing what was, to them, a long spear. These they carried to Glisnak, who directed his companions to set them against the pillar, points out.

The dragon roared again, then charged at them, impaling itself on the spears. Several snapped off, but at least two dug deep, and the winged creature backed up, blood running freely.

The deep-one thundered past Althea yet again, and this time she noted chunks of stone torn away, revealing a glowing orange skin beneath, with molten stone seeping from the wounds. It barrelled into the dragon, and a great hissing noise arose, followed by the smell of burning flesh.

The dragon reared up, letting out a roar that shook the very room, small stones and dust falling from the ceiling. It thrashed around and then finally collapsed, burying the deep-one beneath its body.

More bolts sank into the scaled skin, but nothing moved. The dragon of Tor-Maldrin was dead. Althea closed her eyes, her chin falling to her chest.

A shadow loomed over Althea, and she looked up to see Lochlan.

"Are you injured?" he asked.

"Nothing a good deal of rest won't solve," she replied.

Behind him was a most curious sound. She tilted to the side to see Dwarves hacking away at the body. "What in Malin's name are they doing?"

"Looking for the deep-one. It's buried somewhere beneath the dragon."

Brogar hobbled over, his leg in a makeshift splint. "That looks nasty," he said as he stared at her head. "You should see about getting someone to look after that."

"I should love to," she replied, "but I think there are more pressing matters at present, don't you?"

Lochlan cast his gaze about the room. "Remarkable. I would never have imagined it possible."

"It was your decision to come here and rid the place of the dragon."

"It was, yet if I'm being honest, I thought we'd only manage to drive it away. You must admit, the odds of succeeding were slim."

"Your plan was what did it," she persisted.

"And your bravery brought it to fruition."

"I couldn't have done it without Glisnak and his Goblins."

Behind him, the Dwarves backed up.

"Lord!" called out Haldrim. "You may want to see this."

Lochlan helped Althea to her feet, and together they approached the great carcass. The Dwarves had cut off the creature's neck and dragged it to one side, no easy task considering its massive size. Beneath, they found not the deep-one's body but a collection of stones of various sizes, each partially melted as if hot tin had been dropped from a fire.

"It seems neither survived," said Lochlan.

"Just as well," said Brogar. "I didn't fancy the idea of trying to lure that thing back down into the deep."

"I'm not exactly an expert on things like this. How long will it take to clear away the carcass?"

"Quite a while. And the rest of this place also looks like it could use a good cleanup. Not that we'll likely be the ones taking care of it."

"Why would you say that?"

"I'd assumed you'd want to get back to Dungannon," replied Brogar. "If you recall, there's still the matter of dealing with the boatholders?"

"Oh yes," said Lochlan. "In all the excitement, I'd forgotten all about them."

"I doubt they'd give you much trouble now," said Althea. "Not after word gets out you killed a dragon."

"I did little to kill that thing; the rest of you slew it."

"But the plan was yours, and without your wisdom to guide us, we might all have perished. You shall forever be remembered now as Lochlan the Dragonslayer. As for the boatholders, I have an idea how we could change their opinion of us."

"Oh? Do tell?"

"We convince them to carry trade goods to Weldwyn and Merceria."

"But it's river boats they use, not seagoing ships."

"True," said Althea, "but sailing along the southern coast of the Clanholdings would be safe enough. They could easily stay within sight of the shore, following the coast. I'm sure they can sell much of what the Twelve Clans make, at a substantial profit."

"Such as?"

"Linen is the first thing that comes to mind with all that flax we've got growing. There's a high demand for it in Weldwyn, especially amongst the wealthier folk."

"What do I do about the attempt on my life?"

"You tell me. What would your sister have done?"

Lochlan thought it over carefully. "She would have demanded blood, but I'm not sure that's the best solution. I fear such action would inevitably lead to more death. The would-be murderers are both dead. Perhaps we should leave it at that."

"You are a remarkable man," said Brogar, "but if you wish to last long as chieftain, you must make it clear you'll not put up with any further attacks, else they'll think you weak."

"If there's one thing I've learned these last few months, it's that ruling over a Clan is much more complicated than I ever believed possible. Very well. I shall consider your advice, Master Brogar."

"Master, is it, now? You flatter me."

"You've earned it, my friend."

A shout from outside drew their attention. Shortly thereafter, a Dwarf ran into the hall. "A band of Humans approaches, Lord. I believe they came from Drakewell."

"Then let us go greet them," said Lochlan.

They stepped out into the sunshine to see a group of armed men making their way towards the mine. It took only a moment to recognize their leader, and then Lochlan finally relaxed.

"Neasa!" he called out. "What brings you to Tor-Maldrin?"

"We came to lend what assistance we could. When you marched your company off to battle, many felt we should accompany you and do our part. I scraped together quite a few volunteers, but it appears we came too late. I assume the dragon is dead?"

"It is indeed."

"Yes," added Althea. "And it's all due to Lochlan."

Neasa bowed. "We shall be forever in your debt, Lochlan of Dungannon. How can we ever repay you?"

"The mine sits as an empty shell," he replied. "Yet we have defeated the very thing that drove the original occupants from it all those years ago. I speak not of the dragon but rather the deep-one, what we would call an elemental."

"And you vanquished both? Is there no end to your prowess?"

"I did not break their hold on this place alone—it was a combined effort. Were it not for the valiant Dwarves of the Dragon Company and the Goblins of Tor-Maldrin, we would surely have failed."

"Goblins of Tor-Maldrin?" said Neasa. "Are you now to award those creatures possession of the mine?"

"That is for you to decide, but before you make up your mind, I would have you listen to my reasoning."

"Very well. Go on."

"We both know Clansmen will not willingly work in such a place, yet there are surely riches here waiting to be unlocked. I propose you permit Glisnak and his people to live here and mine. They can then trade what riches they find for goods the people of Drakewell make."

"Such as?"

"Decent weapons, for one thing, clothing, for another. They also have the advantage of being smaller in stature than us, meaning they would consume far less food than Humans. I suspect such an arrangement could prove most profitable to both parties."

"Then we shall do as you suggest, although it may take some time to get the idea across to them."

"I suggest we stay awhile," said Althea. "Glisnak and I have come to understand each other quite well, and it would prove helpful to learn more of their language or even teach them ours."

Neasa looked doubtful. "And you believe these primitive creatures are intelligent enough to learn our ways?"

"They are not primitive by desire, merely by circumstance. I think you'll find they will adapt to our ways easily enough, given a chance."

"Yes," added Lochlan. "And the Gods know we have few allies these days."

"Allies," said Neasa. "Let us hope they serve us better than the last. The Kurathians certainly didn't have our best interests at heart."

"At the risk of sounding insulting," said Althea, "it's not only your interest that's important here. To build a strong alliance, you must both prosper."

"I see she has your gift of speech, Lochlan. Very well, I'll keep your words in mind as we move forward." She cast her gaze over the entrance to the mine and shuddered. "I will never understand the fascination with tunnelling beneath the ground."

"And yet, your own sister maintains the archives," said Lochlan.

"You outwitted me. Very well, I concede the point. Now, what of you? You've added dragon slaying to your list of accomplishments. What's next?"

"We shall stay here for a while, assuming we're welcome. I want to learn more about this place, and as my good wife mentioned, it would be helpful to understand more of Glisnak's language."

"What is it you hope to discover in that mine?"

"That I cannot say, but over the years, I've come to realize knowledge for its own sake is often enough. This was once a thriving mine, maybe even a city, for we know not how deep it burrows. Imagine what they must have learned over the centuries!"

Neasa shook her head. "You amaze me. Any other chieftain would be parading the head of the dragon all across the Clanholdings, bragging about their accomplishments, but not you. All you want to do is learn more about the mountain folk who lived in the mine."

"What can I say? I'm a scholar at heart."

The men of Drakewell came closer, peering in through the great doorway, but none would enter, save one.

"Who's that?" asked Althea. "I don't remember seeing him in town."

"He showed up early this morning," replied Neasa, "just after your

Dwarves left to march here. He introduced himself as Vadym and claims to have come from afar."

"You mean Merceria, or Norland?"

"That was what I thought at first, but he states otherwise."

The individual in question walked amongst the Dwarves as they continued cutting up the dragon's carcass.

"Curious," said Lochlan. "He's dressed like no trader I've ever seen."

"Nor I," added Althea. "Did he come with a wagon of goods?"

"No," said Neasa. "As far as I know, he arrived with no more than the clothes on his back."

"By boat?"

"No, that's even more curious. He came by foot."

"Perhaps he's down from Strathlade," said Lochlan. "That lies north of here, though from what I recall from maps, that would mean he came through some fairly difficult terrain. Did he travel alone?"

"He did."

"This fellow grows more mysterious by the moment. Would you introduce us?"

"By all means," said Neasa. She turned to one of her men. "Go and fetch the visitor, will you? We'd like to have a chat with him."

The fellow ran off, though he paused at the entrance to the mine, clearly hesitant to enter.

"In you go," called out his chief. "You won't find him lurking by the door."

He disappeared inside.

"I assume he speaks our language?" said Althea.

"He does. Quite well, though he's not familiar with some of our local terms for things. I suspect he comes from a large city, if his manner of speaking is any indication. In that regard, he's like you, Princess."

"There's an entire Continent to the east of us. He could be from there."

"If that's true," said Lochlan, "then what's he doing all the way over here?"

"Could he be from farther west?"

"I doubt it. From what I've read, beyond those mountains is little save for the sea. They say ships out of Windbourne tried sailing into the region centuries ago only to be driven back by storms."

"What about the north?" asked Brogar. "Any idea what's up there?"

"Strathlade is the northernmost town in the Clanholdings. If there's anything past that, it has not seen fit to make its way into our written history."

The stranger appeared at the entrance, his cloak thrown back over his shoulders, revealing a coat of mail glistening in the sun. He looked around the area, and then his gaze stopped on the group.

"Ah," he called out. "I see my presence has been noted." The fellow came closer, walking at a brisk pace. "You must be Lochlan and Althea of Dungannon. The townsfolk have talked of little else since my arrival."

"Greetings," said Althea. "And allow me to introduce Master Brogar, a warrior of some renown."

"Pleased I am to make your acquaintance, Master Dwarf, though I must admit to knowing very little of your people."

"And you might be?" asked Lochlan.

The stranger smiled. "My name is Vadym. Vadym Stormwind."

Epilogue

FALL 967 MC

"Are you sure about this?" asked Beverly.

Revi Bloom looked like someone had slapped him. "Of course I'm sure. What kind of question is that? I've studied the Saurian gates in exacting detail. There are no more secrets to unlock."

"Don't worry," said Aubrey. "All we're going to do is step through the gate and look around a little, and then I'll return us to Wincaster by using the spell of recall."

Beverly was having trouble understanding what her cousin was suggesting. "But don't we have to take the gate to Erssa Saka'am first?"

"Ah," said Revi. "That's the beauty of it. My research indicates we can use the gates to travel to any confluence."

"Which is?" asked Aldwin.

A look of annoyance crossed Revi's face.

"Come now," said Aubrey. "He has a right to know where you're sending us."

"Very well. Let me explain this as simply as possible. We mages have known for years that lines of force exist."

"Lines of force?" said the smith.

"Think of them as channels of magical energy. The gates the Saurians built employ them to travel over great distances."

"That much I understand, but why are we here in Queenston?"

"Because the Queenston gate is much easier to get to."

"But Uxley is closer to Wincaster."

"I understand that, but it's hidden down in a well. I don't much fancy the idea of getting horses down there, do you?"

"No, I suppose not."

"Now, where was I? Oh yes, the gates. For many generations, mages believed the ley lines only ran north-south, but recent discoveries by yours truly indicate a second set runs roughly east-west. My research has led me to believe I can now send you anywhere these lines converge, whether there's an actual Saurian gate there or not."

"And that's why I'm going," added Aubrey. "To make sure we can get back safely."

"My intention," continued Revi, "is to send you eastward, where you can learn more about this place called Halvaria."

"That sounds dangerous," said Aldwin.

"That's why Dame Beverly is going."

"That's Lady Beverly now."

"Yes, of course. In any case, you're going to look around, get a feel for the area, and then return. This is only our first peek at what lies in that direction. You should be back before dinner-time."

"And the sickness the gates induce?"

"Only prolonged exposure causes problems," said Aubrey. "And upon our return, Kraloch and I will remove any ill-effects we may suffer."

"You don't have to go if you don't want to," said Revi.

"No, I'm fine," said Aldwin. "It'll make a nice change to accompany my wife for once."

"Oh, one more thing. You can ride your horses through the gate."

"Isn't that dangerous?" said Beverly.

"That's what I thought at first, but I now believe I mistranslated the ancient Saurian language. I am certain there is no danger to you or your mounts."

"Couldn't we all go through at the same time?"

"I'm afraid that wouldn't work. As soon as it transports someone, the flame diminishes. I suppose, if you were walking, you could hold hands and go through, but the flame isn't big enough for two people and their horses." He paused a moment, looking over the trio. "Well?" he said. "What are you waiting for?"

"I'll go first," offered Beverly.

The Saurian gate was a magical green flame standing atop a pedestal marked with magical runes. A wooden ramp had been added to make it easier to ride horses through the portal.

Beverly positioned Lightning on the ramp, then ducked her head, prepared to ride through once it was ready. Revi Bloom touched the runes, calling on his magical power. The strange symbols glowed, and the green flame grew from candle-sized to a roaring bonfire.

A pleasant-looking countryside was visible through the green flame, and then Beverly urged her horse forward. As soon as Lightning's nose touched the flame, they both disappeared, reappearing a moment later in the field beyond. The fire, as expected, reduced once more to a tiny flicker.

"It still has to recharge," explained Revi. "It shouldn't take too long."

"I wonder what lies on the other side?" said Aldwin.

"You'll find out soon enough."

Once Revi pronounced the flame ready to use again, he repeated the process, then had Aldwin ride through.

Aldwin felt a brief moment of cold, and then his entire body seized up, his vision blurred, and he was plunged into darkness for the smallest of interludes. The next thing he knew, he sat on his horse atop a slight rise, looking down into a green field. His mind struggled to come to grips with this suddenly changed environment, and then Beverly rode into view.

"I see you made it," she said. "What did you think?"

"It was a little disorienting, to be honest."

"Take a look behind you."

He turned to see two great upright stones with a third lying sideways across their top, creating a doorway.

"Much different from the gates we found in Merceria," said Beverly.

"I hope that doesn't bode ill," he replied.

The area between the two upright pillars glowed faintly before a green flame appeared, floating in the air. It grew, filling the gap, and then Aubrey could be seen on the other side, guiding her mount towards the flame. Her horse's nose touched the flame and then disappeared, along with its rider.

Aldwin watched as they reappeared on his side of the gate. "That was incredible," he said.

Aubrey took a deep breath, then looked at Beverly. "Did you feel that?" she asked.

"Feel what?" replied her cousin.

"As I was pulled through, I felt a strange vibration."

Aldwin's gaze went to the stones. "Stand back," he warned. "I hear something."

Aubrey moved away from the gate as a loud crack emanated from the archway, followed in quick succession by several more until the top of the right-hand stone pillar split from the rest, crashing to the ground. The top, unable to support its own weight, soon followed, its collapse forcing the second pillar to topple as well.

"That doesn't look good," said Aldwin. "I suppose this means we won't be able to return here in future?"

"Haven't a clue," said Aubrey. "This is an unexpected turn of events."

"What do we do now?"

"I'll notify Kraloch about what has happened, and he'll pass it on to Master Revi."

"But we can still return to Wincaster, can't we?"

"Using my recall spell, yes."

"Tell me," said Beverly. "Do you know how far we've travelled?"

"I suppose I could cast the first part of the spell and contact the Wincaster gate, but that won't give us any sense of direction."

"We were travelling east, according to Revi's calculations."

"Very well. I'll try, but it'll only give me a rough estimate." Aubrey closed her eyes and began the incantation. The spell went on for some time, and the wind picked up, forming a small vortex around her, but nothing else happened. Eventually, the mage ceased her spell and turned to her cousin, a worried expression on her face.

"What's wrong?" asked Beverly.

"I can't contact Wincaster. Wherever we are, it's too far for my spell to reach the circle."

"But you've travelled from Wincaster to Ironcliff before, haven't you? That must be hundreds of miles?"

"It is, yet Wincaster now lies beyond my reach. I'm afraid wherever we are, we're here to stay."

<<<<>>>>

READ ENEMY OF THE CROWN

∾

SHARE YOUR THOUGHTS ABOUT GUARDIAN OF THE CROWN

∾

If you liked *Guardian of the Crown*, then *Ashes*, the first book in *The Frozen Flame* series awaits.

START ASHES

Cast of Characters

Major Characters:

Merceria:
Anna – Queen, married to Prince Alric, mother of Braedon
Aubrey Brandon - Baroness of Hawksburg, Life Mage
Beverly Fitzwilliam - Knight Commander, married to Aldwin Fitzwilliam
Gerald Matheson - Duke of Wincaster, Marshal of the Army
Hayley Chambers - Baroness of Queenston, High Ranger
Randolf Blackburn - Knight of the Hound, brother of Celia

Weldwyn:
Alric - Prince, married to Queen Anna, father of Braedon
Althea – Princess, daughter of King Leofric and Queen Igraine
Brogar Hammerhand - Dwarf, Warrior, bodyguard to Princess Althea
Elgin Warford - Earl of Riversend
Godfrey Hammond - Noble, friend of James Goodwin
Jack Marlowe - Viscount of Aynsbury, cavalier
James Goodwin - Noble, son of Jane Goodwin
Jane Goodwin – Noble, mother of James Goodwin
Lindsey Martindale - Viscountess of Talburn
Tulfar Axehand – Dwarf, Baron of Mirstone

The Twelve Clans:
Glisnak - Goblin
Lochlan - Clan Chief of Dungannon
Camrath - Scholar of Glanfraydon

Secondary Characters
Merceria:
Albreda - Mistress of the Whitewood, Earth Mage
Aldus Hearn - Earth Mage
Aldwin Fitzwilliam - Master Smith, married to Beverly Fitzwilliam
Alexander Stanton - Earl of Tewsbury
Alexander Stanton (Deceased) - Former Earl of Tewsbury
Andred IV (Deceased) - Former King of Merceria
Arandil Greycloak - Elven ruler of the Darkwood, Fire Mage/Enchanter

Arnim Caster - Viscount of Haverston, Knight of the Hound, married to Nikki

Bertram Ayles - Ranger

Braedon Gerald - Prince of Merceria, son of Queen Anna and Prince Alric

Califax (Deceased) - Mercerian poet and playwright

Carlson - Commander of Wincaster Light Horse

Clara - Conservatory student, Life Mage in training

Cooper (Deceased) - Warrior, Bodden

Draven - Troublemaker in Kingsford

Durwin - Conservatory student, Earth Mage in training

Edgar Greenfield - Retired Bodden warrior, queen's courier

Edward Fitzwilliam (Deceased) - Previous Baron of Bodden

Evard Brenton - Royal Guardsman

Fletcher - Warrior, Bodden

Gardner - Sergeant, Wincaster Light Horse

Graves (Deceased) - Warrior, Bodden

Gryph - Young wolf, companion of Hayley Chambers

Henry (Deceased) - First son of Andred IV, previous King of Merceria

Herdwin Steelarm - Wincaster, Smith, Friend of Queen Anna

Heward 'The Axe' Manton - Knight of the Hound, Northern Commander

Horace Spencer - Earl of Eastwood

James - Knight of Bodden

Kiren-Jool - Kurathian Enchanter

Lanaka - Kurathian Commander of Light Horse

Lightning - Beverly's Mercerian Charger

Markham Anglesley - Duke of Colbridge

Matron Crawley - Nanny to Prince Braedon

Nicole 'Nikki' Arendale - Advisor to Queen Anna, Married to Arnim Caster

Preston Wright - Baron of Wickfield, Knight of the Hound, married to Sophie Wright

Randolf of Burrstoke - Old Knight of the Sword

Revi Bloom - Royal Life Mage, Enchanter

Richard 'Fitz' Fitzwilliam - Baron of Bodden, father of Beverly Fitzwilliam

Roland Valmar (Deceased) - Marshal General

Samantha 'Sam' - Queen's Ranger

Shellbreaker 'Jamie' - Revi Bloom's avian familiar

Snarl - Large wolf of Albreda's pack

Sophie Wright - Queen Anna's Lady-in-Waiting, married to Sir Preston

Storm - Kurathian Mastiff, Qeen Anna's pet

Tempus (Deceased)- Kurathian Mastiff, Queen Anna's pet

Tog - Earl of Trollden, Leader of the Trolls

William Blackwood - Bodden Sergeant-at-Arms

Parvan Luminor - Elf, Baron of Tivilton
Roxanne Fortuna (Deceased) - Life Mage
Thomas (Deceased) - FormerEarl of Riversend
Tyrell Caracticus (deceased) - Water Mage, Grand Mage
Walsh - Guard, Summersgate

THE TWELVE CLANS:
Brida (Deceased) - High Queen of the Twelve Clans, daughter of Dathen
Carmus (Deceased) - Fire Mage
Daragh - Senior oathman of Clan Dungannon
Dathen (Deceased) - High King of the Twelve Clans
Derdra - Keeper of knowledge, Drakewell
Kendrick - Warrior, Drakewell
Mirala - Herbalist, cousin to Lochlan, Dungannon
Neasa - Clan chief of Drakewell, daughter of Warnoch
Raurig - Clan chief of Banburn
Raurig 'the elder' (Deceased) - Former Clan chief of Banburn
Warnoch (Deceased) - Former clan chief of Drakewell

NORLAND:
Asher - Earl of Beaconsgate, nephew of Lord Hollis
Barden - Trader, Harrowsbrook
Beatrice - Trader,Harrowsbrook
Bronwyn - Queen of Norland
Caldwell - Holy Brother, Beaconsgate
Celia Blackburn (Deceased) - Knight of the Hound
Elder Roswald - Retired Holy Father in Beaconsgate
Hollis (Deceased) - Former Earl of Beaconsgate
Naran - Captain, Queen Bronwyn's guards
Rosella Blackburn - Mother of Randolf Blackburn
Sidonia (Deceased) - Aunt of Asher

THE OTHERS:
Aeldred - First King of Therengia
Gundar - God of the Earth
Kasri Ironheart - Warrior, Daughter of the Vard of Ironcliff
Khazad - Vard of Stonecastle
Kythelia 'Dark Queen' (Deceased) - Elf, Necromancer
Lysandil - Elf Emissary to the court of the Twelve Clans
Malin - God of Wisdom, revered by the people of Weldwyn
Melethandil - Dragon, Mountains near Ironcliff

Saxnor - God of Strength, revered by the Mercerians
Tarak - Kurathian Prince of Kouras
Tauril - Goddess of the Woods
Vadym Stormwind - Foreign visitor to the Twelve Clans

PLACES
MERCERIA:
Artisan Hills - Hills east of Eastwood
Bodden - Town, Barony
Colbridge - City, Dukedom
Darkwood - Forest east of Wincaster
Eastwood - City, Earldom
Erssa-Saka'am – City, Great Swamp, home to the Saurians
Glowan Hills – Near Burrstoke
Great Swamp - The southern edge of Merceria
Haverston - Town, Viscountcy
Hawksburg - Town, Barony
Kingsford - City, Dukedom
Lucky Duck - Tavern in Kingsford
Redridge – Town, Barony
River Snake - Tavern in Falford
Shrewesdale - City, Earldom
Tewsbury - City, Earldom
The Grand - Theatre in Wincaster
Trollden - Town, Great Swamp, mainly Trolls, Earldom
Weasel - Tavern in Wincaster
Whitewood - Forest north of Bodden
Wickfield – Town, Barony
Wincaster - Capital City

NORLAND:
Beaconsgate – City, Earldom
Galburn's Ridge - Capital of Norland
Harrowsbrook – Town
Ravensguard - Fortress city, Earldom
The Black Crow - Tavern in Beaconsgate

THE TWELVE CLANS:
Banburn - Town
Clearwater - Eastern most river of the clanholdings
Drakewell - Town

Dungannon - Town on the Clearwater river
Galcrest - Town
Glanfraydon - Town
Halsworth - Town
Lanton - Town
Redwater River - Western most river of the clanholdings
Strathlade - Town
Tor-Maldrin - Abandoned Dwarf city near Drakewell
White River - River that flows through Dungannon
Windbourne - Port Town

WLEDWYN:
Abermore – Town, Viscountcy
Almswell - Town, Barony
Amber Shard - Tavern in Summersgate
Barren Hills – Near Aynsbury
Falford - City, Earldom
Faltingham - City, Earldom
Grand Edifice of the Arcane Wizards Council 'The Dome' - Home to the
mages of Weldwyn
Hanwick – Town, Barony
Kinsley - Town, Barony
Loranguard - City, Earldom
Mirstone - Town, Dwarven Barony
Norwatch - Town, Barony
Quarry - Tavern
Riversend - Large port city, Earldom
Sea of Storms - Sea to the south of Weldwyn
Siren - Tavern in Summersgate
Southport - Large port city, Earldom
Summersgate - Capital City
The Drake – Tavern, SUmmersgate
The Serpent - Tavern in Summersgate
Tivilton - City, Elven Barony

OTHER LOCATIONS:
Erssa Saka'am - Ancient home of the Saurian race
Halvaria - Large Empire to the east
Ironcliff - Dwarven Stronghold, Kingdom
Kurathia - Collection of Island principalities
Petty Kingdoms - Collection of Kingdoms on the Continent

Stonecastle - Dwarven Stronghold, Kingdom

BATTLES:
Siege of Bodden (933) – Second siege, death of Edward Fitzwiliam
Siege of Summersgate (966) – Defeat of the Twelve Clans

OTHER THINGS:
Deep-one - Elemental creature from deep within Eiddenwerthe
Dragonweed - Toxic weed
Fantine - Halvarian merchant vessel
Numbleaf - Herb that supresses pain
Saurian Gates – Magical portals allowing instantaneous travel
Saurians – Elder race, small lizard like creatures
Stonecakes - Dwarven travelling ration
The King's Mistress - A play by Califax

A Few Words from Paul

It's never easy to say goodbye to a beloved character, but the fate of Lord Richard Fitzwilliam was set in motion years ago, back when I was still working on Servant of the Crown. He was, in a sense, responsible for the entire sequence of events leading to this point, for without him, there would be no Gerald or Beverly and thus, no one to save Anna from a life of exile. Fitz may be dead, but his spirit lives on in those who survive him.

For those interested, there was indeed someone carried from the field of battle that day, leading to the question of whether or not it was Lord Edward. In answer to that, I will only say, like many historical events, the truth is shrouded in mystery, and will remain so.

The story of Lord James, and by extension, Lord Godfrey, was, in a sense, a holdover from the last book's events. In their case, justice was served, although if you look closely, you might note that not everyone received the punishment they were due. This will have ramifications in the future.

While the storylines of Fitz and Lord James have ended, that of Althea is only just beginning. Her fight to bring the Twelve Clans closer to Weldwyn has only started, yet the spectre of war looms in the east. Will the Twelve Clans once more seek to take advantage of their traditional enemy, or will the warrior princess succeed in doing what no one else has been able to— unite them in peace?

The story continues in Heir to the Crown, Book 12: Enemy of the Crown

No author's notes would be complete without acknowledging the contributions of others. To begin with, I must thank my wife, Carol, without whom none of these tales would have made it to completion. Were it not for her tireless efforts in editing and promotion, I would have given up writing altogether.

I would also like to thank Amanda Bennett, Christie Bennett and Stephanie Sandrock for their encouragement and support. In addition, a debt of gratitude is due to Brad Aitken, Stephen Brown, and the late Jeffrey Parker, for their contributions.

This finished manuscript also owes much to the feedback provided by my BETA team. So thank you, also, to Rachel Deibler, Michael Rhew, Phyllis Simpson, Don Hinckley, Charles Mohapel, Debra Reeves, Mitchell

Schneidkraut, Susan Young, Joanna Smith, Keven Hutchinson, and Anna Ostberg

Last but certainly not least, I must thank you, my readers. Your response to my work has been an endless source of encouragement, and I look forward to entertaining you with more tales of Eiddenwerthe.

About the Author

Paul J Bennett (b. 1961) emigrated from England to Canada in 1967. His father served in the British Royal Navy, and his mother worked for the BBC in London. As a young man, Paul followed in his father's footsteps, joining the Canadian Armed Forces in 1983. He is married to Carol Bennett and has three daughters who are all creative in their own right.

Paul's interest in writing started in his teen years when he discovered the roleplaying game, Dungeons & Dragons (D & D). What attracted him to this new hobby was the creativity it required; the need to create realms, worlds and adventures that pulled the gamers into his stories.

In his 30's, Paul started to dabble in designing his own roleplaying system, using the Peninsular War in Portugal as his backdrop. His regular gaming group were willing victims, er, participants in helping to playtest this new system. A few years later, he added additional settings to his game, including Science Fiction, Post-Apocalyptic, World War II, and the all-important Fantasy Realm where his stories take place.

The beginnings of his first book 'Servant to the Crown' originated over five years ago when he began a new fantasy campaign. For the world that the Kingdom of Merceria is in, he ran his adventures like a TV show, with seasons that each had twelve episodes, and an overarching plot. When the campaign ended, he knew all the characters, what they had to accomplish, what needed to happen to move the plot along, and it was this that inspired to sit down to write his first novel.

Paul now has four series based in Eiddenwerthe, his fantasy realm and is looking forward to sharing many more books with his readers over the coming years.